BY VIC JAMES

BRIGHT RUIN

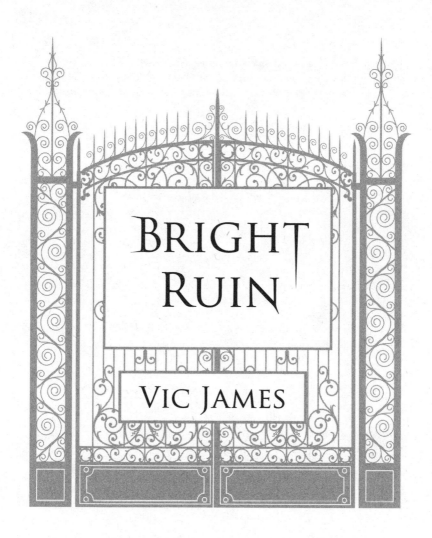

BRIGHT RUIN

VIC JAMES

DEL REY

NEW YORK

Copyright © 2018 by Vic James Ltd.
Map copyright © 2017 by David Lindroth Inc.

Published in the United States by Del Rey, an imprint of Random House, a division of Penguin Random House LLC, New York.

DEL REY and the HOUSE colophon are registered trademarks of Penguin Random House LLC.

Originally published in the United Kingdom by Pan Books, an imprint of Pan Macmillan, London.

The map in this work originally appeared in slightly different form in *Tarnished City* by Vic James, published by Del Rey, an imprint of Random House, a division of Penguin Random House LLC, in 2017.

LIBRARY OF CONGRESS CATALOGING-IN-PUBLICATION DATA
Names: James, Vic, author.
Title: Bright ruin / Vic James.
Description: First edition. | New York : Del Rey, [2018] | Series: Dark gifts; 3
Identifiers: LCCN 2018018901 | ISBN 9780425284186 (Hardcover) |
ISBN 9780425284193 (Ebook)
Subjects: LCSH: Aristocracy (Social class)—England—Fiction. | BISAC:
FICTION / Fantasy / Contemporary. | FICTION / Action & Adventure. |
FICTION / Fantasy / General. | GSAFD: Fantasy fiction.
Classification: LCC PR6110.A493 B75 2018 | DDC 823/.92—dc23
LC record available at https://lccn.loc.gov/2018018901

Printed in the United States of America on acid-free paper

randomhousebooks.com

987654321

First U.S. Edition

Series book design by Christopher M. Zucker

For Hilary and Giles.
Old friends, dear friends.
Thank you for believing in me.

CONTENTS

THE EQUAL REPUBLIC OF GREAT BRITAIN

Semper Excelsius

THE
EQUAL REPUBLIC
OF
GREAT BRITAIN

🏛 Estate   🏚 Slavetown

• City

Inverness

Eilean Dòchais
CROVAN

SCOTLAND

NORTH SEA

Newcastle
Riverhead

UNITED
KINGDOM
Fullthorpe Secure Unit

Millmoor

PROVINCES
OF
IRELAND
Dubhlinn

IRISH
SEA

Manchester

Lindum
ZELSTON

THE BORE

ENGLAND

Far Carr
JARDINE

WALES

Oxford

London

Kyneston
JARDINE

Orpen Mote
JARDINE

Highwithel
TRESCO

Scilly
Islands

Penzance

FRANCE

English Channel

BRIGHT
RUIN

MIDSUMMER

The Snubbing Post, down by the river in Vauxhall, was a useful sort of place when the whole of London was looking for you. The pub was centuries old, its small windows opaque from years of pipe smoke within and traffic fumes without.

In the upper room, six people sat around a large table.

One person was missing, and Midsummer was trying not to feel anxious about her absence.

Renie had been given clear instructions on how to find the place. But the kid was now a quarter of an hour late. Well, Renie was a law unto herself. She'd surely be along soon.

Her uncle Wesley was here, as was Speaker Dawson. The other three were Midsummer's most trusted slavetown contacts: Emily from Exton, down in Devon; Mac from Auld Reekie, the slavetown of Edinburgh; and Bhadveer from Portisbury, the hellhole between Bristol and Cardiff. They were smugglers—of goods in, and people out. Occasionally, they were saboteurs—of faulty equipment, or the careers of brutal guards.

But open revolt had never been on their to-do lists. Could Midsummer change that?

"I'll get straight to it," she told them. "The Blood Fair was monstrous. Whispers in parliament say that what comes next will be worse. We need to end this.

"Meilyr Tresco and Dina Matravers are dead. My dear uncle, who was Chancellor, is dead. Not one of us Equals has got it right or done enough. I need to apologize for our arrogance in thinking this was our fight to win. Because Jardine is justifying his clampdown on all of *you,* because of *us.*"

Mac was watching her, his blue eyes flat and hard. Emily nodded.

"But I'm not giving up," Midsummer continued. "My girl-friend is expecting our first child in a couple of months, and our baby will be Skilless. I'm not here as an Equal, trying to command you. I'm here as a mother, and as a woman who has seen too many lives broken by the slavedays, to ask if you'll let me fight *with* you. To work *for* you, to mend this broken coun-try."

Stop there, Midsummer told herself. *Don't do that Equal thing of imposing your will. Listen.*

She sat back in the pub chair and tried not to fiddle with her lip ring while she waited.

And when they spoke, she listened, as they asked *what, where, when*—and most of all, *how?*

"Folk back in Scotland are already wondering when we'll be getting a Blood Fair of our own," Mac said.

"Here's what I'm thinking," said Emily, leaning forward.

Which was when Midsummer's left-hip-pocket phone

buzzed. She carried three phones and knew exactly who had the numbers of each one. The left-hip phone was for clandestine contacts outside her immediate circle in the Bore. She took the call.

"They've got Renie."

"Jon—is that you?"

She saw Speaker Dawson sit up at the sound of her son's name.

"Security have got the kid down by the rivergate of the House of Light. I'm heading there now. Can you come?" he said.

"Tricky. I'm your boss's public enemy number one."

But Midsummer's brain was already racing for a solution. She went to the pub's antiquated sash window and, with her free hand, hauled it open. Yep. The fire escape that led down from the roof was still in place. She clamped the phone against her shoulder and swung herself out and up.

"Where are you?" said Jon, huffing down the phone as he ran. "They'll recognize Renie from the Blood Fair—take her straight to Bouda. But maybe I can intercept them and get her out. If Bouda hears about it, I'll say it was mistaken identity. She'll believe me over some guards."

"What the hell is Renie doing over there?" Midsummer demanded.

Then she realized—and it pierced her. The kid would be looking for Abigail.

Renie had been inconsolable in the safe house, following their escape from Gorregan Square this morning. She blamed herself for not being able to pull her friend onto one of the lions, and was convinced that Abi was back in Security's custody. Renie had talked about cells beneath Bouda's offices, in which she and the men of the Bore had spent the night before the Blood Fair. Scouting out a rescue must have drawn her back to parliament.

"I'll try a distraction—buy you time. Hang up. Go—*go!*" Midsummer told him, before stuffing the phone back in its pocket and clambering onto the roof.

The Snubbing Post was an old bargemen's pub, and it stood almost flush to the Thames. From here, you could see across the river to the crenelated facade of the House of Light.

Down near the muddy water margin, Midsummer made out three struggling figures. Renie was putting up a fight, but they had hold of her, so it would be over soon.

The Equal lifted her eyes to the roof of the great debating chamber, saw what she needed, and launched her Skill across the river. The target was crouched at one end of the roof gable, and Midsummer flinched as her Skillful awareness slammed into it, waking it. It was much bigger than the lions she'd animated at Gorregan Square: long and powerful. She felt it shake out heavy hind limbs, claws raking the chamber roof, its massive jaws unhinged.

Midsummer trembled as her Skill flowed into a pair of wide wings. As her power filled the creature from snout to scaly tail, she drove the wings down.

She heard an intake of breath beside her. Dawson and Emily were standing there, gaping.

"Is that . . ." came Mac's voice over the edge of the roof. "Is that a *dragon* now?"

He hooted in amazement, but Midsummer hardly heard it. The Security officers were already dragging Renie back toward the parliamentary rivergate.

Faster. It needed to be faster. Yet she had to be certain of her control. If she mishandled the dragon, it might smash into the building—could crush Renie, and the guards, whom she had no desire to harm.

Hurry up, Jon, Midsummer thought, as she sent her beast arching over the parliamentary quadrangle.

The guards had halted, staring upward, dumbstruck. But she didn't want to risk snatching Renie up in the creature's claws. The talons might rake the girl's skinny body or pierce her skull. They might break her or drop her.

Midsummer didn't *want* to risk it, but she *would,* if that was the only way Renie was getting out of there.

She turned the dragon and sent it lower. Renie was still struggling. The girl would be looking for any opening to kick a shin or bite a hand, and escape.

Then Jon burst onto the terrace.

His hands cupped his mouth as he yelled something— presumably a command for the guards to release Renie. Midsummer's heart soared along with her gilded beast. He could take it from here. He'd get the kid away safely. Bouda could be fobbed off with a line about mistaken identity: the child wasn't the Blood Fair fugitive, just a teen trespassing for a dare.

Which was when Midsummer caught a flash of white-blond out of the corner of her eye.

And something rocketed up from the river and slammed into her dragon.

Midsummer twisted and groaned. Her chest felt suddenly constricted, and acrid panic burned her throat. She smacked her forehead to bring herself back to the moment.

Focus.

On the terrace stood Bouda Matravers, her hands upraised as if conducting the wind and sky.

But air wasn't the element she was bidding. Bouda had torn a strip from the river itself. Twisted it into a coiling serpent, and sent it aloft.

Wickedly curved barbs ran the length of the monster's spine, and a lizard's frills fanned about its head. Between teeth like icicles, a forked tongue flicked. Two broad wings spread from its back, while an endless tail thrashed in the river beneath.

A wyvern.

Who had known Bouda could do such a thing? Not Midsummer. No one had seen what the woman was capable of, before the rippling wall of water and the crushing wave in Gorregan Square this morning. And now this. A dazzling beast, veined with incandescent Skill that refracted through its watery body.

It was awe-inspiring. And it was going to ruin everything.

Sweat rolled down Midsummer's brow and prickled her shaved scalp as her dragon writhed in the wyvern's grip. Bouda would have seen the girl, and not even Jon's smooth excuses would be able to deceive her now. The guards had woken from their stupor and were dragging Renie up the steps from the shore. The only chance for the girl would be if Midsummer's dragon could free itself and snatch her away.

Midsummer lashed out with hind claws. The wyvern's screech beat ripples into the river and it bent its frilled head, snapping. Some of those icicle teeth found their mark and Midsummer bit her tongue hard to stifle a scream, blood filling her mouth. Was this as bad for Bouda? Did she also have to inhabit her creature to master it, or was her wyvern merely a weapon?

Time was running out. The guards had Renie up on the terrace now, and though Jon was arguing with them, he couldn't bar their way—one was waving a gun. Midsummer's strength was leaching away.

The wyvern, as if sensing victory, coiled tighter. And in that moment, Midsummer realized what she could do.

She let the dragon sag. Allowed its wings to droop. Hauled in a rasping breath as she made the wyvern work to hold the dragon's body aloft. Felt the serpent's grip loosen as it slid up to capture the faltering, failing wings.

As the coils contracted in triumph, Midsummer flexed the dragon's massive pinions and the wings ripped up and *through* the shining serpent. The wyvern exploded in a spray of shimmering droplets that rainbowed the air.

Midsummer staggered and felt arms reach for her—the others on the roof, holding her up. But there was no time to gloat, or to spare Bouda a glance. Chest heaving, Midsummer turned to look for Renie. She no longer doubted her mastery of the dragon, and could pluck the girl to safety.

But Renie, and the guards, were gone.

ONE

ABI

"You're awake!" said a voice as Abi opened her eyes. Daisy leapt onto the bed and hugged her. "You've slept till teatime."

Abi shifted to dislodge her sister—then recoiled as she noticed the other people standing in the bedroom.

"I don't usually wake up to an audience."

"You see," Gavar Jardine said to the woman next to him, "I told you she'd be back to her usual self."

The old lady smiled, and her face was full of kindness, which was when everything came back to Abi in a rush: Gavar pulling her from the wreckage of Gorregan Square. The motorbike ride. This house in the countryside, lived in by Gavar's old nanny, his little daughter, Libby—and, just as he had promised, Daisy. The disbelieving joy of seeing her sister again.

Abi had taken a boiling hot shower and scrubbed off the filth and blood of Gorregan Square. But she hadn't been able to scour away the bone-deep stain of witnessing people ripping like animals at someone who was helpless to resist—whatever his alleged crimes. Nor could she purge the breath-stealing terror of knowing she was next.

Worst of all was the hollow ache in her chest at the memory of Jenner's betrayal—promising her safety, then turning her over to his father. Despite her escape from the crowd's knives at the Blood Fair, something had been torn out of Abi after all: her heart.

She hadn't been able to control her tears, until this old woman had appeared at her shoulder with a soft, laundered nightdress, a mug of chamomile tea, and two sleeping tablets.

Abi had taken them, gone upstairs to this small guest room, and fallen unconscious for several hours.

"Thank you," she said, looking over her sister's shoulder at the old woman. Mrs. Griffith was her name. "That was just what I needed. And thank you for having me in your home."

"Don't thank me," said Griffith, her lined face crinkling. "Thank Master Gavar."

Abi turned to Gavar. That proud face and the size of him were as intimidating as ever, but his expression wasn't the blank hauteur to which she was accustomed. In his arms, he held his little daughter.

"I'm not sure I've the words for that," Abi said eventually. "You didn't just rescue me. You saved all of us by putting a stop to the Blood Fair."

Abi felt her sister's arms tighten around her. The heir of Kyneston ducked his head.

"It was what anyone would have done."

"But no one else did. Only you."

"Well." Gavar cleared his throat. "Griff has found some clothes for you. Then come downstairs for some food and we can talk about what's next."

When they'd all trooped out, Abi washed and pulled on the skirt and frumpy cardigan Griff had laid out. She looked in the mirror and saw the mass of hair extensions with which she'd disguised herself.

Some people, though, concealed their true self inwardly, not outwardly. How had she got Jenner so wrong? *How?*

She knew how. She had fed herself with fairy tales. All those novels about handsome Equal boys—Jenner had walked straight out of their pages, his Skillessness a tragic flaw that only made him more vulnerable. More lovable. What a fool she'd been.

She wasn't "back to her usual self" after finding refuge and having a few hours of sleep. She never would be again. That Abi had died in Gorregan Square, betrayed by her own romantic illusions.

Abi forgave her past self for her naivety, but wouldn't mourn her.

The kitchen downstairs contained a surreally domestic scene. The foursome could have been a family: a young father with his two daughters, a grandmother at the stove scrambling eggs. Abi went to join her.

"Can I help?"

"Bless you. Sit down and eat."

So she did. The eggs were just how Mum did them, with lots of butter. Abi used to fuss about the cholesterol and saturated fat, but she'd learned there were worse ways to die, so she piled her toast high.

Mum wouldn't be cooking like this in Millmoor, judging by what Luke had told them of life inside the slavetown. Were she and Dad even housed together? Married couples usually were, but there was no underestimating the sheer vindictiveness of the people who'd sent them there.

Wherever her parents were, together or apart, Abi devoutly hoped they hadn't been watching the television recently. For Mum and Dad to know that Luke was Condemned and detained by Crovan had been terrible enough. She didn't want to think what learning of her own intended fate would do to them—because she doubted very much that the Jardines were broadcasting her escape.

"What are they saying about it?" she asked. "Everything that happened this morning. Because I bet no one's talking about how Midsummer Zelston brought bronze lions to life and we all got away."

Gavar scowled. "My brother read the official statement a few hours ago. He's getting good at making my family's excuses."

Jenner, Abi thought. *He means Jenner.*

She pressed her thumb against the sharp tines of her fork and waited for her racing heart to slow, while Gavar sent the two girls into the garden to play.

"He called my intervention 'a doting father's mistake,'" Gavar continued. "Apparently, I erroneously thought I'd seen my daughter in the crowd, and merely wanted to pause proceedings while she was removed. Terrorists seized that opportunity to firebomb the platform and the crowd. And my wife saved the day by Skillfully cracking open the fountain to douse the flames and trap the suspects, who were promptly recaptured. There were lots of pictures of that wall of water, of course. The cameras love Bouda."

"And people believe it?"

"The media is repeating it, which is what counts. Anyone who was there can say otherwise, but they won't get the airtime. And those contradicting it too loudly will be hauled off to Astrid Halfdan and Silenced. Or worse."

As cover stories went, it was paper-thin. But backed by Jardine control of the media and the rapid shutting down of alternative versions? Well, it'd probably do the job.

"We need to talk about you," Gavar said. "Here's what I think. I can get you over the water to one of the Irish provinces. You could enroll at university in Dubhlinn, under a false name. People are going to be looking for you, Abi. My father and Bouda don't like loose ends. They'll hunt you, and all the others who escaped. Midsummer Zelston will have a price on her head bigger than the amount I owe my wine merchant."

"That much, huh?"

They exchanged glances, but the jokes weren't enough to raise one smile between them.

"I don't think I can," said Abi. "My brother is still imprisoned by Crovan for a crime he didn't commit. How can I abandon him?"

"But what can you do for him, Abigail? Nothing. That castle is under ancient Crovan family enchantments. No one in their right mind would even think of a rescue."

"Meilyr Tresco did. And he died there for it."

There. Abi had said it. Meilyr was gone now. Dina, too. Neither of them could be hurt any more by someone knowing the truth about how Meilyr died.

"You mean it wasn't *suicide*? I thought he couldn't go on because of what was done to his Skill. . . ."

Gavar listened in silence as Abi told the story of the botched rescue and its terrible, needless ending. When she was done, the heir of Kyneston ran a hand through that famous copper hair. It was a gesture momentarily like Jenner's, and she winced.

"Abi, I'm sorry, but your brother's not getting out of that castle. I can't save him, but I can save you. And maybe in a few years, when all this has died down, I can get your parents out of Millmoor early and send them over to join you. Daisy, too, when Libby's a bit older. That's the least I can do after what your family's suffered thanks to mine. But Luke . . ."

And Abi's heart must still be beneath her ribs after all, because a corner of it iced over at Gavar's words. Yes, he wasn't as bad as she'd thought. Yes, he had shreds and tatters of decency. But he wouldn't make an effort for a boy he knew was innocent. And any future in which Gavar had influence to release her parents from Millmoor was a future in which the Jardines still ruled.

She'd imagined, as they'd sped away from Gorregan on his motorbike, that Gavar might have it in him to make a stand against his family. But it looked like she was wrong.

"Think it over," Gavar said. "You can stay while you do. You're safe here—let me show you."

He led her outside into the late-afternoon light. Daisy and Libby were playing a noisy game of tag, and Gavar reached down to scoop up his daughter as she ran. The little girl screamed with delight as he tossed her in the air.

"Time to show Abigail the sparkly fence thing," he told Libby, bumping their noses together. "Will you help me?"

The little girl nodded, her curls flying, and Gavar led her to the fence around the house. The fence itself was a standard-issue picket-post, neatly painted. Gavar crouched alongside it, folding Libby's tiny hand in his.

"It's so cool," Daisy breathed into Abi's ear. "Just watch."

"It's not exactly Kyneston's wall," Gavar said, "but it serves its purpose. It hides this place. People walk straight past. I based it on something Silyen did for my London apartment one time, when I had a few too many ex-girlfriends turning up at awkward moments."

He placed his daughter's hand against the fence and covered

it with his own. A moment later, flickers of Skill-light wreathed his fingers, and a glow like sunset outlined the fence posts.

"Griff, Libby, and your sister can come and go freely," Gavar explained, straightening up. "But you should keep a low profile for the couple of days you're here."

Couple of days.

He expected her to make up her mind quickly, then. He expected her to accept his offer.

She should. It was the most sensible thing to do. And she should press him to let Daisy come with her now, not at some vague point in the future. Gavar might think his precautions kept Abi's sister and Libby safe, but the Jardines were a dangerous family to be around.

Could she do that—buy Daisy's safety at the expense of abandoning Luke?

"Help me pick some vegetables," said Griffith, as the heir of Kyneston launched into some kind of energetic rugby-for-toddlers with the two girls.

Small talk would be a welcome distraction from her circling thoughts, Abi decided. She followed the old lady around the side of the old timber-framed house toward a kitchen garden, where climbing sweet peas wound around raspberry canes, and the soil smelled thick and wholesome. This was a tranquil place, set apart from the cruel, corrupt world just beyond its fence.

"Your house is beautiful. Have you always lived here?"

"Heir Gavar bought it for me when my days were done. He'd visit occasionally, and since little Libby was born he's brought her, too, whenever his father is in a rage about baseborns and blood purity. Bless his heart, he even gives me a pension."

Griffith named a sum that Abi recognized from Gavar's column in the Kyneston accounts book—except there, it was
itemized as the monthly storage fee for his cigar collection.

"You only looked after Gavar, or all three of the Jardine
boys? I can't imagine any of them as children."

Griffith smiled. "I still find it hard to believe they're grown
men—or nearly. I had the older two, then when Silyen came
along, a younger woman took over for him and Jenner."

Abi tried to picture them. Gavar would have kept a watchful
eye as Silyen rampaged round the garden, just as Abi had
watched over Daisy.

And Jenner. Had he looked on, Skilless and envious? The
question came out of her unbidden.

"Do you think Jenner ever had Skill?"

Griffith sighed.

"Not one of us who slaved in that place hasn't wondered
that, Abigail. We're no experts, but I never suspected anything
was wrong with him in those early years. Odd things happened
around Jenner, just as they did around his brothers. The gardeners would joke that all they had to do to get Lady Thalia's
cut flowers to bloom, or the breakfast bowl of fruit to ripen,
was to leave them in Master Jenner's room overnight."

"When did the odd things stop?"

"I couldn't say." Griffith shook her head. "Silyen was just as
demanding as Gavar, in his own way. So little by little, Jenner
just faded into the background.

"Then people started to notice that he wasn't doing anything Skillful, and he got some attention at last—but not the
sort any child would want. He'd be tested: made to stand in
front of the gate and attempt to open it. Jenner got attached to
the woman who looked after him, as little ones do. Well, Lord
Whittam would beat her and taunt Jenner to make him stop, or

to heal her, but he never could. You'd go past a door and hear her moaning and Jenner sobbing. Ahh . . ."

Griffith pulled a hanky from her cardigan sleeve and passed it to Abi. Ugh, was she crying again?

"People criticize my Gavar. But I tell you, that boy is unusual among his family: what you see is what you get. Which is a virtue, even if you don't much like what you see. All the rest of the Jardines, you never really know what's going on behind those bright eyes and perfect smiles."

And wasn't that the truth? Abi wiped at her face—which was when the yelling started.

It was Gavar, and he sounded furious.

Abi darted round the side of the house, then froze at the corner. In the middle of the front garden, beneath the willow trees where they'd been playing, stood Daisy with her arm protectively around Libby. Her sister saw her approach and waved frantically, motioning for her to stay back. Gavar must be outside the front gate with a visitor. Whoever it was wouldn't be able to see Abi or the two girls.

Abi strained to listen, then wished she hadn't. Her terror was immediate and absolute.

"I know the Hadley girl is here," said Bouda Matravers.

"I don't know what you're talking about."

"Don't waste my time, Gavar. She's your daughter's caregiver, and I distinctly heard that awful Manchester accent prattling."

Wait. Bouda was talking about a "Hadley girl," but . . . *Daisy*?

She exchanged glances with her little sister. Pure fear was etched on Daisy's face.

That was enough. Abi crept forward, keeping out of Bouda's sight line from the gate, till she reached her sister and Libby.

She shook Daisy, who seemed rooted to the spot, then pointed to where Griffith stood, beckoning. "Go!" Abi mouthed, giving her sister a little shove. She watched as the old lady took the two girls inside through the back door. Griff would draw all the bolts.

And then—because dammit, what could Bouda Matravers want with Daisy?—Abi crept closer. Gavar was no longer shouting; instead he spat his words out as though they tasted sour.

". . . understand why Father wants me in London. He wants to show that though I interrupted that atrocity this morning, I'm still part of Team Jardine. But he doesn't need my daughter and whoever you think is looking after her."

"You don't seem to grasp the gravity of the situation, Gavar. First: the unified family front is *essential* after what you did. Second: those prisoners got away. *All* of them. One I recaptured a few hours ago—that grimy brat. We need the rest. And here's the interesting thing: the reason Renie was prowling round parliament? She thought *we* had Abigail. Therefore, the girl isn't with Midsummer. She must be hiding out in London. So if her sister is at Aston House with us, she may try and make contact."

"You're crazy," Gavar said, though Abi barely heard him because she was shaking all over. She'd just worked out that they had Renie when it hit her that Bouda wanted to use Daisy as bait . . . to trap Abi herself?

"Why do you even need Abigail?" Gavar continued. "You've plenty more locked up for your next Blood Fair."

"You heard the story Jenner put out—that they were all recaptured. That's our version, and it's holding, for now. But we need to produce those prisoners again before people start questioning what really happened. The Blood Fair was a showpiece, Gavar. One that *you* ruined."

"So, Father wants me to come back and play happy families— and bring Daisy Hadley with me. What if I don't? Maybe I like my quiet life in the country."

"Then the next step is simple. I'm having the parents moved from Millmoor to a secure facility. If we've not recaptured Abigail soon, I'll announce that we're bringing them to Astrid's suite for interrogation—unless she hands herself in."

Abi bit her knuckles to stop herself crying out, or flying at Bouda, fingers clawing. Her mum and dad, in the hands of Astrid Halfdan?

"That's all I had to say," Bouda said. "I'd better get back. Midsummer Zelston put on some ridiculous show earlier—a direct threat to parliament. When we get her, she'll receive the same justice as Meilyr. Trust me, you don't want to be on the wrong side in this, Gavar. And you won't be able to hide out here in the countryside, pretending none of it is happening."

She called to someone just out of sight, and a car engine started up.

"Well, hiding obviously isn't an option, as this place is *supposed* to be concealed. How did you find it?"

Abi could just picture Bouda pivoting back on those high heels she always wore, smiling with that perfectly lipsticked mouth.

"We've always known you come to this village, we've just never needed to find the house before. Even now, I can't see it. But have you forgotten that we're married? Our Skill touched on our wedding day. Which means I can tell that right behind you is an enclosure infused with your Skill. And you know what?" Bouda's voice pitched lower. "It's strong. *You're* so strong. You are your father's heir. My husband. We're your family, Gavar. Imagine what we could do together if you stopped treating us like your enemies."

In the brief silence that followed, Abi pictured Bouda's fingertips brushing Gavar's face; her lips, red like a wound, pressing against his.

Then a car door slammed, and Bouda was gone.

A few moments later, Abi saw Gavar Jardine storm back to the house, drawing the back of his hand across his mouth. She hurried after him.

"You were listening?" His expression was ferocious. "Why can't they leave me alone? Why can't *all* of you leave me alone?"

"I didn't ask you to bring me here! And are you really going to run back to your family when your wife whistles and your father clicks his fingers?"

Gavar whipped around with a speed unthinkable for someone of his size and bulk. Abi recoiled, throwing up her arm to ward off a blow that never came. But the heir gripped her wrist and leaned in close—she could see the purple-red flush of his blood beneath his skin.

"The only family I have is my daughter. Nobody and nothing else matters. Not *them*. Not *you*. You go to Dubhlinn tomorrow. I'll make the arrangements tonight. I'm through with all this."

He released her. The imprint of his fingers was on her wrist, a white shadow of his rage.

The house was almost unbearable for the rest of the day. While Gavar was bathing his daughter before dinner, Abi took Daisy outside. They walked together round the neat pathways of the vegetable garden, and Abi explained that Gavar wanted her to go to Ireland.

"It's a good idea," said Daisy, nodding. "You'll be safe."

"But what about Luke?"

"Think about it. If Gavar's dad is as mad and evil as all that, how long can he last? Gavar and Bouda will take over, then he'll release Luke. He got him out of Millmoor before, didn't he? Gavar just doesn't like people *expecting* things of him."

Abi stared at her sister.

"You're eleven. How are you even thinking about politics?"

"It isn't politics, is it, really? Just family. Specially with this lot. I want you to be okay, Abi."

And as Daisy's arms went around her, it was easier to remember that she was only eleven. A kid, thrust into a ruthless adult world whose rules she'd had to learn too well. Abi squeezed her sister, and dropped a kiss on her head.

Back inside, she told Gavar that she'd go over the water, and the sooner the better. The heir looked relieved, and went to call someone—Abi suspected his contact had fixed up more than a few illicit requests in Gavar's drug-taking, playboy past.

With that resolved, dinner was surprisingly relaxed. Afterward they played a simple board game, letting Libby win. As Daisy put the tot to bed, Griffith took Abi round the house, picking out items to get her through the first few days of her exile: clothes, toiletries, a roll of banknotes.

"You'll need a book to take your mind off seasickness on the boat over," she said. "A smart girl like you must be a reader." Abi dutifully looked at the shelves.

They were crammed with chunky paperbacks. Evidently Griff had a taste for crime fiction. Abi grimaced. The last thing she needed was tales of how Security doggedly tracked people down. She dropped to her knees to inspect the lowest shelf. It held storybooks—several that she recognized from her own childhood.

"I remember this one," she said, pulling out *Mishaps of the*

Monarchs. Cartoonishly illustrated, it retold farcical stories from the time of the kings: deluded King Canute, who imagined he had Skill and attempted to turn back the tide. Gluttonous Henry I, who had choked to death eating eels. (Abi remembered Luke's cries of disgust at that tale.)

"Ahh, the boys loved that one. Heir Gavar used to laugh till he went purple, and little Master Silyen, well, he would have been too young for all the jokes, but he'd be so transfixed he'd finally stop fidgeting."

"You read this to them?"

"That's the Kyneston bedtime-story library down there."

Abi looked at the book in her hand, trying and failing to imagine it in such circumstances, then crouched to replace it.

"No, no," said Griffith. "It caught your eye, so you keep it. A familiar book may be just the comforting sort of thing you need right now. And maybe when you look at it, you'll remember that all three of them were just children once. We are what life makes us, Abigail."

Which sounded like wisdom if you didn't examine it too closely. Because the world was full of people who had been dealt harsher hands in life than the Jardine boys but who had turned out rather better. Abi bit her lip and slid the book into the bag.

The bag went on the chair beside her bed when she turned in that night. She dozed fitfully, and when she woke, it was still dark.

Abi sat up and looked around the cozy room—this refuge so unexpectedly offered by Gavar Jardine, which would continue to shelter Daisy.

But this cottage wasn't the place for her, and neither was Dubhlinn. London was where she needed to be.

There'd be no more hiding, and no more running. Now was for fighting.

Lord Jardine and Bouda would subject this whole country to a Blood Fair if they could. Britain itself, pinned down and torn at by the Equals for their sport.

Time to smash the country's chains and set it free.

Abi dressed and hefted the bag. She'd stomped up the stairs earlier to test the stairwell treads. The second from the bottom squeaked, so she skipped it on the way down. In the kitchen, she paused to write a few lines to Gavar.

Tell Daisy I'm in Dubhlinn, she finished. *That we decided me going at night was safer.*

She folded the piece of paper. Paused. Reopened it and added a final line.

You are better than your family. I believe this, and I hope one day you will, too.

She hooked the bag over her shoulders, took what she needed from the dish by the back door, and let herself out.

In the moonlit garden, she gripped the pilfered keys tightly. There were advantages to being a vehicle mechanic's daughter.

Though if there was one thing Gavar would never forgive her for, it was this.

A few minutes later, his motorbike roared away down the lane.

TWO

LUKE

There were advantages to being a vehicle mechanic's son.

Luke may not have had formal driving lessons, but he was the best qualified of the three of them to be behind the wheel— albeit that wasn't saying much. He swore as another car cut them off at the Colchester turnoff. The sudden movement raised a moan from Silyen, who was slumped in the passenger seat, his forehead resting against the window. A rasping laugh came from the back of the vehicle, where Dog was curled up like any real canine on a road trip.

Luke tried to steady his trembling hands on the wheel, and wiped his sweaty palm on his sodden knee before changing gear. But as he stared at the road, he couldn't stop his mind re-playing horrific images: Julian, being led out and chained, begging and pleading, in the middle of Gorregan Square. The blood and the screaming that followed. Then Abi, brought onto the platform to take his place.

Everything after that was like a dream: the fire, the lions, the geysering water that blasted it all away and slammed Luke across the square and into the marble balustrade. He'd blacked out as he hit it.

A slap from Silyen had brought him round, and Dog hauled him to his feet. Luke had searched desperately for Abi, frantic at having missed his chance to save her. But she'd been rescued already, Silyen had said. By Gavar Jardine.

Luke darted a look at the Equal in the passenger seat next to him. Could he believe Silyen? The boy had no reason to lie. Yet why would Gavar rescue Abi?

The heir had stopped the Blood Fair, though, hadn't he? Had called a halt to it after seeing Renie brought onto the scaffold. Maybe it really had been too much, even for a Jardine.

Silyen had dragged Luke to the nearest road with traffic, where he had raised a hand to bring a car screeching to a halt. Dog had yanked out the hapless driver, shoved Luke behind the wheel—and they were off on the weirdest road trip in history, to Silyen's estate of Far Carr.

Luke drummed his fingers on the wheel, trying to process his new reality. He'd seen bronze lions come to life, springing across the square to rescue the prisoners—Renie among them. Silyen had said the creatures' animation was the work of another Equal, Midsummer Zelston. (The surname made Luke wince. She was apparently the niece of the Chancellor he had been compelled to kill.) And she had snatched Luke's friend and the other prisoners away to safety.

Could it really have ended like that—with everyone safe except for the Blood Fair's first two victims? If only he dared believe it.

"You're quiet," he said to Silyen, who was huddled against the window. "It's making me nervous."

"Carsick," the boy replied wanly. "Technology. Ugh."

"And you're *sure* it was Gavar? Why would he take Abi?"

Silyen looked over. The skin was clammy around his dark eyes, but he still managed to roll them.

"Belatedly developing a sense of chivalry? Giving the finger to our father? Gavar doesn't even understand himself, so I gave up trying long ago."

"Is she safe with him?"

Silyen turned away. "Safer than she was with the rest of my family."

Which was true. Luke tried to push down his fear and frustration that, after escaping Crovan's castle thanks to Coira, he had still managed to lose his sister at the very moment he could have reached her.

He had only Silyen's word for where she was now. But it was the best he had to go on, which was why he was in this car. That, plus the fact that he was a convicted murderer and escaped convict. As such, a public square swarming with Security in the aftermath of a major incident wasn't the best place to linger.

Far Carr lay on the coast, several hours to the east. Perhaps Abi could come and join them—the isolated estate would be a good place to hide her.

And what about Coira? She was still at Eilean Dòchais, determined to confront the monster who was also her father— Lord Crovan. How would Crovan react? Would he throw her out? Lock her up? Worse? If only Luke could persuade her to come to Far Carr, too.

Of course, it was hardly his place to be inviting guests to Silyen's estate, much less a fugitive rebel and a runaway secret heir. Luke still didn't trust the boy—he knew too little of his true interests and motives. But he didn't feel in imminent danger around him, which was a massive improvement on the company he'd kept for most of the past year.

Distracted, he was evidently driving too slowly, because another driver leaned on the horn while overtaking them. Luke snapped his attention back to the road. He had to get them to Far Carr in one piece first.

The road crossed the river estuary south of Ipswich, and the sun dazzled off the sheet metal sides of the canneries. Luke couldn't remember the name of the slavezone here, but it operated fishing fleets and processed the catch—another way of doing your days that had once seemed preferable to the decrepit factories and offices of Millmoor. It was a neat trick, he thought: as if one kind of slavery could be preferable to any other, when it was the servitude itself that was so wrenchingly wrong.

Eventually, the landscape gentled. The sky was low-lying, with only thick hedgerows and a few buildings to interrupt the horizon. Roads dwindled to single-track lanes, canopied with trees, and light filtered down in every shade of green. The GPS failed, and Silyen sat up and gave Luke directions. They passed an empty, woodchip-strewn parking lot. Surely local people didn't walk their dogs here?

Then the vehicle stopped dead and Luke understood. This was the closest you were permitted to the estate.

"Home sweet home," Silyen announced, visibly brightening now the journey was over. "I wonder what my staff will make of their lord's new retainers: his faithful hound and his gentleman companion."

Luke choked. "His *what*?"

On the backseat, Dog rasped with hilarity.

It was one more twist of weirdness to an already bizarre situation. Luke would be walking into an Equal estate neither as a slave nor as a prisoner, but as a guest.

Or, apparently, a gentleman companion. He cringed.

"I could give you your own butler," said Silyen. "Would you like that? Rix has hundreds of slaves. Must have been his way of trying to spare them a worktown. Goodness knows what they all do. Cut the grass with nail scissors, I imagine."

"Why do you need slaves at all?" Luke asked. "I mean, even leaving aside the whole *slavery-is-wrong* thing, it's not like the three of us need looking after. And it might be good to have privacy."

No one to tell tales if Abi came here. No one to snoop if Coira turned up. That would be perfect.

"No slaves?" said the Equal thoughtfully. "Privacy. Hmm, why might we need that, Luke?"

There was a disconcerting gleam in his eye, and Dog huffed again on the backseat. *Please,* thought Luke, screwing his eyes shut. *Please let Silyen Jardine not be flirting with me.*

"It's more the centuries of exploitation and servitude I was thinking of," he said carefully. "Not very nice, really."

"Well, when you put it like that . . . It would be fairly straightforward. A legal precedent exists. But I warn you, pizza delivery won't be able to make it out here, and after a week of Dog's rabbit pie you might be begging me to reconsider."

Silyen swung his legs out of the car and walked off toward the woods.

Luke twisted over his shoulder to look at Dog. "What's so funny?"

"No slaves? That's you doing the housework forever, Hadley."

The man bared his teeth in his feral grin and slid off the backseat.

Luke hastily pocketed the car key—though not before checking the fuel gauge. Just under half a tank. Enough to get

him far from here, if needed. Then he hurried into the woods
after them.

The trio followed a track that Luke tried to memorize, until
they reached Far Carr's perimeter wall. It was brick, like the
one at Kyneston, but it flexed in and out in sinuous curves. As
they drew closer, he saw that the bricks were chalky and crum-
bling, the Skill-glow faint. There was a small, top-heavy lodge
alongside a low iron gate.

"Right," said Silyen. "You two duck out of the way while I
do this. Turning up with one escaped murderer might be cool,
but two implies a lack of imagination."

"You're really going to set them free?"

"Well, you asked nicely."

"You know," Luke said, "I think world peace, women's
equality, and an end to global hunger would also be great."

Silyen smirked. "Don't push it, Hadley."

Dog prodded him into the gatehouse—a dusty, disused
space that made Luke sneeze—and the two of them watched
through the grimy window as a brilliant flare went up from the
gate. Soon after, Far Carr's workers began to arrive, plainly
drawn by some Skillful summons. A number were breathing
heavily as they came to a halt in front of Silyen, having run
from distant corners of the large estate. Among the assembling
crowd were a number of children. Evidently Rix had tried to
offer families a sanctuary in which to do their days.

Yet he had also hijacked Luke's body to kill Chancellor
Zelston. Luke's skin crawled even though he had no memory
of it, because a violation was still a violation, even if the victim
couldn't remember a thing. What Rix had done was wrong on
every level. But it had also been before Jackson's punishment
and death. Before Crovan and Eilean Dòchais. Before the Blood
Fair.

If Luke was handed a gun and placed before Whittam Jardine again, would Skillful compulsion be required to make him pull the trigger?

Or would he do it willingly?

The idea was disturbing, and Luke was glad when a brisk handclap from Silyen interrupted his thoughts. Several hundred people were now gathered around the Equal. Seeing them, Luke was struck by a fresh, horrible thought. Where would they go now? Would they be sent south, to the fish factories? North, to the Bore? Children forced into those awful places, which were much worse than service at Far Carr—was this Silyen's idea of a cruel joke?

Too late. Should have thought of that before being smart, Luke.

Silyen opened his hands wide like a conjurer at a trick's conclusion, waiting for the audience to applaud.

"I free you," the Equal said. "Your days are done. No matter how long your service here, even if you came only last week, you have no further debt to pay."

Luke blinked, stunned. Free? Done? As simply as that? Plainly the crowd felt the same, because a disbelieving hubbub arose—one that quieted instantly when Silyen raised a hand.

"A condition," he said, with his mocking smile. "Not unreasonable, in the circumstances. You go now. *Right* now. Anyone still inside this boundary wall within two hours I will personally have chauffeured to the Bore."

The scene degenerated into farce rather quickly after that. Most of the people turned and ran back in the direction of the house. A few tried to thank Silyen, who looked flummoxed when one middle-aged woman bent to kiss his hand. Parents shepherded their children through the gate immediately, taking no chances. Luke could hear them issuing stern instructions that their offspring wait and not move an inch, before turning back to the house to gather their belongings. It was what Mum and Dad would have done.

Luke didn't let himself think much about his parents. It was too hard. They were in Millmoor and safe. Daisy and Abi, though, were with Gavar Jardine. Still at the heart of that poisonous family. Where were they? Surely not still in London, at Aston House.

Luke felt for the car key in his pocket. Would Silyen let him walk out of the estate gate as easily as he'd released Rix's old retainers?

Why was Silyen so interested in him anyway?

Luke had one idea why, based on the times he'd caught the Equal staring a little too long in his direction, or sensed a certain sly insinuation in the boy's words. But disconcerting though it was to think that Silyen fancied him, it was a lot less disturbing than any other reasons why one might catch the interest of a magical sociopath.

Reasons that could include some sort of Skillful interference or experimentation—beginning that night he'd first been dumped outside Kyneston gate, when he'd felt the Equal's Skill reach right inside him.

Or reasons that might explain the eerie episode at Eilean Dòchais, when Crovan had attempted to access Luke's memories of Zelston's murder by breaking down a barrier in his mind that was Rix's Silence. In the hallucinatory landscape where that had happened, a sun-bright, silk-fine thread had connected Luke to a blazing presence that could only have been Silyen Jardine. What *was* that connection?

At any rate, Silyen evidently wanted him around.

Did Luke want to stay around?

He wanted desperately to get back to Coira. But she wasn't the only person he had to think about. Most obviously, Silyen was his connection to Gavar, who now had both of Luke's sisters.

And the Equal had just freed hundreds of people with three simple words. Luke's hunch was that Silyen believed reliance on the slavedays system made the Equals weak, and led them to neglect their Skillful gifts. And the boy appeared to have little love or respect for his family—in particular, his father.

Were those things enough to build a common cause? To win Silyen over to outright opposition of his father's cruel regime? Because with someone like him on the side of justice, the Equals would have to take notice—and change might finally become possible.

"You can come out now." Silyen stepped into the gatehouse. "They're busy packing up and running away. We need to walk the boundary. As soon as that lot reach the first village, word will get out about what I've done. And once my father hears the news, you can bet we'll have visitors. Rix never did a thing about the wall here, so the residual ingrained Skill is all there is. I need to fix that."

"And us? You'll bind us, like you did at Kyneston?"

Silyen tipped his head on one side. The effect was so birdlike that Luke half expected his eyelids to blink upward, or for him to shake out glossy black wings.

"Do I need to, Luke?"

Luke let out a long breath. He couldn't put this off any longer. Because Silyen's chatty manner, his acts of rescue and release—none of that wiped out the one thing for which Luke still needed an explanation.

"Why did you let Crovan take me? You know what he does to people—how horrific that castle is. You worked out what Rix did on the night Zelston died, and you could have told your father, or parliament. Then maybe I wouldn't have been

Condemned, and maybe Jackson wouldn't have lost his Skill. Perhaps he'd still be alive."

To his horror, Luke's voice tore down the middle like a piece of paper. His eyes prickled and he blinked, but it didn't check the tears. He saw Jackson on his hands and knees, howling, bleeding gold from his eyes as Crovan ripped out his Skill. Saw him dead in the hallway of Eilean Dòchais, his blood spilling across the flagstones.

Luke would never forget those moments as long as he lived. Yes, he wanted to fight against the Equal regime because it was the right thing to do. And because he wanted revenge for the cruelty he'd suffered and had watched others suffer: Abi, offered up to die. Renie's stolen childhood. Even Dog, his wife abused and his grief twisted into horror.

But "the right thing" was just an idea. "Revenge" was only anger. In Luke's heart, driving him on, was all that he owed Jackson, and all that he had learned from him. He would never forget his mentor, who had befriended a frightened teenager alone in a slavetown, and taught him to dream bigger and dare more.

Silyen was staring at Luke like he was seeing him for the first time. Well, let him.

When the Equal spoke, he sounded defensive.

"I made sure you were never at risk of . . . ill treatment. I told Father that what we needed to know from you made you too valuable to damage. He sent Crovan special instructions."

"Damage? He *tortures* people. He does it over and over and over again, and makes them forget each time. Did you know that? You certainly know what he did to Dog. And yet you dropped in for tea like you were the best of friends."

"Coffee, actually."

Luke swung at Silyen before his brain registered what he was doing, because it would have told him it was pointless, that you couldn't land blows on Equals. And sure enough, Luke staggered sideways, falling heavily against the gatehouse wall.

He held himself there a moment, to regain his breath. Then twisted to face Silyen, his back against the bricks. He felt completely vulnerable and knew he must look crazed, but he didn't care. The Equal needed to see this. Needed to understand that what had been mischief or intrigue to him had caused pain and suffering for others. Had meant, quite literally, life or death. Because if Silyen couldn't grasp that, then there was no hope for him—and no point in Luke trying to win him over.

Silyen looked . . . uncertain.

"Luke, if you hadn't turned up in Gorregan Square—and I still want to know how you managed that—I would have taken you away from Crovan any day now. I admit, I should have done it sooner."

"What was it *for*?" Luke said, looking the boy straight in the eye.

"I told you on the morning of the trial, and again when you left Kyneston. I said you were going somewhere you'd be useful, because there were questions I needed answered. You know what those questions were: about how the act of Silence works."

"*Useful?* Questions and answers? You sent me to a madman just so you could find stuff out?"

"*Finding stuff out* is the best reason there is for doing anything."

"Really? What about because it's right? Or to make the world a better place?"

There was that uncertainty on Silyen's face again. Luke could imagine the Equal's brain whirring through all sorts of smart retorts: *How would you define "right"? A better place for whom?*

But Silyen didn't say either of those things.

He didn't say anything at all.

Well, perhaps that was a start.

"This is going to be—a party," growled Dog, stepping past them out of the gatehouse.

Luke let his arms flop to his side, willing away the tension that gripped him. He eyed Silyen warily, and followed Dog. The Equal was close behind.

Silyen remained silent as he directed them round the back of the small lodge. Then he issued terse instructions.

"Here will do. Hands on the wall, please."

Please.

Luke laid his palms against it, as if waiting to be frisked by Security. The brick was soft, chalky, and warm. Was that warmth from the sunlight? Or was it Skill? His pulse beat in his fingertips.

"It's so old."

"One of the oldest in Britain, if you discount the Zelston estate, which is built from a Roman ruin. Most of the estate walls went up after Black Billy's Revolt, but Far Carr dates from the time of the kings and queens. What's now the hall was once a royal hunting lodge, and this was to keep the game in—deer, boar—so the local people wouldn't poach them."

Was Luke imagining it, or was Silyen's tone particularly pointed? He knew what the boy was implying: *Before the Equals oppressed you, your own monarchs did, too.*

How had it even happened that England had been ruled by unSkilled kings and queens, and not by the Equals from the start? Luke knew what he'd been taught at school: that those with gifts had kept to themselves, believing that unSkilled monarchs were best placed to rule over unSkilled people. They only took action when rulers were reckless or incompetent, like King John, who had been forced by the Equals to sign the

Magna Carta and follow their guidance. Lycus Parva's revolution, according to Luke's textbooks for his now long-distant exams, happened because of King Charles I's feebleness, not the Equal's ambition.

Was that how the Equals saw history, too? Or were they honest, among themselves, about what they had done? How they had stolen a country from its people.

"Ahh!" Something fizzed in Luke's veins.

It wasn't electricity. Not quite. Though maybe it was a little like a school experiment—the one where a current was passed through a bowl of water and the teacher invited you to stick your hand in. The hair tingled on his scalp and the blood throbbed beneath his toenails.

Luke was a *conduit*. Whatever this was, it was passing through him.

It was Skill, of course. Was this what Silyen had stored up inside himself, like some kind of magical battery? No wonder the boy was permanently wired, his knees perpetually jiggling, feet and fingers tapping.

The sensation wasn't unpleasant. It was strangely intimate—like being resuscitated, with someone else's breath inflating your lungs. Dog wasn't enjoying it much. A low growl came from the man's throat, and he ground his teeth together. Was he reliving years of Skillful manipulation by Crovan? There were times Luke was glad he had no memory of Rix's possession of his body. He remembered his interrogation by Crovan and Whittam Jardine in the aftermath of the Kyneston ball, and that was horrendous enough. Skill could twist you up from the inside. Could scour out your thoughts and leave you filled with nothing but pain.

But this was . . .

This was over. The current switched off. Silyen raked a hand through his messy hair and frowned at the wall.

"You can step away."

"What did you—just do?" said Dog hoarsely.

"I've made sure that the wall knows you, obviously. This will ensure that you'll be able to see the wall and pass in and out of the gate, even if you're not with me."

Silyen's definition of "obvious" was different from most people's. Rather like his definition of "right" and "wrong." A *Concise Silyen Dictionary* would be a handy thing, Luke thought.

"We saw it before," Dog pointed out. "When we arrived."

"Indeed. There was nothing special about the boundary under Rix's stewardship. He wanted this estate to be accessible. I don't, and I'm going to make some changes. I did something like this for Gavar's London apartment a few years ago, when he had about three girlfriends too many. The problem was, none of his staff could find the place. When the cook never showed, he ordered takeout, but of course the delivery guy never made it, either. The way Gavar tells the story, it's a miracle he didn't starve to death."

"You're going to . . . hide it?" said Luke. "An entire estate?"

"Just the wall, which has the secondary effect of hiding the estate. And it's not so much hiding as making people forget that they've seen it. There's an element that's like a Silence, but instead of being laid onto a person, I'm weaving it into an object." Silyen patted the brickwork. "The act will be lodged right here in these bricks."

"So, all the people leaving—the staff—they won't be able to find their way back?"

"No. And if my father sends someone when he finds out what I've done, they won't be able to disturb us, either. You two can come and go, but you won't be able to bring anyone else in—only I can do that. You did say you wanted privacy, Luke. Well, now you've got it."

The smile that slid across Silyen's face was the least reassuring thing Luke had ever seen.

No one had seen Luke and Dog leave Gorregan Square with Silyen Jardine. And none of the slaves had seen the pair of them at Far Carr. The only people who knew that Luke was here were the two standing right next to him. One of them a deranged killer, the other an Equal who had traded Luke's pain for answers to his research—and still had him inexplicably, Skillfully, tethered.

For everyone else, Luke had effectively disappeared.

The thought was disturbing. And yet Silyen had promised that he was free to leave. Instead of feeling threatened by the concealment of Far Carr, shouldn't Luke be thinking about its potential? A whole estate that no one could find.

Yes, Abi could hide out here. He'd get Silyen to contact Gavar just as soon as they were done with this boundary. And Coira would be safe here, too. The two girls were his priority.

But why stop with them? Mum and Dad could be smuggled out of Millmoor and brought to Far Carr. Renie could come. Their other friends from the Millmoor Games and Social Club, too, if Luke could find them. Hilda, Tilda, and Asif could bring in their tech. What about stockpiling guns? Because even Equal reflexes couldn't prevent something they didn't see coming, like a bullet.

Yes, you could plan an entire revolution from behind these hidden walls.

If their lord could be made to agree.

THREE

SILYEN

At Silyen's back, Luke was brooding in silence. What was going through his head?

The boy just seemed to *care* so much. About his family, his friends—especially the late lamented Meilyr Tresco, aka Doc Jackson—and about quaint notions of freedom.

Was that some kind of commoner thing, caring so intensely? Was it something they developed to fill up their otherwise empty lives, in the absence of Skill and power?

Or was it, perhaps, that the Skill and power possessed by the Equals had squeezed out their ability to care about much else?

It was an interesting question. Luke was an interesting boy. There were layers to him that it might be intriguing to peel back—and not only the ones he was wearing.

Silyen smirked, and let the fraying threads of Far Carr's wall enchantment run through his fingers as he tested them, weaving the strands together into something stronger, more complex.

He closed his eyes to the everyday world, and opened them into the bright-and-dark realm of Skill to inspect his handiwork.

And gazed, astonished, at the sight. It looked as though he was braiding fire. Spitting, fizzing, flickering fire.

He blinked it away again. It was less daunting to do it by sense alone, as he had his whole life.

But the sight made him think of the fine, bright thread that had stretched between him and Luke at Eilean Dòchais, when Crovan had attempted to destroy Rix's Silence. The three of them had been in a golden land, lofty and open, with wide plains and forests and rivers—Luke's mind, although he doubted the boy had realized that was what it was. (The mountains had been a little over the top. Silyen wondered where Luke had dreamed those up from.)

Sil's connection with Luke wasn't the simple constraint that, as Kyneston's gatekeeper, he laid on all the Jardine slaves. The standard binding merely prevented them from harming family members. He enacted it on each person individually at the gate. And when they left the household—as Luke, his elder sister, and their parents had done—the act was dissolved. It wasn't about keeping people in or out. That wasn't necessary, as at Kyneston you needed both Jardine blood to wake the gate and Skill to open it.

What he was doing here at Far Carr was entirely different. Both simpler and far more ambitious. Forcing an act applied to people—an act of forgetting—into an inanimate structure.

It was hard to explain to others the sensation of crafting Skill. The only person he knew to be interested in such things was Arailt Crovan, plus Sil's ancestor Cadmus, whose journals he'd studied. Sadly, sharing an interest with a psychopath and a dead man offered few opportunities for discussing new ideas and intriguing theories.

And what of the figure Luke had spoken to in that amber-lit world? The man with the crown and the stag.

Mindscapes were malleable. You could raise and level mountains. Make gardens grow and bloom and die. If you wanted a castle or a horse, a hammock or a cup of tea, then one would appear. They were spaces of pure imagination.

But you couldn't dream up people.

Crovan had pushed himself into Luke's mind, and Silyen had slipped in after, to observe. Luke himself was present in his own head. But there was no reason for a fourth person to be there.

And how had it been *him*? Because there was only one person that figure could be, crowned with twigs and accompanied by a stag: the Wonder King.

Myth. Legend. Forgotten folktale.

The only monarch—ever—with Skill.

Silyen staggered as someone grabbed him from behind.

"Whoa!" That was Luke, his breath warm against Silyen's neck. "Unless you were planning a dip?"

They had reached the beach. Silyen looked down. The sea was licking his boots. He'd been so absorbed in his thoughts, and in the painstaking craft of his hands, that he'd lost all sense of where they were.

The wall ran out at the seashore, and the beauty of the expanse before them stole Silyen's breath away. He inhaled deeply, letting the salt air sting his nostrils and throat.

The North Sea was notoriously dismal, but the alchemy of the late afternoon sun had transmuted it into shining metal. An immense gravel spit jutted parallel to the coast, and the water trapped between it and the shore gleamed like a polished blade.

"Are we done? There's no more wall." Luke's feet slid on the shingle bank.

Silyen looked around for Dog, but he wasn't there.

"He got bored and went hunting in the woods," Luke said. "Said we'd need some rabbits for dinner. I presume he was joking. I *hope* he was joking."

"He wasn't joking. Personally, I'm hoping my departing servants left without emptying the refrigerator."

"I could do you my Millmoor Special," Luke said, scrubbing his fingers through that short, exasperatingly blond hair. "Spaghetti on toast. Authentic cuisine of the working classes."

Silyen laughed. "I'll see your spaghetti on toast and raise you a frozen ready meal, if you can show me how to operate a microwave."

"Unbelievable. You really can be normal sometimes. When you're not being all-powerful and super creepy."

Silyen drew himself up to his full—superior—height. "I refuse to dignify that with a response. But to answer your earlier question: *Are we done?* No, we are not. There's no more wall, but there is more boundary."

Silyen pointed out to sea, blinked—it was as easy as that now—and the world flipped from light to dark.

Not entirely dark. The water gleamed faintly. The land, too. He'd not noticed that initially. After that first day at the House of Light, and then later at Orpen, all he had discerned were the brightly burning traces of human-wrought Skill. Now, more accustomed to this strange alternate vision, he perceived the truth of the world. Skill suffused every part of it, as integral as carbon and oxygen.

Far Carr's Skillful boundary extended far into the water— the coastline must have eroded since its creation, leaving it lying offshore. Weak golden ripples marked the outline beneath the waves. It had been abysmally maintained for at least a century.

Well, there was nothing for it. Silyen started into the water, the crunch of pebbles giving way to the smush of sand beneath his heels.

"You're going in?"

"*We* are," Silyen corrected. He put two fingers to his mouth and whistled for Dog. "Don't worry, you won't get wet."

"Will it be like Crovan's loch?"

And gone was the humor of just a moment ago. Luke sounded subdued, maybe even scared. And dammit, Silyen had thought he'd made it clear that Luke wasn't to be harmed at Crovan's castle. Not in any way that Crovan couldn't repair. What had happened there, to produce this sort of reaction?

"*Not* like Crovan's loch," he said firmly. "It will be less sparkly, definitely less painful, and you're a guest here, not a prisoner. Now come on, I want to finish this boundary by nightfall."

He checked that Dog was following, then turned his back on the pair of them and walked into the sea.

Stepping into another person's mind was nothing remarkable. Silyen had been doing it from childhood, when he had found his way into the rose garden of Aunt Euterpe's memories. But to push aside the sea and walk into it? To hear the susurrus of Skill in the air. To see the glowing outline of a boundary laid down hundreds of years before you were born, and which would persist hundreds of years after you were gone, your own Skill now blended into it. It was astonishing.

People claimed love was the supreme human experience. Silyen begged to differ. The greatest gift was wonder.

He reached into the wall of water, aware, as he never had been before, of the Skill within it. Dragging his hand through as they walked, he felt the salt sting his skin and the sea's tingling power flow over it. His kind had once commanded the sea. The women who had wrecked Napoleon's fleet at Gorregan had rolled up the waves before the French navy as it sailed to invade England.

There was nothing like war to make the Equals remember what they were capable of.

He hadn't wanted war, of course, when he had engineered Zelston's abolition proposal a year ago. Just . . . trouble. With a pinch of mayhem.

Though Meilyr's uprising in Millmoor had fizzled out, Father's ambitions were presenting all sorts of opportunities for the vigorous exercise of Skill. Look at Gavar, incinerating things left, right, and center, plus detonating a bomb and hunting down the culprit who'd thrown it. Silyen highly doubted that before that day, his eldest brother had used his Skill for anything more consequential than seducing women and cheating at cards. Now, thanks to Silyen's intervention, Gavar was discovering the true extent of his powers.

Midsummer's lions in the square had also been impressive, though Silyen was certain they had been mere automata, rather than endowed with any kind of life. In all his experiments, including the deer and the cherry tree, the creation of life—or its restoration to a thing dead—remained beyond the reach of Skill.

And then there was his sister-in-law, Bouda. He'd initially wondered if her hunger for political power masked weak Skill. But he'd sized her up during her visits to Kyneston—and of course, he'd examined Abi Hadley after Bouda's brutal Silencing all those months ago. No, the woman was strongly Skilled. And with her spectacular command of the Gorregan fountains, she'd finally had a public opportunity to display that strength. He fully expected her to find other opportunities soon.

He wondered if even Bouda knew how impressive her Skill was. Those fountains drew on London's deep watercourses. His sister-in-law had reached into a vast source and controlled it.

Yes, with her Skill that powerful and her ambition that naked, Father would do well to keep an eye on Bouda. Sil doubted the man had any idea what she might be capable of.

And Silyen certainly wasn't going to tell him.

As they continued walking, one slow step at a time, the water rose high above their heads. They had been at this for hours, and night was drawing on. Above them, the black walls of water revealed only a shining strip of sky, thick with stars. On this wild coast, they were far from the light pollution of any city or slavetown. The evening air had been mild on the beach, but here, deep within the sea, it was damp and chill. Dog was grumbling and growling to himself discontentedly. Luke had remained entirely mute, perhaps lost in memories of Eilean Dòchais.

Their progress was painstaking. Silyen's mind whirled with everything from Gavar's unexpected interruption of the Blood Fair and Father's next move, to what Luke's hair would feel like to touch and whether the Far Carr pantry would contain anything appetizing. He forced himself to still the distracting maelstrom. Such thoughts were all so unnecessary.

Superfluous.

This was the only thing that mattered. This song of Skill in his blood—and threading its melody into the boundary of his ancient estate.

His violin had lain untouched at Kyneston all year. He no longer needed it. *This* music was all there was.

The seabed beneath their feet was sloping upward now as they neared the shore. The fine sand coarsened to gravel; then came the grudging slip of small stones on the beach. The shallows eddied and sucked around his boots, chilling his feet where water flowed over the leather. At his back, Luke gasped, and Silyen turned.

"What?"

But he could tell what it was, from the glow that bathed Luke's face. Silyen looked down at his hands. His skin gave off a faint miasma of light. Wonderingly, he stroked the fingers of one hand along the back of the other. Brilliance flared in their wake, and subsided.

The expression on Luke's face was almost fearful. "Are you okay? Should we stop?"

"Stop?" Silyen felt more than okay. He had never felt better.

"It's just you look like . . . *him,* when Crovan . . ."

Him? Then he realized. Meilyr Tresco.

"When Crovan removed his Skill?"

"He didn't *remove* it," Luke cried. "You make it sound like something surgical. Something clean. He *bled* it out of him. It was dripping . . . oozing out of his pores. His eyes. *Silyen?*"

Silyen had pushed the sleeves of his hoodie up to his elbows. His forearms gleamed with the same gentle phosphorescence. He lifted the hem of his T-shirt to inspect his stomach, and really, he knew his complexion tended toward the "pasty" end of the spectrum of "pale and interesting," but he had never been quite so *luminous.*

"Your eyes," rasped Dog.

"What about them?"

"Gold," said Luke. "They're gold. Is it coming out of you? Have you been pouring too much of your Skill into the wall? I mean, I know you rebuilt the Kyneston ballroom, and you told me about Orpen Mote. Those were huge things. But you've been working on miles and miles of this, for hours now. You must be exhausted."

Silyen turned his hands over, palms up. The veins in his wrists shone. But the glow of his skin was already fading.

"It's not coming *out* of me," he said slowly.

He blinked, exchanging the dying evening light of the world around him for the bright-and-dark of Skill. And he saw it, falling toward him like snow. Like ash. Infinitesimal specks of pure light.

Of pure Skill.

He stood there, mesmerized, as the particles landed on his skin and disappeared. Melting snowflakes. Bright spirals of Skill eddied down, like the sunshine-trapped dust motes of Orpen library. He could watch it fall for hours. Forever.

Someone was shaking his arm. Silyen cursed them and closed his eyes, dismissing the vision.

He opened his eyes to find Luke's face far too close. The boy blinked and took a step backward.

"We should go to the house."

"We're not done here yet."

Luke studied him, Dog shifting discontentedly on the shore behind.

"You're not . . . hurting yourself, doing this? Because I've really had enough of seeing people hurt, thanks very much."

"How touching. But no."

And he reached past Luke, making the boy sidestep, and grasped again the flimsy threads of the estate's ancient boundary enchantment. How tattered they were. How ragged. How threadbare.

His hands resumed their braiding. This boundary had been woven long ago, and it had slowly worn out. Even acts of Skill decayed over time.

But not only acts. If the Equals neglected their powers, how long would it be until their Skillful *ability* likewise declined and disappeared?

This country's Equals ought to be grateful for the wake-up call Silyen had given them—though he wasn't going to hold his breath waiting for the thank-you notes to arrive. There had been so many wheels already turning, to which he'd delivered an extra spin. Bouda's schemes and Father's coup. The laughable "secret" of Meilyr's activism, and the existence of a commoner network primed for unrest. Gavar's anger, and his divided sympathies because of baby Libby. The opportunity for Silyen to demonstrate his own power, with the awakening of Aunt Euterpe.

There was just as much that he had not foreseen. Zelston's murder and Midsummer's daring. How swiftly and savagely Father would enforce his new regime.

And there were new opportunities every day. Luke's suggestion of freeing the slaves of Far Carr had been inspired—albeit by motives rather different from Silyen's own. Once news of it spread beyond the estate wall, who knew what would result? Perhaps the Zelstons would follow suit. Maybe the Trescos would. Father might dismiss them, but they were two of the great old families. Their actions still counted.

The Blood Fair had proved every bit as spectacular as he'd anticipated when he stood in the crowd, hoodie pulled up, waiting for a show. Gavar, Midsummer, and Bouda had excelled. There would be more to come, he didn't doubt it. And when the dust finally settled, one way or another, the Equals of Great Britain would have remembered their true identity: as wonder-workers.

And who knew, in a country newly mindful of the power of Skill, people might turn for leadership to the strongest Skill-worker among them.

Take a bow, Lord Silyen Jardine of Far Carr.

The thought struck him as unspeakably ridiculous. The more he fought down laughter, the more uncontrollable it became. He sank to his knees, gasping. He felt dizzy and light-headed, and pawed at the cold ground and chalky brick for support.

The other two were talking. He could hear them, as if from a distance.

"Mad bastard."

That would be his ever-loyal retainer, Dog. When Silyen was king of England, he could elevate him to the peerage. The Lord Dog. Maybe he'd give him Eilean Dòchais.

". . . no food. And he's been at it for hours. Seven? Eight?"

Luke Hadley. For honorable Sir Luke there would be a royal pardon. And the king's favor.

Silyen doubled over. He was laughing so much his ribs hurt. He should get a grip. It wasn't very seemly for a future monarch to be kneeling in the dirt, huddled against his own wall.

". . . well, he's not bloody indestructible." A hand shook his shoulder. Then the same voice, closer. "Silyen? We're almost back at the gate—just fifty meters or so."

Silyen looked up, tears of hilarity leaking from the corners of his eyes. He was shaking his head.

"I don't want any of it, you know. None of that trash my family loves."

"No, no, of course you don't. Can you stand up? Dog, a hand, please."

Strong hands gripped under Silyen's armpits and hauled him upright. Someone else's fingers brushed the tangle of hair off his face, and Silyen peered out owlishly. Everything was dark. It must be nighttime.

But it was *too* dark. It should be golden. Sparks whirling in every breath you took. Why was Luke talking about food? Silyen could eat the air, promise-crammed with Skill.

Luke waved in front of his face. Silyen swatted at the movement, but Luke—he was strong, for a commoner—caught his
hand and crushed the fingers together.

"You're freezing. You're dehydrated and shaking. And
you're really not making a lot of sense. My sister would start
talking about blood glucose. I don't have the faintest idea, but I
reckon a bacon sandwich and a sit-down in your mansion
would be in order—once you've finished."

Silyen didn't need a bacon sandwich. He didn't need any of
it. Not even a crown.

"A shed would have been enough."

"What?"

"Don't need a *mansion*. Would be fine as lord of a shed in a
field, if it came with a seat in the House of Light."

"Is that so? Well, I hate to break it to you, but you've got a
pretty big shed."

Silyen shook himself. He was babbling. He was quite ex-
traordinarily tired. How was it possible to be this exhausted
and not be dead? Cousin Ragnarr had once ridden one of his
horses so hard it had simply dropped dead beneath him. But
then, Cousin Ragnarr had been an utter shit. Silyen was glad
Dog had killed him. And so spectacularly, too.

Focus, Sil. You had something to do.

Yes. A wall to complete.

Silyen peered past Luke. There was the lumpy outline of the
gatehouse. No slaves lingering there now, needless to say. Such
a short distance. He could do it.

"Better finish," he told Luke.

"Right you are. Come on then."

And with Luke at his side, Silyen reached a final time for the
fraying boundary magic. *Reach. Splay. Thread. Twist. Repeat.* He
took that which was threadbare and made it shining and strong.

Splay. Thread. Twist.

Some unknowable time later, they stood in front of the gate. Adrenaline surged through Silyen.

He'd done it. It had been more exhausting than rebuilding the Kyneston ballroom and restoring Orpen Mote. More dizzying than swallowing down Aunt Euterpe's power.

He blinked into bright-and-dark and saw, in his right hand, the cabled end of the thick Skill-rope. It seethed and spat with energy, as if he held a lit firework. In front of him was the end from which he'd begun. He grasped it.

As he wove the two ends together, they flared like flame, but it didn't dazzle him, because he was Skill itself. Brilliance through and through.

The loop closed. Silyen's hands fell away from the girdle of power he'd wound around his estate. He stepped backward— and dropped into darkness.

When he opened his eyes, there was still fire. But it was burning in the hearth of Far Carr's great hall, warming him along one side. A blanket had been laid over him. By his side, a tray stood on a low table, bearing the oddest assortment of drinks Silyen had ever seen, even for someone who had grown up with Gavar. Gin, lemonade, a teapot, and a moldy bottle of champagne so old it was either undrinkable or very, very expensive, quite possibly both.

Curled up on the rug before the fire, and sound asleep, was Dog.

"How are you feeling?"

Luke Hadley. The boy was in an armchair drawn close to where Silyen lay. He had a blanket, too, as though he'd slept there. His blond hair was sticking up, vivid in the firelight.

"You certainly look better," Luke said brightly. "Which is good, because you need to call your brother."

"My brother?"

Silyen rubbed his forehead. Perhaps he wasn't as awake as he thought.

"Gavar. You said he took Abi from Gorregan Square. I need to know that's what actually happened, and that she's safe, and what her plans are. I'd like her to come here, if that's okay with you, because she'll need somewhere to hide. That's why I didn't ask the minute we arrived—so you could get the boundary secured."

Abigail Hadley a houseguest? Silyen didn't think he'd signed on for that.

"I don't have a mobile, Luke. You know technology doesn't like me."

"I have a phone right here." Luke waved a cordless handset. "The Far Carr house line, used by Rix's steward. And look, I can even show you how to press buttons with numbers on them, in case you're struggling with that concept."

"I'm not sure I remember Gavar's number. And it's . . ." Silyen squinted at the ugly grandfather clock in one corner. "Quarter past six in the morning. I'm not sure my brother would appreciate it."

"He's got a little kid, so I'm sure he knows what an early start is. And if you really don't know his number, someone at Kyneston will be able to tell you. Or your other brother. *Please,* Silyen. I need to hear Abi's voice. She nearly died at the Blood Fair."

Silyen wanted nothing more than to pull up the blanket and roll over. But Luke had a point.

And annoying Gavar was always a mindless kind of fun.

He took the phone.

FOUR

GAVAR

The girl was gone.

Phone in one hand, Gavar pulled back her duvet with the other. The bare sheets were cold.

The girl was bloody well *long* gone.

Gavar had trained himself to swear less since Libby was born. But that went out of the fucking window with the discovery that Abi Hadley had done a runner.

Which also meant that the sound that had woken him up a few hours ago, the sound a lot like his own motorbike engine, maybe *had* been his motorbike. He had dismissed the idea, because he was in bed and who else would be riding it? He took the stairs two at a time to the kitchen. The bike keys were gone. Fuck.

"Gavar? What's going on?" His brother's voice down the other end of the phone was sharp.

Why was Silyen calling at some ungodly hour to ask about

Abigail Hadley anyway? And so soon after Bouda's visit and her not-so-veiled threats. Yet he couldn't imagine his brother and wife as allies. So Gavar belatedly asked the question he should have started with, had it not been *quarter past six* in the bloody morning when his phone rang.

"Why do you want to know?"

"Just curious about Gorregan. Because I *thought* I saw you rescuing a girl that our brother betrayed and our father condemned to death, and it seemed an improbably decent thing to do."

Fuck it. Gavar was through with trying to second-guess the motives of everyone in his family. He'd taken Abi Hadley. It had been a spur-of-the-moment decision, in revulsion at the murderfest going down in the square. There was no shame in owning that action.

"Yes, I took her. She would have been recaptured otherwise. But Bouda came snooping round here yesterday, so Abigail must have spooked. She's gone."

"Gone?"

In the background of Silyen's call, Gavar thought he heard someone else speaking angrily. The sounds went muffled, as if Sil had placed his hand over the receiver. Was Silyen in London, at Aston House with the rest of the family? Was this call a trap?

"Explain?" Sil was back, sounding breathless.

"She's vanished in the night. And she's stolen my motorbike," Gavar snarled, "so I don't think she's popped out to buy a pint of fucking milk."

He terminated the call and shoved the phone into his dressing gown pocket.

Fine. Abi Hadley could do what she wanted, and good luck to her. He ran a hand across his face and exhaled.

The girl had overheard Bouda yesterday. She'd been standing there, just behind the hedge within the fence's protection. She knew that Bouda and Father wanted her back, and that they would threaten her family to get her to comply. Had she gone to turn herself in? She'd be handing herself back to more horror and pain.

Gavar had told Griff to empty the house of alcohol a few months back, wanting to make sure Libby never saw him drunk. Right now, it was a decision he was regretting. He opened all the kitchen cabinets. Nothing. Crouched to search the lower cupboards. Nothing.

His movements wafted a piece of paper onto the floor. Seeing his own name written there, Gavar unfolded it. He read the note twice, then screwed it up furiously. It told him only what he already knew—that Abigail Hadley wasn't as clever as she thought she was.

And nothing proved it more than the last line she'd written: *You are better than your family.*

What a joke. He was a Jardine, and a mediocre one at that.

He remembered Griff's bureau in the sitting room. He could have sworn he'd seen his old nanny once pour herself a nightcap from a bottle in there.

He was in luck. And a shake suggested the bottle was almost full. It was a coffee cream liqueur, sickly sweet, but it'd do. Gavar wedged himself into Griff's favorite armchair and tipped back his head.

Sometime later, his phone went again. He would have ignored it, but the insistent buzz was annoying.

"Yes?"

"Gavar?"

"Dearest wife. Missing me already?"

"Are you drunk? It's barely seven in the morning."

Bouda's disgust was palpable. Had he slurred? Who the fuck cared? Not Gavar.

"S'just strong coffee." He peered into the bottle. Dismayingly, it was empty. "*Was* strong coffee."

"Well, you'll sober up on the journey. I've dispatched a car already, and it'll be with you within the hour, so get Libby and the Hadley girl ready. You're to come to London immediately."

What on earth? Had Abigail gone straight to London to give herself up? But in that case, there'd be no need for Daisy to bait her sister to Aston House.

He emitted a croak, which Bouda correctly deciphered.

"Because of your brother, that's why. Do you know what Mad Lord Silyen of Far Carr has done? He's manumitted his entire estate."

Manumitted. It had too many syllables for Gavar to pronounce right now, but he knew what it meant.

"Freed them."

"Yes, *freed them*. Every single slave. Which rather puts a new spin on things. Your father and I have some ideas about what we do next. We'll see you later."

Bouda hung up, and Gavar sat there as the silence whirred in his ear. *Silyen*. His entire sodding family was a nightmare. Would it never end?

So much for his carefully calculated insobriety. He went to the kitchen and downed three glasses of water, while urging his Equal metabolism to burn through the alcohol he'd just consumed. Then he stomped upstairs to get the girls woken and washed—and to deliver the news to Daisy that her sister had left in the middle of the night, to go over the water to Dubhlinn.

★   ★   ★

They were waiting for him in the Damask Salon of Aston House.

Father, Mother, Bouda, and Jenner were seated on a long couch, like a jury. The one person Gavar might have counted on for a "not guilty" verdict, or at least a "case dismissed," was Mother, who of course excused herself immediately. She administered a dry peck to each cheek and left to settle Libby and Daisy into the nursery quarters. Gavar had considered leaving the girls behind with Griff. But now that the cottage's location was common knowledge, he would prefer to keep them close.

Gavar made for the adjoining armchair.

"Did I give you permission to sit?" Father barely turned his head as he spoke.

Gavar paused. He'd been made to stand for reprimands from his father since he was four years old. Possibly younger. Possibly even before he could stand. He pictured Father grasping him by the hands as he wobbled on thick toddler legs, delivering a rebuke on the slovenliness of his romper suit or his disreputable teddy bear.

But he'd never stood for a scolding in front of his younger brother and wife. And he certainly wasn't starting now.

He sat and pulled out a packet of Sobranies, lighting up. His family was always on at him to stop smoking, which was ironic, given that they were the reason he needed to.

"I said—" Father surged from his seat, smashing the ciggy from Gavar's mouth, his nails stinging Gavar's lips. *"Did I give you permission to sit?"*

Something ignited in Gavar, hot and hating. Father was a bully, nothing more. The man bullied his wife, his children, his slaves, and now an entire country—which he doubtless also regarded as *his*. It was pathetic.

"I wasn't aware that I needed permission for such a mundane

activity," he said, as calmly as he could. Aston House had been done up in Mother's favorite flimsy French style. The furniture was all spindly legs and satin cushions, which would be matchwood and kindling to Gavar's incendiary Skill. "Do I need to ask your permission for breathing, perhaps? Or breaking wind? Let's test that, shall we?"

He leaned sideways in his chair—only for Father to haul him the rest of the way out of it.

"Degenerate puppy!" Father's spittle landed on Gavar's face as he shouted. "You mocked my authority in Gorregan Square, and now you mock me in my own home. How dare you? Do you not realize how precarious your position is?"

"Precarious?"

It was to be this again. Hollow threats of disinheritance. Gavar almost sighed at the familiarity of it all. He had, over the years, had ample reason to research the process by which an heir could be disinherited. It was all but impossible.

Not *entirely* impossible—and as any disavowal had to be authorized by the Chancellor, Father could both act and approve. But the bar was set high. The only crime for which disinheritance was automatically enforced was premeditated murder of an Equal, which was one of the very few sins of which Gavar was assuredly innocent.

"I think you'll find the laws around disinheritance are pretty tight," he told Father. "So don't trot that one out."

"Gavar, Gavar." Father spoke as if to an especially slow and stupid child. "We are still in an emergency Chancellorship. I *am* the law. Everything can be changed to suit the needs of the time."

"All right, a question: where are you going to find a replacement heir for Kyneston? I hear my insane little brother has just freed his entire staff. We all know what that means—the 'great penalty,' isn't it called? No slaves can ever again be allocated to Far Carr. Silyen has just doomed his estate. He and his inheritors can sell off land to pay people to work there. But sooner or later, when they've pawned the last candlestick, Far Carr will be ruined. You'd never entrust Kyneston to him and risk the same."

"I'm not intending to entrust Kyneston to him. But you seem to have overlooked other deserving candidates."

"There are no other . . ."

The scoff on Gavar's lips died as Father turned toward the couch and with one hand gestured toward Bouda, and with the other, toward Jenner.

Was he serious?

Gavar looked at the pair of them. Really looked at them. Jenner was tense and pale beneath his freckles. The skin was ivory and dull around his eyes, which regarded Gavar with a mixture of defensiveness and resentment. As for Bouda—his wife had always been a woman of sharp edges, from her fine cheekbones to her cutting tongue. Now, grief over her dead sister Dina had ground her to a knife edge.

"A woman with none of our blood, or a Jardine with no Skill," he told Father. "Nice try, but I'm not buying it."

"More fool you," said Father. He walked round to the back of the couch and stood between the two of them, resting a hand on Bouda's shoulder. "Spouses can act as surrogates in the event of an inheritor's mental incapacity—until such time as their offspring are of age to succeed. Bouda could perfectly legally be heir and lady of Kyneston, until your eldest child reaches eighteen."

"There aren't any children—and won't be, as long as I have to worry about my wife sinking a knife in my back when we're in bed."

"Oh, I don't know," said Father. His hand slid from Bouda's shoulder up the back of her slender neck. His meaty fingers rested there at the base of her skull. Bouda's expression never altered, though Gavar was sure he saw her flinch. "When a man gets drunk as often as you do, he might do all sorts of things that he doesn't remember. I wouldn't be at all surprised if there wasn't a new generation of Jardines before too long. Am I right, dear daughter?"

Those fingers squeezed. Bouda had become so thin it looked like her neck might snap with no effort at all.

What was Father implying? That he'd ordered Gavar's wife to seduce him next time he was so pissed he didn't know what he was doing?

Or . . . something worse? That hand was blatantly proprietorial. Would Bouda really submit to Father just to have a shot at stealing Gavar's position? It was unthinkable. But then, sitting beside her was Jenner, proof of just how far members of this family were prepared to go to get what they wanted.

Too revolted to look at his wife, Gavar turned to his brother. He'd told Abigail Hadley that Jenner's betrayal could have been the result of their father's control. But she'd shaken her head and told him that she had looked at Jenner in the Equals' viewing box in Gorregan as she was led onto the platform. He had been unable to meet her eye. He wasn't dull or blank. Not acting under his father's compulsion. Jenner knew what he had done, Abigail said.

Looking at him fidgeting on the couch, nervy and drawn, Gavar knew she was right. Jenner had lured her in and turned her over. And now Gavar understood why. He didn't know whether to feel sick or sorry.

"Your brother, of course," Father continued, "is *presently* Skilless. But this, also, may soon change. Arailt Crovan has graciously agreed to remain in London a few days longer, to examine Jenner."

"You can't believe this bullshit," Gavar told his brother. "No one's been able to create or transfer Skill. Ever. You sold out Abi Hadley for an absolute fantasy. That girl really cared for you."

Jenner's brown eyes were bloodshot, and his skin flushed angrily beneath the freckles.

"Don't lecture me. We all know what *you* did to the girl who loved you. I was there when you shot her dead."

And that was a low blow. One Gavar was still wholly defenseless against, because it was true.

"What has he promised you? Because everyone did all they could when you were little to try and get Skill into you. I saw it. It wasn't pleasant, but they tried, and nothing worked. Now Father tells you he can do it, right when he needs something? He's only dangling it because he's finally found a use for you—to put pressure on me."

"Screw you, Gavar. You think this is about you? Oh, I forgot—*everything* is about you. The heir. The golden boy, even when you were snorting drugs and failing your exams at Oxford. Well, who's in the Family Office every day, keeping Kyneston running? Me. Do you know how many tenants we have? How many slaves? How many properties? Do you know the first thing about the estate you've always blithely assumed you're going to inherit, even while you stagger about with women and booze and disgrace the family name?"

Gavar clenched his fists. He could feel his Skill roil angrily in his chest, like flame in the heart of a dragon, ready to pour out of him. This was one fucked-up family reunion, even by Father's standards. The man was watching him with a predator's lazy interest, and Gavar's temper flared.

"You've really told him you can give him Skill? I know you're a bastard, but that's cruel even for you."

Father kept his cool. "You've seen what Crovan can do. He can manipulate Skill. Draw it out."

"I saw him *destroy* it. Breaking things is easy."

"You'd know." That was Bouda, primly folding her hands in her lap. "You've made rather an art out of wrecking things for the rest of us. Soiling the Jardine name. Being a neglectful husband. Ruining the Blood Fair. Remember what I told you yesterday? It's time you started working *with* us."

"Father's making threats, you and Jenner are circling like I'm some kind of wounded animal. That's your definition of playing happy families?"

Father moved from behind the couch—after what looked like a final caress to Bouda's neck—and came to stand very close to Gavar, their chests almost touching, like prizefighters before a bout. Gavar had several inches on his father, but the man radiated menace.

"Gavar, none of us wants to see you replaced as heir. Jenner will be content to have Skill, and Bouda will be content with her position at your side—as long as you don't force our hand. But your wife is correct. We need you to show your loyalty and work with us. We want you to go to Midsummer Zelston."

"Midsummer?" Gavar stared at them. Of all the things he'd anticipated, that wasn't one. "If you want an assassin, I think Astrid Halfdan would be rather less conspicuous and a whole lot more effective. Or if you want a diplomat, then Jenner's shown himself pretty good with the oily excuses."

"We don't want you to be an assassin or a diplomat," said Bouda, smiling for the first time. "We want you to be a traitor."

Father patted his shoulder and, dumbfounded, Gavar sat down to listen as they unfolded their plans.

He wasn't sure what he was hearing at first. Midsummer's "ridiculous show" that Bouda had mentioned yesterday turned out to be some sort of spectacular attack involving . . . a dragon. A sculpture from the roof of the House of Light, but astonishing nonetheless.

"If she's got you that worried, why don't you simply arrest her?" he said.

"Because we have to eradicate not just her, but this cancerous emancipation movement," Bouda replied. "I knew Midsummer was part of it, thanks to one of my sources, but I had no idea she would step up like this. It seems that every time someone who's involved comes to grief, there's another person waiting to take over: after Meilyr died, my sister. After DiDi . . ."

And there it was, a crack in her composure that betrayed that Bouda was, after all, only human. Her hands knotted together, the knuckles white.

"After my sister, Midsummer Zelston. Given that Silyen has just freed every slave at Far Carr, he might be part of it, too, and we all know how dangerous that could be, with his power and his unpredictability. We need to find out everything we can. Need to know how far it goes, then end it, root and branch. This country needs to be *cleansed,* Gavar. Then we can heal it. Reunite it. Make it our own."

Gavar nodded. That all made sense—if you looked at the world from Bouda's perspective.

"I can see your logic. But . . . *me*? You seriously think she'll fall for that? What about these other 'sources' of yours?"

"But you're perfect," said Jenner, sitting forward. "Don't

you see? You derailed the Blood Fair. You're known to have a rocky relationship with your father. Your weakness for commoner women is notorious. You even have a baseborn child. What would be more understandable than you taking up the cause of ending the slavedays, partly to spite your father but mostly out of love for your daughter?"

It was the worst idea Gavar had ever heard. Or the worst since a university teammate had suggested climbing Magdalen Tower at dawn one May morning, gagging the choir singing there, and bellowing obscene rugby songs instead. He'd been rusticated from Oxford for a term for that.

"It's ridiculous," he said. "Anyway, Midsummer hates me. Until Rix's confession, she was convinced that Father and I had conspired to murder her uncle, and that I fetched the Hadley boy out of Millmoor to do it."

"Until Rix's confession," said Bouda. "She doesn't think that now. Besides, we'll make sure she believes you. Just wait till you tell her how your cruel father has your little daughter under lock and key at Aston House, and is still drafting the Bill of Succession that will send her to a slavetown."

At Bouda's slow smile, Gavar's guts knotted in a way that usually took two bottles of whisky to achieve.

"Libby," he said urgently. "Where is she?"

"Safe, Gavar. She's perfectly safe." Father was nodding his great lion-maned head. "And we'll keep her that way while you do this. Then when it's over, we will *all* be family together. I could even issue a writ of legitimization for her—although of course her lack of Skill would disbar her from succession."

The door opened and closed behind him, and Gavar twisted around. It was Mother. She didn't look at him, but walked straight to Father and slipped a hand into the pocket of her silky housecoat.

"All done," she said, handing a small key to Father. Only then did she turn to Gavar with a gentle, vague smile. "She'll have a lovely time while you're away, darling. I've had all sorts of new toys delivered. It was such a good idea of yours, to bring that Daisy girl to look after her while you help your father."

Gavar gripped the arms of the chair so tightly he expected to be clutching splinters any minute.

What was this?

His family had well and truly done a number on him, that was what. They had found every one of his weak spots, his hopes and his fears, and dug in their sharp claws. For all that he'd spent his entire life wishing to be free of his estate responsibilities, if he was not heir of Kyneston, then what was the point of him? Who was he?

He was Libby's daddy. And that meant both keeping her safe and securing her future.

And all he had to do was win the confidence of—and then betray—a woman who hated him.

It should have been the easiest decision ever.

It *was* the easiest decision ever, he told himself fiercely. He owed Midsummer nothing. He'd be protecting his daughter and her interests. Gavar didn't believe Father's insinuations about legitimizing her, but he owed it to Libby to maintain his own position at the heart of the family, because that was what kept her safe.

He drew in a deep breath. Unpeeled his fingers from the arms of the chair.

"Yes, Libby will have a wonderful time staying with her grandmother," he said, giving his mother his most winning smile, "while her daddy takes care of some family business."

FIVE

ABI

The thing about fear is that no one tells you how big it is. How hungry.

Two things have the power to eat you alive. To swallow up everything else, until you're just scraps and leftovers: love and fear.

Abi knew. They had feasted on her down to the bones. She could feel her ribs and sharp elbows as she slid the bag off her back to retrieve her shopping.

Thank goodness for Griff's little roll of banknotes. She'd changed into the jeans in the loo of the supermarket where she'd bought them, but had wanted to get away from anywhere with security cameras before using the other two items. Which was why she'd pulled the bike into an overgrown motorway rest area, too run-down even to host a burger van.

The scissors first. The stupid hair extensions had been the last look she'd worn in public, at the Blood Fair. Off they came, the blades close to her scalp. Abi doubted she was rocking the pixie-crop look, but who cared. Jenner had liked her long hair, and it felt weirdly liberating having the weight lifted from her neck. She rolled it all into a plastic bag and stuffed it into the trash bin.

Then the phone.

She'd had a cup of tea in the supermarket's dingy cafe while it charged, and had repeated to herself two numbers. She had been petrified she'd forgotten them in those final moments of the Blood Fair, up on the platform, when everything had been driven out of her mind except how much she loved her family and how afraid she was to die. But no, they'd been stored away safely in a brain well trained by years of studying for exams.

Jon's number. And Midsummer's.

She'd nearly called one of them after the safe-house raid that had picked up Renie and the men from the Bore. But she had rung Jenner instead. The mistake had almost cost her her life.

Which of these numbers would be the right one this time? Her fingers paused over the buttons.

"You're left-hip phone," Midsummer had told her, laughingly pulling out a handset, then producing two more from other pockets. "That's your hotline. Zero-seven-nine . . ."

. . . *seven-nine-seven-five* . . . Abi's fingers moved across the keys. The call connected after a few rings.

"Hello?"

"Midsummer. It's Abigail."

There was a moment's pause, then a throaty, disbelieving laugh.

"You're safe?"

"I am."

"When I realized I couldn't see you, I—"

"It's okay," Abi said. "I'm safe. You didn't see me because someone rescued me."

"Who?"

"You wouldn't believe. No, *really* you wouldn't. I'll explain when I see you. Midsummer, I overheard Bouda saying something yesterday. I think they have Renie back in custody. And they've . . . they've got my parents, too. Pulled them out of Millmoor, and they plan to start interrogating them if I don't turn myself in."

Midsummer made a noise of disgust.

"I know about Renie—Jon alerted me and I watched it happen, but I was on the other side of the river and couldn't stop them taking her. Abi, there's a lot to do. Almost too much: Renie and your parents. The dozens of people taken at Riverhead are being detained at Fullthorpe maximum security unit, and I'm worried they're destined for another Blood Fair."

"My brother's still with Crovan," Abi said. "Even my little sis is being hauled back to Aston House. They think that'll lure me to make contact, so they can recapture me."

Down the phone, Midsummer exhaled.

"They know what they're doing. They've got us racing round trying to put out small fires so we won't notice the massive bonfire of freedoms and rights they're planning."

"Can you help me?"

And Abi fought to keep her voice level when she asked, because everything rode on this question. What she was up against now—her whole family scattered and in danger—was more than she could tackle alone.

"Abi, that's not how it's going to work. Can *you* help *me*? Because the only way we're going to win this thing is by putting out that bonfire before it catches hold. Resisting Jardine's regime has to take priority. There will be choices—hard ones. Can you accept that?"

Abi held the phone away from her ear for a moment as she

took in those words. Choices. How could she choose between the commoner cause and her family?

But then, without Midsummer, she'd have no way to reach any of them, and so no choices at all. She put the phone back to her ear.

"I can accept that."

"Good. We'll do all that we can. We have people working on this all over the country, Abi. In Exton, Portisbury, Auld Reekie, and more. Jardine's regime has to end before it becomes our new normal."

The Equal gave her a time and a place, and hung up.

It didn't take Abi long to get there—an abandoned industrial park on the outskirts of Harlesden, North London. The time on the phone said she was an hour early. Abi made sure the bike was concealed, sank down against a wall, and hugged her knees. She'd had a sleep earlier that morning—a few hours round the back of a farm outbuilding, not long after leaving Griff's cottage—so she wasn't tired, and her thoughts were as restless as ever. They circled round and round the moment when she had watched a man ripped to pieces by a crowd and had known that she would be next. Even though she'd escaped, the terror of it had marked her forever. Turned out you could scar on the inside.

You learned in school about countries that went backward. Peaceful nations that flared up in civil war. Democracies that fell under the sway of fanatics. You never imagined such a thing might happen here in Britain. But it could. It was happening right now.

Could it be stopped? Or was it part of some great cycle of history?

No, Abi refused to believe that. History only appeared inevitable because it was written in a world where it had already
happened.

The bag lay at her feet, and to while away time she pulled
out Griff's book—the comical tales of England's kings and
queens. Here was the story of vain and foolish Queen Elizabeth, who never married after rejecting every one of her Equal
suitors. Idiotic Henry V, who thought he could take on a
French army four times bigger than his own at Agincourt, and
only escaped annihilation when his Equal adviser wove illusions to suggest that the English forces were superior, making
the French retreat.

Could there ever have been an England in which Elizabeth
was admired as a strong and independent ruler? In which Henry
V was the daring hero of Agincourt, and not a cocky dunce? It
didn't seem likely, but then this book had been written in a
country that had known three centuries of Equal rule. Who
knew how these feckless monarchs had really lived?

Two hours later, she was through with the book and Midsummer still hadn't arrived. Abi decided to stay put. Being a
rebel leader in a police state wasn't the sort of job where you
could leave the office on time, was it? And an hour after that,
Midsummer turned up, striding through the tangle of brick,
weeds, frayed wires, and broken office furniture.

"Sorry I'm late. It's been a strange morning. But it's *so* good
to see you." She pulled Abi into a hug, then put her at arm's
length to inspect her. "I like the haircut. Joining the sisterhood?"

Abi laughed. "Something like that."

"What happened in the square? When the lion came back
without you, I was frantic. You said someone rescued you?
Who?"

"I'll show you."

Abi walked into the darkness of the ruined warehouse, started up the bike engine, and wheeled it to where Midsummer stood. Her reaction wasn't what Abi expected, her face screwing up with suspicion.

"Gavar Jardine? Are you serious?"

"I know, I know. I almost thought I was hallucinating because of concussion. But he did it on the spur of the moment, just like he stopped the fair. He's not a good person, Midsummer, but his heart's in the right place."

"Well, that just made my complicated morning even messier."

"What do you mean?"

"He's been in touch—Gavar. He did it via Speaker Dawson. Told her that he wanted to meet me. That his father's mad, he's had enough of his family's cruelty, he's worried about his daughter, and—I'm reading between the lines here, but I don't think I'm wrong—that he hates his wife."

Despite herself, Abi laughed. "You're not wrong." She told Midsummer everything that had happened since the Blood Fair, and the Equal listened in silence.

"So, what does he want?" Abi asked, when she'd finished. "Apart from family counseling. Why did he contact the Speaker?"

"He wants to join us, Abi." The Equal's fingers worried at her lip ring. "I honestly don't think I can trust him, though. Yet he's so Skilled, and it would be such a PR coup to have the Chancellor's own son turn on him. I've arranged a meeting this evening—though if there's any sign he's accompanied, we abort. I've let him know we'll have a gun on him, if he makes any unexpected moves. He'll meet me and a couple of the others. Jon will keep away—we can't have his involvement revealed to Gavar."

"I need to be there," said Abi.

"I thought you'd say that. Come on then. Time to show you our new digs."

By the time of Gavar's arrival, Abi had taken in so many faces and names at Midsummer's new HQ that it'd be a challenge to memorize them all. She would, though. At school, she'd always memorized everyone's names by the end of the first day of a new term. At the time, she'd imagined it'd be good practice for when she was a doctor, with a ward full of patients. Ah well, transferable skills.

Midsummer had taken over an antiquated factory building on the outskirts of London—doubtless one of those built privately last century, before its commoner owners realized they couldn't compete with Equal industrialists using unpaid labor. In its repurposed rooms were gathered people from around the country, with links to slavetowns from Penzance to Aberdeen.

Some were barely older than Abi herself—students with laptops and multiple mobile phones, sitting in the corner. She spotted one group in a circle around Luke's techie friends from Millmoor—Hilda, Tilda, and Asif—and gave the trio a wave. They'd be hoping to rescue their friends Jess and Oz, taken at Riverhead and held at Fullthorpe secure unit—where it seemed likely Abi's parents also were.

There were others here whose reasons for fighting were more visible: on their skin, or in their wary eyes. A lean woman from Exton, her face and neck a mass of ropy scar tissue. A burly Scotsman whose rolled-up tracksuit bottoms revealed a prosthetic lower leg. A sad-eyed man from Portisbury whose wrist bore a series of faded woven bracelets and a tattoo with two dates just twelve years apart. Had he lost a child in a slavetown—one he had taken in young to give a good start in life, just as Mum and Dad had done with Daisy? Abi shivered.

But for all the anger and tragedy in these people's pasts, the factory space hummed with a sense of purpose, and Abi felt good being part of it. No matter how determined you were, no matter how resourceful you tried to be, you'd never achieve as much alone as when part of something bigger. Was this what Luke had discovered in Millmoor?

Could Abi fill the hole left inside her by Jenner's betrayal with the fellowship of these people?

"It's time," Midsummer said, when afternoon had turned to evening. "We're meeting Gavar a long way from here. I'm not having this place put at risk."

At her side was a woman Abi had seen on and off throughout the afternoon, petite and curved in every place, from her wide hips to her smiling mouth, and in what looked like the middle stages of pregnancy. She wasn't smiling now, though, and she held tight to Midsummer's arm.

"If you think it's a risk," the woman said, her Brummie accent making her sound even more urgent, "then why're you going at all?"

"Layla, darling, it's Gavar bloody Jardine." Midsummer wound her fingers in the woman's glossy hair. "He could be what swings this thing our way. We've secured the place and we'll be checking out every vehicle and person that comes close."

She bent down and kissed her girlfriend, and Abi's heart clenched. Not even Equals were indestructible, and Layla would have an anxious few hours ahead.

Renie's uncle Wesley handed Midsummer a closed-circuit radio.

"My boys have been scoping the place out," he said. "No sign of anything fishy."

"Thanks, Wes."

"You should join us," Abi said to him. "I mean, Midsummer, it's your call. But Gavar stopped the Blood Fair because he saw Renie. Wesley being there, like me, would show that you're putting some faith in his good intentions."

Midsummer thought about it for a few moments, then nodded. She was decisive. She was *good* at this.

They traveled by car across London, west to east. Though it was just after six in the evening, their route kept them far from the city center, and the roads and pavements were half empty. Wesley spoke from time to time via the radio. The driver turned down a gravel track, then pulled over.

"Right." Midsummer inhaled deeply. "Here we go."

While the Equal was plainly tense, Abi felt a strange sense of calm. She'd been impressed by Midsummer's level of organization and support, and she believed that Gavar could be won for the cause. The burly heir had spirited Luke out of Millmoor simply because Daisy asked, and had sped Abi away from Gorregan without anyone asking at all. If these two Equals could just manage to trust each other, who knew what might become possible?

The air was brackish in her nostrils, and wind blew round Abi's newly bared ears as she surveyed their surroundings. You'd hardly know you were in London. They'd driven to the edge of Walthamstow Marshes, and blue-black water pooled in reservoirs all around. It was a clever choice. The space was wide open, and only narrow raised paths divided one lake from the next. They were meeting Gavar where three lakes adjoined, and when a man nodded to Wesley as the trio stepped onto a path, Abi realized that there were two more lookouts stationed at the entrance to the other paths.

Farther out, where the raised banks converged, Gavar was

waiting. He stood brooding in a black leather overcoat that hung from his wide shoulders down to the tops of his biker boots.

"This is Wesley," Midsummer said, presenting him to Gavar. "He would have died at the Blood Fair if you hadn't intervened. More important, his niece, Renie, would also have died. She's the girl you interrupted it for."

"I owe you one," Wesley said, extending a hand to Gavar, who simply stared before Wes shrugged and withdrew it again. "You stood up to your family for that. It was a brave thing to do."

Gavar made a dismissive sound, then transferred his gaze to Abi.

"You've come to return my motorbike, I presume."

"I appreciated the loan."

The heir scowled. "I didn't."

"Did you find my note?"

"Yes, and I told your sister what you asked me to."

"Thank you. But that's not the bit I was referring to. What I said at the end—about you and your family, that bit. I meant it."

Gavar shifted his gaze to Midsummer. "Congratulations. You seem to have found the only two enrolled members of the Gavar Jardine Fan Club."

"I'm pretty sure my little sister is one, too," Abi said. "Founding member, in fact."

Gavar snorted at that.

"All right," said Midsummer. "Time to get real. Come with me."

SIX

ABI

Gavar sat in a chair in the middle of the dripping, strip-lit concrete space—the boiler room of a disused pumping station, back from when the reservoirs had been London's emergency water supply. If he was intimidated to find himself ringed by half a dozen people, he didn't show it.

Abi suspected he wasn't intimidated in the slightest. Gavar had little reason to fear anyone.

Anyone except, perhaps, his father.

"You expect us to believe you?" said Bhadveer, the guy with the bracelets, his tone that of a teacher hearing another the-dog-ate-my-homework excuse. "Well, maybe we do. Maybe you yourself believe it right now: that you hate your father, and think his and your wife's policies are cruel and misguided. But you are a hothead. Impulsive. You may be with us today, then regret this conversation tomorrow, and then the day after that be our enemy again."

He turned away to Midsummer. "I'm sorry, Midsummer. I do believe he's genuine, but I don't believe he's reliable. The risk's too great."

"Genuine?" It was the Scottish bloke with one leg. "You're off your head. His daddy's our entire fackin' problem. His wifey's near as bad. I don't believe a word of it. This whole thing stinks." He spat angrily onto the floor at Gavar's feet and the heir reacted at last, his face flushing with that Jardine rage. But he remained in his seat.

"Isn't the point," asked the woman from Exton, Emily, "that this is *the people* asserting themselves against our masters? I know you're our leader, Midsummer, but you're practically one of us. You've lived among commoners for years, you love one of us, you've faced prejudice because of that love, and for the color of your skin. Your and Layla's child will be common-born. But if Gavar joins us, doesn't this just become a power struggle between Equals?"

Abi winced. That was exactly how she'd felt, during the past months, watching Meilyr Tresco and Dina Matravers lay their doomed plans at Highwithel. This battle belonged to the common folk of Britain. There was a reason you talked about *winning* freedom, not *accepting* freedom, or *being given* it by the very people who'd chained you.

But Gorregan had changed her. The white-hot terror of the execution scaffold and the realization that she was about to die had burned away some of her scruples about *how* you won.

"It's still a victory, if you use your enemy's weapon against him," Abi told them. "Anything that helps us win, we need. Gavar could be the game changer."

Several people started talking at once: disagreeing, offering opinions. Then one voice cut through them all and the room fell quiet.

"He can go get my Renie," said Wesley. "To prove it. She's being held in those cells beneath parliament, where they kept us before the Blood Fair."

"In Astrid Halfdan's suite?" Gavar said, appalled. "I knew she'd been retaken, but—*there?*"

How could anyone fail to see that his horror was genuine?

"Why do you think I lifted the dragon off the roof of the House of Light?" asked Midsummer. "Or didn't they tell you about that, either?"

"Threats," said Gavar. "The way Bouda described it, she said you were threatening the House. Menacing it with your Skill."

"A rescue," said Midsummer grimly. "One that failed. That's a good idea, Wes, and goodness knows I want that kid back, but it'd blow Gavar's cover pretty quickly if he just walks in there and walks out with her."

"He can take me," Abi heard herself say. "We can make it seem like an arrest—then an escape."

She looked at the floor to steady herself before continuing, willing herself to believe that this wasn't the worst idea she'd ever had.

"His family thinks I'm on the run," she said, "and that I'll try and contact my little sister, who works for him. So it's only what they'll be expecting if he says he caught me trying to sneak in to see her. I'm guessing not even Astrid runs a twenty-four-hour operation down in that basement, so if he took me in late tonight there'd be fewer guards. He could take me down to the cells, go to put me in the same one as Renie, then we could . . ."

Abi's voice trailed off as she saw her plan fall apart. How could she and Renie believably appear to overpower Gavar Jardine?

"You'd trust him enough to let him do that?" asked the Exton woman incredulously.

Wesley had also seen the obstacle in the plan. "He could take me, too," said Wesley. "Say he'd caught both of us, then when he unlocks Renie's cell for you, I could hit him or something. Apologies," he said, turning to Gavar.

"That wouldn't be necessary," said the heir, sitting forward on the edge of the chair and rocking it onto two legs. His expression was grim. "There's another thing Astrid has that would do the job."

Gavar sketched out the route from the cells to freedom, explaining where each door led to, and that his parliamentary pass should open them.

"But you'd need to use a taser on any Security we meet," he told Abi. "Would you be up to that?"

The guards would be commoners. Just normal people, doing their jobs. *Do no harm, do no harm, do no harm* . . . The doctor's vow beat in Abi's brain. *But I'm* not *a doctor,* she told herself firmly. *I'm an outlaw, because they made me one.*

"I'm prepared to use a taser," she said. "Tell me about the other thing."

Gavar did. He told them how it could be managed. Abi made some counter-suggestions. And at the end, Midsummer nodded.

"If you're still willing, Abi, let's do it. Gavar, you say you want a better world for your daughter—I want the same for my kid. So I'm taking a chance on you, for the sake of both our children. Get Renie and Abi back to us safely, and that'll make you one of us."

A look of understanding passed between the two Equals, then Midsummer turned to bark instructions down the radio to have a boat ready on the Thames for later that evening.

Abi's eyes met Gavar's. She thought she saw her own uncertainty reflected there. It was oddly reassuring—the impulsive heir considering his actions, for once. But Abi couldn't quite swallow down the bitter memory of the last time she had trusted a Jardine boy.

She wished she could see Jenner. Talk to him. Rage and shout at his betrayal, and demand to know whether Skill was so much more precious to him than she was. But she couldn't. And deep down, she didn't really want to. The answers would be nothing she wanted to hear.

Instead, when it was time to go, she walked with Gavar to his motorbike. It was a final opportunity to get the measure of him, and to stifle the choking fear that she was making another terrible mistake.

"We're sure this will work?" she asked for the millionth time. "Silyen lifted the slave binding on me and my parents when we left Kyneston, so there's nothing to prevent me acting against you, but surely your Equal reflexes will interfere?"

"You can suppress the reflex," Gavar said. "It's something you learn at school—imagine trying to play rugby otherwise. It's a matter of pride to be the first to manage it. I was only third in my year, so when I got home that holiday Father made me demonstrate, then beat me with a belt buckle. At least the bruises disappear fast, too."

"Won't they be able to tell from the CCTV that you've let your defenses down? That you're allowing me to do it?"

But Gavar seemed unconcerned. "I can't imagine anyone will notice," he said. "The reflex only works against an attack we see coming, so just be sure to get me from behind."

They'd reached the bike on which he'd come to the rendez-vous spot. It was a massive Union American–imported Harley-Davidson.

"My second-best bike," he said, swinging his leg over. "We'll have to get you out in one piece, won't we, because otherwise I'll never get back my favorite, the Norton Triumph. I'll see you later, Abi Hadley."

He nodded at her, and roared away.

Two hours later, as sweat rolled down her forehead, Abi fought against choking panic. It was only an instinctive reaction to the obstruction of her airways, she told herself. Gavar had stuffed a handkerchief in her mouth—one of those Jardine salamander-print ones, which was hilariously symbolic, except she *really* wasn't seeing the joke right now—and was dragging her by the scruff of her neck. She could feel how he'd tried to bunch up the back of the borrowed jacket she wore, so it wouldn't constrict her throat, but it was still terrifying. Her feet stumbled and scrabbled as she tried to keep upright.

"Caught her sneaking round the back entrance of Aston House," Gavar told the two Security officers on duty at the main entrance to the parliamentary complex. The sodium yellow from the lamp light, and the flickering radiance cast by the looming House of Light, gave them a ghastly appearance, as if this whole charade weren't awful enough already. "I'm taking her to the Office of Public Safety."

"Your wife's office? Yes, yes, of course, Heir Gavar."

"*My* office," snapped Gavar. "We were tasked jointly by my father. Just because I don't swan around here with paperwork doesn't mean . . ."

But the guard was already cringing and swinging open the gate.

"Who should I notify . . . ?" the guard called feebly after them, but Gavar was dragging her forward.

"You okay?" he asked quietly, once they were out of earshot of the entrance and into the long shadow of the outer quadrangle wall. Abi could only make a moan of agreement.

She was dragged into a second quad, and across to a heavy oak door with a security-fob panel set incongruously next to it. Gavar touched his parliamentary pass to it, and when the door gave an electronic beep, he shouldered it open and thrust Abi through ahead of him—

—right against the chest of a massive Security guard. She grunted as they collided, and her heart accelerated. The plan hadn't anticipated an obstacle already.

"Heir Gavar. An unexpected pleasure, sir. And who's this?"

A baton prodded Abi painfully in the chest. As she arched backward, she saw first the bull neck, then the brutish face.

Kessler.

The one who had ripped Luke away from them all and hauled him off to Millmoor. The one who had barked orders as his goons manhandled Renie out of the safe house. The one who'd led them all onto the platform at the Blood Fair. Abi's hatred for him throbbed like a pulpy bruise beneath her skin.

Kessler's baton trailed lingeringly across her breasts, then up her throat, forcing her head back. The tip of it tapped her lips and prodded at the handkerchief in her mouth.

"That's enough," Gavar said, his voice tight. "You know who this is. You were there at the Blood Fair—I've not forgotten."

Kessler was the one who had sworn Renie was old enough to die, and Gavar had overruled him. The man scowled, and thrust his baton roughly into Abi's mouth. Her gag reflex made saliva well into the handkerchief, and she coughed and gasped for air.

"Abigail Hadley," he said. "Where did you find her?"

"Trying to break into Aston House to see her sister, the stupid little bitch."

"Not so smart after all, Miss Hadley." Kessler gave a wide, thin-lipped smile. "I'll enjoy having you back with us."

Well, this had to look convincing. Abi kicked the man in the crotch as hard as she could.

Kessler howled and lashed out, and Abi actually *heard her nose crunch* as, for a moment, everything went red.

"Fucking hell!" Gavar yelled. "Give me your taser, Kessler. Make sure it's ready to fire." He held his hand out for the plastic device, which the guard, still doubled over, slammed into his hand.

"Zap her on max," Kessler moaned.

Abi's eyes were watering from the pain of her smashed nose, so she only blurrily made out Gavar holding the device up in front of her face. This whole corridor was under camera surveillance. Kessler was Bouda's creature and would doubtless relay a full account back to his mistress. She and Gavar had discussed beforehand how every detail of this would have to appear authentic. And right now, Abi's fear was as authentic as could be.

"You try anything, and you'll get some of this," Gavar warned her. "Now hold still."

He jammed the taser in his belt. Then his fingers touched Abi's nose, pinching on either side, and it *hurt* almost unbearably. And then it didn't.

He'd healed her. The thing she'd one day dreamed of studying had actually happened to her. And she was so scared and strung out on adrenaline she'd barely been aware of a thing. Gavar yanked her arm.

"You *fixed* the bitch?" Kessler spat.

"I'm about to lock her in a cell. I don't want her falling unconscious and choking on her own blood. Now, do you want my magic hands on you where it hurts? No, I thought not." Gavar laughed nastily. "Take me through."

And Kessler dragged himself upright, hatred in those piggy eyes, and led them down the corridor. Abi counted the doors as they went.

"That's the way to the rivergate," Gavar sneered, as they passed an otherwise nondescript door. It tallied with the one Abi had memorized from his instructions. "That's where my wife caught your little friend. And now we've got you back, too. Maybe I'll put you both in the same cell so you can swap your sad stories."

Kessler snorted. He wouldn't be smiling if he knew the real reason Gavar had pointed it out. That was her escape route. Abi was stumble-dragged past the door to Bouda's Office of Public Safety, her eyes rolling to absorb every detail and store it away.

"I'm not letting go of this one," Gavar told Kessler, when they reached a metal door set into the end of the corridor. "You open it."

The outer door opened with a card like Gavar's, and led into a small holding area with sparse metal seating molded to the floor and walls. The next door had both a card panel and a numeric keypad. Kessler's fingers moved swiftly across the keys, shielded by his bulk. Gavar had told Abi the code was the day, month, and year of the very first Blood Fair. A nice touch.

"The runt is the only detainee we have right now," Kessler said as they walked along a narrow corridor. "So there's only one of my boys on watch down here. Shah!"

He bellowed down a metal staircase into the darkness below, his voice muffled by the soundproofing all around. Abi's fear welled up again. There was a reason it was soundproofed. This was where Astrid Halfdan did the dirtiest work of Whittam Jardine's regime. Yet torture wasn't just inhumane—it was pointless. You'd never know if your victim's confession was reliable, or simply screamed out to make the pain stop. Abi suspected that getting at the truth was only part of what drove Astrid.

As the new guard appeared up the stairs, Gavar dismissed Kessler. The man hesitated, but not even he was fool enough to contradict an Equal—especially one who was his match in size and his master in power.

"Heir Gavar," said the new Security man fawningly. He held a large gun across his body.

"You've got a new prisoner," Gavar told him. "You have keys to these cells. Where are they?"

"Right here." Shah patted his belt.

"Good. Now wait here at the top of the stairs." Gavar gave a predatory smile. "I want a little privacy with the prisoner before you lock her up, if you get my drift. Watch the corridor."

That fear again. That *fear*. Because in just a few moments, it would be Abi's turn to take over this rescue. Gavar had been chillingly convincing. Abi suspected that the roles of autocrat and brute hadn't required much acting.

Shah obeyed. Gavar marched Abi down the stairs, then opened a door—and pushed her into a room that stole her breath with horror. It was a steel-and-white operating theater.

Not equipped to take away pain, but to inflict it.

"Look at all of Astrid's toys," Gavar said, running his fingers along a metal trolley where trays of sterilized instruments waited. "Not that, though. That sends you to sleep—which would be a shame with what I've got in mind."

His touch rested on some syringes, each sealed in a sterile packet and containing a premeasured dose. When he turned away toward a surgical trolley, as if to test the mattress, Abi knew it was down to her now.

She snatched up a syringe, ripped the packet, and lunged for Gavar. When they'd spoken, she'd argued that she didn't want to have to actually inject him, but he'd insisted. Its effects would last ten minutes at the most, thanks to his Equal metabolism. She sank the plunger into his neck and, clawing at the trolley so he didn't make a sound, he fell to his knees.

Abi pulled the handkerchief from her mouth, then bent to tug Gavar's pass from his pocket and the taser from his belt. He'd told Kessler to make sure the gun was active, so all she needed to do was pull the blocky trigger. Creeping up the stairs, she took aim at Shah, whose back was turned as he watched the corridor. For a few moments, Abi didn't breathe. This was it. Another boundary crossed.

Then she remembered the easy way Shah had turned away when Gavar had asked for "privacy," knowing full well what he was implying. No regrets. Abi squeezed the trigger.

The tiny metal harpoons hooked into the guard's back, electric threads unspooling, and Shah went down with a cry. Thank goodness for the soundproofing. Abi dropped the weapon, now useless with its spent single-use cartridge. Gavar had tricked the man into revealing where the keys were on his belt—and Abi unclipped his taser, too, in case Kessler was in the corridor.

Her hands hovered a moment over the gun. But it was too heavy, too complicated. Too lethal.

Speed was all that mattered. She went back down the stairs to where six cells ringed the hallway around the door to Astrid's chamber of horrors. Renie's face was pressed against a tiny window in one, her expression frantic. Abi put a finger to her lips, then tried the keys in turn, her hands shaking. The third one did it, the cell door sprang open, and Renie thudded into Abi's chest with a hug hard enough to wind her.

"Come with me," Abi whispered. "Keep quiet, and stick on my heels."

"One sec," Renie hissed.

She darted into the white room. She emerged seconds later with a flash of metal that she slipped into her pocket. They ran up the stairs and stepped over the groaning guard. Shah made a feeble swipe at Renie's heels, and the kid stamped on his throat without hesitation. Then they fled along the corridor. Abi stabbed in the numbers, pressed the card to the panel, and ran to the outer door once it opened. When the hydraulic bolts hissed back, Abi motioned Renie behind her, then cracked it open to peer through.

Empty.

Abi slipped out, tugging Renie behind her. And it was the hardest thing in the world to walk up the corridor, instead of running. Wherever Kessler was, he was nearby, and running feet in this tomb-quiet wing of parliamentary offices would be a giveaway. Abi could only pray he wasn't monitoring the CCTV somewhere.

"D'you hear that?" Renie said.

Abi strained. A crackle. A Security radio. *Someone,* somewhere, must be watching the security cameras—and was notifying Kessler.

She sprinted for the door that would lead, eventually, to the rivergate. They were nearly there when Kessler came charging out of the Office of Public Safety at the other end. Abi slammed the pass against the touchpad as Renie yanked at the handle, and as one, they dove through.

"Gerrof!" Renie cried, and Abi saw Kessler's hand reaching through the doorway to claw at the kid's back.

She threw her shoulder against the door. It was too much to hope that she'd break the bastard's wrist—but maybe she had come close, as he yelled and his fingers uncurled.

"I said, *gerrof,* you git," Renie hissed, and with a flash of metal, she jammed a scalpel into Kessler's palm.

He roared and burst through the door, sending Abi spinning back against the wall. But Renie had bought the time Abi needed to steady her backup taser, and she squeezed the trigger, having dialed the voltage up to maximum. It was a fierce satisfaction to watch Kessler jerk as the energy discharged.

"Simple," she told him. The word he'd used to explain their family's nonexistent choice between resisting and submitting, when they were first picked up to do their slavedays. "That's for Luke, you bastard."

She tossed down the spent device. If CCTV had caught their escape, then it would catch their felling of Kessler, too. Not to mention that the guy was now lying pretty conspicuously half in and half out of the open doorway, and they weren't stupid enough to try to move him and risk him regaining consciousness.

She remembered the instructions Gavar had drilled into her, and let her feet lead her. Had Luke run like this, in Millmoor, with this tough kid by his side? People who just wanted to be free, and the world to be fair—they were always running.

Renie grabbed Abi's jacket and she nearly fell over, until the girl's scrawny arms went around her middle and pulled her behind a doorway. A moment later, voices and feet passed by. Not Security, it sounded like, but voices deep in conversation. Parliamentary staffers, working late. Abi's heart was hammering, and who knew that just breathing was so noisy? She held her breath until Renie nudged her back out again.

Gavar's pass got them through another exit. Beyond it, steps led down into darkness, ending at a heavy oak door that reminded Abi of the ones at Crovan's castle. She shuddered. Her brother was still there. And she felt a momentary surge of resentment at Wesley, for being quick enough to suggest freeing

Renie as Gavar's proof of good faith. If Abi had been thinking ahead, she could have suggested a rescue of Luke, instead.

But then Abi felt Renie's springy hair brush her arm as she bent to inspect the door. Remembered that the kid had only been retaken because she'd come here looking for Abi after they'd been separated in Gorregan Square. Her face heated with shame.

Midsummer had promised Abi hard choices. This was what they looked like.

"It's just a bolt and a latch," said Renie, "then we're out on the terrace, by the river. But we'll have to go up to the bridge, 'cause I can't swim."

"No need," said Abi. "They're waiting for us."

On the lapping shore of the Thames, the air thick with tidal brine, the pair watched the masked light of a boat ripple across the water toward them.

Abi nudged Renie into the shallows, and when the kid was knee-deep, hands reached over and hauled her on board.

"I can do it myself," Abi said as they stretched for her, too.

But all of a sudden, the strength had leached from her, and she let Wesley's strong arms pull her up. Abi lay propped against the shallow hull as the oars dipped in and out and sped them upstream to Vauxhall. The night sky was dark, the moon barely a sliver, and the facade of parliament was a long, low silhouette broken only by its clock tower.

But there at the heart of the Westminster complex, burning with a fire that never went out, was the House of Light. Abi didn't take her eyes off it as the boat moved away.

SEVEN

SILYEN

"I'm sorry," said Silyen, barely glancing up from his book. "I'm a prodigy of Skill, not a missing persons' database. Here's an idea: do you have any of your sister's clothing? Dog could sniff it and go track her scent."

From the rug by the fireplace, Dog wheezed with amusement. Perhaps he'd enjoy sniffing Abigail's clothes. Silyen winced. Not a good mental image. And Luke, as ever, wasn't getting the joke. He was pacing up and down in a way that made it difficult to concentrate on one's reading.

"If you won't help, then fine. I don't know why I even thought you might. But I can't sit around not knowing where she is."

"You know, I'm spotting a problem right there: you *don't know where she is*. Our island is eighty thousand square miles. In which of them do you propose beginning your search?"

Luke's chest was rising and falling, his blue eyes blazing. The boy really was distracting when angry. But on balance, Silyen preferred it when he wasn't. This was the third time they'd had this row since the conversation with Gavar, and it was getting tiresome.

"Look, your sister is resourceful. You describe her as the clever one of the family—which I can well believe, though you should give yourself more credit. Yet you're carrying on as if she's run blindly into danger and needs you to rescue her." Luke's hands flexed and those eyes narrowed. Yes, that point had struck home. "When I said in Gorregan Square that you can't save everybody? Well, I should also have said that not everybody *needs* you to save them."

"You're hardly the authority on saving people. You wouldn't piss on your own family if they were on fire." Luke paused reflectively. "In fact, you'd probably be responsible for the fire."

"If you had my relatives, you would be, too."

"If I had your relatives, I would have stockpiled every box of matches in the country."

And there, at last, was a smile. A halfhearted one, but still . . .

"But what can I *do*?" the boy cried, scrubbing a hand through his hair and flopping into one of Far Carr's soft leather armchairs. "Maybe my sister has a plan and is fine. Maybe the rest of my family is fine-*ish,* too, though I doubt it. But there's a friend I left behind at Eilean Dòchais, and other folk from Millmoor I need to know about. Meanwhile your father is massacring people in the middle of London, and I want to help stop him but I don't know *how* anymore. I've been locked up for months, and the Equals I knew are dead."

The boy looked frustrated. Exhausted. At his wits' end.

Luckily, Silyen had wits enough for both of them.

Prior to Luke's interruption he'd been enjoying a curious account of the history of his estate, accompanied by a pot of surprisingly good coffee from the Far Carr pantry. Now he set down the book and slid off the sofa, crossing to perch on the arm of Luke's chair. Perhaps this would distract the boy. At the least, it might stop him yet again tiresomely mentioning this female "friend" at Crovan's castle.

"What if I told you there was something more important than any of that?"

"I'd say that I'm really not interested in how, five hundred years ago, Lord So-and-So did such-and-such a Skillful thing that no one had ever done before. I'm sure old books are fascinating, Silyen, but people are dying out there, and—"

"What if I told you about the king? The one we saw at Eilean Dòchais."

That got a reaction. Luke looked up warily.

"The one with the stag? In that golden place?"

"The very same. Do you know where *that place* was?"

Luke shook his head. "Nowhere. Some kind of hallucination, caused by the pain. I figured it was my brain trying to make sense of what was happening. There were walls, which I guess represented Silences, and Crovan was attacking one. . . ."

"It was *you,* Luke."

"*Me?*"

"It's your . . ." Sil waved a hand. None of the treatises in English had words for it that didn't sound incredibly lame. His favorite was from a bonkers memoir by a nineteenth-century Bavarian Equal, but that might be because clever things usually sounded even cleverer in German. "Your *Selbst-Welt,* you could say. It means *self-world.* A 'mindscape,' if you like, but philosophy of mind is frightfully muddled—I blame Wittgenstein and his steaming pot."

Luke's eyebrows were halfway up his forehead. "Do excuse my lack of education," the boy drawled, in a voice that had better not be a *rubbish* impersonation of Sil. "My schooling was regrettably interrupted by my enslavement. But—what the bloody hell are you talking about?"

"I can take you there again."

Luke stood up so abruptly that Silyen nearly toppled off the arm of the chair. The boy headed to the fireplace, almost as far from Sil as he could get without leaving the room, and hunched over, hugging himself.

"Luke?"

Silyen recoiled at the expression on his face, half fear, half hate.

"Forget it, Silyen."

"What?"

"I remember when *he* did it. Crovan. It was so excruciating that I almost broke my back straining away from his hands. It felt like my brain was melting. And you were just *watching* with your chin in your hand like it was something fancy at the ballet. So no, you can't take me there again."

What was Luke talking about? Yes, Silyen could remember the boy gasping and twitching. And yes, repeated Silencing broke brains—he had told Luke as much. But not this sort of Skillwork.

"It might feel strange, but it shouldn't *hurt,* Luke. Was it painful when we did the boundary wall yesterday? Or when I first bound you to the Kyneston estate?"

"With Crovan," Dog rasped, "it hurt. Always."

Silyen's glance darted between the two of them. Dog's ribs were heaving, and Luke was actually trembling.

Sil had always thought anger was almost as pointless as regret. He'd look on with contempt as his father and brothers vented their rage. But he dug his fingers into the armchair's yielding leather, wishing it were Arailt Crovan's neck.

Yes, he knew the man did ghastly things in that castle, but only to people who deserved it—either for their crime, or for their stupidity in making a powerful enemy.

Skill, though, was almost a miracle. The greatest wonder of this world. Granted, certain acts were intrinsically harmful: the Silence, and anything intended to cause pain, like Gavar's showboating in Millmoor. But to inflict agony gratuitously, in the mere exercise of Skill, was obscene. It was like crafting a flower out of razor blades, or making belladonna jam.

He looked at Luke and the boy held his gaze defiantly. What he had endured was plain in those wide blue eyes. And Silyen found that there were words on the tip of his tongue. Words he'd not been able to bring himself to say when they'd argued in the gatehouse.

He thought he could get them out now.

"I'm sorry, Luke. I really am."

At that, something seemed to go out of the boy. His arms fell to his sides. His whole body loosened. He shook himself like a horse when you took off its saddle.

"Words I never thought I'd hear."

Dog stirred on the rug. "How touching."

"Oh, go chase a bloody stick or something," Luke said, and Silyen snorted.

"No apology—for me?"

Silyen studied Dog warily. He was still dangerous. Not merely damaged, but without any desire to be repaired. The people who truly owed Dog an apology he had killed long ago—and he had then committed crimes that more than merited his punishment.

"I gave you freedom—and you'll have the other thing you want, too." Dog held his gaze a beat too long, and it was Silyen who looked away first. "Luke, I want to take you back to that golden place, your self-world. And it won't hurt, I promise. If it does, if you say 'ouch' even once, I give Dog full permission to sharpen his claws on me."

"What's so special about the inside of my head?"

"Because we met someone there who died one and a half thousand years ago—if he ever lived at all."

"The king. But if the place is only my imagination, surely he's something I dreamed up?"

"When you're talking about Skill, there's no such thing as 'only imagination.' That place is real, just not in the same way that this hall or this furniture is real. And *he* is, too. Here, let me show you something."

Sil snatched up a candelabra, and with the lightest caress of the air above it, five flames flickered into existence.

Most of Far Carr's furniture had been under dust sheets when they arrived, Rix having preferred the smaller rooms of his house—or, even better, the hospitality of other people's. Suits of armor stood bagged in each corner, like the victims of a particularly thorough kidnapping. But Sil had peeked beneath the covers of two huge canvases, one on either wall.

"Have a look at this."

He lifted one drape to reveal a fanciful nineteenth-century depiction of the construction of Stonehenge. The book Sil had just put down informed him that the artist—whose signature was painted carefully in the corner—was the younger brother of the twenty-second Lord of Far Carr. In his vivid brushstrokes, a Skill-worker clad in druid's robes marshaled an airborne array of megaliths into their famous circle.

Luke tipped his head to examine the painting.

"I never saw you rebuild Kyneston after your aunt blew it apart," he said. "But I heard what you did. Moving blocks of stone. It must have looked a bit like this."

Oh. That was a comparison Silyen hadn't considered before. Rather a gratifying one.

"Would you call this scene history—or myth?" he asked Luke.

"Um, we don't really know, do we? I mean, Stonehenge got built, but we've no idea how."

"Indeed. So, what about this one?"

He led him to the opposite side of the hall and unveiled the second canvas. It was a large, luminous landscape by the same painter, but compared to its dramatic companion piece, it was oddly bare of detail and event.

It depicted dawn, somewhere by the sea. Silver-barked trees thinned out amid wide reed beds that stretched to the shore. The artist had chosen a palette of washed-out colors: pale brown stalks, pale blue sky, pale gray water. The world was radiantly threadbare, like old cloth that the light shone through.

It was only when Silyen moved the candelabra that the others noticed the figure, and Luke gasped.

The king stood at the shoreline, his tattered red robe as fine as shadow, his hand resting on the scruff of the beast at his side. Their silhouettes on the brilliant water were made jagged by branching antlers and a crown of twigs. The man appeared to be speaking softly to his creature—or perhaps only to the air.

It seemed as though at any minute the thin sky might tear and they would step through it.

"It's him," Luke breathed. "But I've never seen this picture before, so I couldn't have imagined . . ."

Dog was bending over the label at the bottom of the frame.

"There's no title," he growled.

"It's been gilded over. But if you squint, you can make out the original letters underneath. It's called *The King's Farewell*."

"This picture looks like the beach here, but we saw him at Eilean Dòchais," said Luke. "Who is he?"

"He was the only Skillful monarch this country has ever had."

"I didn't think there were any at all."

"Exactly. So, you see why I want us to find him again—if you agree?"

Luke leaned against the table that took up the length of the hall, staring at the painting.

"Why does he matter? You said earlier that this was more important than my family's safety, or my friends, or your father's murders, or anything else that's going on out there."

Silyen's throat was absurdly tight as he set down the candlestick. He'd always pursued his researches alone in the library or in the woods. Scholarship was a solitary act.

And yet . . .

"There are two things I've always wanted to know," Silyen replied. "Where does Skill come from? And why were there ever unSkilled queens and kings, rather than my kind ruling from the beginning? I think the answer to both lies with the Wonder King—as he's known in tales.

"There are traces of him, here and there. I showed your sister the Chancellor's Chair at Kyneston—there are carvings on it that I believe depict parts of his story. And my aunt and I used to read to each other from *Tales of the King,* a beautiful medieval poem-cycle about his deeds. There was a copy in the lost library at Orpen, but I've never found another complete one.

"Which begs the question: *why* is there so little trace of him? I used to think he'd been deliberately suppressed, because we've not forgotten the rest of the monarchy. Yes, we mock it in bedtime storybooks, and deface it, like the poor old Last King's statue with its face chiseled off. But every schoolchild can name the kings and queens." He caught Luke grimacing, and corrected himself. "Every *diligent* schoolchild can name them. But someone as unique as the *Wundorcyning*? All we have are echoes and fragments, like this painting, or the poem, or the chair."

Luke had been listening hard. He swallowed, and Silyen saw his throat bob.

"And you think that the answers might be somewhere in my head?"

"It's where we saw him. More than that—we met him. You *spoke* to him."

Silyen hadn't forgotten a moment of it. Luke asking the king if he was dead, or imagining their encounter, and the king telling him: *Neither.* Luke asking where they were, and the king saying: *Right here.* The door outlined in light, through which they had seen themselves in Eilean Dòchais. The king's promise: *You see how close we are.* Then his command: *Go now.*

It had been the most astonishing moment of Sil's life. He had dreamed of it ever since.

Luke was absorbed in thought. Judging from his expression, Silyen would swear the boy was . . . *scheming?*

He was.

"If we do this, then you need to do something for me. I have to get back to Eilean Dòchais to check on a friend—you might be interested to meet her, too. So when you've done looking in my head, I want you to call your family and find out if Crovan is still in London. If he is, we go to Scotland."

"Anxious to introduce me to your friends, Luke? How delightful." He grinned as the boy flushed bright red. "Deal."

So many promises. So many bargains. People and politics. Motives and maneuverings. It was all such fun.

And yet, compared to the perfection that was the practice of Skill, all such utter dross.

"Right," said Luke, pale but determined. "Let's do it."

As the boy settled back in the armchair, Dog curled up on the rug to watch the entertainment. He'd find it rather dull. Their bodies would fall comatose, as if in a deep sleep. Their eyes would roll up. (Sil knew this from repeated requests from Mama that he not go into his own mind when the staff were around, because it frightened the maids.)

Sil pressed his fingers to Luke's forehead, closed his eyes—

—and opened them.

The first thing he saw was a golden thread, spider-fine, that spun out of him. The second thing, as he lifted his head, was the sunlit grasslands that stretched endlessly away on all sides. The third, the eagles that circled overhead.

At the other end of the thread was a boy, kneeling. Luke's clothes were different: a pair of American-brand jeans and a T-shirt with the tour logo of a Canadian band. The band was a good one, if a little too grime for Silyen's tastes. Luke wouldn't have been able to buy either item in Britain—they would be things he coveted. Sil checked himself to see if the boy had put him in anything ridiculous, but no. It wasn't his hoodie and sneakers, though, but his riding jacket and boots. The boy plainly still saw him as an Equal, but hey, it was a good look.

Luke got to his feet and the golden thread that joined them disappeared. He frowned and reached for it. Under his touch, brightness streaked between them. When he removed his hand, it vanished again.

"You're a person," Luke said, evidently surprised. "You look like yourself."

"What on earth was I last time?"

"To me, you were . . ." The boy shaped something vague in the air. "Light. You were just light. Skill, I guess."

"And now?"

"Lord of the manor."

"That's me." Sil raked back his hair and stared around them. Broken up by cloud, thick bands of sunlight passed across the plains, which changed from bright to dark and back in an instant. A distant mountain range was creased blue and gold between the ridges. Snow glittered on its peaks. As birds wheeled overhead, their eerily magnified shadows fell blackly on the ground beneath. The colors were saturated. Intense. The air rippled as if in a haze, though it wasn't hot.

Luke was gazing in astonishment at the endless grasslands, the bubbling river, the cloud-heaped sky.

"And you say that my mind created this? The way it looks? Because it's epic. Reminds me of my favorite games, like Age of Awe. I would have expected more cars and girls, to be honest. Something more . . . mundane."

"I think a lot of people would find if they looked, *really* looked, inside themselves, that they're more than they imagine, Luke."

"Now you're sounding like Jackson."

Luke's tone was wistful. That was quite enough of that.

"I suppose we should start by looking for the wall—Rix's Silence. That's where we were last time, when the king appeared."

Silyen turned on his heel, surveying the expanse. Between the rippling plains and the moving shadow, it was hard to make out anything. Except . . . was that a sinuous shape in the grass? The scale of this terrain was so vast that for a moment he couldn't get a fix on what he'd seen. Could it be a snake? But it didn't move, and he realized that he was looking at a wall, a long way away.

It was low and somehow dappled, blending into the surrounding trees and grasses. You could barely see it was there. But something about it felt familiar.

Luke had seen it, too. "Let's go," he said.

The waist-high grasses snagged Sil's trousers and scratched the sleeves of his jacket as they walked. Glancing over, he saw that Luke had acquired a hoodie that covered his arms. Had the boy done that consciously? Was he learning that this space was his to shape? Side by side, they fell into a rhythm and Sil lost track of time. At one point, he glanced up to see if the sun had moved, then realized why everything here felt so bright and the shadows so strong and slanting: there were two suns in the sky.

"Nice touch," he said, pointing.

Luke looked thrilled as he shaded his eyes and glanced up. Sunglasses appeared on Luke's nose, and Silyen blinked as his eyes acquired a pair, too.

"We've still got ages to go," Luke complained, peering ahead to where the wall was becoming clearer, but not significantly closer.

"You know, I think you could do something about that."

"Bring it nearer?" Luke looked dubious.

"Perhaps. Or maybe get us there faster."

"Oh. Whoa!"

Luke jumped back as a road unrolled at their feet, stretching away across the grasslands. Then grinned as a sports car appeared in the middle of it. Sil didn't know the first thing about cars, but this one was shiny new and looked sickeningly fast. Gavar would have drooled at the sight of it. Silyen just felt queasy.

"I'll go slowly, I promise," Luke said, climbing in.

And he was as good as his word, keeping the speedometer at a steady thirty miles an hour.

"This is astonishing." Luke's eyes traveled over the car's sleek interior. The dirty beats of the grime crew were playing through the sound system. "Is this what it feels like to have Skill, back in the real world?"

"I hate to break it to you, but I can't create Lamborghinis out of thin air. More's the pity. If everyone in Britain had one, maybe people wouldn't moan so much."

"You still don't get it, do you?" Luke said.

"Get what?" *Ugh, please, not another Meilyr-inspired sermon.* Sil turned his head discreetly before administering side-eye.

"Shall I tell you what I thought," Luke continued, "when I realized that I control how we appear in this place? I thought about putting you in something ridiculous. Humiliating. A bikini, or a gorilla suit—or even making you an actual animal, because if I can make you appear like a golden cloud, I'm pretty sure I could make you a pig or a dog.

"But then I realized, no, that's how you lot think—you Equals. That's what it means to have power. Being constantly tempted to use it and abuse it. In fact, to not be able to tell where power ends and abuse begins. And then I had a really weird thought."

Silyen gritted his teeth for whatever judgy pronouncement was coming next.

"I thought that in a way—and obviously with exceptions, like your father and Bouda Matravers—you could all be a lot worse."

Unexpected.

"Thanks for the vote of confidence."

"Sil, this Wonder King . . ." Luke's fingers were tapping the steering wheel and he was staring straight ahead. "When we met him, I felt awe. Felt respect. But what if there's a good reason he's been erased from history? What if he was dangerous, or ridiculously powerful? Perhaps we shouldn't be looking for someone who's been forgotten. I mean, isn't he *dead*?"

The hairs prickled up the back of Silyen's neck. He thought it entirely possible that the *Wundorcyning* was all of those things.

Which was exactly why Silyen wanted to find him.

"Ahh!"

Silyen jerked forward as Luke slammed on the brakes and the car screeched to a halt. They'd reached the wall.

And it was nothing like Sil had imagined.

EIGHT

LUKE

The wall was too old to be Rix's Silence.

"It's not the same one Crovan was attacking," Luke told Silyen.

It was more than old. It was ancient. It was a dry-stone wall, made without mortar. Rocks were piled on top of one another and fitted painstakingly together, each piebald with white lichen and green moss. It stood as high as Luke's shoulder, though appeared taller because of grasses sprouting from the top. A butterfly, its wings flimsy and near-transparent, flitted among the seed-heavy stalks as they whisked in the breeze.

It looked like nothing so much as Hadrian's Wall, built by the Romans to keep out marauders from the north. When Luke was younger, they'd visited it a few times on family holidays. Mum was a keen walker, though Daisy was usually begging to be picked up before they'd gone a mile. Luke ran his hands over the wall, marveling at the contrast between the prickly velvet of the moss and the rough stone beneath.

Silyen, though, was frowning. The Equal seemed displeased as he looked one way along the length of it, then turned to survey the other direction.

"Problem?" Luke asked eventually.

"It's straight."

"And?"

"How do you keep things in if it's straight? It should be an enclosure."

Luke got what he meant. If a Silence was a way to contain memories, it made sense it would enclose them, like a wall around a fortress.

"The one before, that Rix laid on you, was round," Silyen said. "Like a city wall. Break through the wall, and you're into whatever's kept behind it. But this . . ."

The Equal tailed off, looking at the structure reproachfully.

"Perhaps it's not a Silence at all," Luke suggested. "Perhaps it's just a wall that my brain thought would look good. It's like somewhere I used to visit with my family. So if it's that . . ."

If it was that, then he should be able to change it, just as he had with the clothes they were wearing and the road they'd driven on. Luke looked at the wall and imagined it taller. Pictured the stones more neatly aligned.

Nothing altered. So, this wasn't his creation. But it wasn't Rix's black wall, either. The only other person who Luke knew had Silenced him was Crovan. Was this his handiwork?

But then why did it appear as though it had been here for centuries?

"It must have been made looking this way, right? Because otherwise it's definitely older than me, and no one could have Silenced me before I was even born."

"There are hereditary Quiets that pass down the genera-tions," Silyen said. "Families use them to hide their dirty secrets—the true parentage of a child, which might permanently disbar a line of succession, that sort of thing. My mother's family has a Quiet. My aunt Euterpe told me about it in the library at Orpen—that was her mindscape, a perfect re-creation of the Orpen Mote of her childhood, before it burned down. But the Quiet has a different shape. It's a locked box to which she had a key."

"So this is Crovan's work?"

Silyen shook his head, in either disagreement or bafflement. Luke didn't know whether to be reassured or scared that the Equal was just as much at a loss.

"It just . . . goes on," Silyen said, casting his eyes along the expanse of it. "No secret could be that big."

"So it can't be one," said Luke. "And look."

He pointed to where, a short distance farther along, the wall had broken down. A fall of stones had left a breach in the length of it, wide enough for a person to squeeze through.

On inspection, it looked like a normal gap in a normal wall. The sort of thing where a storm knocked a few stones off the top, then sheep took to jumping over the low part, and stone by stone, a hole opened up. It didn't look as though it had been smashed down by a raging Skillful fury, like Crovan's. Simply something that had come apart with age.

Luke had learned his lesson on the shore of Eilean Dòchais, when he'd thrust his hand into Loch nan Deur and had his curiosity rewarded by excruciating pain. But he could see no danger here. This place was Luke himself, Silyen had said, and he sensed that that was true.

"You let me go to Crovan because you both wanted to learn how to break down a Silence as a way to discover the concealed memory," he told Silyen. "So if this is a Silence, then what— the memory comes back on the other side? We should try."

Silyen nibbled his fingernails. It was strange to see him so uncertain—Silyen, who had answers for every question you could think of, and ten more you hadn't.

"We should. Shall I go first?"

"No thanks. My mind, my memories."

Silyen nodded as Luke squared his shoulders and looked at the gap. Luke couldn't believe he was feeling so tense. Couldn't believe that this was all real—in a manner of speaking—when he was actually sitting in an armchair at Far Carr. Couldn't believe that the whole of this past year hadn't just been some astonishingly detailed bad dream from beginning to end.

Could he be hurt, in this place? If his clothes here weren't exactly real, then was his body? Could he die here?

Luke reached cautiously into the space between the stones. Something lifted and tickled the hairs on his arms, but so lightly it might have been merely a breeze. There was no pain, no sense of threat or malevolence. As he stepped through, his scalp tingled. He felt his pulse throb beneath his fingernails. His heart sped up. Was that only adrenaline or something more?

As Luke stood there trying to see if any thoughts or memories had come back into his head that hadn't been there a few moments ago, Silyen nudged him aside from the gap. And as the Equal stepped across, too, he gasped so loudly that Luke thought he must have sliced an artery on a jagged bit of rock.

"What? Are you okay?"

"Skill," Silyen hissed. His eyes had gone very wide. "Ahh, so much."

Luke shook his shoulder and could feel the boy's heartbeat thrumming through him as if he were as fragile as a bird. Silyen splayed a palm on his chest, catching his breath.

"But I don't remember anything," Luke told him. "No memories have come back to me. And they should, shouldn't they?"

They stared at each other. The Equal's confusion was evident—and disconcerting. Luke had relied on Silyen to be a kind of guide in this place, he realized. Now it seemed that it was equally new territory to him.

"Let's start from what we know," Silyen said. "Here, in your mind, is some kind of act. In certain respects, it resembles a Silence—a wall or barrier. However, in one important regard, it is different: it's not an enclosure. It appears to be old. It also appears to be broken—or at least, breaking down. It was created using an act of immense Skill, or by a very powerfully Skilled person."

Luke's mind raced. When he examined where it had brought him, he almost stopped breathing.

"Maybe it's him? The Wonder King? The name's a bit of a clue that he's incredibly powerful. He lived a long time ago, which is why the wall would be old. And you said that he was forgotten—*almost* forgotten, with just bits and pieces of memories. Would that be what happened if a Silence broke down, like a wall with gaps and holes? Something—or someone—who's not quite remembered, but not quite forgotten, either?"

Luke realized he was trembling. What did it all mean? Silyen had raked his hair over his face, as if giving himself privacy to think.

"Can you take us up there?" the Equal said after a while, pointing to the top of one of the tallest, snowiest mountains. "Because we need to see . . ."

Luke looked. The peaks were a long way away and a *long* way up. Definitely higher than the hills in the Peak District that Mum and Dad used to drag them up in the summer.

"Do I dream up a plane or something? Give us wings? Maybe get a giant eagle to come and pick us up—I'm pretty sure I've seen that in a movie. . . ."

"Eagles are always good." Silyen was grinning. "But there's an easier way, now that you're more accustomed to how this place works. You simply think it."

"*Think* it?"

"Well, this is your mind, Hadley, and most of us use our minds for thinking, though you may be an exception."

"Just when I was *thinking* you might not be a colossal git, Silyen."

The Equal spread his hands wide. But Luke got his point. How would it work? Would they fly up into the air?—because that would be both cool and terrifying. Why on earth had his stupid brain created a landscape like this anyway, and not . . . Then his stomach lurched and everything swirled as if the world were a painting whose colors had run. He staggered and his feet slipped beneath him. Two hands grabbed his wrists and held on tight.

Luke blinked and opened his eyes.

"If I might suggest . . ." Silyen murmured. "More suitable footwear?"

They were now high on a mountain peak. The sky up here was blue-pink and stung with each breath, and snow-covered ice crunched beneath their feet. They were so high that condors circled below them.

"Better," the Equal said, stamping his feet with satisfaction.

Luke examined himself. He was clad in a mountaineer's down suit, as garishly red as a London bus. Silyen was in some historical version, complete with tweed trousers tucked into thick socks, round tinted goggles, and a scarf that muffled him to the nose. Great—even in Luke's imagination the Equal was the cool one.

Sil pulled Luke to his side and pointed to the grassy plains below, threaded through with a golden ribbon of river.

"Look, you can see Crovan's handiwork from here. Each one of those he laid on you after your interrogation sessions." The Equal's voice hesitated a moment. "So many . . ."

Scattered across the landscape at intervals, like cattle corrals or city walls with no city inside, were small enclosures. They were constructed from smooth blocks that reminded Luke of the sheer sides of Eilean Dòchais castle, and they pitted the landscape. He couldn't imagine what the minds of those kept prisoner for years must look like, if Crovan hurt them and Silenced them over and over again. Their minds would be an expanse of pitiless little citadels, locking away horror and pain.

Luke *had* to get back to Eilean Dòchais. He had to know that Coira was okay. He desperately hoped that she had reconsidered her plan to wait and confront Crovan, and had instead fled the castle—along with whomever else among its prisoners she chose to get to safety.

"And there," Silyen continued. "That's the Silence Rix put in place when he used you to kill Zelston. The one Crovan was trying to tear down, to find out how to break through Silences laid by others."

The walls of this one were taller, thicker, blacker; the whole structure had a lopsided appearance, as if thrown up quickly. But it was still a strong enclosure, and sealed behind it were Luke's memories of those minutes in Kyneston's ballroom that had wrecked his life and ended Chancellor Zelston's.

"Those are what Silences usually look like . . ." Silyen said.

". . . and then there's that."

Luke finished the sentence as they both stared at the wall that meandered through the great plain. It wove close to the river, looking just as much a part of the landscape. From up here, you could mistake it for a natural feature, like the incredible gritstone edges Dad had once shown them in the Peak District national park.

"It looks like it *belongs*. You'd almost not notice it, unless you walked into it," Luke said.

"Hmm . . ."

Silyen sounded abstracted. Then the Equal spun on his heel and reached into the air, grasping the handle of a door that hadn't been there moments earlier, and which Luke was pretty sure he hadn't imagined. It was made of slatted wood and painted a thick, glossy white.

Silyen pushed it open. "Excuse the mess. I'm not one for entertaining visitors."

A "mess" was one way of putting it. The high, sunlit room resembled an explosion in a library. There were books everywhere. Piled on the floor and on shelves—in both neat rows and more haphazard stacks. Books were stuffed under cushions and down the sides of posh but knackered sofas and armchairs.

The Equal made a gallant "after you" gesture, and Luke stepped through—hesitantly, because he knew where they must be now. If the vast landscape was somehow, mystifyingly, *Luke,* then this unexpectedly cheerful, white-walled room overflowing with books must be . . . *Silyen.*

He glanced back. Through the doorway he could see the frosted sky of the mountain peak; their footprints were still visible in the snow crust. The door swung shut—then disappeared. Luke took a deep breath and looked around.

"It's not as sinister as I would have imagined," he conceded.

Silyen smirked, and picked a path through the scattered books to a large table with not an inch of visible surface space. Among the litter of books, cups, and several French coffee presses was a wooden box the color of cinnamon.

Silyen patted it. "My family's Quiet. Gavar has one, and Jenner, and my mother, of course. It's how I knew of the existence of my ancestor Cadmus's journals. It doesn't contain them, of course. Only my aunt's memory of Orpen actually held the books. But the knowledge of them is locked away in here.

"Just as Silences are walls that encircle a memory that's hidden, Quiets take the form of closable objects: boxes, bags, chests, safes, wardrobes, you name it. We can open them, but we can't show their contents to anyone else. That's the difference between the two acts. A Quiet bestowed on Equals doesn't rob us of our memories, but prevents us from sharing them. A Silence laid on commoners conceals your memory from you.

"Quiets are mostly used in families, but they're also used by groups. Say a bunch of friends commits a murder one drunken night: you can all accept a Quiet. None of you will forget the deed, but you'll each be prevented from talking about it. Or two people having an affair could agree to conceal it with a Quiet. The only one who can lift a Quiet is the one who bestows it, presumably the person with most to lose. So, you can see why Crovan and I thought it would be valuable to know how to break down those walls and open those boxes. Just imagine what you might discover."

Silyen's eyes gleamed. His enthusiasm would be infectious— were it not for the inconvenient fact that this research was why he'd allowed Luke to be sent to Crovan. The Equal had seemed genuinely contrite about that earlier, but presumably only because he'd taken a shine to Luke, rather than because he'd grown any morals.

And yet Luke planned to use Silyen, too, if he could. To get to Eilean Dòchais. To help Coira escape safely if there was any trouble, and maybe to show her how to wake the Skill she surely possessed. He even dreamed of Silyen pitching his weight behind the struggle against his father. None of those things would cancel out what Silyen had done to him. But Luke knew now that the world was grayer than it had appeared when he first joined the Millmoor Games and Social Club. And when he and his friends had sat in disused offices, planning their latest strike-backs against a faceless regime.

And sometimes the person who benefited most, when you forgave someone, was yourself.

"There's something I need to show you," the Equal said, throwing an arm round Luke's shoulder and steering him toward the far wall of the library, which was floor-to-ceiling French doors. "And the view is amazing."

It was. Sil led Luke onto a terrace strewn with tropical flowers. The air was warm and heavy with vanilla, coconut, and sea salt, and glittering water stretched away to the horizon. The terrace was raised above a sandy beach, and from the water's edge, the sea darkened from turquoise to deepest navy blue.

Luke had never left Britain, and the unfamiliar scents and sights were almost overwhelming. It was one more thing the Equals denied the common people—the right to see anything beyond their own small corner of the wide, vast world. Luke had created his inner world from the fantasy realms of video games, but Silyen's perfect place had a real-world counterpart.

"My family has an estate on one of the Confederate-controlled islands in the Caribbean," the Equal said. "We don't go there much, because, ugh, airplanes, and also truly loathsome politics. But it's beautiful and inspired me, I guess. Oh, hello."

Luke glanced down. Their clothing had changed to better suit the outdoors. Silyen was in a buttoned black linen shirt, while Luke was . . .

Luke was topless.

"A shirt would be nice," he said through gritted teeth.

Silyen's grin was diabolical, but a moment later Luke was clothed. In an extremely tight white T-shirt. Luke rolled his eyes. If this was Silyen's mind, he should be grateful not to be naked.

"The wardrobe opportunities honestly aren't why I've brought you here."

The Equal nudged Luke around to where a riotous tropical garden met the sea. You could hardly tell it was a garden, because the flowers were so overgrown, but the wall gave it away. It was in a tumbledown state, thanks no doubt to the climate, and cut through the bright blooms to run right into the sea.

"I never realized," said Silyen. "Because it doesn't look at all out of place. But that's the same wall, I swear. Watch."

And as Luke did, Silyen altered the landscape around them, just as Luke had been able to manipulate his own world. The sprawling foliage shrank back; the shoreline retreated, leaving an exposed seabed. Coral stood in the sunlight like petrified trees, sprouting from seaweed grass. But just as when Luke had attempted the same thing, the wall remained unchanged.

Luke's spine prickled.

"I don't get it. Someone's Silenced both of us, in the same way?"

"It's stranger than that. I've told you that my aunt's mindscape was the Orpen Mote of her childhood. We'd walk round it and talk and laugh and argue. Over the years, I got to know every corner of it. There was a wall that ran through the water meadow beyond the moat—an odd place for one. Then I realized how ancient it was, and decided it must have belonged to some vanished building, or been the boundary of a long-lost field.

"But when I was at Orpen a few months ago, there in the real world, in Kent, helping her rebuild the ruins . . ." The

Equal paused, momentarily stricken. "The wall wasn't there. It had no real-world counterpart."

"It was only in her mind," Luke breathed. "And you first saw it years ago, before you ever met me. So this isn't just about us, or because of things that have happened recently."

"I'd lay money on the fact that we're not the only ones with this wall running through them. I'm trying to remember if anyone else . . ."

Luke wondered into how many minds the Equal had trespassed. It wasn't a comforting thought.

And then just like Dad doing the final tuning on a car engine, to send it sputtering into life, a connection sparked in Luke's brain. What all this was, and what it could mean.

"Maybe *everyone* has it. The Silence is how you make people forget things—it only doesn't get used on Equals because of some weird etiquette, right? And your family Quiets tell us that forgetting can be made to pass down, to last for years. So maybe if this is the work of the king, and he's that powerful, he's come up with some combination of the two—and the thing we've forgotten is *him*."

Silyen stared at him and Luke thought he might laugh till he bust a rib, because he had actually come up with an idea about Skill that Silyen Jardine hadn't thought of. The Equal shoved his hair off his face. His speech and his breathing had sped up.

"Right. And because he did it so long ago, the act has slowly been breaking down. You can see it right there in the wall, which is pretty much coming apart."

They both looked across Silyen's beach to where the wall, stripped bare of flowers, seaweed, and sand, looked like the bleached remains of a long-lost Atlantis. The cracks and gaps in it were plain to see.

"Yes!" Luke crowed. They were on a roll with this. "Which

is why he's remembered from time to time. Because the forgetting is disintegrating, every now and then a memory slips through. Someone writes a poem about him, or carves an image, or paints a picture. . . . What? Why are you shaking your head?"

Silyen couldn't be having second thoughts. This was all making sense—inasmuch as anything Skillful ever would.

"I get how it might work, that it might decay, et cetera. But, Luke, nothing could be done on that scale. Silences are laid individually. Yes, family Quiets are inherited, but even those start with a small group of people, the original family members. You couldn't do it to an entire country. Even assuming that the population of Britain back then was much smaller, you'd still be talking more than a million people. Dammit."

Silyen squatted on his haunches, chewing his fingernails. The wind stirred that messy hair.

They'd been close to something, Luke thought. So close.

But they weren't there yet. And in the meantime, having given Silyen what he wanted—the chance to step back into Luke's mind—it was time for the Equal to keep his side of the bargain.

"Would this be the moment to remind you that I want to check on my friend at Eilean Dòchais? I mean, who knows, it might even help us with this, because that's where we were when we first saw him, and . . ."

Luke stopped, his mouth going dry. Silyen arched an eyebrow.

"And?"

It came back to Luke with the intensity of a hallucination. After just a few days away, his time at the castle already resembled a feverish nightmare.

He remembered standing by the Last Door only half conscious, his mind cut loose by Crovan's interrogations. He'd been clutching the doorframe—and the deadly door was open. Coira had found him there, staring out, babbling about the king and his stag.

He was insisting that he'd find them there, on the other side of the door.

Coira had snapped her fingers next to his ear. Had looked like she wanted to slap him. Had grabbed his shirt and pulled him back from danger.

And then, at the end of her patience, she had told him *Be my guest* if he still wanted to risk his life by chancing the Door. And Luke had stepped through the Last Door onto Crovan's rocky island—and lived.

The first thing that had gone through Luke's mind was astonishment at still being alive. The second thing was what that meant about Coira's parentage—that she was a Crovan. Only family could give a person permission to step through the castle's Last Door.

But this third thing, he had only remembered now: his conviction that the king was out there, just through the door.

Had he been? And if so . . . why?

As the salt-sweet breeze of Sil's improbable mindscape blew around them, Luke pulled Silyen to his feet.

"There's more I need to tell you," he said. "And we *really* need to get to Eilean Dòchais."

NINE

BOUDA

"Who thought that putting your husband into Midsummer's circle was a good idea?" Jon Faiers demanded before the office door had barely closed behind him. "Because as far as I can see, his contribution so far has been failing to capture one prisoner and releasing another. Not to mention seriously limiting my usefulness. While he's close to Midsummer, she'll keep me away because she won't want to, as she thinks, betray me as her spy in your office."

Jon's eyes flashed with anger, but Bouda let neither their fury nor their gorgeous baby-blueness distract her.

"Sit down," she said, motioning to the armchair on the other side of her desk. "I said, *sit down*. I know what this is: it's jealousy. And it's pointless. Gavar has explained that the staged escape was necessary to win Midsummer's trust. I wasn't happy, but it makes sense. We give up one prisoner to get Gavar into a position that enables us to sweep up them all.

"As for how his work affects your position, don't be ridiculous. You couldn't plausibly spend much time with these ragbag rebels anyway. Midsummer's no fool. She'd realize you were absent from this office to a degree I'd never tolerate, and quickly come to the conclusion that I *did* tolerate it, and that you were a traitor. More important, you and Gavar have different roles. His job is to bring us information *from* their camp, and yours is to plant misinformation *into* their camp. You'll have your part to play in our endgame."

Jon didn't seem mollified.

"And you think Gavar will be able to keep up the pretense?" he protested. "He's hardly a master of subtlety. You're talking about someone who shot his mistress because he wasn't articulate enough to persuade her not to leave him. He's dumb and dangerous."

Bouda leapt to her feet, incensed.

"How dare you speak of my husband like that? He's the Chancellor's heir. Show some respect."

"Your husband he may be, but has he laid a hand on you since your wedding? At least when he was sober he was able to tell the difference between you and one of his commoner pickups. Ah!"

There was a crack like a handclap, and Faiers staggered back, palm pressed to his face. Blood trickled from between his fingers. What on earth had just happened?

Slowly, Jon lifted his hand away and Bouda saw it—a shard of glass embedded in his cheek, beneath the eye. Then she noticed that the front of his shirt was soaked through, and that the water stain was pinked in places. More blood.

The remains of the water glass that had stood on her desk until a moment ago lay scattered across the floor. A surge of Skillful anger had shattered the glass.

No. Bouda flexed her fingers and knew what she'd done. She had exploded the *water*.

She hadn't intended to hurt Faiers, and yet her Skill's reaction had been honest. Why did these men feel entitled to perpetually question her judgment? Even this man, whose mind and body were so attractive, even though his Skillessness should have repulsed her.

Well, maybe this would be a lesson for him. Argument was one thing—she valued his counsel and opinions. But defiance and disrespect were not to be tolerated.

"Let me see," she said, pushing his hands away as she examined the damage. A few shards hadn't penetrated his suit jacket, but there was one nasty needle of glass jabbed close to his collarbone. Bouda tweezered it out with her lacquered nails and heard Faiers gasp.

She needed to see the wound, so she tugged off his tie and unbuttoned the neck of his shirt. Which was when she noticed that his breath was coming even faster and his heartbeat was hammering. He tipped his head forward, so his mouth rested against her forehead.

"You," he breathed, as she touched her fingers to the puncture and felt the skin beneath them heat up. His exhale was long and sensuous, and one hand came up to the back of her neck. He was finding this arousing.

Bouda was, too.

She lifted her mouth close to his.

"Say that you're sorry," she said. "For disobeying me."

"I'm sorry, Heir Bouda."

As their lips met, hot and hungry, Bouda thought it wasn't absurd that she felt like this about a commoner. It was almost perfect. This was how things should be, between the Equals and the commoners. The people might be defiant, but were easily reminded of their place—and would love and admire their masters all the more for it.

Bouda pulled back to inspect the wound on Jon's face. It was a nasty slice, and she flinched to see how close it had come to his eye. Just as well that she used only fine Prussian glassware. She saw a slender shard still embedded deep in his cheek. Her nails plucked it out, and it left a welling red seam some two inches long.

She licked her finger and wiped away the blood, watching the cut close up in its wake. Healing was no talent of hers, but every Equal child knew how to fix cuts and grazes so they didn't scar.

When she took her hand off Jon's face, though, there was still a faint red line marking his cheekbone—and always would be. It would be good for him to remember both who had injured him and who had healed him.

The country would do the same, once Bouda was through with it.

"Jon," she told him, stroking the mark she had left, "let me explain why it's irrelevant whether or not Gavar 'keeps up the pretense.' I suggested to my father-in-law that Gavar go to Midsummer. If he succeeds in sustaining his deception, then we have her trapped and can end this cancer of commoner revolt. If he fails, then he's finally out of his father's good graces. Either way, one of my rivals falls."

Which would leave only one more person to deal with.

There was a reason Bouda had suggested to Whittam that he be the one to task Gavar with infiltrating Midsummer's camp. A reason why Bouda ensured that Lady Thalia be the one to secure Gavar's child, and why Bouda herself had sat there cringing submissively as Whittam stroked her like a pet and made vile insinuations about the Kyneston succession.

Midsummer, Gavar . . . and Whittam. If the trio could somehow be made to take out each other, Bouda would be the last one standing.

Faiers was watching her as if hypnotized. She remembered the evening they had first met, at Grendelsham. How smoothly he had intervened when Whittam was groping her. His frank declaration on the clifftop. For all his faults—not least this possessiveness that ran through men like blood—he wanted the same things she did and would take risks to achieve them.

And to have a commoner at her side when the dust settled would be a valuable thing. He could never be more than a lover—to have an unSkilled child would be unthinkable. But he could be a partner in power.

"Come down to the river with me," she said, refastening his shirt and ignoring his pout. "We need to talk where we won't be interrupted, and there's something I want to try."

As they descended the final stairs to the rivergate exit, Bouda remembered the CCTV of Abigail Hadley and the feral child from the Blood Fair, drawing back the bolt and running for freedom. Gavar's "capture" of Abigail had been a well-choreographed piece of fakery—one designed to deceive both the Westminster guards and, more important, Midsummer's supporters. Bouda had watched it several times. The CCTV coverage was incomplete, but she saw the small giveaways: the moment Gavar twisted the girl's neck to show her the door leading to the exit corridor; whatever it was he said to the guard in Astrid's detention rooms, to get the imbecile to wait at the top of the stairs, back turned.

No, Gavar might be many things—crass, brutish, and oblivious—but he wasn't stupid.

Then she and Faiers were out of that same door and on to the parliamentary terrace, and Bouda's head swam with the zing of ozone from the river. She was giddy with the sense of her own power, tingling through her.

Faiers steadied her elbow.

"You were magnificent that day," he murmured. "The creature you conjured out of the river to throttle Midsummer's dragon. I've never seen anything so incredible."

"You'll see something much better, if I have anything to do with it. And I'll need your help."

And she told him what she was thinking.

That was the thing about winning a game. It wasn't enough to have your own strategies and tactics; you had to learn everyone else's, too.

And then there was Silyen Jardine. Bouda wasn't sure that he was even playing a game—it certainly wasn't the same one as the rest of them. But he was too powerful to ignore. She had watched him rise. First his impressive feats at Kyneston, then his irregular inheritance of Far Carr. And finally, by sheer accident (*surely* sheer accident, because the person responsible for it was Bouda herself, when she arrested Rix), his elevation to be its lord. No one had seen him since before the Blood Fair. The day of the Fair, he had inexplicably freed every slave on his estate.

Bouda had no idea what Silyen was up to. But she'd learned one thing from him. Skill was so much more than any of them had appreciated. All her life, Bouda had used her Skill in petty ways. Now, in this turmoil, it was finding outlets she'd never imagined. She was finally understanding that, like a muscle, her connection with her Skill strengthened and developed with use. As an Equal, it was thrilling to feel the potential tingling in her veins. As a politician, it was an unrivaled opportunity to inspire both obedience and admiration.

And wonder. Surely better than either fear or love, because it contained both.

"Keep an eye on me," Bouda instructed Faiers, as she stood on the gritty river shore where the Thames alternately challenged and retreated from the terrace wall. She needed to know how far she could go. How far before the river escaped her control. How far before she was lost.

She sent her Skillful awareness coiling out into the water like a sinuous, infiltrating weed. When she'd first felt this, drawing water from the Bore's canals onto its burning fields, she'd been afraid of the way the water tugged at her, as if her very self might be one more piece of flotsam to be washed away.

But not here. Not now. She sent her Skill deep into the Thames.

This was London's lifeblood. From the time of the Romans, the river had quenched the thirst of this settlement, carried away its filth, borne the trading vessels that helped it grow, and, just occasionally, poisoned it.

But there was far more than simply this central channel. London's lost rivers flowed far beneath the stone and tarmac. They crisscrossed below the city, an alternate, subterranean map. Their interlocking branches and tributaries were a net of water, spread out under the capital. If you could draw it tight enough, you would capture the whole city.

Bouda was uncertain if she was breathing anymore—or if she was, whether it was air or water. She could still feel Jon's hand on her elbow, and yet it was as though she were at a distance, looking at him holding someone else. She was immersed in Skill. Was this what it had been like for Silyen Jardine all these years? No wonder he had been strange and separate and self-absorbed.

She flowed through the river—and the river flowed through her.

In Gorregan, she had pulled the water up through the fountain. Had drawn it spouting into the sky to extinguish the flaming platform, and create a barrier for Midsummer's wretched metal lions. Now, she wanted to *push* the water upward. Through the soil, through the cracked mains pipes and the straitjacketing tarmac. Through every crevice and chink it could find. And though she couldn't see it, Bouda could feel it, as she made the streets of London ooze and run. Far from where she stood, puddles welled in Oxford Street and storm drains slopped over along the Mall.

It was there. She could reach it. Her plan could work.

"Bouda?"

That wasn't Faiers.

"Bouda?"

"She was feeling a little tired—we've been working through the night on new security measures—and came out for some air. Can I help, Jenner?"

Bouda reeled herself back into her body, and wanted to cry with the smallness of it. She shook herself. Blinked.

"Jenner. What can I do for you?"

"Father wishes to see us. Crovan's with him, and Gavar will be coming soon with news."

Very well. While Bouda planned her next move, the other players had been busy with theirs. Time to find out what they were.

"You're dismissed, Faiers. Thank you."

And without a backward glance at Jon, Bouda walked with Jenner to the Chancellor's suite in New Westminster Tower.

Her brother-in-law at least waited until they were out of earshot before he began wheedling and beseeching. How had she not noticed before that beneath that blandly pleasant exterior, Jenner was just as hungry as the rest of the Jardine men?

But not for power—or rather, only for that power the rest of them took for granted: Skill.

"Crovan wants to go back to Scotland, but we have to keep him here in London. Father promised me that he'd research Skill restoration, or transferral. I need you to help me make sure he stays."

"And how do you propose I do that? More to the point, *why* would I? Just a few days ago, your father was using the prospect of you, with Skill, to threaten my husband with disinheritance. As long as you're Skilless, that's an empty threat."

"Bouda." Jenner took her elbow and pulled her to one side in the corridor, beside a long tapestry. She shook him off. Men didn't touch each other when trying to make a point, so why touch her? "I'm no threat to Gavar, or to you. There's only one thing I want—that I've ever wanted, although I've tried to pretend to myself otherwise. Whoever gives me that, I'll be in their debt forever."

And something that could have been pity welled up in Bouda. It had felt extraordinary, down there on the Thames shore, filled with the immensity of both the river and her Skill. To never know that? What kind of a third-rate life would it be? Commoners at least had little idea of what they lacked. But Jenner? Faiers?

Faiers.

"People have attempted it for thousands of years," Bouda told her brother-in-law. "And if anyone ever discovered how, they kept it very quiet. But I agree, if anyone in this country can, it will be Arailt Crovan. I'll do my bit to try and persuade him. And if he succeeds, well, it'd be nice to think there's one Jardine who keeps their word and pays their debts."

"I won't forget it," Jenner said. "You'll see."

     ★   ★   ★

Whittam was sprawled on the sofa when the pair of them reached the Chancellor's suite at the top of the tower. Bouda blinked away the distasteful memory of the half-naked woman she had once seen lounging in the same spot. Whittam had a whisky glass in his hand—he was rarely seen without one these days—and his face was beginning to look puffy, his skin coarse. It was just as well the public only saw him from a distance, on the balcony of Aston House, or behind the tinted glass of the state cars.

Crovan was at the vast paned windows, looking across the Westminster complex. Many floors below lay Bouda's Office of Public Safety, but Crovan, like most visitors to these rooms, had eyes for only one thing. The golden coruscations of the House of Light played over his face, turning the lenses of his glasses into dazzling discs. Bouda ignored Whittam's slurred greeting, and went to Crovan's side.

"Impressive, that trick with the dragon," Crovan said, lifting his chin in the direction of the crenelated roof of the House. He glanced briefly at Bouda. "Yours, too, of course. At Gorregan you displayed the sort of elemental manipulation that has a long history in these isles. Of course there are similarities with your ancestor, Harding the Voyager. But to animate those creatures . . ."

Dragons crouched on each end of the House's roof. From up here, you could see how big they really were. Almost the size of legendary dragons. Bouda imagined them sailing across the skies of London. That would be an impressive sight. The people would stand openmouthed in the streets.

No, the sooner Midsummer was dealt with, the better. Getting Gavar in had been the right thing to do—his information would enable this to be brought to a swift conclusion.

"You're so right," she murmured, looking up at Crovan

through her lashes. He was one of the few who had always been immune to her small charms and flirtations. Was he gay? Asexual? She had never heard the slightest breath of intrigue around his personal life. "It would be fascinating to discover how she does it, wouldn't it? Very rewarding research."

Crovan snorted. "I doubt she'd cooperate with any research, Bouda."

"Do your prisoners at Eilean Dòchais cooperate, Arailt? And yet you study them nonetheless. Midsummer is a criminal, and I imagine her punishment would be for the Chancellor to decide, just as it was with Meilyr Tresco. Perhaps unlike his, it might be carried out in an environment better suited to . . . thorough evaluation."

Crovan turned to her then, and as the light slid from his lenses, she glimpsed his eyes: pale gray and coolly assessing. She stood her ground. Whittam had given this man Meilyr, but Bouda could give him Midsummer.

And if Jenner wanted to believe she was doing it so Crovan could rip out Midsummer's Skill and hand it to Jenner like a coat for him to slip into, then so much the better.

The door being thrown open behind them made Bouda jump. It was her man-child husband, who had so much promise, yet seemed determined to deliver on absolutely none of it.

"You do realize," Gavar said, crossing to the small table where the whisky decanter stood and pouring himself a glass, "that I'm supposed to be *in revolt* from my family. *Disgusted* by my father's regime. Not popping round for tea."

"That doesn't look like tea," remarked Jenner.

Gavar muttered something coarse and tossed back the drink.

"The explanation Midsummer gets is that you're here for a dressing-down over your botched arrest, which enabled a prisoner to escape," Whittam said, holding out his glass for Gavar to refill as if he were a butler at Kyneston. "So, what news do you have for us?"

"Two things. One is a prison breakout at Fullthorpe super-max, to free those taken at Riverhead and other political prisoners: the ones from Millmoor, the Bore, the Hadley parents, et cetera."

Jenner flinched at the name. Bouda suspected he'd been relieved when the eldest Hadley girl had escaped the Blood Fair. She had briefly wondered if he'd been responsible for spiriting her out of the square, because she hadn't seen the girl on the back of any of the bronze lions. But Midsummer must have got to her somehow, given Abigail's participation in Gavar's sham rescue. Ah well, Abigail Hadley was one more loose end that would soon be tied up.

"The other thing is a day of protest across London. She's had that in the works for a while."

"Protest?" You could see Whittam's lip curl. "As if anything was ever achieved by banners and placards."

"How does she propose to get into Fullthorpe?" Bouda asked. Jon had told her about the planned protest, but the Fullthorpe jailbreak was new information. It must have been a recent decision. "It's our most secure. She'd need an army."

"No idea," said Gavar. "Facilitating that fake escape has got me access, but there's still resistance to my presence and she has a pretty tight inner circle."

"Perhaps," Crovan said, leaning forward, interest evident on his face, "she intends to use *you*. It was your Skill that destroyed the Blood Fair platform, you who knocked a whole square of rioters and Security to their knees in Millmoor."

Gavar shrugged. "Maybe. But like I said, I don't know. I presume you'll want me to go along with whatever it is, rather than try and prevent it?"

"Indeed, for appearances. And because we need her to commit an unambiguous, high-profile criminal act. Do you know what she intends to do with those released?"

"They have well-developed smuggling networks for getting people out of Britain. Her allies are from a number of slave-towns and regions, so they could be sending people out in any direction, though my bet would be on Holland, and over the water to the Irish provinces."

"Interesting." Whittam sat back, steepling his fingers over his whisky glass. "Well, if further details come to light, be sure to pass them on. In the meantime, this is all useful. When these pitiful disturbances have been taken care of, and we have Midsummer under lock and key, your mother will be delighted to welcome you back to Aston House—to be reunited with your daughter."

"You bastard," said Gavar. He ground his cigarette into the side table, and the varnish gave off an acrid stink. "I guess if Midsummer decides she wants your head on a spike, I'd have to go along with that, too. *For appearances.*"

With a swirl of black leather coat around the door, he was gone.

"It seems that Midsummer has ambitions," Crovan said. "However, I see nothing here that requires my immediate participation. I should get back to my castle, which I've left in my steward's hands for several days now. It's always amusing to see how my guests have passed their time in my absence—they tend to make their own entertainment. But to delay longer might be imprudent."

"Perhaps you might join me for dinner tonight," Bouda said, "then make your journey tomorrow, when rested? There's so much we could discuss." She darted a conspiratorial glance at

Jenner, who looked like someone had handed him a puppy for Christmas.

"Very well, that sounds agreeable." Crovan was smiling thinly. Perhaps he was already imagining Midsummer delivered to him for her Skill to be excised and examined. He rose and bowed courteously before departing.

Bouda wasn't relishing the thought of a few hours alone with the man. But she needed to discover how he might align in the various possible configurations of a final power struggle. Would he support her? Remain a neutral observer? Or even prove to be another late contender?

"Protests!" Whittam burst out contemptuously, once the door was closed. "Is that the best the whore can do? We need more than that. I can't flay her in the public square for a bit of fist-waving and window-smashing."

"I agree," said Bouda. "She wants to go high and portray us as going low. We'll never provoke her into plotting something like an assassination attempt—"

Jenner nodded. "But we could insinuate that she was behind her uncle's slaying, because she knew that if he married Aunt Euterpe, she'd be out of the Zelston line of succession."

"That might work. What's more important than beating her—at least at the moment—is dragging her down. She wants the moral high ground and we can't let her have it. So, we let her win Fullthorpe—but we make sure she'll lose it, too. Then in London, we bring her down. Here's what I'm thinking."

She leaned in on the sofa, and told father and son precisely half of her plans.

TEN

ABI

Abi ran a comforting hand down Renie's back as the girl gazed out of the car window. They'd been on the road for several hours, but had left London before dawn, so the sun wasn't long risen as they neared the Zelston family seat of Lindum.

They'd just passed Lincoln—the city to which the original Roman settlement of Lindum had given its name. This was farming country, hard against the perimeter of the Bore. Was Renie thinking of her brother, who had died there in the agricultural slavezone? Of her uncle Wesley's years of harsh labor?

Abi was thinking of her mum and dad.

She let her hand rest on Renie's back. She never wanted to let the girl out of her sight again, yet here they were, about to take on the supermax facility of Fullthorpe to rescue their loved ones. Abi's parents, Renie's friends Oz and Jess, as well as the others taken at Riverhead and rounded up in the Bore.

Her stomach had been knotted the whole journey just thinking about it. There were so many things that might go wrong between now and the moment Abi could put her arms around her mum and dad again. Every minute of the drive up had been excruciating. Abi's senses were strung out from straining for the distant whoop of a siren, or the flash of red and blue lights from a pursuit car. And even now it wasn't over. What if there was a cordon around the estate, or officers at the gate?

Abi tried to smother her anxiety. If she didn't, it would swell and swell until there was room for nothing else inside her skull, and she needed her wits now more than ever. Midsummer had promised that once they reached Lindum, Abi would understand how they could get in and out of Fullthorpe to rescue so many. Did the Equal have a private platoon of tanks? Because otherwise Abi didn't see how they could manage the kind of assault that would be needed. This wasn't trickery, to smuggle out a prisoner or two, as with Renie's retrieval or Oz's rescue from Millmoor. This was releasing *dozens* of people. What secret concealed there would make that possible?

Midsummer pulled the beaten-up old car—it was her girlfriend's—off the road and onto overgrown tractor ruts. As they bumped along the farm track, Abi glimpsed far ahead, rising above a double row of cypress trees, two towers of neat Roman brick. The electricity of Skill thrilled across her skin as the car passed through the trees, and she knew that they'd crossed the estate boundary. The excitement was a welcome distraction.

A sturdy two-door wooden gate was dead ahead.

"Can you give me a hand, Abi?" asked Midsummer's girlfriend, Layla, from the passenger seat. "I'm usually fine, but right now . . ."

The woman unfastened her seatbelt and swiveled out, the bump of her pregnancy plainly visible. At the gates, Abi lifted the bar under Layla's direction, then set her shoulder to the left panel. She gave a grunt of effort—just as the gate swung open of its own accord. Midsummer beeped the car horn jauntily, and they heard Renie's laughter through the car window.

"She always likes to make her guests work for it first." Layla rolled her kohl-lined eyes, though she was smiling. She jerked a brilliantly manicured thumb over her shoulder at the mansion now revealed behind them. "This place is something else, isn't it? Given the state of that ruddy track, we'll do better walking from here."

Every schoolchild saw pictures of it in textbooks, but nothing could have prepared Abi for Lindum. Even by the standards of Equal estates, it was jawdropping, fashioned from the remains of an immense ancient bathhouse, like that of the Emperor Caracalla in Rome.

Abi remembered what she'd read of its history. The baths had slipped into slow decay following the empire's abandonment of Britain. But two hundred years ago, a Zelston ancestor had decided to mark her family's Roman-era lineage by remodeling the complex into a livable estate. It turned out that abandonment had been the saving of it. Concealed beneath strata of leaf mulch, bird droppings, and blown topsoil were glass mosaics, monumental statuary, and bright tiles—all intact.

Restored, it was spectacular. Abi's head turned as she took in Lindum in pieces, because the whole was too incredible. They were approaching a pillared courtyard, once the bathers' exercise yard. Above it rose the famous dome, pierced with an oculus that opened to the sky. Everywhere, the structure glittered: red and white tesserae surfaced the courtyard walks, while the dome's rim was banded with blue and yellow tiles. Sculptures of strange beasts peered from nooks and crannies, or loomed along sight lines in the formal gardens.

"I still pinch myself whenever I'm here," murmured Layla. "Luckily, her mum, Lady Flora, is a sweetheart, otherwise it'd all be a bit much. Needless to say, I had no idea Midsummer was an Equal when she picked me up in a dark nightclub four years ago. Ugh, she's *killing* the suspension on that."

The car was making jerky progress along the track. Abi focused on the ghastly scraping of the exhaust box against the ground, as distraction from a pang of jealousy that this commoner girl had found an Equal who thought she was worth loving back.

"It's good to have you with us, Abi." Layla patted her arm in a maternal fashion. "You and Renie both. I still can't quite believe it's come to this—and so soon. Midsummer's been working quietly for years. She was just the obscure child of a third-born Equal, and didn't want anything to do with their screwed-up, backstabby world. She loved her uncle, and hoped he was going to make change happen in his own way. But he was forever being blocked, and when things weren't moving fast enough, the other two—Meilyr and Dina—wanted to put on more pressure."

Layla paused, her hands dropping to the round of her stomach. She was maybe six months along, or a little more, Abi estimated.

"We decided to start a family, with the help of a friend of ours, and amazingly it all went right first time. But it feels like everything's been going wrong ever since. Her uncle was shot. Jardine's back in power and worse than ever. And suddenly Midsummer is an heir and leading a resistance. I'd be lying if I said I wasn't scared for her, Abi. Scared for all of us."

Perhaps it was hearing Layla name her fear that brought it welling back up in Abi. It clawed its way up her throat so her breath came hard, and flooded her stomach with bile. She'd read that people who'd cheated the odds—walked away from a car crash or defied a bleak medical diagnosis—often underwent a change in attitude. They became more carefree, more able to live in the moment. Well, Abi was still waiting for that to happen. It felt like the moment she lived in most often was the one in which she stood on the platform at the Blood Fair, awaiting the knives.

"I sometimes feel like I'm second-guessing everything," Abi confided. "And that whatever I choose, it will be the wrong decision."

Layla nodded. "Like Gavar Jardine. I thought Midsummer should have sent him packing. I still do, most of the time. But then I think: what if he's the one that'll make the difference? His Skill is so powerful. His *name* is so powerful. What if it's not her that changes it all, but *him*?"

Abi was nodding in agreement when the car door banged and she nearly jumped out of her skin. *Get a grip,* she told herself. What use would she be to her parents' rescue if she startled at every sound?

"Welcome to Chez Zelston," said Midsummer, snagging Layla round the waist for a quick kiss before dropping the car keys into her hand and whispering, "Sorry, babes, I busted the exhaust box."

"Whoa." Renie spun on her heel to take it all in. "What *is* this place?"

"It's home sweet home. I came here when I was ten, after spending my childhood in Abyssinia, where my father's from. When my parents split up, Mum brought me to Britain and my two little brothers stayed with him. That was really tough for both of us, as you can imagine, so she moved in with her brother. Uncle Winter had never got married, still pining after

Euterpe Parva, so he became a father figure for me. There's not a day I don't miss him, especially here."

"That's the abbreviated family history," said Layla, leaning into her partner's side. "But yeah, if you've wondered why my girl thinks a bit differently from all these stuck-up, inbred British Equals . . ."

Midsummer laughed—that frank, throaty sound Abi had liked since she'd first heard it.

"Here's the funny thing. My father let me go because when I was little, I was regarded as a bit of a dud. I never showed any particularly interesting Skill and he practically disowned me. It's how I ended up with my mum's surname rather than his. But the minute I got here: bam! It all started happening."

"What started—"

Midsummer pursed her lips and an earsplitting whistle interrupted Renie's question. The Equal held up her wrist like a falconer.

It was a moment before Abi spotted the white shape that lifted up from Lindum's roof, spread immense wings, and swooped toward where the four of them stood. The silhouette was recognizable as it flew—a barn owl, with thick trousered legs. Midsummer's wrist dipped beneath its weight as the bird settled there.

Which was when Abi saw that it wasn't white because it was a barn owl. It was white because it was made of marble.

"Alba was the first," said Midsummer, petting the owl's head. "I'd only been here a few months when she came to me. Owls are the patron bird of the Roman goddess Minerva, to whom the hot springs here were dedicated. The Minerva statue was smashed to bits long ago, but Alba survived." She raked her fingers through the bird's downy marble breast.

"And as you can see, lots of other statues also made it. I spent the rest of my childhood trying to coax them all to life, and one by one, they woke for me." Midsummer clicked the fingers of her free hand. "So, yeah, Gavar Jardine can explode things, and Meilyr could heal any injury short of death, and DiDi was one of the most charmingly deceptive people I've ever met—no wonder even her sister never knew about her double life. But me? I get to animate weird old statues."

She laughed again, and her right hand came down to pat the creature that had padded across the lawns at her summons. It was a massive gray marble wolf. Abi had never seen a real wolf before, but this was surely larger than life-size. Its ears were raised and alert, and a tongue lolled from a sharp-toothed jaw. The row of teats sagging from its belly promised a mother's ferocious protectiveness.

"I call her Leto," said Midsummer. "Named for the mother of Apollo, though she's obviously the she-wolf that suckled Romulus and Remus."

It was extraordinary, Abi thought. Why couldn't all Equals be like this, using their gifts to arouse wonder and admiration? Why use their ability for sordid power games, when they could use it for miracles?

"The lions must have been easy," Abi breathed, daring to reach out to stroke the owl. Its wings were snow-white and snow-cold.

"At first, I could only work with creatures roughly my size or smaller," said Midsummer. "Leto here, or a satyr or a faun. No problem. Something like Tom, Dick, and Harry over there? Forget it."

The Equal pointed to a monstrous creature the size of a rhinoceros, with the body of a lion and three ferocious eagle heads, each looking in a different direction. A gryphon. The heads had curved beaks, and the lifted left foreleg bore wicked claws. The thought of it coming to life made Abi shiver.

"Then I got better. Bigger creatures, and more than one at a time. Now, I can manage seven or eight, depending on their size." Midsummer whistled sharply, and as Abi watched, mesmerized, all three heads of the gryphon snapped around. The creature lowered its leg, and stalked toward them with a predator's grace. At Abi's side, she heard Renie squeak with excitement. Or possibly terror.

When the gryphon reached them, Layla and Renie barely came up to the beast's shoulder. Leto the wolf huffed and padded away as Midsummer reached up to scratch behind the ears of each head. "They love the attention," she said. "But be careful, if you spend too long on one of them, the others will nip."

Abi warily watched the other two heads as she reached up to scratch between the eyes of Tom—or was it Dick, or Harry? The creature's eyelids lifted upward in sleepy pleasure.

As she gazed around at Lindum's courtyard and grounds, many more sculptures caught Abi's eye. A gargantuan female torso with a ravishingly beautiful face and a lower body comprised of two thick, reptilian tails. The muscly figure of a man, more than ten feet tall, clad in a lion skin and resting on a club. A sphinx, with a lion's supple body, arcing wings, and a woman's wise visage. There were dozens of them. A veritable army.

Which was when Abi realized exactly how Midsummer Zelston planned to break eighty prisoners out of Fullthorpe supermax jail.

Others of Midsummer's team arrived through the morning, a few vehicles at a time to avoid any impression of a convoy. The Equal and her mother took it in turns to wait at the end of the track and bring them through the gate, while Abi stayed at the great house, to help Layla greet and settle in the new arrivals.

There would be some thirty people coming in all, with around twenty taking part in the assault on Fullthorpe the next day. The estate's burly gardeners were expanding their job description by carrying in bags and gear. (Lindum did have people doing days, Layla had explained, but only the minimum required to keep the estate maintained, and Midsummer paid a wage equivalent into a savings account for each of them.)

"What's that?" Layla looked up fearfully as a loud sound thudded overhead, growing louder.

"Helicopter?" Abi said.

She remembered the last time she'd been in one, with Dina at the controls, her beautiful face a rigid mask as she flew them away from Eilean Dòchais, carrying with them the body of the man she'd loved, who'd been shot dead in Crovan's hallway. This couldn't be Dina.

Was it Security, knowing they wouldn't get past Lindum's boundary, coming by air instead? Abi ran outside, Layla at her heels, and they looked up.

When she saw the yellow and black colors of the chopper, she understood.

"Do you see where it says 'Air and Sea Rescue'?" she yelled over the din. "It's come from Highwithel."

The craft settled and the rotors stopped. The pilot that hopped out of the cockpit wasn't much older than Abi, and her tanned and wind-creased skin and auburn plait marked her as a Tresco, one of Meilyr's sisters. The girl opened the door of her chopper, and Abi helped the passengers clamber out.

"Abigail, hen, how did you get here?" the first one asked.

Abi was hugged to an ample matronly bosom, then squished from behind by an equally suffocating pressure.

"Hilda, Tilda," she said, when the gray-haired twins parted and she came up for air. "It's so good to see you."

Keeping a safe distance from the hugging, Asif gave a nervy little wave.

"Reunited," crowed Renie, running up to join them. "Or we will be, once we get Oz and Jess. And then Luke."

Abi's optimism had been buoyant since seeing Midsummer's marble army, and it soared with the arrival of the techie trio. The twins, with evident pleasure, marshaled a couple of Lindum's hunkiest gardeners to unload crates of gear from the chopper, and soon they'd taken over a room as a surveillance hub.

In London, Midsummer had shown the team aerial photographs of Fullthorpe, thanks to her unrestricted access to the Internet. These revealed a square compound, subdivided like a Japanese lunchbox into smaller walled sections: a grass exercise field, workshops and outbuildings, a large warehouse or factory, and, behind double walls, four residential blocks. But now a more detailed picture emerged.

"I used to tell Jackson that the success of any operation was one percent inspiration, nine percent perspiration, and ninety percent information," joked Tilda as the trio fired up their gear. "He said that was about right, though the percentage for information should be higher."

As soon as their equipment was up and running, Asif began a deep dive to locate the Fullthorpe CCTV network. Tilda hunted for the data servers that held detailed maps and information on staff routines and prisoner holding locations. Hilda worked on satellite enhancement, to generate images clear enough that they could observe in real time the jail's routine of meals, work, exercise, and patrols. Abi's heart was in her throat— might she glimpse her mum and dad on one of those feeds?

It was complex work, yet just a few hours later, Asif punched the air with a cry of triumph.

"They're still using the same setup as for Riverhead and Millmoor," he said, shaking his head. "It's on a different location within the servers, because this is a jail rather than a slave-town security facility, but it's all going to be here somewhere. They haven't even tightened their access protocols much since I last went looking. An extra layer of encryption, and the authorization codes will be different, but no surprises."

"How stupid are they?" Renie scoffed.

"It's less stupidity than arrogance," said Midsummer, peering over Asif's shoulder. "The people who run this country feel secure in the strength of their Skill. To them, technology is flimsy by comparison, like putting up a wooden fence behind a stone wall."

"They don't worry about how to prevent people discovering stuff," said Abi. "They rely on fear to keep people from looking for it in the first place."

Fear was the thing the Equals used best of all, she'd come to realize, in all the hours she'd lain sleepless since escaping the Blood Fair. More than their Skill, political power, or wealth. Fear of a harsh assignment if you questioned the slavedays. Fear of loved ones getting even worse treatment if you challenged their conditions. Fear of Security. Of more years on your days. Of the Blood Fair.

Fear was the superpower they all possessed. And unlike Midsummer's monsters, there was no limit to the number of people they could control with it.

A servant bent to whisper in Midsummer's ear, and one of the Equal's pierced brows arched upward. She caught Abi's eye and motioned toward the doorway.

"Uh-oh," Layla whispered. "You're being summoned."

"It's Gavar," Midsummer hissed, as the pair of them walked down one of Lindum's echoing, vaulted corridors. "I wasn't sure if he was going to show up—which is why I made sure he knows no specifics of what we're planning at Fullthorpe. I've been wondering ever since he got in touch whether he really came to us of his own accord, or if it was some kind of deception."

Midsummer's ambivalence was perfectly logical. But it was misplaced, Abi was certain.

"I get it," she told the Equal. "I really do. I lived at Kyneston for months, and I thought he was the worst of the lot: cruel and childish. But I was wrong. My little sister trusted him from the start. He got Luke out of Millmoor for her. He stopped the Blood Fair, got me away from Gorregan, wanted to send me over the water to Dubhlinn. Even now, I'm not sure if he's a 'good' person, but I do know that he loves his daughter and he hates his father. And both those things put him with us, not them."

"The pair of you going in for Renie? That was fantastic," Midsummer agreed. "But Jon called me earlier and said that Gavar was at Westminster this morning, meeting his father and Bouda. What if him joining us is something they've cooked up together? So far, Gavar only knows about the handful of people he met, and they're all 'persons of interest' to Security anyway. But I'm exposing a lot more people if I bring him in closer."

What should she say? Abi was convinced that Gavar's heart was in the right place. But did she *want* to believe that, because her chances of freeing her parents were better with two Equals on their side, rather than just one? Midsummer's judgment was hers to make.

"Jon didn't say how long Gavar was with them, or what it was about?"

"I asked, but it wasn't on Bouda's official schedule. Seems Jenner came and fetched her."

The mere mention of his name, out of nowhere, slipped a needle between Abi's ribs and deep into her unprepared heart. So Jenner had moved from the fringes of his family to its center? Doubtless he felt her betrayal had been worth it.

"I'm sorry," Midsummer said, rubbing Abi's shoulder comfortingly. "I know what he meant to you. But it shows how treacherous that family is."

Abi winced. "It says a lot about Jenner, and nothing about Gavar. Do you know what Layla told me earlier? She said that she's uncertain and afraid, too, but wonders if Gavar might be the one to tip the balance.

"Right now, Midsummer, you're the only Equal on the front line of our side in this. I know your mother's part of it behind the scenes, and Armeria Tresco. And I know you feel as strongly as I do that a rising of the people has to come from the people. But I've seen how your leadership gives everyone hope. Ninety percent of that is you being awesome, but some of it is because you've got Skill. To have someone else like that? It might make all the difference."

"Hmm . . ."

Midsummer was deep in thought. *Please let her agree and not turn Gavar away,* Abi prayed, as they stepped out of Lindum's front door and walked to the formal estate entrance. It was another wrought-iron gate, like Kyneston's—and on the other side was a parked Harley-Davidson and one huffy owner.

"Gavar. What do you want?"

"I'm sorry?"

Gavar didn't sound sorry. He sounded pissed off at such a greeting. Abi didn't blame him.

"Or another question: what were you doing with your father this morning?"

"Getting a roasting for not only letting this one slip between my fingers"—he pointed at Abi—"but allowing the kid to escape, too. You can imagine it's not made me popular."

"Abigail tells me you wanted her to go to Dubhlinn. Is that true?"

"No, Midsummer, I wanted to lure her to a gingerbread house and eat her. What is this? Didn't I prove myself with rescuing the girl? Either you trust me, or you don't."

"Let me think about that. Maybe I don't trust you because you're a daddy's boy, and your daddy is the worst human being alive. Maybe I don't trust you because you shot dead the slave-girl you abused, when she tried to flee with the child you knocked her up with. Would I be wrong?"

Abi was grateful, at that moment, that a gate stood between them—though Gavar could have blasted it off its hinges if he wished, and he looked like he wanted to.

He didn't. He gripped the ironwork and stared at Midsummer.

"Look, both those things are true—but they're not the only truth."

"So, I'm right . . . but I'm still wrong?"

"You know what he means." Abi's heart was hammering at this unexpected confrontation. Was Midsummer really going to throw away all the possibilities that Gavar represented? She tried not to see her chance of freeing her parents slipping away, too. "You can do awful things and still be capable of good ones. He helped me and my siblings. He *stopped the Blood Fair.*"

"He's the heir of Kyneston. On a fast track to the Chancellorship. Why would anyone jeopardize a future like that?"

"Maybe," Gavar snarled, looking like a blood vessel was going to burst in his temple, "someone who was never asked if he wanted it."

Midsummer took a step back. Then she put her hand to the gates of Lindum—and pulled them open.

"I wasn't sure if I could trust you, Gavar. But I figured I could trust your temper to tell me the truth. Come on in. We've got a jailbreak to plan."

Gavar rolled his eyes as he wheeled his bike forward.

This pair were the most unlikely of allies, Abi thought as she watched them walk to the imposing red-brick mansion. But if this alliance could hold, they might just win.

ELEVEN

LUKE

As the chopper lifted and spun, Luke fought down panic. The last time he'd been in a helicopter was when Crovan had taken him to Eilean Dòchais. Luke had been collared at Kyneston's gate, then strapped into his seat for the flight to an unknown fate in Scotland. His hand slipped down to the buckle of the belt restraining him now, and he clicked it in and out a few times, just to reassure himself that he was free.

Headphones over his ears muffled the noise of the rotor blades—then emitted a whine of feedback.

"I've changed my mind," came Silyen's voice, somehow managing a bored, aristocratic drawl despite the static. "Amsterdam is *so* dull. Let's go to Scotland instead. The liquor is better."

"My lord?" Luke could hear the pilot's uncertainty. Poor sod. At the private airfield, Silyen had asked for someone discreet. The man presumably thought he was taking a spoiled young aristo and his friends on a debauched day trip, where they'd smoke pot and visit the red-light district away from the disapproving eyes of Equal society.

"Scotland," said Silyen airily. "Head for the Isle of Skye. I'll give you more precise directions when we get closer."

"My lord, we've not cleared the flight path. The weather conditions could—"

"Scotland." Silyen's voice this time brooked no argument. "And no need to radio back to base. We'll be fine. My father *is* the Chancellor, you know."

At Luke's side, the Equal pulled off his headphones and fell back against his seat with a groan.

"Are there any of those paper bags?" he asked Luke. His pale skin was already sheened with perspiration. "You might want to have one ready, just in case. I find cars bad enough, but these things are the worst. You wouldn't want to turn up to see Coira covered in my puke."

Luke really wouldn't. He rummaged around the cabin for the sick bags, handed two to Silyen, and kept two for himself. Seated on his other side, Dog was looking avidly out of the window. Luke proffered a bag.

"No thanks," the man rasped. "I like—choppers. Was airborne for my—tours of duty—in Mesopotamia."

What a jolly trio they were: Silyen, tech-sick; Luke, having flashbacks; and Dog, fondly dreaming of the days he rode helicopters into the killing fields of desert combat.

Luke hoped to goodness that Crovan was still in London. What had happened at the castle in the days since he left? Coira had wanted to get others away from the island, too—the "servants" she sheltered belowstairs. Had she managed it, or had Crovan's steward, Devin, and the "guests" who lived upstairs, prevented her? Maybe she had been able to connect with her Skill.

Whether she had or hadn't, would Coira want to come with them now? Luke couldn't assume that she would. She had no memory of any life outside the castle. Had never left the island it stood on. You sometimes heard in the news about girls abducted and locked away for years. Of the children born to them who'd never known life beyond a basement, until one day their mothers escaped into the sunlight, yelling for help.

They were strong, those women and children. They found deep sources of resilience. And Coira was the most resilient person Luke had ever met.

His flight north with Crovan had been through the night, until they arrived at Eilean Dòchais in the flaming dawn, so Luke had never seen Britain from the air before. During school holidays, his parents had tried to show their three kids the loveliest parts of the country: the Lake District, the Peak District, and the Yorkshire Dales. Dad had herded them yelping into the chilly sea on the North Wales coast for a swim; Mum had chivvied them up Mount Snowdon, with the promise of hot chocolate at the top.

The absence of his family pierced Luke. He was still worried sick about Abi, who was who knew where after running away from Gavar Jardine. He hoped the heir was doing a better job of protecting Daisy. Although they were in the dump that was Millmoor, Mum and Dad were the safest of the lot of them.

Luke suddenly missed them desperately. He thumbed the two-way button on his headset and spoke to the pilot.

"Can you fly over Manchester? Over Millmoor?"

"There's a no-fly zone over slavetowns. But I'll let you know when we're close."

Luke clicked off the connection and sat there with his eyes shut, trying to calm himself by working through all the potential scenarios at Eilean Dòchais. There was one crucial thing to remember: they wouldn't be able to leave the castle without Coira's permission. They had to know she was inside before they entered.

"Millmoor on your right," crackled the headset, some time later.

Luke leaned over Silyen—who complained feebly—and looked down. The pilot banked the copter to give a better view.

Tears welled in Luke's eyes. He could see it perfectly now, this city that he'd learned street by street under Renie and Jackson's tutelage. There were its quartered districts: the Machine Park, where he'd labored in Zone D; the Comms Zone with its hangar-like call centers. In one of those, he'd first met the club: Jackson and Oz, Hilda and Tilda, Jess and Asif. There was the meatpacking district and there the derelict old quarter, Britain's first industrial zone, where the slavedays had taken on their brutal modern form as backbreaking factory work.

Those vast tarmac squares were the vehicle depots, hopefully Dad's workplace. Luke had no idea which of the low white buildings was the admission clinic, or the hospital, but Mum would be in one of them, he was sure.

Within the outer zones was the ring of housing. And nestled at the heart of it all, the bull's-eye at which Jackson had taken aim: the administration hub. That had been Luke's last sight of Millmoor, before Gavar Jardine had spirited him away with the best of intentions and the worst of outcomes.

Silyen was pawing at him and Luke jerked back.

"I said," the Equal grumbled, still looking wan, "what's so interesting? Or are you actually trying to smother me?"

"Millmoor," Luke said, subsiding into his seat, overwhelmed by memories. Silyen barely spared a glance down.

Not long after, the window filled up with blue as sky merged with sea. When they next crossed green, it was Galloway, and Scotland lay beneath them. And when blue appeared a second time, Silyen murmured, "The Firth of Clyde," and stirred himself to give the pilot instructions on their true destination.

"That's an estate," replied the man, apprehension plain in his voice despite the crackle and rotor noise. "They're all no-fly, except for authorized approaches."

"This is authorized."

"You only changed your mind once we were in the air, how can it—"

"I'm authorizing it now. Eilean Dòchais is a few kilometers east of the Skye Bridge."

"I'll need to radio for coordinates."

Something in the cockpit control panel popped and sizzled. Silyen reeled off a string of numbers, then leaned back, evidently over the worst of his airsickness. A metallic scraping on Luke's other side made him glance down, and he saw in all its hideous glory something he'd not laid eyes on since the Blood Fair, when it had been dripping with what could have been Julian's viscera: Dog's glove of knives.

What if Crovan was at home? They'd be screwed, wouldn't they? Knives or no knives.

Silyen had telephoned his mother and asked artless questions about Crovan's whereabouts. Lady Thalia had sounded distracted, but confirmed that he was dining with Bouda, and would return to Scotland the next day. It had been too late to rouse a helicopter for a night flight, but Silyen had evidently thrown enough Jardine money at the problem that a chopper had been found for them at the crack of dawn. Depending on how early a riser Crovan was, they could have a day, or merely hours.

"There's the helipad," Silyen said.

And as the chopper spun, Luke saw it: Eilean Dòchais, sitting tight against its own reflection in the glittering waters of Loch nan Deur. It was as beautiful as when he'd first spied it, and almost as terrifying, even though this time he was in the company of a freakishly Skilled Equal and a vengeful madman armed to the teeth and they were both, somehow, on his side.

"Fascinating," Silyen said as they stood on the shore of Loch nan Deur, after leaving the helicopter beyond the estate's wards. "Those glints in the water are Skill, but constrained to a single purpose: to cause pain. Such a clever trick, used for such a petty purpose." He wrinkled his nose disapprovingly.

Dog jumped back as the boat, called by Silyen's Skill, scraped onto the gravel shore. He plainly knew the water's properties, too.

Luke glanced up at the castle windows as they crossed over, hoping for a glimpse of Coira's face. But the panes were too thickly leaded, the glass too old and clouded, to see clearly. Silyen was hanging over the side of the boat as it moved, and Luke wondered if he got boat-sick as well. But it turned out he was studying the lazy swirl and sparkle of Skill in the water. Luke didn't know whether to smile or despair at how easily distracted the Equal was. Then the boat bumped against the island and Luke wished for distraction himself, to postpone what was coming next.

Outside the Door of Hours he squared back his shoulders purposefully and knocked. There was no answer. Luke knocked again, louder and longer. They waited.

His heart was in his throat. What did this mean? Was there nobody in the castle at all? Had Coira got them all away, even the mad and bad ones? Or in Crovan's absence, had the place sunk into anarchy? Maybe Coira was gone and the remainder had killed one another. He stepped right up to the door and hammered desperately on it with both hands—

—then staggered over the threshold as it swung open beneath his fists.

Well, shit.

He'd been hoping for so many reasons that Coira was inside, but now he had one more reason. If she wasn't, he'd be stuck here until Crovan came home. And given that he didn't know Luke had ever left, odds were the man wouldn't happily show Luke out the door.

"Luke?" a voice called out from the dim recesses of the entrance hall. It sounded familiar, but altered. Who was it?

From under the archway that led to the castle's great central atrium and square staircase shambled a human figure. With it came an unpleasant odor blended from sweat, stale smoke, and booze.

"Luke Hadley? You've come back. What about the others?"

Others had got away, too, then. Had Coira gone with them? Luke gestured over his shoulder to Silyen and Dog. They needed to stay outside.

The shaft of light from the doorway fell onto the advancing figure and Luke tensed, ready for trouble. But he recognized who it was at the same time as his brain processed the voice. *Not a nice man,* his memory whispered—words he'd written in the journal he'd kept while incarcerated here.

"Devin?"

Crovan's steward, whose position nonetheless did not spare him his master's sadistic attention, was a wreck. He was still in formalwear, but everything that should have been tucked in hung out. He wore no jacket. His hair was plastered to his skull on one side and stuck up on the other. He looked like he hadn't slept since Luke had left, and that the hours he should have spent sleeping had instead been spent drinking.

"Have you all come back?" Devin slurred, blinking his eyes against the light from the doorway, and peering to see who stood there. Silyen and Dog were just silhouettes. "He's going to be so angry with you. With all of you. Not with me. It wasn't my fault. No one's supposed to be able to leave. But with her they can."

He hiccupped disconsolately, and raised a port bottle to his lips.

"Has she gone, too?" Luke asked urgently. No need to check who that *her* was.

Devin's only answer was a mournful braying that was either laughter or despair.

"Upstairs," he said eventually. "She's upstairs. But she's not coming out. So now you're back, you can't leave, either." He hiccupped again. "One less lash for poor old Devin when the master gets home."

"Coira is upstairs?" Luke asked again, wanting to be completely sure before he waved Dog and Silyen in.

"Locked herself in the master's rooms," Devin confided. "Don't know how. So disobedient. She'll get more lashes than poor Devin when the master's back. *Y-y-y-you?*"

The steward stuttered and stumbled backward, eyes going wide at whatever he'd seen over Luke's shoulder. The deceptively gentle scrape of steel on steel told Luke what it was.

"Me," rasped Dog.

And Dog reached past with a movement so fast that Luke didn't know what had happened, until the blood sprayed him full in the face and something plopped wet and stinking at his feet. He cried out in disgust and wiped at his eyes with his sleeve. Dog was laughing.

In the gloom it took Luke's eyes a moment to adjust. But his other senses told him what had happened. At his feet was what had, until a few moments ago, been Devin. The body gaped like an open purse, slit from throat to groin.

Luke swallowed down bile.

"What the hell?" he yelled at Dog. "That wasn't necessary."

"You're here," Dog growled, "for the girl. Silyen's here—for this king. What did you think—*I* came for?"

Luke knew. Revenge.

"When I was a bad Dog," the man said, "Devin filled my—water bowl. Crovan let him get it—from the loch. Drink that or nothing, he said. He got what he deserved."

As Luke stood there in horrified silence, trying to imagine what it would be like to drink the acid waters of Loch nan Deur, Silyen simply stepped over the pooling mess and headed deeper into the castle.

"Wait," Luke called after him. "You can't just stroll in. We've no idea what the situation is. There are nearly fifty prisoners in this place, and they've all been locked up for a reason."

"The situation is: Crovan's not here. Therefore, the situation is: there's no problem. Who'll challenge us? One powerful Skill-worker." Silyen pointed to himself. "One maniac with an excessive number of knives. And one . . . well, you might want to keep close, Hadley. Now come on. We'll get this girl first, then I want to see if we can find any trace of the king."

The Equal strode into the castle's central atrium. The wide staircase wound its way around all four sides, up to the higher floors. The place was in an absolute state. Empty bottles and broken glasses littered the floor. Items of furniture had been smashed and one of the great landscape paintings was slashed from side to side. Pieces of antique weaponry had been pulled from the walls—and where were they? Luke wondered warily.

He knew what this looked like. Every now and then, you'd be invited to a party thrown by kids whose parents had gone off to start their days. There'd usually be an older sibling in their twenties, whom the parents had judged sufficiently mature to watch over the younger ones, who were maybe just finishing school. Houses got trashed. Everyone pretended the parties were about celebrating freedom from parental supervision, though you'd often find one of the host kids crying quietly in a corner somewhere.

The destruction wrought on Crovan's immaculate castle was gobsmacking. How long had it been since Luke left here? Incredibly, he realized it was only a few days. So much had happened: the journey to London, the Blood Fair, and the Skillful clash in Gorregan Square. The drive to Far Carr and everything that had occurred there: renewing the boundary and walking in the dreamscape of his own mind.

He tried to remember whether or not he had actually seen the king in the castle hallway. He had *wanted* to, when he'd stood at the Last Door in some kind of trance and looked out. He'd been about to step through when Coira had interrupted him, and then Crovan had caught them and Luke had deduced her secret—that she was his daughter.

Luke looked back over his shoulder to the entrance hall. Now that they were inside, the Door of Hours would have disappeared, and the Last Door should have become visible, but it was too dim to make anything out.

"What did I just say, Luke?" Silyen was starting up the stairs two at a time. "Keep up."

The higher they went, the louder the noise grew. A steady

thump-thump-thump from the top floor, and the raucous sound of many men's voices. People were moving as though stupefied through the upper rooms: the library and the billiard room, where they gathered for "champagne o'clock." Mostly the men were Crovan's "guests" in their country-house tweeds or dress suits, but a few wore the gray tunics of the "servants" from belowstairs. Whatever division had existed between the two groups was evidently suspended.

Everywhere, the castle was in disarray: food ground into carpets, ornaments smashed or overturned. What the hell had happened here?

Luke tried to piece it together. It was clear from Devin's words that Coira had led some of the castle's prisoners to safety, as she had told Luke she would. Then she had come back, again just as she had said. She had wanted to speak to Crovan—to her father—and to discover from him the secret of her birth.

Luke imagined that in the first hours after Crovan's departure, the castle's residents allowed themselves some license, just like kids when their parents were gone. So Coira's freeing of her chosen few might have gone unnoticed. But all it would have taken would be one of those she'd left behind to notice her crossing the loch.

On her return to the castle, they'd all be clamoring for freedom. Many of them most likely people who should never see the outside of a secure facility. Luke knew that Coira felt as he did, that the punishments endured here violated any standard of civilization. But she couldn't simply release dangerous criminals into an unsuspecting community. So . . . what? She had taken refuge in Crovan's private quarters. The door to that was Skillfully warded, but evidently it recognized her blood, just as the Last Door and the moat did.

So, the banging and thumping above? That would be those

still trapped in the castle, trying to break in to her. The dismembered furniture was presumably being used to batter the door down; the missing weapons would be to threaten her when they did. And because forty people couldn't be attacking one door at the same time, the bottles and cigar ends ground into the carpet were how the rest were passing the time. Maybe they were keeping up their assault round the clock, depriving Coira of sleep until she gave in.

That sounded like a rational and plausible scenario—but all Luke's rational thinking went out the window the minute the woman started screaming.

"No! Please," came her high panicked voice. "I'm begging you. Coira—help me!"

"Here's what we'll do," bellowed a man's voice, followed by a heavy thump on a door. "If you don't open up for us, you scrawny bitch, then this one's gonna pay. We'll all have her, two at a time. And you know how many of us there are. We'll make her scream a little louder each time until you stop pretending you can't hear us."

The woman's wail was hideous, raw and ragged. "No! Coira! Please!" Then it broke off in sobs.

Luke met Dog's eyes, and for all the madness in them, Luke saw the same clear understanding of what was about to happen. As one, they sprinted for the final turn of the staircase that would take them to the topmost floor—

—only to fall as something caught their ankles and slammed them down. Luke's jaw banged a carpeted stair and he felt blood fill his mouth, but that wasn't why he was furious.

"What are you doing?" He spat blood from where he'd bitten his tongue, and swore at Silyen as the Equal walked up to them. He'd tripped them up with Skill. "She needs help. Now."

"Get a grip on your 'saving everybody' thing, Luke. At least our friend here has a reason for his hair trigger where rapists are concerned, but you spent months here among these people. You should know better."

"Know better?"

The woman upstairs was whimpering now, and there was the sound of ripping fabric.

"Last chance," the man called to Coira. "There are plenty of us, so you'll be listening for quite some time. I'd hate you to lose your beauty sleep—not least 'cause when we're done with this one, and we finally get that door down, you'll be next. Unless you come out now and take us all off this island."

At the threat to Coira, Luke made a dash for the stairs, only for Silyen to grab him. Those skinny arms were stronger than they looked. *Bloody unfair Equal strength,* Luke thought, his mind boiling with rage as he struggled against the restraint.

Then Silyen put his mouth close to Luke's ear and whispered.

"It's. Not. Real."

What? Luke's chin jerked up. He looked at Dog, whose eyes still burned, but who had cocked his head to one side to listen.

Silyen clamped a hand over Luke's mouth as the woman above gave another scream, then began a nauseatingly rhythmic series of sobs and groans and muttered pleading.

"Shhh . . ." Silyen admonished.

He removed his hand and beckoned the pair of them to follow. Where the stairs turned into a landing, Silyen pressed Luke back against the wall. He put a finger to his lips, shot Luke a meaningful look, then pointed over his shoulder.

There was a semicircle of them gathered around the finely carved door of Crovan's suite, all men—more than a dozen—plus one woman. Tossed to one side just outside the group was a torn curtain. The woman was not only fully clothed, she was grinning as she uttered the obscene noises. She paused for breath, and to gulp from a bottle she held, and the men covered her silence with crude jeering and noises of encouragement. Several of them were armed with the spears and swords missing from their place in the staircase weaponry displays.

Luke felt sick. He'd known what sort of people were condemned here. The worst of the worst. He should have learned that lesson with Julian. But this was grotesque: to fake a rape in order to draw Coira out of safety. After which, these creatures would compel her to make their escape.

When he saw the door slowly open, his veins iced up.

"Stop it," said Coira.

Her voice was as quiet and commanding as ever, and for a moment Luke wondered if her Skill had woken, that she could speak with such assurance. But then as she took in the scene around her, and understood that she had been tricked, fear came into the girl's eyes.

He saw Coira's shoulder turn and her fingers scrabble uselessly for the handle. But the largest of the men, the one who had been hammering the door and leading the charade, leaned against the door. Its lock shut behind her with an audible click.

"Oh no, you don't," he said.

Which was when Luke let loose a bellow of fury and charged.

TWELVE

LUKE

His momentum, and the surprise, carried Luke through the circle of men to where Coira stood by the door. The onlookers stepped back, startled, then closed in again to watch what would happen next.

"Who've we got here?" the man sneered. He was powerfully built, and Luke recognized him from the confrontation in the kitchen, the night he and Coira had run afoul of three of the castle's worst. "Little I-Didn't-Do-It assassin boy. Back for another clip round the head with a saucepan? I'll do it harder this time."

"Luke, what are you doing here?" Coira's eyes inspected him swiftly. "Your sister?"

"She escaped the Blood Fair."

"Why did you come back?"

"For you."

"Touching," the man sneered, jostling Luke intimidatingly.

"We're gonna have some fun here first. I'll let you watch, then maybe you can join in."

"Give it over," Luke said, with a momentary giddy rush of relief as he remembered Coira's collar protected her from harm. "You know you can't hurt her."

"Who's talking about *hurting* her . . . ?" The man leered and grabbed his crotch.

Luke didn't let him finish. He drove his fist hard into the man's belly and watched him double over, grunting. It felt like Luke had broken all his fingers, but he swung a second blow up against the man's chin and watched his head fly back. He'd grown strong in Millmoor and at Kyneston, and hadn't lost it in the few months he'd spent in this castle—unlike the men around him. Their long incarceration and Crovan's formal dinners had rendered the prisoners flabby and unfit.

There were, though, many, many more of them.

"Get back in," he urged Coira, as the circle around them tightened—but it was too late. The woman made a grab for Coira's hair and twisted, making Coira cry out in pain. And as Luke looked over, something heavy and hard smashed into the side of his skull and he reeled back against the door.

"You little—" roared the man Luke had punched, now hefting a chair leg.

But the rest of what he said was lost in the resonant zing of steel drawn across steel, followed by a ripping sound that was most definitely not curtains. One of the onlookers let out a yell of horror as the man standing next to him crumpled to the ground, scarlet cascading down his front. Dog stood there, blood dripping from the lethal fingers of his metal hand.

"Bad doggy," scoffed the ringleader. He tipped back his head and emitted a few derisory barks and howls. "I remember you, you mad bastard. Get him, lads."

But nobody moved.

Dog's blades flashed forward, so close that Luke felt the air passing over them and flinched. The Condemned woman screamed.

"Now—go," Dog growled.

Luke saw that the woman's hand—still attached to her body—clutched a length of thick dark hair. Coira's hair. The woman recoiled, dropped the severed tresses, and pushed her way through the pack of onlookers. Her feet thumped the stairs as she ran.

Freed, Coira pulled back and began wrestling with the handle. But the door opened outward and the press of bodies made it impossible to open. The men were wary of Dog's blades, but there were nearly twenty of them. Where was Silyen? Why wasn't he coming to their aid?

"No one else will die," Luke said, lifting his hands partly in appeal, partly as a warning. "Just leave Coira alone."

"Who *are* you, girl?" called an older man who wore a servant's tunic. The look in his eye was desperate and Luke wondered what he'd done that Coira hadn't selected him for freedom. "How can you get in there, to his private rooms? You was downstairs with us, in the kitchens. And now you can get people out of this place? We only want you to take us, too."

All eyes turned to Coira. Luke's heart was in his mouth as he wondered what she'd say, what pretext she'd come up with.

"I'm his daughter," Coira said. "Now let me and my friends pass."

And the men's hostility turned to something that Luke sensed was fear. As they shuffled imperceptibly away, there was finally enough space for Coira to wrench open the door.

"Bravo," said a voice from behind them all as Silyen stepped out of the shadows. "I was wondering how you'd manage that."

"And who the fuck are you?" said the ringleader, spitting bloodily onto the carpet.

"Family friend," said Silyen. "Just stopping by. If you could bring me some coffee, I'd appreciate it. Thirsty journey."

Silyen knew how to turn his creepy superwattage up for an audience, because you could actually see Skill fizzing and spitting from him as he walked through the pack of desperate prisoners. When he reached the door, he put his arms around Luke's and Coira's shoulders.

"Great work," he murmured as he steered the pair of them into Crovan's apartments. "Nicely done. Just one thing."

"What's that?" said Luke, suddenly apprehensive.

"Never make promises of good behavior on others' behalf."

The door smacked shut behind the three of them. Through the thick paneled wood, the sing of metal on metal was plainly audible. Luke heard Dog's rasping laugh.

Then the screaming began.

Luke could feel Coira, on Silyen's other side, twist in his hold. But the Equal's grip was unyielding.

"Forget them," Silyen told her. "You had your chance and you made your choices. They're the ones you chose not to save."

Coira struggled against him.

"That didn't mean abandoning them to be murdered."

"Killed fast or killed slow." Silyen shrugged. "Amounts to the same thing. You know what Crovan does to them. At least Dog's no sadist."

"When Crovan gets back, when I've had a chance to speak to him, I'll persuade him to do it differently. Those people can't be let out, but they could be kept here without such cruelty."

"Not as long as Arailt Crovan keeps them," said Silyen.

The screaming outside had stopped. Presumably most of their would-be assailants had fled after seeing that Dog meant business. Luke didn't want Dog anywhere near him—or Coira. But it would be better for him to stay with them, rather than roam the castle picking off its inmates one by one.

"It's over," he told Coira.

Her nod told him she'd thought the same, and she shook Silyen off and went to the door. A further two corpses were visible on the carpet outside—one of them the ringleader. Dog was almost at the landing but he turned at Coira's whistle, short and sharp, like you'd use with a real dog. Shivers ran down Luke's spine at the thought of the pair of them here, for the years of Dog's incarceration, when Coira would have been just a child. What history did they share?

"Let's get you cleaned up," Coira said, ushering Dog inside the apartment and closing the door. As he stood on the doormat, she inspected him and sighed. "It's good to see you."

Unbelievably, she went up on tiptoe and—very briefly—put her arms around his neck and squeezed.

Coira led Dog to Crovan's bathroom, then went to locate some clothes. Silyen appeared untroubled by any notions of privacy. He strolled through the rooms running his hands over everything, picking things up before carelessly putting them down again.

"So much history," the Equal said, breathless.

"This isn't a trip to the museum, Silyen. Your mother said Crovan is coming back today. He could arrive at any time. We have to be quick."

"No, we don't. We may not get another chance like this. You've got what you came for—that girl. Now I want what I came for—to know why our king walked into your mind here, and why you saw him at the doorway downstairs."

The Equal pushed open the door to a small sitting room. Books lined the far wall, and a cushion and blanket on the sofa

showed that this was where Coira had been sleeping. But Silyen's eye was caught by the tapestries that covered the room's
two long sides.

"Look at those. I'm pretty sure that's where the inspiration
for the prisoners' collars came from. Do you remember me asking Crovan about 'Gruach's necklace'? My ancestor Cadmus
speculated on the story in his journals. It's what first got me
interested in Skillful bindings."

The tapestries must have been hundreds of years old, but the
colors were still bright, doubtless preserved by Skill. One
showed a handsome young couple in a boat. The girl had red
hair to her waist, and beside her sat a bearded young man.
Above them, a storm raged and lightning forked. The tapestry
opposite showed the same girl standing on the shore, with Eilean Dòchais looming behind. At her side was not the young
man, but an old woman with a braid of white hair. Around the
girl's neck was a necklace of twisted gold—a toque, stitched in
thick gilt thread to look almost real.

"The legend of Fair Elspet and Bold Alane," said Silyen.
"Rather romantic, if you can imagine applying such a word to
a Crovan." He raised an eyebrow at Luke, who cringed.

"Elspet was the granddaughter of the *mormaer* Crovan who
built this castle. He believed Scotland needed no high lord, and
turned hostage keeper to end the Earl's War, after his son died
fighting. But his adored granddaughter Elspet fell in love with
the son of the man who killed her father—a young noble
named Alane.

"Knowing the *mormaer* would never agree to their marriage,
they murdered him in this castle one night, then fled across the
lake. But Elspet's great-aunt Gruach discovered their crime,
and from the battlements she called down lightning and struck
their boat."

"The coat of arms," Coira said, behind them, making Luke jump. "The lightning-struck boat is the Crovan emblem. I never knew the story."

Luke suppressed a ripple of jealousy, that Silyen could give Coira this gift of knowledge of her family lore.

What would her Equal status mean? She'd talked of staying here to speak with Crovan, but after what had just happened, surely she'd now leave with them. Perhaps at Far Carr Silyen could work with her to unlock her Skill.

And after that . . . ? There was a seat in the House of Light that belonged to Coira: the heir's chair of Eilean Dòchais. Could she still claim it, even if her father never acknowledged her? Would Equal society embrace her? Luke's imagination conjured Coira in a pale silk gown, waltzing across a ballroom in the arms of a dashing young heir. It wasn't a comforting image.

"And the necklace?" Coira asked, touching the golden band around her own neck. "The other half of the story?"

"Ahh." Silyen smiled. "Not a happy ending. When the boat sank, Alane drowned. And once her great-aunt Gruach got to her, Elspet wished she had, too. Hers were the first tears to fall into Loch nan Deur—the Lake of Tears. The pain the water causes is said to be her grief and anguish—though presumably it's just a prosaic old enchantment to protect the island. And to prevent Elspet fleeing a second time, Gruach wrought a necklace that bound her to the castle."

"What happened to her?"

"I tend to lose interest in legends once the Skillful bits are over. But I've not read that Elspet's necklace came off, or that she ever left the island again."

"I can leave the island," said Coira. "Or I can get to the far shore, at least. That's where I took Luke, and then the others. I never tried going along the track to the village, but I made it across the loch."

Silyen flapped his hand impatiently. "You're not wearing the *actual* necklace, are you? You're simply subject to a Skillful binding that takes the *form* of a golden collar, presumably in homage to this charming bit of family history. In your case, if you are who events seem to suggest you are—Crovan's daughter—I'm guessing it constrains your Skill. That wouldn't affect your power over the castle itself, though, or the loch and the Last Door, which respond to the family blood. May I take a look at it? Luke has been badgering me to see if I can take it off."

"I'd wondered why you came," Coira said, turning to Luke. "I can't imagine anyone ever wanting to see this place again."

"I wanted to see *you* again," Luke said—and please, no, let him *not* be blushing as the pair of them stared at him.

"Touching," Silyen said dryly, after a pause that was precisely long enough to be awkward.

Luke waited for Coira to say something like "I missed you, too," but of course she didn't. She blinked.

"Did you never notice?" Silyen asked. "All those years alongside him. Knowing you were treated differently from the rest. The resemblance that Luke saw—did *you* really never see it? Did nobody else see it, before now?"

Coira looked pained.

"In my imaginings, I've been everybody's daughter: from your father's, sent here to avoid disgrace to the family name, to the cruelest prisoner's. And yes, Crovan's. But I never thought seriously about him, because who would treat their daughter like this? And he always told me I was guilty of a crime, just like everyone else. The worst crime, he said.

"Yes, we look a little alike, but I've found bits of myself in all sorts of people before: eye color, body shape, hands, noses, you name it. When you want to see a resemblance that badly, you can find one anywhere. I've had these questions my whole life. And now I want answers—it's what I stayed here for."

"Well, I could take a quick look and see if there are any answers in there?" Silyen tapped the side of his skull.

"Surely Far Carr would be a better place to . . ." Luke started, turning to Silyen, but he had already taken Coira's hand and was leading her to the sofa.

What was Sil playing at? He knew that Crovan was heading back, and he had told Luke he was here to investigate any trace of the Wonder King, not to concern himself with Coira. This was no time for Silyen to get distracted.

But the Equal was already murmuring instructions as Coira closed her eyes. Silyen took one of her hands and pressed the fingertips of his other hand to her forehead. Luke recognized it as what the Equal had done to him, but seen from this perspective, it looked weirdly intimate. Something that even Luke's inarticulate boy-brain could recognize as jealousy prickled through him.

Well, he wasn't here to be the third wheel on the world's most introverted first date. He'd have a dig around. If he could turn up something like the painting at Far Carr, anything that hinted of the Wonder King, then perhaps Silyen would agree to getting the hell out of here sooner rather than later.

What he saw behind the first door he tried, he wished immediately to unsee. It was the bathroom, and contained a pile of blood-drenched clothes, the glove of knives, meticulously cleaned and drying on a towel, and Dog, neck-deep in suds in Crovan's bathtub. Hastily Luke closed the door again and crept along the corridor.

Here was the largest room, where Crovan and Silyen had

forced their way into Luke's mind on that excruciating afternoon. Silyen was now doing the same to Coira next door—
though if he used violence, Luke would make him regret it. He
went to the window to check that their helicopter was still
there, on the moors beyond the loch. It was. Sil had done something to the chopper before they left, presumably to stop the
nervous pilot from flying away without them.

On the desk were stacks of papers and a leather-bound note-
book that, judging from the year stamped in gilt on the corner,
was a diary. Luke's mind boggled at the notion that Crovan had
a schedule of social engagements, and he flipped it open. Except he should have learned the lesson Abi had taught him long
ago, when she'd ripped into him about not peeking at her journal, because the diary was an itemization of horror. Crovan
had recorded, in tiny handwriting so neat it looked typed, exactly what he had done that day to whichever "guest" had been
summoned to his rooms.

Luke's gorge rose as he read a couple of pages, and he
slammed the book shut. Coira had this man's blood in her veins.
At school, in biology class, they'd once had the nature-versus-
nurture debate: how much of who you were was set by your
genes, inherited from your parents, and how much was because
of how you were raised? Half of Coira's genes had come from
Arailt Crovan, and she'd been raised in a castle prison. How had
she turned out so decent and so brave?

Sickened, he looked around. Was this search pointless without Silyen? Would Luke even recognize what he should be
looking for? The door on the far wall was ajar—practically an
invitation to pry. Luke went over and pushed it a little wider.

Crovan's bedroom.

Given the luxury of the rest of the castle's furnishings, the
austerity of this room was a surprise. The walls were white-

washed and bare of pictures, the floor merely stripped boards covered by a faded and homely rug. The bed was made with military fastidiousness, with a single navy-blue blanket tucked in on all sides. A bedside table held a small brass nightlight and three books. A plain window looked out to the loch.

Luke sat on the edge of the bed and picked up the books. What were these, the only items Crovan chose to have close to him in his most private space? He tipped them sideways to examine the spines. The first was a history of Scotland, in which Crovan's family no doubt featured extensively. Might it contain any clues about the Wonder King? The second was a copy of *Powrie's Peerage,* which proclaimed itself the official genealogy of Scotland's Equals.

The third, startlingly, was a book that Luke recognized: a swoony classic novel in which an orphan girl fell in love with the master she went to slave for, only to discover that he was a raging alcoholic with a mad wife locked in the attic. It was one of Abi's favorites. Luke couldn't imagine it was Crovan's sort of book at all, but the copy was well worn. He flipped it open, and there in the front was a date, more than twenty years earlier, and an inscription: *To darling Rhona, with all my love, Arailt.*

Repellent though it was to think of Crovan calling anyone "darling," this proved it: he *had* been married and had a wife. This book must have belonged to Coira's mother. She would want to see it, he was sure.

It was with a sense of triumph that Luke tucked the book under his arm. Silyen might be showing Coira how to use her Skill, but Luke had something even more precious—a clue to her family. Because one thing was for sure: whatever Coira hoped, Luke was certain Crovan wasn't going to spit out the story of her birth and upbringing just because she asked nicely.

He swiped the history and genealogy books, too, because
Rhona sounded like a Scottish name, so maybe these pages
would hold more clues. He fanned through the tissue-thin,
close-typed sheets, and sighed at the scale of the task.

Then gaped as something fell out and wafted to the floor. A
photograph. Luke snatched it up—and the elation he felt at
seeing a female face that looked just like Coira's drained away in
an instant as he realized what he was looking at.

The picture showed four figures posed formally on the great
staircase of Eilean Dòchais. The girl looked a little older than
Daisy. The young man beside her was perhaps a decade older,
in his early twenties. Stood behind were an older couple: she
wore a sash to which was pinned a brooch in the shape of a
lightning-struck boat; he a kilt, in the tartan that was all over
the castle.

It had to be a family portrait. The young man was Crovan.
The girl at his side, who looked so much like Coira, was far too
young to be a wife or fiancée. With shaking hands, Luke turned
the photograph over and there it was. The date was twenty-five
years earlier. The inscription: *Lord Fionnlagh Crovan; Lady
Fenella; Heir Arailt, aet. 21; Rhona, aet. 12.* Luke didn't recognize
"*aet.,*" but it had to mean "age."

Horrified, Luke clutched at the very last straw. Perhaps this
was some sort of creepy arranged-marriage setup. Rhona was a
girl from another family, brought to Eilean Dòchais to meet
the man she would one day marry. But the straw twirled from
his grasp as his eyes darted frantically around the picture. Family resemblances blended between all four: the father's mouth
on the daughter, the mother's nose on the son, both children
with their mother's cool gray eyes.

Coira's mother was Crovan's sister.

Sickened, Luke put down the books. Much though he knew

Coira yearned to discover her family, he hoped she never found this out.

They needed to get away from here *right now*. Coira's intention to stay and wait for Crovan was a monumentally bad idea. Luke had always thought that, but given what he knew now, it was doubly so. He hurried out of the bedroom to go and break up whatever Skillful love-in she and Silyen were conducting, glancing out of the window en route to check on the chopper again.

And saw that where one helicopter had been sitting on the distant helipad, there were now two.

Luke's heart lurched. He hurtled into the corridor and collided with Dog, newly dressed in Crovan's clothes, the glove laced back onto his hand.

"I heard—a chopper," the man rasped. "Ours?"

Luke shook his head. "His."

Under other circumstances, the scene that greeted him in the sitting room—Silyen so close to Coira that their knees touched, his fingers against her cheek as if he was moving in for a snog—would have been the last thing Luke wanted to see. But it barely registered in the urgency of Crovan's return.

"He's back—Crovan. His helicopter's out there. We need to go. Hide while he comes in, then make a run for it."

The two broke apart. Silyen's eyes were shining. Coira looked up.

"I need to talk to him, Luke."

"You can't. He won't let you go. There's a reason you've been locked up here all your life."

"Which is? What have you found?"

She was up on her feet, her expression both fierce and pleading, and Luke could see that she wanted more than anything to know who she was. But how could he tell her like this?

"Please, let's just go to Far Carr. I'll explain there, and then you can arrange to meet him in London perhaps. But if you confront him here, now, it'll be disastrous. Will you trust me?"

Coira thought for a moment, then nodded.

"And you?" Luke asked Silyen. "You're being suspiciously quiet. No objections?"

"Oh, my investigations have been most rewarding." The Equal smirked. "We'll have to compare notes on our theories. In fact, I'd love to ask Arailt about them, but if you're going to insist on this *running-and-hiding* thing . . ."

"I'm insisting," Luke said firmly. "If we hide near the Last Door, once we've seen him come inside, we can leg it out."

He pulled them down the apartment hallway, and stuck his head out first once Coira opened the door, checking that none of the prisoners from earlier were going to try to bar their way.

"I could—kill him," rasped Dog.

"No! Not an option." Coira shook him by the arm. "I know where we can wait."

As they reached the ground floor, she directed them through a doorway to one side. It was some sort of utility room, filled with household cleaning items. A couple of tarnished silver candlesticks sat on a sideboard, and on a narrow shelf above lay two halves of a broken rifle. It was the rifle used to kill Jackson, Luke realized, feeling it like a fresh blow—and would there ever be a time when thinking of the man didn't hurt?

Coira was peering through the crack in the door, and Silyen was listening intently with those superfine Equal senses. But Luke didn't need either to know when Crovan arrived. A roar of disgust told them he'd discovered Devin's gutted corpse.

The scene of chaos he saw as he made his way into the central atrium and stairwell of his castle must have infuriated him further, and as he mounted the stairs his voice could be heard bellowing for Coira.

"Now!" she whispered, and they slipped from the utility room. Devin's pooled blood made the floor sticky beneath their feet as they hurried to the Last Door. Coira stood in front of it, her breathing tense and shallow.

"We know it works," Luke said, touching her arm. "We did it before. You've done it again since. I'll go first."

Coira nodded, and her hands smoothed out her skirt. Then she reached for the door and pulled it open. Beyond the still water, they could see a solitary helicopter on the rise of the heather heath. Theirs. Crovan's had departed to wherever it went when he didn't need it.

"Luke, I give you permission to leave."

He stepped over the threshold and into the warm, clean air. But Crovan's yell from the floor above was so loud that Luke heard it even outside. Crovan must have sensed Skillful activity at the door.

"Dog, I give you permission to leave."

Dog's lips drew back from his teeth—was he remembering the last time he crossed this threshold? Had he been chained and naked and on all fours? He hesitated a moment. But they didn't have moments to spare.

"Come on!"

At Luke's urging, the man stepped through. Silyen was already waiting, toes on the threshold, as Coira spoke his permission—but over his shoulder Luke saw Crovan appear, pale and furious.

Silyen made it out and Coira followed, but as she stepped through, her feet hitting the rock outside and the sun falling on her face, Crovan reached through after her and grabbed her sleeve—

and pulled her back into the castle—

—and Coira stumbled and staggered backward through the door into—

—nothing.

She fell into nothing.

Crovan's hand dropped uselessly to his side. Luke stared at the open, impossibly empty doorway. For a moment, it shimmered in a color that Luke couldn't name. He heard a cry that wasn't Coira's voice, but wasn't anything else he could identify. Gentle warmth bathed his face—then it was gone.

He blinked and saw Crovan standing in his bloodstained hall, shaking with something more than fury. Dog had fallen entirely silent, not even his blades scraping.

Luke and Crovan had stood like this before, on either side of this door—the night Luke had worked out Coira's secret. Except that night, Crovan had caught her *inside* and kept hold of her. When Luke had tried to go back through the door, it had been impossible.

What had Crovan said about the Last Door, the day Luke arrived? *It only goes one way.*

"Where is she?" he heard himself scream at Crovan, because he didn't want what he suspected to be the truth. "You said this door only goes one way, so where has she gone?"

"This is the door between life and death," Crovan said tightly. He looked as disbelieving as Luke felt. "You can't go the other way."

Luke trembled, trying to calm himself, when he noticed Silyen's beatific smile.

"I love the word 'can't,'" said Silyen Jardine. "I find it the most stimulating in the English language."

THIRTEEN

SILYEN

You can meant that a thing was permitted, or known, or done before. None of those things held the slightest appeal for Silyen.

You can't was the beginning of everything worth attempting.

Luke was having a meltdown. Crovan, disappointingly, looked tense and furious rather than thrilled at the small miracle that had just taken place at his own front door.

Silyen's day, though, had gone from *fascinating* to *absolutely incredible*.

Crovan surged across the threshold and grabbed Luke by the throat.

"What. Has. Happened. Here?"

The boy struggled, dropping the books he'd been clutching. Silyen had taken the opportunity to inspect them while they waited: a history of Scotland, *Powrie's Peerage,* and a rather intense novel that Silyen had enjoyed enormously when younger, even though the hero reminded him of Gavar.

Crovan had noticed the books, too, and Luke choked as the man tightened his grip.

"Where did you get those? How *dare* you!"

At Sil's side, Dog rasped his knives together, but their threat was impotent given that Crovan's Skillful reflexes would be primed for any attack.

Silyen bent to inspect the books. Something was protruding from one of them—a photograph. And, oh goodness, it was *interesting*. He turned it over and couldn't suppress a grin as he saw the names inscribed on the back. Out of the several hypotheses Sil had constructed to explain what had just happened at the door, what he'd discovered in Coira's mind, and the existence of Coira herself—one of them began to coalesce from theory into fact.

A ghastly gurgling noise from Luke interrupted his thoughts. The boy's eyes bulged at his former jailer. It was hard to say which of the two of them was redder in the face.

"Devin's guts are leaking all over my hall," Crovan hissed. "Half my servants are nowhere to be found. And now this. The girl is gone."

"Girl?" Luke tried to yell, but it barely came out as a wheeze. "Don't you mean *your daughter*? And with your own sister. You sick bastard."

"You don't know what you're talking about!"

"Is he talking about this?" Silyen said innocently.

He held up the photograph.

"Don't touch that. Give it back."

"Well, I would, but you have your hands full. It would be terrible if—whoops!"

The photograph slipped from Silyen's fingers and did a

breezy zigzag toward the loch, even though the air was as still as if the world held its breath.

Crovan lunged for it, and in the same instant, Silyen grabbed Luke and pulled him behind him. For someone without Skill, the boy's lack of self-preservation instincts was deplorable. With Luke safe, he tugged Dog to his side, too. It was a lord's duty to protect his retainers.

The picture was now in Crovan's hands. He retrieved the three books and tucked the photo back between the pages.

"Do you think I would treat my own daughter like that?" the lord of Eilean Dòchais sneered at Luke. "She's no child of mine."

"She has to be—she's your *heir*," Luke said. Silyen could feel the boy behind him radiating anger, and held out an arm to keep him back. "She can give people permission to leave through the Last Door. That's where your servants have gone. She released all those she didn't think deserved to be here. The castle obeys her because she's a *Crovan*."

Luke spat out the last word as if it tasted disgusting. The pair of them stared at each other, breathing hard. It would all be rather entertaining were Crovan not so dangerous and Silyen not so invested in Luke remaining unharmed. Time to try civilized conversation instead.

"I'd always wondered about the collars," Silyen said. "Everyone thinks they're just a kind of shackle for your Condemned prisoners. But the necklace Fair Elspet wore wasn't that, was it? It was her punishment, and it was *personal*. Seeing the tapestry helped me make the connections. Before the Condemned, and before Coira, you collared her mother for the same crime as Elspet: a love that her family didn't approve of."

"Whatever you think you know," said Crovan coldly, "is of no interest to me. Now remove yourself from my island, Silyen. I may have tolerated your presence before, in the interests of research, but our collaboration is at an end. Hadley, get back inside."

At Sil's back, Luke flinched. Of course, Crovan had no idea that Luke had ever left the castle. Didn't know that he had stood in Gorregan Square, or driven to Far Carr.

"I said," Crovan growled, "get. Inside."

Silyen reached for Luke's throat. The boy's skin was tantalizingly warm and beginning to bruise where Crovan had choked him. Sil drew down his fingers slower than was strictly necessary, and tugged open the neck of Luke's sweater to show that he was uncollared.

"You like controlling people, don't you, Arailt? Except it's not always possible, is it?"

"Spare me the amateur psychology, Silyen. With or without a collar, the boy is Condemned and belongs in my custody."

"Oh, you know." Silyen shrugged. "You've mislaid so many prisoners that I can't imagine you'll miss one more. Tell me, did your sister manage to take off her collar to sneak out and meet her lover? Or did you only put it on her when you discovered she was pregnant? Did you consider the child's father unsuitable—or is Luke on the right track, and you wished it had been you? Naughty Arailt."

Crovan's face contorted in fury. His hand slashed through the air—but when the lightning struck, Silyen let out a laugh that was one part fear to nine parts exhilaration. He had been braced for attack from the moment he had pulled Luke and Dog to him. The air hissed as the electricity crackled and dissipated, his Skillful wards protecting all three of them.

"A nice touch," he crowed. "But you should have given us time to get in the boat if you wanted to uphold family tradition."

"Are you fucking nuts?" Luke cried.

The boy was shaking violently—shock from near-incineration by lightning would do that. Silyen wasn't sure if he meant Crovan or himself. Possibly both.

Luke still hadn't figured it out—which was fair enough, given that he hadn't seen what Silyen had inside Coira's head. Her mindscape was a version of Eilean Dòchais and its surroundings. But the castle had been transformed into an impossibly tall and airy version of itself. Its sparkling windows were alight with candles and lamps, and both doors stood welcomingly ajar. The pair of them had walked through room after room made bright and hospitable, the furnishings cheerful, the walls hung with paintings and photographs rather than weapons and stuffed animal trophies.

Aunty Terpy's memory-Orpen was an exact reproduction of its original, because his aunt's loving childhood had been everything she had wanted. Coira, though, had taken the only place she had ever known and made it the warm, inviting inverse of its cruel reality. Her island, unlike the barren promontory on which the four of them now stood, was bursting with life. It was studded with rock primroses and tiny pink-petaled alpines; swifts and martins dived and spun around the castle walls.

It had been enchanting—and none of it had interested Silyen in the slightest.

There were two things that had captured his attention. The first was glaringly obvious: the loch around the castle was drained of its cruel, Skill-infused waters. Coira's Eilean Dòchais stood ringed by a dry, stony bed. Silyen knew what that symbolized, and he had ached for Coira's loss.

And the second thing . . . Ahh, what to make of the second thing?

Coira herself had been oblivious. But Silyen had been acutely aware of the presence—perhaps vaguer than a presence, perhaps merely the sensation—of a person just out of sight. Throughout his time in Coira's mindscape, Silyen hadn't been able to shake the notion that if he could cross the dry loch and peer over the rise of the heather moor, or scramble to the high battlements and look out, then he would see . . . someone else.

Someone searching for Coira's castle, but unable to find it.

Someone he and Luke had met once before at Eilean Dòchais, that time in Luke's mind, when he had been accompanied by an eagle and a stag. The king.

Silyen shook his head, to get his thoughts straight. Given the Crovan family history that was unraveling right here on the shore, there was a reason why that person could be looking for Coira: because he was her father. But there was also a reason why that was impossible: because he had died more than a thousand years ago.

It was just as well that Silyen had never taken the division between possible and impossible too seriously.

"You know what?" Luke was saying. "I don't really care who her parents are. We just need to get her back."

"Back?" Crovan's lip curled. "Why on earth would I want her back? My sister died giving birth to her, and I've had to endure her presence for seventeen years. I sent her belowstairs so I didn't have to see Rhona in her face every day. Now she's gone through the door. Good riddance."

And you could see Luke putting it together himself, patching up the holes in what he knew with these scraps of information.

"When you told her she'd committed 'the worst crime,'" the boy said, "you meant her mother's death. You let an innocent girl grow up thinking she was as bad as everyone else in your castle, just because she was motherless. You made her live as a servant, cooking and cleaning and waiting on those scumbag prisoners."

"I did my duty by her. While she lived, I protected her, for Rhona's sake. You know that none of the Condemned could lay a finger on her. But now that she is dead . . ."

Crovan opened his empty hands, a conjurer relieved that his dove has disappeared.

"She's *not dead*."

Luke was practically howling, and he really needed to stop before Crovan lashed out again. The boy didn't know how much danger he was in. If Luke took a step out of Silyen's protection and the Equal struck in that instant . . . Sil gripped Luke's wrist tightly to restrain him, and conversationally changed the topic.

"I initially thought you used the collar to lock away her Skill," he remarked. "But you didn't, did you? You drained it. I might have guessed that your showstopper with Meilyr wasn't the first time you'd attempted that. You wouldn't have risked your peers seeing you fail."

"She neither needed nor deserved to have Skill," Crovan snapped.

The lord of Eilean Dòchais was going to throw them off this island any minute now—or try the fuss-free option of incinerating them again. This called for desperate measures. Flattery.

"A remarkable thing to do," he said. "Unprecedented. I'd love to know how you managed it."

Crovan's expression turned wolfish. "Common belief is that you are already well acquainted with *how*, Silyen. There is the curious case of your Skilless middle brother—though your sister-in-law was asking me only last night if I thought that might be remedied. And the sad demise of your aunt Euterpe, who could have had her Skill destroyed and, once defenseless, been murdered. The only people present, of course, were you and your hound there. One of you rumored to have stripped Skill before, the other with a talent for killing. Strange coincidence."

Silyen's neck prickled. As far as Sil knew, the man couldn't take Skill, only destroy it—and he evidently believed Silyen to be capable of the same. It would be unwise to get into a contest with him. Sil doubted that Crovan could touch him or his power, but the man might discover that he actually *retained* what Skill he took. Silyen didn't want that to be common knowledge. He was well aware that his fellow Equals tolerated him as an eccentric. But if they knew the truth, how could they not regard him as a threat?

No, risks were all very well, but only when the reward was worth it.

But Sil wasn't going anywhere without discovering what Crovan knew of Coira's impossible paternity. Which was when Luke opened his big gob, and Silyen—even more so than usual—could have kissed him.

"But who was her father? Please. She spent her whole life wondering. And if she really is dead, then there's no harm in us knowing."

Crovan regarded Luke coldly, the lenses of his glasses reflecting only the blank gray-white of the cloudy sky.

"I have no idea. The only man I ever saw was some tramp I spotted her walking with out on the moors one day. The arrival of a child was an unpleasant surprise. Its possession of Skill even more so."

"A tramp? With Skill? Are you joking?"

"He wore a ragged cloak." Crovan's lip thinned. "It would have been a disguise, of course. Someone she'd met at one of the debutante balls in Edinburgh—perhaps an inappropriate second or third son, rather than an heir. Rhona was eighteen and our mother was launching her into society. All the daughters of the old *mormaer* clans were there, trussed up in virginal white—though that color may have been a lie from the moment my sister put it on. It certainly was by the time she lay bleeding nine months later."

Luke's breath was coming fast and angry, while Crovan stood immobile, as if turned to stone.

"You made Coira live like a servant, and took her Skill to punish her for how you felt about her mother," Luke said. "And now she's gone, too. What's broken inside you that you could do that?"

"My parents ran their car off the road hurrying back here, when Rhona's labor started. So my whorish sister's bastard child killed my entire family. The brat and her mother got what they deserved."

Silyen reached back a warning hand, to keep Luke where he was. He could feel the boy's chest rising and falling as he struggled to control himself.

"Charming though this has been," Sil said, once satisfied that Luke wasn't going to try something really stupid, "I think we'll get going. If you don't say a word about our visit, we won't say a word about the disorderly state of affairs that we found here. Is that fair?"

Crovan's lips twitched. His thin little mustache really was horrid.

"Your father wouldn't care if I tossed every prisoner in this castle off my battlements wrapped in chains. No, I think you'll find he's rather more interested in what you're up to at Far Carr, on an estate that's now without a single slave. You can't imagine that he and your sister-in-law approve of your recent actions."

"Not in my wildest dreams. Well, goodbye, Arailt. I daresay our paths will cross again soon."

Sil extended a hand, and wasn't offended when Crovan didn't take it. The man huffed, an arid sound with no mirth in it.

"We can't go and leave her behind!" Luke was resisting Silyen's efforts to prod him toward the jetty steps.

"We're not 'leaving her behind.' She's not *here*."

"And you're each just letting the other *walk away*?" Luke looked between Sil and Crovan in disbelief.

"Zero-sum game," growled Dog.

"I beg your pardon?"

"Stalemate. Mutually assured destruction. Python eats alligator." The man gave that batshit laugh that was really starting to get on Silyen's nerves.

"What our friend is trying to say, Luke, is that if the lord of Eilean Dòchais and I were to allow things to turn nasty, neither of us could feel assured of victory, and therefore we are choosing to avoid conflict. Well, give or take a lightning bolt or two, eh, Arailt? Please don't strike the boat while it takes us back across, there's a good chap."

Luke looked like he was going to keep on fighting this every step of the way, so Silyen touched his forehead and sent him down into unconsciousness. Dog scooped up the boy and carried him in a fireman's lift to the boat. Crovan watched as the vessel crossed the loch to the shore, and he was still there when Dog, grumbling, dumped Luke into the cabin of their helicopter.

It wasn't until the craft had lifted off the ground that Silyen leaned over Luke and brought him round.

The boy looked at him and then Dog, then out of the chopper windows, where Eilean Dòchais had already disappeared. He gave Silyen what he doubtless intended to be a furious glare, but which was obviously the verge of tears, then hunched over in his seat.

Silyen wasn't in touch with his own emotions, let alone anyone else's, and it was tiring just looking at Luke. But then, he did still want to keep looking.

"She can't be dead," Luke burst out. None of them wore the headsets, so the pilot couldn't hear what they said, and the noise of the engine and rotors was almost deafening.

"She isn't," said Silyen. "If you go out of that door without permission: dead. She went the other way: not dead."

Luke was red-eyed and suspicious. "Now's really not the time to be dicking about. You may not have noticed, but I'm finding what happened back there rather hard to deal with. Coira's amazing. Of course I want to believe she's not dead. But if she isn't, then where is she?"

"She's somewhere else. And, no, I've no idea where."

"No body," rasped Dog. "When the Last Door kills—there's always a body."

"Precisely. Thank you, Dog."

Luke fell silent, trying to process it all.

If Silyen was honest, he was still trying to work through the details, too. They had seen a living girl simply step into thin air—and disappear.

And that changed everything. Not everything that Silyen had *thought* about, because he had sent his mind into every dark corner of the unimaginable and improbable. But it went way beyond what he had *experienced*.

"Hear me out," Luke said beside him, as quietly as the rotor noise permitted. "I know I'll sound like an idiot to you, but I'm trying to understand."

That's fine, it was on the tip of Sil's tongue to say. *Everyone sounds like an idiot to me.* But he stopped himself.

In the past year, this boy had been on a learning curve far steeper than any Silyen had undergone, with his life frequently in danger along the way. Sil not only had never faced such risks, he also had the security of the Skill that thrummed through him. A power that could attack, defend, and heal. Without it, he would be as vulnerable as if he ran barefoot in the dark across a floor of knives. And that was how Luke lived, every day. In that state of vulnerability he had joined Meilyr's uprising in Millmoor, and survived Crovan's castle.

He wasn't an idiot. In his own earnest way, Luke was remarkable.

"Tell me what you're thinking," Sil said.

"The way I see it," the boy began, "some aspects of Skill are how the body works, just done better, like your physical strength or ability to heal. The mental stuff is freakier, but also understandable. Persuasion or influencing people? The rest of us can do that, too. As for examining or hiding memories, well, scientists say that one day we'll be able to store our thoughts digitally, or erase them, so again, I get it.

"Even the weirdest thing—those mindscapes, mine and yours? Mine didn't just *look* like the setting of one of my console games, it's kind of the same thing: a world you create with your imagination and spend time in. Having you there with me, or Crovan building walls within it, it's like a multiplayer game. I can accept all that, just about.

"But when we're in my mindscape, or yours, our bodies are still right here in the real world. Coira *disappeared,* Silyen. She went through a doorway and didn't come out the other side. And I've no idea what that means, and I'm actually kind of terrified that I don't know what anything means anymore. Crovan's interrogations in that place scrambled my brain. It was getting difficult to make sense of things, so I had to write stuff down, like a journal. And now I'm afraid I'll wake up any minute and find that I'm back there, slobbering into my pillow, with only half a brain."

Luke's hands were shaking. Silyen took them and squeezed until he heard the bones click. Then he pulled Luke's head against his shoulder and held the boy there while he drew in great heaving breaths.

"I don't have all the answers," Sil told him. "But I do have the next best thing, which is questions."

"Questions?" the boy mumbled against his jacket.

"Do you believe in fairy tales, Luke?"

He huffed. "Would you, if you were me? I don't know. Maybe when I was little."

"I think I've done it all backward. When I was younger, my aunt and I used to read *Tales of the King* to each other. They were about the king battling monsters, working wonders, and walking in strange worlds, and I knew they were just stories. But the older I've grown, the more I've come to believe they were real.

"I wanted a peerage so I could get inside the House of Light—that was my price for staying hush about what Rix did to you." Silyen felt Luke pull away from his side, and knew he deserved it. "Here's why. When you're outside the House, you see Skillful brilliance pulsing within the chamber. I needed to know what you see from the inside. Turns out it's exactly the same: radiance *on the opposite side*. The parliamentarians talk about a 'world beyond,' but it's not beyond—it's always on whichever side you're not.

"Except when Rix adopted me, a great flare of Skill burst *through* the glass walls. It went straight into my heart, like someone had stuck jumper cables in me, or as if Crovan's lightning bolt had hit. They all saw it. I heard Gavar and some others freaking out."

"So it goes both ways, too," Luke said, straightening up.

"What?"

"The Last Door. Crovan always said it only went one way. But it doesn't—we just saw that. Coira went *the other way*. The night we both discovered Coira could command the Last Door, she'd found me staring out of it. I was sort of sleepwalking, and was convinced I could see somewhere else. Not Loch nan Deur at all, but another place—and I thought the king was in it. Don't laugh at me for wishful thinking, but what if the door is like the House of Light, and there's somewhere else on the other side, whichever way you go? What if she's *there,* just waiting for us to find her?"

Silyen didn't laugh. Nothing killed an idea faster than mockery. And this was a *good* idea.

But everything was jumbled up: the Wonder King, Skill, other worlds, doors that went both ways, and Silences that were centuries old.

Coira, Luke, and Silyen.

He knew the connections between some of these things. Guessed at others.

But the bigger picture was still just out of reach.

"When I was in Coira's mind—which looked like the castle, but a jollier version of it," he told Luke, "I felt as though the king was right there, just out of sight."

"They're connected," said Luke. "Aren't they."

It wasn't a question.

The two of them stared at each other, uncertain. Silyen took a breath. Luke had shared his thoughts, although fearful of being thought an idiot, so Silyen would, too.

"Crovan mentioned seeing his sister with a tramp in a ragged cloak. We've seen that cloak, you and I. Yes, I'm pretty sure the king is Coira's father—and he's been looking for her. But somehow, he found us instead."

"Maybe if we find him," Luke said, "we find her."

Silyen nodded. He couldn't care less about one of them.

But finding the other?

He cared about that very, very much indeed.

FOURTEEN

ABI

They took the time they needed to get it right, with a degree of planning even Abi couldn't fault. The changeover cycles of the Fullthorpe secure unit were watched around the clock, to ensure that it tallied with the schedules Tilda had found. Another team worked on the logistics of getting the rescued prisoners away to safety, once they were free, then out of the country.

Every connection that those already signed up to Midsummer's movement could draw on was utilized. The jail was sixty miles north of Lindum. The nearest major slavetown was in the shadow of Leeds—Hillbeck, reputedly the roughest in the country. But someone there knew someone who knew someone with the right sort of business based close to Fullthorpe, and so three lorries pulled up at Lindum's back gate with the words "Bloomin' Lovely—Creating Gorgeous Gardens" painted brightly on the side.

"Here for your stonework," said the driver of one, a hard-faced guy with a soft moors accent. "Each van's good for twenty-six tons. I hear you'll have no problem loading them in?"

"No problem at all," Midsummer said, smiling, as Abi unbarred the gate and the Equal swung them open for the lorries.

The guy's reaction was priceless as first Leto the wolf, then Tom, Dick, and Harry, the three-headed gryphon, then even more outlandish members of the stone menagerie trotted, stomped, or slithered up the lorry tailgates and lay down inside, turning back into innocuous stone. They would be driven up to the garden center depot and parked overnight, until Midsummer and the assault team arrived the next day.

That was the last time Abi smiled, because next Renie appeared at her elbow to take her to Hilda and Tilda.

"There's something they need you to check," the kid said.

The "something" was a freeze-frame image scaled up from the prison's own CCTV cameras.

"So, hen," said Tilda, pointing out two blurry shapes among a huddle of prisoners. "Is that your ma and da?"

Hilda was ready with a chair as Abi sat down in shock. She had known they were in Fullthorpe. Bouda's words that day at the cottage had threatened it, and Asif's trawl of the prisoner records had confirmed it, when "Hadley, S." and "Hadley, J." were there on the list. But to see them like this . . .

Her fingertips brushed the fuzzy pixels as she strained to make out details. Mum's bob had been shorn up to her ears—the sort of cut she'd said she would never have, because it made her feel "old and sensible." That bright spot was light gleaming off Dad's familiar receding hairline, which Daisy would tease him about while Luke anxiously checked his own hair in the mirror. Dad looked stooped, while Mum, always trim ("Keeping healthy is part of a nurse's job description," she'd say as she urged Abi out for a mother-daughter run), had shrunk and become birdlike.

Abi was heart-struck. What were they doing in there? Being held as leverage for their law-breaking children was what. If Abi had gone meekly to Millmoor with them, after Luke's Condemnation, this wouldn't be happening. The guilt was overwhelming, and anxiety stuffed its fingers down Abi's throat again, blocking her airways and making her gag.

Except *no,* dammit. This wasn't on her, or Luke. This was on no one except the Equals—and specifically on Bouda Matravers and Whittam Jardine.

"That's them," she croaked, and Tilda's arm went around her shoulders and squeezed.

"You'll have 'em back soon enough," the woman promised. "And look, here's Oz and Jess with the rest that got taken at Riverhead."

She pulled up another two pictures, and there was Oz, still bulky in his prison uniform, his dark face an unreadable blur in a line of prisoners in the grainy image. By the time Abi turned to Jess's picture, she was incapable of recognizing anyone at all, given how her eyes filled with tears.

"I'm sorry," she said, mortified, as she realized several had fallen onto the computer keyboard.

"Not long now, lassie," said Tilda. "Don't you worry. We'll get you all in, and get you and them safe back out again."

There was a shared supper that evening, followed by a minute-by-minute briefing led by Renie's uncle Wes and Midsummer. The twins had set up a projector inside Lindum's massive rotunda, and photos of the compound, superimposed blueprints, plans of the surveillance camera locations, and, almost unbearably, the CCTV images Abi had been shown were all thrown onto the faded Roman brickwork. Gavar sat at the front throughout, his face tight with attention. Occasionally he'd lean forward to object or challenge, sweeping that long coat over one knee impatiently. His comments were always blunt and to the point.

Midsummer had given him a crucial role. It was a massive—and public—vote of confidence. Abi didn't think it was misplaced.

She barely slept that night, tossing and turning beneath the blankets in a cool guest room. She climbed out of bed—Renie a dead-to-the-world lump beside her—and padded across to the window. The terra-cotta floor tiling was warm beneath her feet as she stood looking out, the curtain billowing in the breeze. Across Lindum's grounds, statuary gleamed in the moonlight. Then Abi glimpsed the gleam of white wings, and Alba the owl swooped around where Midsummer stood almost invisibly in the night, a smaller figure leaning into her. As the two women kissed, Abi stepped back and pulled the curtain. Hers wasn't the only family with everything on the line tomorrow.

The morning would bring another rehearsal of the plans, carefully timed. When she woke a second time, Abi felt too nauseous for breakfast, but knew she'd have to eat something, so went for a jog around the grounds to try to work up an appetite. Dew flecked her ankles, and birds sang and shrilled as she passed. There was no one out here but her.

Until she saw a familiar figure off by himself, pacing in circles around a tree. It was Gavar, a phone pressed to his ear and evidently agitated. Abi slowed and reconsidered her route—she didn't want to disturb him—when he burst out furiously, ". . . totally unnecessary . . . absolutely not."

Abi's chest tightened, and despite being winded from her

run, she held her breath. What was this? When the heir stabbed his phone to end the call, she had to slide hastily behind a tree as he strode back toward the house.

Thinking quickly, Abi calculated another route, via an old icehouse, that would give the impression of having come from a different direction altogether. Then she took off at a run. Who had Gavar been talking to? And what about?

Her looping route brought her to the back door and into the kitchen at the same time Gavar stepped in from the opposite end, having come through the interior. Midsummer looked up from the long table, where she sat with Layla, Renie, Wesley, and the rest.

"We're almost done," she said, "but there's some scrambled egg on the stove. Where have you both been?"

"Went for a run," Abi said, wiping her sweaty face.

"Calling my daughter," Gavar said, showing the phone in his hand. "I make sure she hears her daddy's voice every day, and we're all going to be busy later."

But his face was grim as he scraped the cast-iron skillet almost empty and took a seat at the bench.

Unease prickled through Abi. What she'd heard had plainly not been a conversation with Libby. Perhaps some sort of disagreement with Griff, or even Daisy? But she'd seen how Gavar was with them, and couldn't imagine him using that furious tone. His other family, then—Whittam or Bouda, or even Jenner? What could it all mean?

If Abi voiced her fears to Midsummer, she might abort the rescue. If she challenged Gavar, he might storm out, and he had a crucial role to play in the plan they'd devised. In fact, Abi couldn't imagine how they'd ever thought it might be possible without him.

But if she said nothing . . . ? What if Gavar had betrayed every detail of the plan, and when they arrived at the prison, there were detachments of Security waiting for them? Gavar might turn on Midsummer, and not only would there be no rescue, but two dozen more prisoners for the Jardine regime. And with Midsummer gone, the network she had drawn tight around her would fall apart.

Stop it, Abi told herself firmly. *Stop catastrophizing and imagining the worst. This is like before your exams—you convinced yourself you'd failed them all, then got top grades for every one.*

But the stakes were too high to do nothing. She went to find the twins and Asif.

"Have you noticed anything odd at Fullthorpe?" she said. "Unusual comings and goings? Comings in particular."

"Like what, love?" Hilda asked.

"Reinforcements. Extra Security, that sort of thing. I mean, I know Midsummer runs a tight ship here, but all it would take would be one person to betray us."

"There's no one here that hasn't suffered a loss at the hands of these bastards, Abi. No one will have said a word."

"But to answer your question," said Asif, leaning over—and Abi blessed his logic and detachment—"it's hard to determine 'unusual' when we've not observed the whole routine. That said, we've seen nothing that looks alarming. One small van coming out this morning, and nothing going in. Certainly nothing either way that looks like Security. But it's on our to-flag list from the minute you all leave here. We'll let Midsummer and Wes know immediately of anything that looks irregular."

Abi's airways opened up a little, and the terrible pressure on her chest eased. "Right. Of course. Thank you."

"Time for the final run-through," Tilda said, grinning. "Would you go grab those nice strong gardeners to help a couple of girls with their gear?"

This briefing was timed. The rotunda had been emptied of all furniture, and as a graphic time-lapse of the rescue plans was animated over the aerial CCTV view, those going into Fullthorpe moved around the space in their groups. A clock counting up from zero was projected onto the far wall. Abi watched the two small dots denoting herself and her companion. Apart from the beginning and the end, they were alone, at some distance from the others, and Abi was able to observe the rest of the rescue unfold. Her stomach lurched as Gavar led his team into the center of the rotunda, a stand-in for the secure wing where some of the prisoners, her dad included, were being kept under twenty-three-hour lockdown.

"Fourteen minutes," Midsummer said, pointing to the clock on the wall. "That's calculated from the time we estimate it'll take from the detection of our intrusion—we'll be pretty noticeable—to full lockdown being complete. There's a free-fire protocol that the guards are supposed to stick to, but once we're in, I doubt any of them will wait for orders. We've got eighty people to get out, and to give them the best chance of getting away, we need to ensure we can't be followed. That means we'll be blocking the compound's main gate, and resealing our entry points at the walls. Any questions?"

Abi raised her hand. "What if . . ." she asked, trying very hard not to look at Gavar as she spoke. "I know we're all tight on this, but what if somehow they've found out about our plans, and battalions of Security roll up, either before we arrive or during the raid?"

Midsummer's face was as hard as one of her marble creatures.

"We abort. But I'm confident that surprise is on our side. I trust everyone in this room"—and was Abi imagining it, or did the Equal's eyes seek out Gavar across the echoing rotunda? "We are planning to get our friends and family out of there, not to leave them behind. But I'm not going to risk adding more to their number. If our observation team spots anything untoward, they'll immediately report their best assessment to me, and I'll decide if we continue or go. But the thing we do *not* do is fight. This is not an attack—it's a liberation."

Abi nodded. You could feel it fill the whole vast space: admiration for this woman, and the shared belief in what they were about to do.

She was ready, too.

Who knew that a marble gryphon's back would be so comfortable—though Abi suspected her thighs would ache chronically tomorrow. Beneath her, supple marble muscles moved as the creature ran, and her fingers were wound into the beast's scruff where cold feathers met cool fur. It was disconcerting to be faced constantly with one of the three fierce heads, either Tom or Harry, constantly scouting backward.

Up in front flew Alba. Midsummer led them, on the powerful shoulders of Leto, as the wolf made speed in silence. Renie was atop the sphinx—which was the size of a small pony—as though she'd been riding one all her life. Plainly a street childhood in Millmoor had made her adaptable to any circumstance.

The sphinx's paws thudded on the ground, but the real earthshaker was the giant, jogging at their side. Abi guessed he was a figure of Hercules, clad in a lion skin, but in place of his marble club he'd been equipped with two twenty-pound sledgehammers, with which he periodically whacked at branches, as

if practicing for what would come next. Weaving in and out of
the trees, barely visible, was the gargantuan snake-bodied creature, whose upper torso was a beautiful woman. Abi was happy
for it to keep its distance. The humanoid animations, even (perhaps especially) Renie's human-headed sphinx, were eerie.

Both Abi's and Renie's mounts responded to simple com-
mands from their riders, but the larger monsters were Midsummer's to control, so their first task was to get the Equal into
the highest perimeter watchtower, which was also the closest
to the residential blocks. From there she would be able to direct
them.

They kept up a pace, marble limbs never tiring, as they
closed in on Fullthorpe. Once the message had come through
that Gavar's team was moving into position, the garden center
vans had driven to a quiet country road a few miles from the
jail. With supermax prisoners not being in high demand as
neighbors, Fullthorpe was mostly surrounded by agricultural
land, an unexpectedly bright patchwork of yellows and greens
on Hilda's images. But the closer they came, the more the tree
cover thinned. It finally dwindled to a mere perimeter screen to
hide the prison from passersby—and which also, just about,
concealed their unnatural menagerie.

There was a faint buzz of traffic noise from the roads. Half a
kilometer away was a light industrial park, where vehicles were
ready for the getaway. The three of them and the beasts halted
in place, listening through their earpieces. Renie was checking
her watch with military precision. And if it was weird having
their movements coordinated by a kid barely in her teens, well,
Renie had been doing this longer than any of them. Knowing
when a patrol passed, or a storeroom door might be open, was
what had kept her alive and free in Millmoor for all those years.

But this would be bigger than anything she'd attempted be-

fore. Midsummer's face was sheened with sweat that was probably down to exertion from controlling the creatures—they'd
brought six rather than seven, so she wasn't permanently
stretched to her limits—but it was doubtless also anxiety. Abi's
hands were slippery and her heart was lodged in her throat.
Every movement or rustle in the woods sent her nerves jarring,
and adrenaline coursed through her.

"Any unusual movement to report?" Midsummer asked into
her mouthpiece. "Arrivals? Departures? Signs of Security being
ready inside the compound? Over."

Please let Gavar not be a traitor, Abi pleaded inwardly. Please let
the conversation she'd heard that morning be merely him keeping up appearances with someone back in London. Perhaps his
mother, or Silyen.

And where *was* Silyen Jardine in all of this? Abi had always
had a sense of him being on the edge of things. Present, but
unnoticed until his grand entrance, as when Kyneston's ballroom blew. But she hadn't seen him at the Blood Fair. Hadn't
heard word of him for weeks.

The crackle in her earpiece brought her back to the present.
It was Hilda's calm voice.

"Nothing to report. All clear to proceed. Repeat, all clear to
proceed. Over."

Abi's fingers gripped the feathered neck of Tom—or was it
Harry?—while the beast's other two heads strained forward.

Other voices came over the headpieces, one after the other,
confirming that they were in position and ready. Abi's heart
rate cranked upward. She felt it throb in her earlobes, the tips
of her fingers, the tensed crook of her ankle.

Hang on, she told her mum and dad silently. *We're coming.*

Then Midsummer, clear and strong: "Let's go, on three . . .
two . . . one . . ."

And Abi was out of time for either fear or hesitation.

The giant hurtled from the treeline faster than seemed possible, his arm windmilling the massive hammers. Behind him slithered the serpent-woman, her thick tails propelling her with unnatural speed. Alba spread her wings and soared into the sky, heading for the central CCTV camera post. When that was destroyed, she'd move on to the others one by one, Tilda counting them off into each team's earpiece as the screens went dead.

The giant had already battered a hole in the perimeter wall and ran to the next position, on the north side. Records showed that thirty of the prisoners they were after should be here, in one of the textile workshops. In the fifty-foot wall, the hole he left behind didn't look large, but it was enough for a giant snake, a wolf, and a sphinx to squeeze through. Not a gryphon, though.

Abi felt the shoulders of Tom, Dick, and Harry flex beneath her as the creature unfolded mighty wings and crouched low on its leonine haunches. Distantly, an explosion blasted from the opposite side of the compound, which could only have been Gavar Jardine taking down the front gates. While the noise echoed, Abi's stomach lurched as her beast leapt into the air.

And this was madness, surely, because Abi felt the wind against her face and knew that she was flying. How did the marble gryphon not simply drop out of the air? Then she remembered that Midsummer had set a metal dragon circling over the Thames. This was Skill incarnate.

She dug her fingers deep into the gryphon's scruff, and between wingbeats tried to make out what was happening below. The giant serpent's coils had flattened the mesh fence around the watchtower, where Midsummer was dismounting, and the creature was sliding toward its next target, the internal double wall around the residential blocks. This was where the majority of the prisoners they were after were held. That was where Gavar Jardine was heading, accompanied by only a few men—the fewer the better, so the Equal could focus on clearing a path in, rather than protecting his companions. There, they would need to break people out of blocks A and D.

The last sounds Abi caught before the gryphon rose too high for hearing were the snarling of Leto, as it bounded into the watchtower ahead of Midsummer, and shots that Abi hoped desperately were for the wolf and not its mistress. She could only imagine the screams of the men who ran from the tower to be confronted by a rearing sphinx with a child on its shoulders.

Midsummer believed they could do this without casualties, not only among their band of rescuers but among the prison officers and Security. Abi wasn't so sure.

She caught a glimpse of the giant and the small team of men pounding along beside it toward the workshop complex. Then the gryphon banked and dipped and Abi was heading toward her own target.

Few walls could resist the combined onslaught of marble monsters and Gavar's incendiary Skill. Which meant that the true challenge wasn't getting the Riverhead prisoners out of the Fullthorpe compound, it was getting them away from the site altogether. Abi knew that the Highwithel chopper, with Meilyr's sister at the controls, had been timed to take off from its refueling spot ten minutes before Midsummer gave the signal. She couldn't spot it just yet, but it would be here shortly. The obstacle was that the exercise field was crisscrossed with steel cables, to prevent exactly such an airborne escape route.

The prison's designers hadn't reckoned on a gryphon, though—an oversight for which Abi felt they could be forgiven. She reached into her backpack and pulled out a hydraulic bolt cutter, acquired from the same industrial suppliers as the giant's outsize hammers. It would cut steel rope up to two centimeters thick. Construction specifications that Hilda had unearthed revealed that the wires across the exercise field were a few millimeters thinner. They were concreted into the top of the yard wall, which stood five meters high and just wide enough for a gryphon to settle all four feet on.

Abi slid off Tom, Dick, and Harry's back and hefted the cutters. Her wrist had recovered from her fall in Gorregan Square, and she'd spent time practicing her technique. She snapped on a pair of gloves to prevent the handles slipping through her fear-greased palms. The cables were tethered in clusters at the four corners of the yard, forming a web as they radiated out. The first corner of cables cut, Abi clambered back onto the gryphon, which flew to the next—Midsummer must be safely in the tower, watching over everything, coordinating her creature's movements.

As she was sweating on the third corner, Abi heard the whump of the chopper and saw it rising over the treeline. Louder than its rotors, though, was the din of shouting, gunfire, explosions, and mayhem that was now erupting all around. Smoke rose in several places, and masonry dust clogged the air. Somewhere down there were her parents. *Please,* was all she could think. *Please, please, please.*

Abi could see the first batch of prisoners—those broken out of the workshop where the records said that Mum should be—being guided out of the hole in the wall's northern side, and counted them as they ran. Thirty-one. But the two leading the way weren't in prison garb; they were rescuers, guiding the inmates to the first wave of getaway vehicles on the industrial park. So: twenty-nine escapees. Their manifest had said thirty.

One was missing. It wouldn't be Mum. It *couldn't* be Mum. Thirty to one it wasn't her—why on earth would it be?

But the giant was already sealing up the gap with rubble to prevent any of the legitimately incarcerated escaping, and there was no time to wonder. The chopper was directly overhead and Abi and her beast moved to the fourth corner. As she bent to sever the final tethers, a gunshot pinged off the gryphon's haunch. Being marble, Tom, Dick, and Harry didn't react, but Abi felt sharp stone fragments whizz past her legs, a few stinging her calf and thigh. The shock, coupled with the weight of the bolt cutters and the downward whirlwind as the chopper descended, threw her off balance.

And Abi fell.

FIFTEEN

ABI

Luckily, she knew *how* to fall.

Mum and Dad had made her and Luke do a basic mountain-safety course a few years ago, during a walking holiday in Wales, and Abi, at least, had paid close attention. She willed herself to go limp, and landed feetfirst but immediately rolled onto her side to distribute impact. It jarred all the way up her legs and spine, but she'd landed on grass. A quick check told her that everything was in working order.

Prisoners were streaming into the yard through the gate that had been thwacked from its hinges by the serpent-woman. They were all women—the female residential block had been the first target of Gavar's team. Abi got shakily to her feet and looked around. Tom, Dick, and Harry were still perched on the wall. Midsummer must not have spotted her fall amid the unfolding chaos.

"Abigail?"

A hand was shaking her arm. Abi blinked. Jessica. Her brother's friend whom she'd met at Highwithel. Oz's partner, who had gone with him to reconnoiter Eilean Dòchais, before the pair of them were captured at Riverhead. Abi began to protest that she was okay, but that wasn't why Jess had stopped her.

"Have you come for all of us?" Jess yelled over the noise of the rotors. "Because we're not all in the residential blocks. There's a whole bunch in the workshops."

"We got them," Abi yelled back. "Thirty of them, right? They've already gone. You need to go, too."

She gave the woman a push toward the chopper, which was filling up, but Jessica didn't move.

"Abi, your mum should have been with them. But she was taken to the hospital wing this morning. Nothing serious."

No.

No, that wasn't true. It *couldn't* be.

She pressed a finger to her earpiece to transmit.

"Emily? Emily, come in." The woman was coordinating the getaways for those escaping through the north wall. "Emily, is my mother with you? Over."

A crackle of static. Then Asif's voice, neutral as ever.

"Abi, essential comms only till we're done or I'll have to mute you. Sorry. Over."

Frustration tore from Abi's lips. She grabbed Jessica's arm and shook it.

"Are you sure? How do you know?"

"I'm sure, because . . ." The woman shook her head. "I'm just sure."

"I've studied the plans. I know the layout of this place. That's the hospital block over there, right?"

She pointed to a low, gray building in the compound's west quadrant.

Jessica nodded. "But you can't—"

"I have to," Abi said. "Now get on that chopper and get out of here."

But Jess didn't budge. Instead, she picked up the bolt cutters from where they'd landed when Abi fell. A monstrous braying sound made them both jump.

"We've got to be quick," said Jess. "That's the lockdown siren. Follow me."

It was blaring from loudspeakers across the prison compound. Every prisoner not in their cell was being returned immediately. Entire wings would be sealed off, enabling Security and prison officer manpower to focus on containing the breach. The drill called for total lockdown to take less than seven minutes. After that, the rescuers would face fiercer opposition than they had so far.

But in nine minutes—according to the plan—they would be gone.

Jess was already running and Abi took off after her. The exercise yard was the northwestern quarter of the complex. The hospital wing was in the southwestern quarter. Between them lay the four residential blocks at the heart of the compound.

It was chaos. The air crackled with static—testament to the amount of Skillful power Gavar Jardine was throwing around. Whole sections of buildings were down, and men and women lay groaning in the rubble, both those in guard uniforms and those in the orange-and-gray jumpsuits of the prisoners. Abi had neither anger nor pity to spare for them. Her whole energy was focused on her mum, and the minutes ticking down until the compound was sealed.

Jess swung the cutters up to slam aside a Security man who had pulled a weapon on them and doubtless expected two women to stop. Abi tracked the gun as it flew from his hands, then sprinted to it.

It was a pistol. She didn't know how to fire it, but even her untrained eyes identified the magazine lodged in the main body of the weapon. She breathed a sigh of relief as it slid out again in her hands, and stuffed both parts into her backpack. Midsummer had told them to avoid fatalities at all costs, and Abi didn't want to make herself a target by running with it openly in her hand, but she'd use it—or try to—if she had to.

Jess hadn't stopped, and Abi raced after her. As they reached the hospital, panting, Abi realized how hard this was going to be without Gavar's Skill or one of Midsummer's monsters.

But the lockdown was working in their favor. Patients had to be secured, the same as everyone else, and the hospital's Security team would have started with the day admissions clinic—where patients would be more mobile and therefore more of a threat—then moved deeper to secure the wards one by one. No patients were held in the reception area, so there was no need for heavily secured doors to the outside. Indeed, the outer doors were easy-release, designed for speedy entry with a casualty, and they flew open after a few hefts of the bolt cutters.

Abi and Jess hurtled inside to find only a receptionist and two prison officers guarding the sealed doors to the day clinic.

The officers were armed with batons and pepper spray. They were the ones in close contact with the prisoners during the day, and the risk of a prisoner wresting a gun away from them was considered greater than the likelihood of them needing to use one. When firepower was required, Security would intervene. The receptionist was unarmed, though presumably equipped with both spray and a panic button. Nobody would be answering that button, Abi thought.

"Where's Jackie Hadley?" she demanded. "Brought in this morning. I'm only here for her. No one will get hurt."

"You're the one who'll get hurt," said one of the officers, slapping the tip of his baton against his palm. "Are you part of whatever's happening out there? You crazy bitch."

"Just let us take her and go," Abi said. "All the CCTV systems are down. No one will be able to see what happened in here. There could be ten of us threatening you. No one will blame you."

"Don't work like that, love," said the officer. "We've got a job to do, and we do it."

"Katie?" Jess appealed to the receptionist. "You know me from when I've been on cleaning detail. You know why Mrs. Hadley's in here, and that she doesn't deserve to be."

The receptionist looked torn, but shook her head.

"Sorry, pet. I know it's tough, but rules is rules."

This was all taking too long—far too long. The lockdown would be nearing completion; the exit holes would soon be sealed back up as the groups of escapees made it out. Abi shrugged off her backpack, reached in, and hoped to goodness she didn't slot the thing together backward.

"We don't have time for this," she said, straightening up, the gun outstretched in both hands so they couldn't see how she was shaking. "I need the three of you over there, now."

She motioned with the gun toward the far wall. The effective range of pepper spray was ten feet, maximum fifteen feet, she knew. Over there, they wouldn't be close enough to try anything.

"Hands up where I can see them. Now!" Was anyone falling for this? Apparently so, because the receptionist got up and joined the guards, and all three began to shuffle along the wall, hands raised. "You, Katie, throw Jessica your pass so she can open that door. And one of you tough guys, give us the keypad code. Jess, get my mum. If there's anyone else in there, make sure they don't get out."

Abi thought she glimpsed her mum's face up against the reinforced glass panels in the door of the dayroom, but couldn't take her eyes off the trio against the wall to check. Jess needed both the pass and the code for the keypad that controlled the secondary locking system. Then with a click and a beep, Mum was out. Her face was badly bruised, and one forearm was in a plaster cast. Her eyes were red and raw in her hollowed-out face.

The sight of her made Abi want to fire every bullet in the gun. Not at the guards, but just to spray them around to relieve her terrible, impotent rage. Instead, she steadied her hand. Just as with the prison break itself, getting *away* was what counted.

"Jess, Mum—to me," Abi said. When they reached her side, she barked at the officers to detach and slide over their canisters of pepper spray.

"Any move to use or open it, and I'll shoot," she said. "Do it one at a time. You first."

She motioned for Jessica to pick up the canisters. Then, with Jess and Mum alongside her, she backed toward the door, murmuring instructions as they went. She nudged Mum out first, stepped through, then watched as Jess emptied one of the spray canisters right inside the doors before slamming them shut. That should discourage the three inside from coming after them. For good measure, she told Jess to wedge the other canister through the exterior handles of the clinic door to secure them, at least momentarily. Even thirty seconds more would help.

"Go!" Abi yelled at her mum and Jess.

Abi cracked the gun apart again with shaking hands and

shoved it in her backpack, then took off down the streets after them. If her legs were running, they couldn't be wobbling.

That must have taken nine minutes, surely. The helicopter was lifting off with its second and final batch of escapees. Dad was scheduled to be among them, and Abi strained to see him, but the prisoners were safe in the chopper's interior. Only Gavar Jardine stood watchfully in the craft's open side, ready to repel any last-minute effort to prevent their departure. Unlike his intervention at the Blood Fair, there'd be no explaining this away to his family.

There had been no last-minute betrayal. No platoons of soldiers waiting. No Kessler and his brutes with their tasers and guns. Abi's bones nearly melted with relief that she hadn't said anything about Gavar's angry call that morning.

With the north wall sealed and the helicopter gone, the hole in the west wall—through which Renie and Midsummer had entered—was the only exit route remaining. Abi zigzagged through the courtyards, trying frantically to map the space onto her memories of the blueprint and what she'd seen from the air.

"Head for the watchtower," she yelled ahead to Jess, realizing that they'd find the breached section of wall there, where Midsummer was commanding her monsters.

And here came one of them. The ground shook and Abi heard Mum stifle a scream as the giant lumbered past, dragging its enormous hammers.

Then her mother screamed again, and fell.

"Mum!"

Abi dropped to her knees by her mother's side.

"Abi?" Jess spun.

"Keep going!" Abi yelled, her hand clasping Mum's good

one. "Or the exit hole will be closed up. It's in the wall next to the watchtower. Go!"

She didn't even look to see if the other woman had obeyed. Instead, Abi put her fingers to her mother's side and they came away red. Mum whimpered, and Abi had never felt so helpless.

"We've got to get you up," she said, ripping at the hole in her mother's prison tunic so she could inspect the wound. A bullet must have gone through, and a runnel of dark blood oozed out. "We're so close, Mum. And Dad will be waiting for us outside."

Her mother hid her face and moaned, and the awfulness of it made Abi shake. She pulled off her hoodie and T-shirt, made a pad with the T-shirt, and pressed it against the bullet wound, then knotted the hoodie round her by its sleeves, as if Mum had just taken it off on a warm day.

"Up," she said. "Come on, Mum, please."

Abi hauled her mother to her feet. She was so light. There was hardly anything to her at all. Was that what Millmoor had done?

But she was still too heavy for Abi to carry any distance. Every step clearly pained her—and on the third one, she cried out and sagged to her knees. Her stifled scream ripped through Abi like a knife.

Abi bent over and reached under Mum's arms, locking her hands together around her chest, and pulled her upright again, grunting with effort. All the while, her mother was protesting feebly, telling Abi to leave her and run. But she wouldn't. She couldn't.

She had failed to rescue Luke. Hadn't persuaded Gavar to send Daisy over the water. She wasn't going to abandon her mum.

The back of Abi's neck went suddenly cold, then pain lanced her shoulders.

She'd been shot, too. This couldn't be happening. They weren't meant to die here. Not like this.

Then Abi felt herself lifted. Her arms reflexively tightened around her mother's chest, fingers locking in a fist. The noise and the yelling all around quieted—even the siren's blare.

More cold needles dug into her thighs—they were claws, she realized. Quickly, she wrapped her legs round her mother's, so the pair of them were stacked up as if tandem skydiving.

It wasn't a parachute that held them up, though. And they weren't falling, but rising. Abi twisted her head sideways and saw the curve of wings alongside. For an insane moment, she wondered if they were both dying, and an angel had come for them. Then she heard a harsh screech, and Tom, Dick, and Harry tossed back their heads as the gryphon bore Abi and her mother higher.

A new terror seized her: she wouldn't be strong enough to keep hold of her mother's limp body. But one of those fierce, beaky heads curved down, and with surprising delicacy Tom (or was it Harry?) gripped Mum's prison tunic by its strong collar. Before Abi had time to cry out, Mum was plucked upward and laid carefully across the creature's broad back.

Abi's view of the ground below was now clear, but she couldn't see through her tears. She blinked and refocused. A woman in prison clothes was sprinting away from a hole in the wall. A black woman was riding a gray wolf, and a brown girl on a white sphinx followed her. A giant forked serpent with the body of a woman slithered in their wake. As it exited the hole, a last flick of its powerful tails brought down the watchtower behind it, the rubble of the ruined structure blocking the gap.

The mounted woman and the girl looked up, and waved.

★ ★ ★

What followed was a blur. The gryphon deposited them at a distance from the prison, at the prearranged rendezvous. Mum was unconscious when they touched down, and Abi checked her pulse: steady, but faint and too slow. Midsummer sent her creatures barreling into the lorries, all except Alba and Leto, then hastened to Abi's side.

"Healing's really not my thing," she said, looking at Mum's twisted face. "Dina was always good—Meilyr the best. I'm worried I'll make it worse if I try."

"She'll die if you don't," Abi whispered, unable to believe it had come to this. Her mother bleeding out on the ground before her. Both the T-shirt and the knotted sleeve of the hoodie were now soaked with blood. "Please."

"You gotta try, Midsummer," said Renie, softer than Abi had ever heard her.

Which was when she looked at Midsummer and realized that the Equal, too, was almost at the end of her strength. Her skin was clammy and gray. She looked barely able to stand, let alone capable of healing another.

Abi had done this. Her decision to run from Kyneston had led her mother here. She gripped her mum's hand tighter.

"I'm sorry," she told her. "This is all my fault. I'm so sorry."

"Shut it!" Renie hissed. "Come on, doctor-girl," she said to Abi. "All right, so Meilyr was the best. But if he was here, he'd be telling you that you can do this, too."

She was right. Abi laid her mum's hand down gently, then pulled away the wadded cloth and inspected the wound. There hadn't been anything on gunshot trauma in the premed textbooks she'd read. The bullet was in there somewhere, but she was pretty sure there was no urgency to remove it—that doing so might actually be dangerous. No, internal bleeding was the risk, and with her weak pulse and lapse from consciousness, Mum was exhibiting the signs. Blood was welling up again, so Abi replaced the T-shirt and reapplied pressure.

"I have to get her to a hospital."

"They'll arrest you both," said Jess.

"But she'll live."

"We need to go," said the guy who was going to drive them back to Lindum, scanning anxiously up and down the road. "This place'll be swarming with Security any minute."

"Wait, I'll try."

Midsummer wiped her brow, then bent over Mum, gently removing the impromptu dressing. She frowned at what she saw, then closed her eyes, brow knitting in concentration.

A few moments later, like something repulsive crawling out of a hole in the ground, a dull, ugly nub breached Mum's skin. The bullet. When Midsummer popped it out, blood welled in its wake, and Abi thought she might throw up. But the Equal laid her palm over the wound, heedless of the blood. Abi watched it spilling blackly over her black skin. The trickle slowed.

Stopped.

Midsummer rocked back on her haunches, utterly spent.

"Help me get her in the front," Renie instructed the driver, and the pair of them hauled Midsummer into the car. Abi and Jess lifted Mum and carefully laid her onto the backseat.

"Leto," Midsummer murmured groggily, her head lolling against her seat.

But the Equal had barely any strength left, and so the faithful wolf had turned back to stone, frozen by the roadside and too heavy to lift. As Abi slipped in to rest Mum's head on her lap, and Jess and Renie squashed in the other side beneath her legs, only Alba's white wings flew down the road ahead of them.

The journey was terrifying as the driver twisted and turned across the moor at speeds that belonged on a racetrack. And yet it was the slowest hour of Abi's life. As with their first arrival at Lindum, she was terrified that the park would be ringed with Security. But they had traveled the fastest, and she remembered that Lady Flora, Midsummer's mother, was protecting the great house. Only an Equal would be able to get close. If Whittam Jardine or Bouda Matravers wanted Midsummer, they would have to come for her themselves.

The gate flew open before them, and people were already running from the front door. Layla went to Midsummer's side, supporting her inside. The Equal waved her mother toward Abi, and Lady Flora commanded two of the staff to carry Mum to the room Abi had been sharing with Renie. They stretched her out on the bed, and it wasn't long before more people were arriving with clean cloths, bowls of steaming water, and a green plastic first-aid box, which Abi tore through.

She undressed Mum and washed her, almost crying with relief to feel her mother's skin warm beneath her touch. There was color in her face again. Lady Flora came back, and volunteered her own services as healer, but Abi's inspection told her that whatever Midsummer had done had been enough. The skin was still raw and puckered, and there was black bruising beneath it where infinitesimal blood vessels had ruptured, but the wound had already drawn together. What Mum needed now was rest.

And so, it seemed, did Abi. The lack of sleep, the adrenaline that had washed through her body nonstop for hours, the strain and the fear, had all taken their toll. And though she'd intended to lie down on top of the coverlet next to Mum for only a few moments, to comfort her with her presence, the next thing she knew, she was blinking awake into darkness.

On the pillow beside her, her mother's breathing was deep and even. And everything that had happened came back to Abi in a rush.

Horrifying and nightmarish though it had been, one strange upside of Mum's rescue had been that Abi had seen her. Been able to hold her. When they'd thrashed out the plans for getting each prisoner safely away, she had asked for Mum and Dad to be taken straight across the country to Liverpool, and from there, over the water to Ulaidh.

Abi had seen the helicopter lift off and away. Dad should be in a safe house in Liverpool by now. Maybe someone there would have a phone. How good it would be to hear his voice and know that he was okay, too.

She swung her legs off the bed, and winced at a sharp pain. Of course. She'd been hit herself, by the whizzing marble shrapnel from the gryphon's flank. She hadn't even noticed it, in the adrenaline rush of everything that had happened.

"Abi," a quiet voice said.

She peered into the darkness.

"Jess?"

The woman made a small, tight sound.

"Were you keeping an eye on us? Thank you."

"I was." Jessica sounded exhausted. Why was she not also asleep? "You seemed the right company. Even if you were unconscious."

Jessica's voice trembled and broke a little, and Abi tried to force down panic, even as sharp talons of fear closed around her heart. There was nothing more to fear. They'd done it. Everyone was safe.

"The right company? Jess, what is it—is Oz okay?"

"Do you know why your mum was in the hospital wing, Abi?"

Abi didn't know. She didn't want to know. Whatever Jessica was about to say would be nothing good. Abi wanted to press her hands to her ears so she wouldn't hear it. To lie back down next to Mum and sleep until whatever Jess was about to say didn't matter anymore.

"She was beaten by the guards when she tried to stop them taking your dad away this morning. They came for him at breakfast time. They took Oz, too, and some others. They put them in a van and drove them away."

Abi's heart imploded. It did whatever black holes did when they were too heavy and just collapsed beneath their own mass. Dad hadn't been rescued?

Wait.

Breakfast time. A van.

Abi remembered Gavar Jardine's mysterious phone call. Asif reassuring her about what they'd seen at Fullthorpe: *Nothing that looks alarming. One small van coming out this morning.*

Had Gavar tipped off his family that the raid was about to happen, so they'd removed a few prisoners? But why only a few? And if the Jardines knew about the rescue, then why hadn't they tried to stop it?

No, this wasn't making sense. None of it made sense.

"So, they took Oz and my dad," she told Jess. "Well, wherever they are, we'll get them. It can't be harder than what we just did."

"Oh, Abi . . ."

Jess broke down, burying her face in her hands. It was raw, animal sobbing.

Abi couldn't bear to hear it. She headed for the door. One of the others would have answers about where Dad was being held.

Downstairs, Lindum's wide brick corridors and tiled floors were eerily empty. Abi hurried toward the rotunda, which had become the hub of Midsummer's team. The furniture that had been cleared out for the drill that morning was back in place, and more than a dozen people were gathered around a television whose flickering images cast blue light up onto the dome.

"What's going on?" she asked the room. "What are they saying about what happened?"

Heads turned. She saw Renie reach for the remote and mute the sound.

A figure in the middle of the group got to her feet.

"This will be the last thing they do," she said. And if Jessica had sounded broken, Midsummer sounded blazingly, incandescently furious. "Abi, I'm so sorry."

All the breath left Abi's chest in that instant. The very last of it came out as words.

"What have they done?"

One by one, those sitting around the screen moved away. The image on the screen was nothing Abi could understand. As if hypnotized, she walked toward it, willing it to become clearer.

Because it looked like . . .

It looked like . . .

Horror slammed like an iron bar into Abi's midriff and she doubled over. Her scream echoed around Lindum's great brick dome, spiraling out into the empty night.

SIXTEEN

BOUDA

The film crew had done a good job, Bouda thought, though there was really no need for the camera to linger on the bodies like that.

"While a small number of prisoners escaped," the reporter could be heard saying, *"they are not believed to represent a danger to the public and a recapture mission is under way. However, these men, identified as the ringleaders, exchanged gunfire with Security during the shocking events that unfolded this afternoon at Fullthorpe secure unit. Eyewitnesses told us that the marksmen who took down these individuals saved many more lives from being lost."*

The gunshot wounds on each man were indeed the work of snipers, though they'd been inflicted from closer quarters and under calmer circumstances than those suggested by the reporter. In a field a few miles distant from Fullthorpe, to be precise, when the handcuffed men had been let out of the van and told to run. The bodies had later been driven back to the wrecked jail, and laid out amid the rubble before the news cameras arrived.

Bouda glanced at the others in the room with her. Astrid wore a thin smile and Whittam's satisfaction was evident. This setup had been his idea. And if Bouda found it distasteful the way the pair of them reached for death at every opportunity—at the Blood Fair, and now Fullthorpe—well, she had to admit it worked.

When a close-up was shown of one wound, though, Bouda had to look away. Such a tiny injury, yet enough to destroy a man. Or woman.

Dina's death from a sniper's bullet on the Tyne Bridge had been a terrible accident. But it was these rebels and their perverted ideas that had put her in harm's way, and Bouda would never forgive them. They had killed her sister, and now they were trying to tear apart the nation. They deserved everything they got.

"Authorities have named them as Oswald Walcott, forty-four, with a history of violent sedition at both Millmoor slavetown and Riverhead . . ."

The photo that flashed up was the one they'd inspected all that time ago in the Justice Council, when Gavar had first been dispatched to Millmoor. The man's brutish appearance spoke for itself. Walcott had got away from them once, thanks to Meilyr's meddling. But not a second time.

"Steven Hadley, forty-nine, is the father of Luke Hadley, the young man Condemned earlier this year for the shocking murder of former Chancellor Zelston."

Whittam grunted with approval that they'd remembered the "former," even though Zelston had been out of office mere hours at the time of his demise. It had been difficult to find a suitably criminal photograph of Hadley. In the end, they'd used the one taken when he was processed upon arrival at Millmoor. The man had been so red-eyed and wild you could easily believe he was high on drugs.

"*Hadley's involvement makes it all the more extraordinary that this devastating assault on a detention facility appears to have been masterminded from Lindum, the Zelston estate. Sources say this throws new light onto precisely how the current titleholder, Lady Flora, and in particular her daughter, Heir Midsummer, attained their positions.*

"*Chancellor Winterbourne Zelston's death came on the same day as he appeared in public for the first time with his betrothed, Euterpe Parva. The motives surrounding the slaying have previously been unclear, with experts believing that Luke Hadley was a lone-wolf terrorist, indoctrinated with classist beliefs in Millmoor slavetown. However, given the Hadley family's involvement with the woman who stood to benefit most from her uncle's untimely demise*"—and that picture of Midsummer, fist raised and ranting at some student protest two years ago was just *perfection,* Bouda thought—"*those links are now being reexamined.*"

Jenner appeared on-screen, offering condemnation and comforting platitudes. He was good at this. He'd won the nation's hearts with his soppy address at his aunt's funeral, and his bravery when the bag containing Ragnarr Vernay's head was lobbed at the grieving family. It helped that he had puppy eyes and was romantically unattached. Even his Skillessness, which Bouda had always considered an insuperable defect, appealed to swaths of commoner women who both pitied him and entertained fantasies that it made him more attainable.

No, Jenner—just like Faiers—would have his uses when Bouda was Chancellor. She would restore the heyday that followed the Revolution, when both Equals and commoners knew their place and worked together for the glory of the nation. The two men, a Skilless Equal and an Equal-sired commoner, would symbolize the new compact between rulers and ruled.

She'd have to make sure Jenner didn't get *too* much screen time, though. He couldn't eclipse Bouda herself. It was so much easier for men, given respect and authority like it was their birthright, while women who sought the same thing were branded ambitious and unnatural. Well, by the time all this was over, Bouda would have both respect and admiration.

Then she could work on winning the country's love.

At the far end of the couch, Whittam grunted and turned off the television.

"Thank you all. Excellently managed. That Zelston bitch looks like a violent seditionist who conspired to bump off her useless uncle to boot. That's worth losing a few prisoners for." He turned those bloodshot blue eyes onto Bouda. "The CCTV cameras were destroyed in the raid, correct? There's nothing showing Gavar's involvement?"

There was. Midsummer had used some kind of *owl* to take out the jail's surveillance cameras, but not before one of them had caught Gavar blasting the perimeter wall through which two dozen prisoners had promptly escaped. Bouda had ordered a copy made, then had the original recording erased.

"Nothing."

"Good. And it ends here, right?" a voice said from the doorway. They all twisted round as Gavar strode into the room. "The investigation finds 'unanswered questions' about Midsummer's role in her uncle's death and she's stripped of her title. Job done."

"It's only just beginning, I'm afraid," Bouda said. "The people need to see her fail. And they need to see us showing our strength."

More to the point, they needed to see Bouda working miracles. Glorious and powerful.

"Showing our strength? Just have another bloody parade or something. I'll stand on the balcony and wave till my hand falls off. She can't come back from this. You've done enough."

"*We've* only got started," Whittam growled, in that way that still made Bouda's scalp prickle.

"Well, I'm not being your go-between anymore. You assured me no one would die, then you killed the *Hadley dad,* for crying out loud. How the fuck am I meant to explain that to Daisy?"

Gavar threw himself into an armchair, raking his fingers through that thick copper hair. Bouda watched his tantrum in disbelief. How could his priorities have become so twisted up that he was upset at having to tell a commoner girl—a murderer's sister—that her seditionist father had been dealt justice? No, Daisy Hadley's presence at the heart of the Jardine household would have to be addressed. How one lowborn family had become so mixed up in the affairs of the nation, Bouda couldn't comprehend.

"I suggest you pull yourself together," she said. "And not undo the credit you've earned with your father. Fullthorpe achieved exactly what we wanted: congratulations. Now your part is finished and Faiers takes over from here."

Gavar looked up as Jon moved to Bouda's side.

"That weasel? If you call Midsummer a class traitor, then he's the pinnacle of treachery. You know his mother is part of Midsummer's inner circle. Can you even trust him?"

Jon looked like he had a retort ready, but Bouda laid a hand on his arm. A row would achieve nothing.

"I trust him. And I'm grateful to you. We all are."

She smiled around the room. Nobody smiled back.

"Has it occurred to you," Gavar said, "that maybe Midsummer's right? That we don't have to be such utter shits all the time. That our Skill would win us all the devotion we could ever want, if we only stopped grinding people's faces into the dirt and let them look up to see us."

"You speak foolishly, Gavar," said Whittam. "And tread dangerously."

"If you've become so fond of her, why don't you go back and join her?"

That was Jenner. Bouda looked up in surprise. There was venom in his voice.

"Do you stop for even a minute to think of all the advantages you have—your position, your *power*?" It was as though he couldn't even bring himself to say "Skill." "And yet you do nothing with it. Nothing at all. You don't deserve any of it."

And right at that moment, Bouda knew that if she ever needed a weapon against Gavar, she would have one in Jenner. He was hardening with each decision he made. Betraying the girl they'd all thought he was sweet on had been the first step. He would betray his brother, too.

She despised him.

"We all have our part to play, Jenner. Gavar performed his, and you performed yours, and everything went according to plan. Gavar, I understand if you're feeling conflicted and don't want to be here for what we're discussing next. It's been quite a day. Why don't you go spend the evening with Libby?"

"Are you giving me permission to spend time *with my own daughter*? Fuck you, Bouda. Whatever you all do now, you can count me out of it."

He slammed the door so hard the rows of Chancellors' portraits on the wall rattled, as though generation after generation of Jardines were expressing their disapproval of him.

"Thank goodness," Astrid drawled. "Maybe now the adults can have a grown-up conversation."

Bouda pressed her lips together. She might think such things, but she didn't like hearing others say them. Not even her own allies.

And yet . . . there could be only one Chancellor. And if it was to be her, it couldn't be Gavar.

"Thanks to Gavar, we know that there's a day of protest planned," she said. "Banners, marching, all the usual nonsense. But that's not enough for our purposes. We need some act of violence that will enable us to crush her publicly. And we need it to happen soon, while Fullthorpe is still fresh in people's minds.

"Hopefully, today's events will have left her furious. Ready to lash out. We know that Midsummer's people have no problem with the destruction of public and private property—remember the arson at the Queen's Chapel, and the stores they firebombed on Mountford Street? We want more of the same. Bigger targets.

"Now, I've drawn up a list of high-visibility targets. And Faiers will put them in front of her. He is uniquely well placed to penetrate Midsummer's circle, thanks to his mother's former position as Speaker. The plan is for Faiers to contact his mother, saying that after Fullthorpe he's not prepared to risk working with me any longer, and to go to them with documents and information. Nothing truly useful, of course. He'll tell them that we are divided and quarreling, split over the actions at Fullthorpe, and that the time to strike is now. He'll suggest these locations."

She tapped the slender file that peeped from her handbag.

"He'll also confirm that Gavar's supposed defection to their camp was done on your orders, Whittam. Even if my husband does have a moment of madness and go to her—though I give him more credit than that—Midsummer will never take him back."

She waited for Whittam's applause. It didn't come, of course. It never did. She and her husband had that in common, at least.

"Surely she'll be suspicious?" Astrid asked. "I mean, swap Gavar out and Faiers in? Isn't it too neat?"

"She'll realize she was wrong to accept Gavar," Jon replied. "But me? I was *born* into their little resistance. Both of my parents—Speaker Dawson and Rix—have worked for the commoner cause all their lives."

"Your father was responsible for her uncle's death," Whittam objected.

"*Accidentally* responsible. My father was actually aiming at you, and yet here I am."

"On my daughter-in-law's recommendation. She evidently trusts you, for whatever private reason . . ." Whittam's gaze swung toward Bouda and she steeled herself not to flinch beneath it. What was he insinuating? "And I tolerate you because I know you know that I could break your neck as easily as I can do *this*."

There was a sharp snap, like a twig underfoot, and Faiers cried out. He stared at his hand in disbelief.

Bouda looked, too. His little finger had been snapped in half like a pencil, the bright core of bone sticking through the skin. It had been done with a practiced efficiency. Bouda remembered Gavar drunk and confiding one night, telling her about his father's war stories, and his boasts of Skillful interrogation.

Clearly mental assault wasn't the only way Whittam had pried secrets from his victims.

"Unnecessary," she hissed. She reached for Faiers's hand. "I can fix it."

And she tried, she really did, but everyone knew that DiDi had been better, and Meilyr the best. The shard of bone tucked itself back under the skin, like a needle disappearing into a fold of cloth, stitching it together from the inside. Stitched together a little wonkily. He'd probably get arthritis there when he was older. Jon didn't look like he was complaining, though. There was a gleam in his eyes that suggested he almost thought the injury worth it to have her Skill upon him again.

And there were more like him, she knew. Many, many more, for whom the demonstration of Skill was a thrill and a wonder. They would all belong to her when this was over.

"Any more questions?" she asked. "Preferably not accompanied by injury to my staff."

"If his story is that he's been working for them inside your office all along, surely they'll want to know why he didn't tip them off about our plans at Fullthorpe?"

Jenner. Even Jenner was presuming to question her.

"That's precisely the cover story. Faiers tells them he wants out from my office because he thinks we're on to him. Case in point is that he knew nothing about our Fullthorpe plans. He'll say that if he's suspected and marginalized, no longer getting useful information, there's no benefit to him staying in Westminster. In fact, there's only risk. If we interrogate him, he might reveal information that endangers all those he knows in Midsummer's network."

Really, this was elementary statecraft. Be plausible. Lie with the truth.

"It's not like she needs to believe me for long," Jon added. "The net is closing. London is where it ends."

Whittam grunted and sat back.

"Good. Fullthorpe delivered, and this will, too. When your little weasel here squeaks all Midsummer's plans in your ear, we'll have her. When she fails in London, it'll be in front of millions. And this pathetic delusion of commoner equality will fail with her."

Bouda returned to Aston House alone. She'd had enough of the lot of them. Jon had suggested they go back to her office, but Bouda knew what that meant, and she really wasn't in the mood. She wanted to avoid any similar "suggestions" from Whittam that might be harder to get around. And Astrid and Jenner? Well, they were like knives she held in each hand: cruel and useful. Neither of them had much to offer beyond that.

Walking through the vast palace's echoing corridors, she instructed a parlor-slave to bring her a chicken salad, no dressing, then shut herself into her apartments.

It was at moments like this that she missed her sister so much it was like a physical pain. She and DiDi had lived separate lives, Bouda busy at parliament, Bodina distracted—so she had thought—with shopping, travel, and parties. And yet just knowing her sister was there had been enough. Bouda's thwarted admirers would call her an ice queen. But three people could always melt her heart: her darling parents and sister. Now she had only one of them left.

She unzipped her dress and stepped out of it, turning in front of the mirror to admire her taut figure. She brushed a hand over her flat stomach. If she had a child, would she love it—and would it love her?

There was a sharp rap at her door. Bouda slipped on a silk dressing gown and went to answer. But it wasn't a slave with a tray.

"Can I come in?" Gavar said.

"Finished lullabying your bastard?" she snapped. Because even if she had a baby with this man, she would always doubt if he could love it as much as he loved his firstborn, the slavegirl's child.

"Just stop it, Bouda. Okay?"

Gavar pushed his hair out of his eyes. He looked subdued, and for once, she couldn't smell booze on him. Bouda hesitated, then opened the door wider to let him in. She locked it after. When the servant came with her supper, he could leave it at the door. She wasn't hungry.

"To what do I owe the pleasure?"

But Gavar didn't snipe back. He just raised a hand—was it a plea for silence or an admission of defeat?—and lowered himself into a chair in Bouda's sitting room.

"Will it end here?" he said. "All this. When Midsummer's protest has been shut down."

"As long as she ceases to stir up classist agitation, yes."

"We don't have to *persecute* them, you know. Just for the crime of being common-born and Skilless. That's a kind of punishment in itself. Your sister—"

"Don't speak about my sister."

Bouda pulled her dressing gown tighter. The rooms of Aston House were horribly drafty. High-ceilinged and impressive, and perpetually cold and empty.

Gavar rubbed his chin. "I was only going to say that your sister was a better person than either of us could ever be."

"I don't need you to tell me that."

"Do you think he knew it was her?"

"What?"

"My father. Do you think he knew it was your sister on the bridge at Riverhead? It's just . . . what happened at Fullthorpe today got me thinking. Snipers, again. That was his suggestion, wasn't it? He liked to use snipers in the desert, when he was on military attachment."

Goosebumps broke out over Bouda's body. The draft in here was absolutely intolerable. If only she had DiDi's snug cashmere robe. But she had ordered the servants to pack it away, along with the rest of her sister's possessions. Of all Bodina's things, only Stinker the pug remained in Papa's care, becoming ever more corpulent and inert in his grief, like Daddy himself.

Bouda was afraid that her three people to love would soon become none.

Her thoughts were racing all over to avoid going back to that bridge. To her sister's passionate pleading and the tears in her eyes. How fragile Dina had looked, yet how strong her voice had been as she told Bouda to break with Whittam and to say "enough."

"Whittam wasn't there. Besides, why would he want my sister dead? She was just a misguided girl. Not a danger to anyone."

"He wasn't there on the bridge, but he would have been watching the cameras. And with our sharp Equal eyes, he could have seen that it was her, even if none of the commoners did. A kill order only takes a moment."

"Why are you saying this, Gavar? Are you trying to get me on your side after that childish display earlier? Or do you finally see how far you've tested your father's patience, and think that the only way you'll get back in his favor is by alienating me from him? What's wrong with you?"

She expected her husband to get angry. Instead, he sounded tired and disbelieving.

"Wrong with *me*? Doesn't it get exhausting, Bouda, thinking that everyone's playing the same pitiful power games that you are? 'Dividing people.' 'Taking sides.' That's talk for playgrounds, not parliaments."

"Governing isn't *easy,* Gavar. But some of us at least have a sense of duty that makes us try."

He still didn't get angry. Just looked at her. And something about his expression reminded her, unbearably, of Dina on the bridge. "Do you really not understand?" her sister had asked.

Bouda understood, all right.

She understood that no one was on your side except yourself. Not really. And that nobody could be trusted. That people would always try to use you for their own ends, and the only way you could prevent that was to be one step ahead, working out better ways of using them instead.

And she understood that she was cold and alone—though neither as cold nor as alone as her sister, lying in the Matravers family mausoleum back at Appledurham.

She'd wanted to be Gavar's wife, once. Had dreamed about it for years, when a teenager. The future they'd build together and the dynasty they would create. Both of them taking turns at that greatest office of state, the Chancellorship, not as rivals but as running mates. Was it too late for that? What if they could still unite and be the First Family that Whittam talked of?

"I don't want to talk about my sister," she said. "Or your father. But . . . perhaps you need not go back to your rooms tonight."

She let the silk robe slip off her shoulder and looked at her husband.

But there was no lustful spark in Gavar's eyes. No indication that he might succumb. Just a bone-deep weariness and that maddening kind of pity.

"I don't think so, Bouda." He hauled himself out of his chair and briefly kissed her cheek as he passed. "Try and get some sleep. I'll show myself out."

He left her standing there in the middle of the room. And something that must have been fury, because it couldn't have been disappointment, roared in her ears.

She never heard the crack like a gunshot—like a sniper's bullet taking down his kill—as the four great fountains in front of Aston House turned, in an instant, to ice.

SEVENTEEN

ABI

Telling Mum had been the hardest thing Abi had ever done. Scarier than running from Kyneston. More terrifying than trying to trick Crovan into releasing Luke from Eilean Dòchais. She'd left out the details, simply saying that Dad had been shot during the escape, and Mum had howled and pummeled her as if Abi was the one that had killed him.

She wasn't. She knew that. The guilt that had choked her before the Fullthorpe raid had been burned away by the pure, blazing hatred she now felt for the regime that had done this.

It burned so fiercely she could barely think. And yes, logically she knew the anger was a way of coping, a displacement mechanism. That had been in the textbooks; every doctor would have to recognize the stages of grief. But rage was better than feeling sad and helpless and utterly, unendingly heartbroken. Rage gave you purpose and a reason to get out of bed.

Abi gave Mum some sleeping pills, then washed her face and

went downstairs, still dressed in the same clothes she'd worn for the raid. Clothes she had put on when her father was still alive. When he was still in the world to sling an arm round her shoulders and kiss the top of her head—the only one in the family tall enough to do so—and proudly call her Daddy's Not-So-Little Genius.

Don't think about Dad. Think about how you can make the people who killed him pay.

It was noon already. And in the rotunda, along with Midsummer and the others, was a new arrival: Jon Faiers.

"Abi," he said, and those brilliant blue eyes were full of compassion. "I'm so sorry for your loss."

"You work in Bouda's office. Didn't you know what they were planning? Couldn't you have stopped it—or warned us, at least?"

"Abi, Jon didn't know anything," Midsummer said. "That's why he's here. He's been worried for a while that they suspect him. The fact that he didn't hear a whisper about their response to Fullthorpe only confirms that. He's come to join us permanently."

Midsummer laid a hand on Jon's arm, and close on his other side sat his mother, Speaker Dawson. Abi felt rebuked, although she knew that hadn't been Midsummer's intention.

"Something's changed in parliament, Abi," Jon said. "It's getting more brutal. More desperate."

"More brutal than the Blood Fair? Yeah, I guess, because this time they actually managed to kill the innocent guys they framed."

This anger. Abi knew it was unfair. But if it wasn't anger, then it would be helplessness and tears. She could feel the salt stinging her throat and the back of her nose as she tried to hold them back. But there was someone more deserving of her anger than Jon, who had merely failed to discover what the Jardines were planning.

"Where's Gavar? I need to know if he knew anything about this."

On Midsummer's other side, Layla sighed. One hand rested on top of her bump and there were dark circles beneath her eyes. She looked like she'd barely slept.

"He's not been back here. He went off in the second chopper lift, you know, and got all those rescued matched with their handlers for the getaways. Then he just disappeared. We know where he went—straight back to Westminster. Jon says he was at a meeting with his father and Bouda last night."

"I'm sorry, Abi," Midsummer added. "He obviously wasn't genuine with us. I know you trusted him, and I did, too. I know you wanted to believe the best of him—so did I. You mustn't blame yourself."

"Blame myself? Why would I *blame myself*?" And here it came, fury bubbling up. She was getting louder, and the noise reverberated round the vast brick dome as if dozens more were adding their voices to hers. "Why should I blame anyone other than the Equals? The Jardines. This has to end, Midsummer. We have to take the fight to them. Hit back."

"We all want change, Abi . . ." Abi could hear the "but" in Midsummer's tone—and here it came. "But we're not going to use their tactics to win it, and we can't beat them like that anyway. They have Skill and they have military power. We have right on our side, and the ninety-nine percent of the population that doesn't have Skill. We have to win with what we have."

"We'd win by killing Whittam Jardine."

And in the echoing chamber that magnified the smallest sound, silence fell.

She'd argued it back and forth with herself, at first unable to believe that this was where her anguish over Dad's death had led her. "First do no harm" was the physician's guiding principle, after all. But she wasn't a doctor, was she? And sometimes you *did* have to cause harm. Surgeons performed amputations to prevent the spread of infection—and Whittam Jardine's regime was pure poison. What if he could be cut away? Then Britain could heal.

Midsummer was looking at her with what Abi suspected was disappointment. Fine. Abi was disappointed, too—that no one was willing to do what was necessary.

"Better futures never begin in blood, Abi."

"One man. The blood of just one man, and it's all over. We do to him what he did to my father—a bullet, from a distance, that he won't see coming."

Please let Dad not have seen it coming.

"There are other ways than killing of showing that we're serious, and that we won't give up," Midsummer said. "We need to get the whole of London out on the streets, Abi. We need to get people coming to the capital to add their voices to ours. You remember what we did in London before—targeting the Queen's Chapel and Mountford Street? We can do that across the city, take out key buildings, show people that you can hit the Equals where it hurts without risking—or taking—lives."

"You'd be risking lives if you're talking about arson. Caretakers or firemen might die. And that still might not be enough to win people over. Yet you won't take out Jardine, when it could put an end to this."

"We *wouldn't* be risking lives, Abi." Jon leaned forward and turned around a stack of folders on the table in front of him, flipping open the one on top. "There wasn't much I could take

from the office—Bouda and Astrid Halfdan don't exactly leave
top-secret files lying around. But look at this: it's a register of
Equal-owned assets. Jardine's no fool. He knows that if you
threaten a person's wealth, you threaten them. Here's the property section. It's got detail on current usage. There are places in
here that are massive, incredibly valuable, but unoccupied. Or
buildings with symbolic significance, which we know will be
empty at night—or would contain so few people that we can
clear them out."

"This sort of thing works, Abi." Midsummer's eyes were
bright. "We've seen that in revolutions in other countries. All it
takes for a tyrant to fall is for the people to rise. They just have
to have the courage and inspiration to do so—and I don't believe a bullet in Whittam Jardine's skull would inspire anyone."

Abi disagreed.

She had a gun—the one she'd picked up in Fullthorpe. Un-
fortunately, she had no idea how to fire it—let alone with
enough accuracy to take down a man from a distance. Could
pistols even do that?

There were two people Abi could think of who would
know. One was Gavar Jardine, so scratch that. The other was
Dog. The man owed her for all the food and antibiotics she'd
taken to him in the Kyneston kennels. And while he loathed all
Equals, he surely hated the Jardines in particular. His tormen-
tors, the Vernays, were a Jardine branch-family. She shuddered
as she recalled their encounter outside Euterpe Parva's funeral,
Dog carrying the severed head of Ragnarr Vernay before he
lobbed it at Jenner and Lady Thalia.

She wasn't sure where he was, but she knew who would
know. She saw in her memory the night that everything
changed: Dog, moving among the ruins of the East Wing,
leash in hand, preparing to choke the life out of Hypatia Ver-

nay. And Silyen's careless "I'll see you later," as though the two were friends arranging to meet after class.

That strange boy was now Lord Silyen of Far Carr. The estate was in East Anglia, a half day's drive from Lindum. Silyen would have no reason to tell her where Dog was—if he knew. But then, he had no reason not to, and the promise of mischief in the offing might be enough to pique his interest. She just wouldn't tell him it was mischief that would end with his father's death.

Though if she was honest, Abi wondered if he would care. Even in those panicked minutes up on the execution platform at the Blood Fair, she'd noticed that Silyen wasn't in the viewing box with the other Jardines. Whatever schemes of his own he was pursuing, his family's sick politics didn't seem to be among them.

"I'm going to take a walk," she told Midsummer and the others gathered in the rotunda. "I want some fresh air and to be by myself for a bit. I hope you don't mind."

"Of course."

Midsummer smiled, and it made her beautiful, despite the sleeplessness and stress etched into her face. Abi desperately wanted to believe that what the Equal was planning was enough. But she'd seen Meilyr fail because he believed the best of people and had tried to do things the right way.

Sometimes the wrong way was the only way to get the job done.

Abi would do it. Then when Whittam was gone, Midsummer and her clean hands could take over and set the country to rights.

She went upstairs to write a note to Mum, telling her how much she loved her, and that she was to lie low in Ulaidh until it was all over. She kissed her mum's brow and tucked the paper beneath her pillow. Who knew when, or even if, she'd be back.

Then she picked up her backpack and checked that the gun was still inside. She should have no problem getting out of Lindum, because while the Zelstons were alerted to anyone arriving if the estate gates weren't opened by Skill, as far as she was aware there were no restrictions on exits.

She'd find out soon enough.

She had to hunt around for the keys to Layla's battered car, trying to remember where the woman had put them. When she eventually located them on a table by the exit to the colonnade, Abi pocketed them with a faint smile. Gavar Jardine's motorbike. Those two boats in Ennor harbor, when she'd been trying to reach Highwithel. Vehicle theft was proving habit-forming.

The downside to Layla's ancient vehicle was that it had no GPS, but Abi knew roughly where Far Carr was, and the cities that would take her in the right direction: Peterborough, then Cambridge, then she'd stop at a petrol station and buy a road atlas.

And if she felt a clench of anxiety and nauseous guilt as she bumped the car across the Lindum estate toward the back gate, taking the most obscure route? Well, both of those things did a good job of blocking out grief—though neither was as effective as anger.

Best of all was the hot burn of revenge.

The watch on her wrist told Abi she'd been driving for more than four hours when she turned over the bridge toward Rindlesham Forest. It was one of the oldest surviving woodlands in the country, she knew. A remnant of the land before Rome's legions came. After the empire left, Britain's history lapsed into obscurity for hundreds of years. A centuries-long silence. And then, gradually, towns appeared again. Roads again. Kings and queens escaped their palaces in London to hunt in these woods.

Until the day the Equals overturned it all.

Far Carr had once been a royal hunting ground, somewhere in this forest. And while Equals didn't exactly hang out banners and put up signs to advertise the whereabouts of their estates, the spaces on maps said as much as the words. She pushed the atlas off her lap and drove on.

Rindlesham was an eerie place of filtered half-light and muffled sound. This deep into the woods, there was no other traffic. The road soon petered out into a track and Abi saw a parking lot on the left, a large, woodchipped space that looked as though it was regularly used. But it was presently empty of all save a luxury sedan. Perhaps the owners were walking their dog, Abi thought as she drove past. That boded well for Lord Silyen not being a paranoid householder who'd surrounded his estate with bear traps.

And then the car engine stalled.

A few turns of the key later, she reached the obvious conclusion. This was Skill—which must mean the estate was near. Slinging the backpack over her shoulder, Abi got out.

The logical thing was to follow the track, so she did. It soon dwindled from track to path, then path to trail—then petered out entirely.

Abi scuffed the leaves on the ground for any trace of footprints, but couldn't see an obvious route. Which was strange, because if this was the main approach to the estate, then this was where goods and supplies, visitors and slaves, would come in and out. The size of the parking lot made it plain that a number of vehicles might be here at any given time. Had she taken a wrong turn?

Backtracking, trying not to panic about getting lost, Abi saw one tree that she recognized, then another—then the parking lot ahead. She must have just taken a fork off the path somehow. She tightened the straps on her backpack and turned back into the forest.

At the last point where the trail was distinguishable, Abi picked up a fallen leafy branch. Fishing a now-useless ponytail band out of her pocket, she secured it to an intact branch so that it hung down in plain view—a marker. She could see the route she'd taken before—what she had imagined was a straight continuation in the direction of the track. This time, she set out at a slight angle to it.

But again, frustratingly, the path soon disappeared. If only she had a compass, because the atlas had been clear: due east of here was the North Sea, and somewhere between it and where Abi stood was the estate.

She kept walking. Far Carr couldn't be *too* far. According to the map there were perhaps six miles to the coast. The seashore formed one stretch of the estate perimeter, and the landward boundary arced out in a semicircle inside the woods.

The afternoon was wearing on, so the sun would be swinging toward the west. The light was still strong enough to cast shadows on the ground, so if she kept the sun at her back and her shadow roughly before her, that meant she was heading eastward, toward the sea. Sooner or later, she'd reach the estate wall.

But she walked until her legs were tired and her shadow di-

luted. When she looked at her watch, an hour had passed. It
had been slow but steady going. How had she not reached the
wall yet?

Should she continue to blunder around, or turn back? Having walked for so long, she must be close to the wall—maybe
just a few hundred meters away. But she couldn't tell, and didn't
want to get lost out here after dark. She needed to retrace her
route while she could still see it. Groaning with the wasted
time and effort, she turned back.

Except her route must have taken some pretty phenomenal
wrong turns, because just five minutes later, while her eyes
were fixed on the ground, something smacked into Abi's face
and she looked up to see the branch that marked her starting
point.

How could she be so rubbish at this? Why was Far Carr's
entrance a million miles away from its parking lot?

Then Abi realized, and didn't know if she wanted to curl up
with dismay or screech with outrage.

Skill. It was Skill.

Silyen had hidden his entire damn estate, just as Gavar concealed the cottage in which he hid his daughter. Far Carr was
right in front of her. She'd probably spent the past hour walking along its wall, like an imbecile, unable to discern that it was
even there.

She hadn't come this close only to give up now. She'd sleep
in the car. Stake out this place. Silyen would have to come out
sooner or later.

First, though, she'd make one last attempt to reach the estate
tonight. She went back to Layla's vehicle, and found that the
engine sputtered to life once she'd put it in reverse gear. She
backed it down the track to the parking lot and boxed in the
swanky sedan. If it was Silyen's, she wasn't having him simply

driving away from here while she blundered around in his woods, hopelessly lost.

Then she headed into the woods for a third time. Did Silyen know she was here? If he'd cocooned his estate in Skill, would it also somehow alert him to her presence, as a spider sensed the thrumming of its web?

The thought gave her goosebumps, but then, she *wanted* him to find her. It was darker now, and cooler, and it turned out that fear was yet another emotion that was pretty good at keeping grief and sorrow at bay.

And just as she was preparing to turn back, because the light had almost gone and it was just too creepy for words, the gate appeared.

There was no Skillful dazzle, like at Kyneston's blazing entrance. Far Carr was barred by just a low iron gate. By the faint glow of Skill-light she saw the estate wall, an unusual design that flexed in and out. There was the dark shadow of a gatehouse, and by it she saw the figure of a man.

It wasn't Silyen Jardine, though.

"Abigail Hadley," rasped Dog. "Fancy seeing you here."

Abi's heart sped up. She would never not find this man alarming.

"I could say the same about you. What are you doing at Far Carr?"

"I'm one of Lord Silyen's—personal retainers."

He laughed and Abi's skin crawled. She was here, in the dark, in a magically unfindable place, with a homicidal madman.

A madman who only kills Equals, she reminded herself. *A madman who adored his dead wife and for her sake would never harm a commoner woman.*

She felt fairly confident on the first point, but the second one could have been wishful thinking.

"A retainer?"

"There are two of us. You know—the other one."

"I don't care about anyone else. I've come for you. I mean, I came to ask Silyen if he knew where you were . . . but here you are." She gripped the gate, and it was cool to the touch, just as it should be, and its solidity was reassuring. "I've been stumbling around in the woods for hours. He's hidden this place, hasn't he? Using Skill. I guess I can only see the wall because you're there at the gate?"

Dog nodded. In the silence, Abi heard a ringing, scraping sound, and looked down to see that the man was running a knife along the middle bar of the gate. He stopped it just a few inches from her hip as she jumped back. Her heart was thudding. Was this some kind of threat?

She looked more closely. It wasn't one knife—it was five. One for each finger of his hand. The blades dripped with blood. And suddenly she wasn't scared—she was absolutely terrified. What the hell was Silyen up to, behind the walls of his concealed estate? Abi remembered when she, Daisy, and baby Libby had stumbled across him in Kyneston's woods one day, after finding the unmarked but nonetheless stone-cold-dead deer that he had claimed was an "experiment."

Had coming here been an awful mistake?

No, it hadn't. She needed Dog. And he would do what she asked, she was sure.

"You told my brother—Luke—that he had to hate the Equals to beat them."

"Yes."

Dog stepped right up against the gate, gripping it with his unsheathed hand. His skin gleamed in the frail moonlight, his fingers scrawny as a skeleton's.

"*I* hate them," Abi said. "And I need your help to beat them."

Dog threw back his head and laughed. Whatever he'd been doing here with Silyen Jardine, becoming more normal hadn't been part of it. But Abi didn't need him to be sane. She just needed him to be deadly.

"Never thought you had it in you—Abigail Hadley."

And Dog stooped over the gate so close she caught the reek of his breath. It smelled like raw meat and she saw traces of blood around his mouth. Had he been catching and eating creatures in the woods?

Well, Abi had better prey for him. The kind that deserved everything it got.

"Come with me to London. I want to find a use for this."

She pulled the gun from her backpack.

EIGHTEEN

RÆDWALD

They were deep in conversation as they came down the beach, and hadn't noticed him yet.

The tall one was the *Searugléaw*, and the strong one at his side his *gesið*.

Rædwald rubbed his chin ruefully. The words of his youth were unknown now. Not entirely vanished, though. *Searu* had become *Skill*. And while men no longer had a *gesið* with whom to stand back-to-back in battle, everyone needed a friend at their side in this world.

In all the worlds.

He should know.

The light was just fading, the day ending. He crouched down on the pebbles and passed his hands over the kindling he'd gathered. Conjuring Skill-light would have done the job, but it felt good to do things the old way. As salt in the driftwood hissed and popped, the pair saw his firelight and hurried toward him on the shifting stones.

"You," said the tall one as they crashed to a stop. A disbelieving smile lit his face. "Right here on my beach."

Rædwald lifted an eyebrow. "I think you'll find it was mine first."

"Indeed it was, Your Majesty. I'm Silyen Jardine. May we join you?"

Rædwald gestured to the opposite side of the fire and the boy flopped down, cross-legged. The blond one was still standing, amazed.

"I'm Luke Hadley," he eventually managed. "Your Majesty."

"None of this 'Majesty.' I'm hardly majestic."

He wasn't. His crown was made of twigs and flowers. His robe had been given to him on his twentieth birthday. It would be fair to say it was showing its age. He plucked its crimson tatters around himself with dignity.

"I am Rædwald. Please, sit."

"Thank you, King Rædwald."

"He's very polite," explained the dark-haired one. Silyen. "He's from the North, where they're well brought up."

"They weren't in my day," Rædwald muttered, thinking darkly of the raiders who had brought this land to its knees. He wondered what he sounded like to this pair. They'd find his accent Germanic, perhaps.

"Silyen, on the other hand," said the blond one, Luke, "often comes across like he was raised by wolves. Though in a way, he was."

The boys scowled at each other. Rædwald remembered the teasing of his own youth, from his hearth-sisters and shield-brothers in King Tytila's hall. How innocent their rivalries had been—until the day that they weren't.

For all their jests, though, the two young men were plainly awed. They sat in silence for a few moments. He expected the *Searugléaw,* the Skilled one, to speak first, but instead it was the other.

"We've been looking for you, to see if you can help us find my friend. Silyen thinks you've been searching for her, too— and found us instead. But you were in my mind, at Eilean Dò- chais. And now you're here in the real world. How is that possible?"

Rædwald smiled. "Because to one who walks in Skill, there is no difference."

"You're the *Wundorcyning,* the Wonder King," said the other, Silyen. And he was confident enough that it wasn't even a ques- tion.

"Among other names. *Cealdcyning. Gastcyning. Cwiccyning.*"

"The Cold King. The Terrible King. The Living King," Sil- yen translated, his face radiant with more than firelight. "And you made us forget you."

"I did."

"But we've started to remember again."

"You have."

Rædwald pulled pinecones from his pocket and tossed them onto the fire. He'd always liked their resinous scent. When he died, they should have laid him in a boat among his furs and jewels and weapons, and covered him in cones and pine branches, and scattered him with incense. Then the boat would have been pushed out to sea, and his *gesið,* his shield-brother Hryth, would have shot a flaming arrow into his heart.

That's what they should have done. If he'd died.

"It's like I've done here at Far Carr," Silyen continued,

"but . . . inside out. And so much bigger. I've enchanted the wall, so no one *outside* can find this place. You enchanted the borders of this entire land, so no one *inside* Britain could remember you. Am I right?"

The boy was so convinced he was right that he waited for nothing more than a nod before continuing.

"We know that magical restrictions can last generations— just like a hereditary Quiet. This forgetting of you stayed intact for centuries, like a strong old wall, with just the occasional crack through which a memory crept in: the person who wrote down *Tales of the King* or the one who painted the picture that hangs in my hall. But it happened so rarely, there was never enough memory of you to be actual history. You were a king of whispers and legends."

Silyen sat back, flushed and triumphant. As he should be, thought Rædwald. He had pieced it out entirely.

"Very good."

The king leaned against his stag's warm flank and petted its neck. He looked at the other one. Luke.

"But *why*?" Luke asked. "Why would you want to be forgotten? And not just by the people who knew you, but by everyone, forever after? Aren't you Coira's father?"

They were a good pair, these boys. A brain and a heart. A *how* and a *why*.

"It is a long story," Rædwald told them. "And it began a long time ago. Let me show you."

He got to his feet and shook out his tattered robe, then reached into the middle of the fire and opened a door.

Through it, Rædwald could see King Tytila's hall by torchlight. He could smell the hog grease of the burning rushes and the juicy stink of meat. There was his mother, the king's wife, pouring wine for the men of the royal bench. There was Rædwald himself, at the king's right hand. On his other side sat his shield-brother Hryth, while Ædla brushed her hip not-so-accidentally against his shoulder as she passed with another steaming dish. It was Rædwald's twentieth birthday, and there was merriment among his assembled friends.

Among those he had thought were his friends. He was heart-sick to see them.

"Come."

He beckoned the two boys. Luke squared back his shoulders and stepped through first.

"Is this real?" the boy asked, once they all stood together and the feast swirled around them in a haze of sweat, smoke, and spilled mead. "Have we . . . gone back in time?"

"This door leads only to memories. Other doors you step through with your whole self. Still others exist in the mind. Real and unreal. Then and now. *Here* and *there*. All of these things are one, if you look at them correctly."

"It's not just you who has Skill," said Silyen. He had been studying the king's bench. "Your mother. Those three men there. That old man—and her."

He was pointing at Ædla. Rædwald had to look away.

"You know how rare this gift is," he told them. "Few possess it, in your time, among such a large population. So think how very few we *Searugléaw* are in this little kingdom, this quarter-ling of Britain, fifteen centuries ago. You have found us all."

They watched as the celebrations continued. As King Tytila rose to his feet, called for his cup, and began the speech that would change everything.

"My mother was a Bavarian princess, a widow, and I was her only child," Rædwald told them. "King Tytila wanted a *Sea-rugléaw* bride to give him status, and my mother's brother wanted British jewels. So, when I was two years old, we were traded. In time, I had three brothers—there they are—but none, of course, were Skilled. I watched over them as they grew, taught them all I knew, and loved them with my whole heart.

"There were two Skilled families within my new father's domain, who served as his advisers and trusted counsel. Good, wise men. Or so I thought. What my father is saying now, I believed he said with their blessing. This is my twentieth birthday, and he is naming me his successor and the girl Ædla as my bride."

"I can see it in their eyes," said Luke. The boy gave a low moan. "Oh."

Rædwald put a hand on the boy's shoulder.

"Then you have seen more than I did."

He walked them through the hall and out, away from the king-stead. Here was the burial field, the humped mounds where warriors and their families rested with honor. It was a freezing night. The stars were sprinkled white across the black sky like flour on a kneading board.

They'd persuaded him to come and make an offering to the ancestors, to seal his confirmation as heir.

Rædwald saw himself throw back his fine new robe and kneel on the frosty grass, his friends in a circle around him. They were his dearest and nearest: his three brothers; the Skilled father and sons who were the king's advisers; Ædla and her father; his shield-brother, Hryth. With Luke and Silyen alongside him, Rædwald watched himself sip from the silver cup, then pour the remaining wine into the earth to honor his people.

Which was when the eldest of his brothers seized him by the hair as the middle one cut his throat.

His brother's hand shook as he slashed. He was the cleverest of the three, but only fifteen. Often, afterward, Rædwald wondered if it had been his idea, and if he had wanted their father's throne for himself. Ædla, too. They had all wanted Ædla—though none of them had loved her like Rædwald did.

This wasn't the first time he had watched this moment. Each time the knife to his heart was worse than the memory of the one that opened his throat like a hog's.

He glanced at the two young men at his side. Luke looked stricken; Silyen, watchful.

That wavering hand meant the slash hadn't killed him, and now his Skillful reflexes were on guard against his brothers' attack. Rædwald watched himself wrench away from his brother's grip, even as the red lips of his wound pursed together. Ædla stepped back, a look of horror on her face, as he clawed the ground for support.

"Hryth!"

He called his shield-brother and the man pushed through the others to his side. Rædwald looked up into the face of the one he trusted above all others—and so never saw or suspected the hand that drove a blade into his side.

Another groan came from Luke; Silyen was ghostly pale. Neither of them looked away as blow after blow, blade after blade, rained down on Rædwald where he lay. For every attack his Skill could repel, there were three more waiting behind.

At last, his new robe slashed to tatters and re-dyed scarlet, Rædwald was rolled onto his back like a butchered sow. He couldn't move, he couldn't speak, he couldn't breathe. He could only look out of eyes that swam in blood. The injuries he'd sustained were too catastrophic for his Skill to repair.

The men around him fell back into a circle, and Ædla crept forward to crouch at his side. Rædwald remembered how that had been his final sadness, that he could not speak to tell her

how much he loved her, and that he was sorry she would belong to one of these butcher-men now.

Ædla tugged at a pin and let down her hair. Those chestnut
waves he had loved to twist around a finger brushed softly
against his cheek like a parting kiss.

"Foreign filth. You'll never have me," she whispered.

Then she slammed the pin down into his eye.

Luke jerked backward in shock. "Why is he showing us
this?" Rædwald heard the boy hiss to his companion, but Silyen shook his head.

As the pin point entered Rædwald's brain, he died.

His body lay on the frost-edged ground, blood leaking
slowly now that the heart no longer beat to pump it out. The
circle of his murderers stayed in place, waiting to be certain of
his demise.

When they were satisfied, the wolf pack moved back toward
the hall. No effort was made to cover or destroy the body. They
wanted his corpse to be seen—a claim and a warning.

Ædla went down first, with a shriek.

"Watch," Rædwald urged the boys.

Bright threads of Skill arced from her mouth to the cooling
corpse, spilling across the body in a wash of gold. The gaping
wounds greedily drank it down.

One of the counsellor's sons went to Ædla's side—and how
had Rædwald not seen *that*? he wondered, even now. But as the
young man stooped to support her, he cried out as his own
Skill burst from his chest and twined with the faltering flame
of his sweetheart's draining power.

"You, too," Silyen breathed, turning to Rædwald. "You can
take it, too."

He nodded. "I never knew till then."

Coils of fire writhed from the other three Skilled, twisting and spiraling up from their screaming mouths. But no flame raced toward him from the hall, from his mother, which was how Rædwald had known that she was already dead. She and her royal husband slain by their treacherous retainers.

"But you were *dead*," Luke said. "They made sure of it before they walked away."

"Nothing can reverse death," said Silyen. "I've tried. I used to experiment in the woods at Kyneston—his sister caught me once. Trees. Animals. Nothing worked. My ancestor Cadmus tried it, too, when his wife was dying in childbirth. Skill can't bring things back to life."

Rædwald gestured around them, at the curves of the grave-barrows and the distant trail of smoke from the king-stead.

"It's not a question of *things*, and *doing*. It's about yourself, and *being*. How would you define this place and your presence here? This is my memory, but it is also a real experience for you, in this moment. You feel cold. You see the stars. You smell our furs and leather. You taste my blood in the air. By every measure, you are *here*. Yet you are also *there*."

He indicated the open doorway that led back to the beach at Far Carr, where their three bodies slumbered around the fire.

"*Here* and *there* are one. Most crossings between are easy. But some are hard—and death is the hardest of all. It requires more Skill than any person has ever been born with.

"Through the centuries, I have watched and laughed as scholars tried to classify our gifts. Some of us master elements; others, objects; others, people. Some become strong, or cause pain; heal or destroy. Sometimes one of these things is done powerfully; sometimes several are done briefly, or weakly."

Silyen was nodding.

"And once or twice over the centuries," Rædwald told the

boy, looking into his dark eyes to be sure that he understood, "there is one whose gift is to take more."

He pointed back toward his cold, gray body. Skill-fire was lancing into it like lightning strikes from the sky.

"I emptied the five who tried to kill me. But the more I took, the more I was able to take. I never knew the women and men it came from, but my need drew it from all of Britain's quarterlings. Until not even that hardest crossing was too difficult anymore."

As they watched, Rædwald's body sat up. He pulled the pin from his eye and wiped it on the frosty ground, then threaded it into his tattered robe as a fastening.

He caught Ædla first, to spare her the pain of watching the others die, because he had loved her. He shattered her rib cage and speared her heart with one stroke of his sword. Next, her lover. Then her elderly father. Her lover's brother. His father. All five of the *Searugléaw* he killed.

Then he went after his brothers. Their father's line ended in the frozen mud, begging for mercy.

His shield-brother, Hryth, was the only one to fight back, and Rædwald was glad of it. He had lain in furs with this man since their boyhood, and beyond. It was a hot, dark joy to open him from throat to belly.

Rædwald felt no joy, seeing it now. Given enough time, both love and hatred died.

The three of them watched as, back in the hall, Rædwald stood over the body of the man who had bought him, but whom he had nonetheless been proud to call Father. He pulled off the murdered king's golden circlet, inlaid with garnet, and settled it on his own brow. Then he cut down any in the hall who were left alive, even the servants and the dogs.

He pulled the torches from the walls and tossed them onto the tables and benches, and the rush-strewn floor. Then he pushed open the great double doors and walked away.

Wide-eyed, the boys watched him go.

"What happened next?" Luke asked.

NINETEEN

RÆDWALD

"Next, I ruled harshly over my traitorous kingdom. I forget for how long, but for many more years than a man should live. I healed and slew, and performed feats of Skill that were accounted miracles: foul water ran clean, crops flourished, storms failed, and boats returned safe to harbor. I have told you the names they gave me: *Cealdcyning. Cwiccyning. Gastcyning.* Cold King. Living King. Terrible King. Then when the raiders came, the North-men, I laid my crown on the seat of my father and walked away. This kingdom hadn't saved me. Let it save itself, if it could.

"It couldn't, of course. Up and down the coast, the little kingdoms burned and fell. I no longer cared. By then I had discovered that there were other places than this."

"Innocent people died," Luke said. "With that much power you could have saved them."

"Innocent people always die, Luke. It's usually the guilty that live."

The boy had thought he was talking to the hero of this story. He was mistaken.

"I roamed for years through this world and others, and at last my anger ended. Mostly I was alone, but sometimes I showed myself to men and women and they opened their doors and beds to me, or walked alongside me awhile, and I allowed myself to be happy. I worked wonders and marvels, and was given my final name, the *Wundorcyning*.

"But wherever I went, people needed me. To find a stolen child, to make a blighted crop whole again, to discover lost treasure, to drive away demons, to cure a barren woman or a maddened man. And great though my power was, I realized that the needs of men and women would always be greater, and that I could never satisfy them, even in all of my lifetimes."

He led Silyen and Luke away from the ruined king-stead and down to the shore. He'd always loved these liminal places the most, where land ended and sea began, and you could cross from one to the other with no more than a boat. Not even that—simply in your naked skin.

Rædwald halted on the shingle bank, before it shelved into sand.

"I resolved to walk away for a second time, and this time for good. I began on the shore of my father Tytila's land, and walked and wove until I ended back there again."

He pointed away along the beach, where his other self came into view. This Rædwald was slowly following the water margin, trailing a thick fiery rope of Skill. His hands worked in the air, knotting together his power and his intentions into an enduring act.

"Like you and the Far Carr boundary," Luke breathed to his companion. "Incredible."

"I've always thought so," the other replied, a smile in his voice. But there was awe, too.

As the man by the water came level with them, he halted. The bright cable he held in one hand fizzed and dripped with Skill. His free hand reached to pull the other end of it out of the darkness. Carefully, he drew the two together.

Rædwald remembered how that had felt. The momentary hesitation before he took himself out of the minds of men and women forever. The feeling of relief and release once he had done so.

Some things, some people, were better forgotten.

The golden cord flared—Luke gasped as it lit up the length of the coast in both directions, as far as the eye could see—and faded. There was nothing left but a ghostly afterimage girdling the sea. Then nothing at all.

Empty-handed, the man reached out again and a doorway limned in light appeared at the water's edge. As he pulled it open, a gentle bronze radiance bathed his weary body and something that sounded like—but was not—birdsong drifted up to the onlookers' ears. Exhausted, both sorry and glad, Rædwald's memory-self stepped out of the world.

The doorway closed, and it was just the three of them standing on the beach.

"You went," said Silyen, "and the memory of you went, too. Objects survived, though. The Chancellor's Chair—that used to be a throne. The carvings on it are of you, aren't they?"

"Those carvings were made during my wandering years, as reports of my deeds reached Britain's new rulers. With no *Searugléaw*—no Skilled—in the realm anymore, I must have appeared even more of a marvel."

"Wait," said Luke. "No Skilled anymore? You took it *all*?"

"There are few enough in your time, Luke. When I lived, Britain was a threadbare place, and we *Searugléaw* were hardly any at all. The Northern raiders who seized this country were warriors. They despised the artifice of Skill, and brought none of its practitioners with them. It wasn't until centuries after that a few of the gifted began to settle these shores again. And as you know, it took hundreds more years until the Skilled were numerous enough and bold enough to wrest back rule of this land from the giftless queens and kings that had ruled it in the meantime."

He could see the boys absorb it—their country's history, made plain at last—as he led them back to the beach of their own time, and their bodies that still sat around the fire.

"So why are you here?" Silyen said, holding his hands to the flames to warm them once they had slipped back into their skins. "Now. With us. Are you repairing those cracks that let the memory of you leak back in, or is there . . . something else?"

"Some*one* else?" Luke added.

Rædwald understood what they were saying: this knife-witted boy, who liked so much to *know,* and this shield-hearted boy, who lived to protect others. They were correct.

"After I left this world, I returned from time to time to patch up my enchantment. And when I did, I would resume my wandering habit—occasionally showing myself to one or another who caught my eye.

"The last time, there was a girl, in a castle. She was lonely and so lovely. Her mother wanted her to wed, and her brother wanted no man to have her but himself. All she wanted was to be free."

"Rhona."

Luke was leaning forward, his expression intent. And hearing that name spoken after all this time was like a blessing.

"Rhona. She came to love me and we would lie down together on the heath. But she never knew who I was, and when she told me she was with child, I knew that any future with her was impossible. How could I stay here: never aging, never dying? I could have taken her with me, but the paths between the worlds are not always easy—and often dangerous. And if I am honest, I relish walking them alone. So, I made a selfish choice, and left once more.

"I never stopped wondering about that child, though. And so I came looking for them both. But time and place are different between *here* and *there,* and finding your way back is hard. When I searched in Skill, I sensed a gift resembling my own and thought it might be hers."

"But it was mine," said Silyen. The boy's black eyes gleamed.

"Yours," Rædwald agreed. "Look."

He lifted a hand and the Skill all around them sparkled into existence. It filled the night sky like stars, part of everything that was. But it also swirled thickly around Rædwald himself, and wrapped Silyen in brilliance. And there—he had seen it that first time they'd met—was the brightly glowing thread that connected the boy to Luke. He had bound this one to him, just as King Tytila would bestow the *bord-gehat,* the oath of protection, upon his favored warriors.

The two boys were transfixed by the eddying radiance as Rædwald concluded his story.

"I found *your* Skill," he told Silyen, before turning to Luke, "and then through *you* I saw the place where you both sat, and recognized it as the castle of Rhona's family. So close. But I could never sense our child, or Rhona herself. I've told myself that they must be dead.

"And so you see me now, my latest repairs accomplished, ready to depart once more. But before I go, I thought what harm would it be, to ask you . . ."

"Rhona's dead," Luke said gently. "But your child, your daughter, she's alive, and she's amazing. Her name is Coira."

"Lord Crovan, Rhona's brother, destroyed your daughter's Skill when she was a baby," Silyen added. "That's why you couldn't sense her."

And Rædwald thought he was done with hurting and was through with pain, but Silyen's words cut as deep as a brother's blade. The one precious thing he had left to his abandoned child—ripped from her and ruined.

"So, where is she?" he asked. "My broken daughter."

"She's not *broken*," Luke said fiercely. "And she's not dead, either, I'm sure of it, even though she went through that door."

That door. He could mean only one. Rhona had spoken of it with pride—and not a little fear. The fatal portal. The *mormaer*'s vow and the hostage's security. The Last Door.

Rædwald knew where it led. Only to death. He had been there himself, though rarely and always reluctantly. Each time, he had felt the place clawing at him, as if he were something that had slipped from its grasp which it wanted back.

"If that's where she's gone, then there'll be no returning."

"You don't understand," said Luke. "She went through *the wrong way*."

The boy described their escape from the castle. How Lord Crovan—Rhona's brother—had discovered their departure and seized Coira when she was neither through nor back. How the girl had gone *through* all the same . . . to somewhere else entirely.

Somewhere else.

Rædwald tossed his last pinecone on the fire. It was gutter-

ing to embers and ashes, and flakes of brightness spiraled upward and died in their ascent.

"Could you find her?" said Luke, leaning forward. "Wherever she's gone? I couldn't see it, but there was . . . a color, I
can't describe it, and a sound I can't explain, either. And it was
warm, but sort of softly so."

"Do you understand how many worlds there are, boy?" he
asked. "As many as this."

He gestured to the eddying sparks of Skill, as numerous as
constellations, and he saw the light dim in Luke's eyes. Silyen
laid a hand on the boy's shoulder, and Luke slumped against
him.

So his daughter had a friend who cared about her. Rædwald
was glad.

"To search through them all would take lifetimes," he told
them. "But then, lifetimes are exactly what I have."

He rose, and his stag huffed up to stand beside him. A pierc-
ing whistle summoned the eagle to his shoulder. He studied the
boys with eyes that had once swum in blood, but now were the
pure gold of Skill-light.

"Thank you for what you've shared. I won't abandon her a
second time. If my girl is out there, I'll walk the worlds until I
find her."

He knew where he'd begin. Rædwald reached into the air
and pulled open a door. The world that lay beyond it was entirely dark, but welcoming. Nameless fragrances drifted
through. In its unseeable depths, a voice spoke a greeting in a
tongue that he alone understood.

"Wait!"

Silyen had scrambled to his feet, boot heels slipping on the
stones.

"You said that you come back to repair your enchantment,

so the boundary is whole again. That means everyone forgets. Will *we*? I don't want to forget this."

"I don't want to forget who Coira really is," Luke added, at Silyen's side. "I thought that Crovan was her father—a monster. But she's *your* daughter, and that's incredible. Someone here should know that."

Could it be managed? These boys, two bricks pulled from the wall to let the light in?

He thought it could. He reached out and touched a hand to Silyen's forehead, and the boy flinched and gasped. Rædwald smiled—it would be the boy's first encounter with a power greater than his own.

When he touched Luke's brow, the boy dropped to one knee. Clearly the habits of majesty died hard.

"Very well. Remember me. And perhaps one day we'll meet again, *here or there*."

Rædwald patted his stag's powerful flank to send it through the door before him. He loosed the eagle into the alien sky.

Silyen watched, golden-eyed and silent, and Luke remained kneeling as Rædwald lifted a hand before following his creatures through.

TWENTY

ABI

Dog looked at the weapon, as if memory was stirring, then reached through the gate with a hand that knew exactly what it was doing.

"Point-four-oh caliber," he said to himself as he banged the magazine into the handgrip. "Nearly full. Who have you got—this for?"

"Whittam Jardine."

Abi's chest tightened. She'd known that naming the deed to Midsummer would meet the response it had. But suggesting it to Dog? That was as good as making it real. Like putting the gun to Whittam's head and pulling the trigger.

Was that really what she wanted?

No. Of course it wasn't what she *wanted*. But it was what had to be done. She'd seen how the Jardine family worked, and how Lord Whittam crouched at the center of it. That night at Aston House when she had gone to Jenner for help, her heart had stopped—actually stopped, who cared if that was a medical impossibility?—when she realized the boy she adored had betrayed her to his father.

How fragile she'd felt, as Lord Whittam gripped her face with thick fingers and pondered her usefulness for the Blood Fair. When he had circled her, weaving plausible lies that she and Luke had been part of a network of rebels scheming violence from the start. The same lies that he had spun around Dad, concealing the kind, decent man that he was in a sticky tangle of falsehood.

Whittam Jardine had to die, because otherwise how could Abi ever clear Dad's name?

And Dog had to do it, so that Midsummer's name wouldn't be dragged into it.

"Thought you were the—good girl," Dog said, not letting go of the weapon. "And your brother—the hothead."

"He . . ."

Abi couldn't say it. The words swelled like a sponge in her throat, and even air could barely get through.

She had to say it. She had to name the crime for which this man would die.

Abi swallowed, and forced the words out. She told Dog about the raid on Fullthorpe, and its aftermath. How they'd thought their plan had worked. And how the Jardines had twisted it to their own ends, after all.

"They shot them, then staged it like the prisoners were the violent ones. My dad, and three others."

Dog looked at her, and Abi braced herself for the inevitable "Sorry for your loss," but it didn't come. Instead he nodded.

Then whisked the gun around so fast Abi didn't even have time to scream, ran his thumb over some catch, and fired up into the trees. A moment later, something small plummeted to the ground. It was amazing Dog had even seen the creature, let alone hit it.

"Whittam's on my list," he said, lips pulling back from bloodstained teeth. "I'll do it. I prefer to be hands-on—with a blade. But this way—has advantages."

"Silyen doesn't need you here? He hasn't bound you to this place, the way we both were at Kyneston? I remember he broke your binding the night the ballroom exploded, and mine was removed when my parents and I left the estate for Millmoor. . . ."

Dog shrugged. "I'm a free man."

Abi stood there, on the other side of that low gate. Could it really be this easy?

"And you can just walk away?"

"That's what he said. I can't let you in. But I can—go."

"Well, let's go now, then. Is there anything you need from the manor house? I have money."

The man waved the glove of knives dismissively. "This is all—I need. If I went back, it'd get—complicated."

Dog set his hand to the latch, and it lifted easily on what was barely more than a simple farm gate. Judging from the parking lot and this casual entryway, and given that the concealment of the estate was Silyen's work, slaves would have come and gone freely when Far Carr belonged to Lord Rix. The man had lived his principles.

Abi shivered. The irony hadn't struck her before now. Rix had used Luke to try to kill Whittam Jardine. It was his actions that had sent everything spiraling into disaster for her family.

Yet here she was, finishing the job for him.

"I've got a car," she told Dog as he swung the gate shut.

And as he dropped the latch, it disappeared: the gate and then the wall, blurring away into nonexistence before her eyes. It was the creepiest thing Abi had ever seen.

Well, Silyen Jardine and whoever else was loopy enough to be in there with him could enjoy their privacy. The lord of Far Carr had a gift for meddling, but from here on, everything needed to unfold as straightforwardly as possible. The farther away Silyen was from what was about to go down in London, the better.

She planned to head for Dalston, where, several blocks away from the old safe house, she'd noticed a row of railway arches housing businesses that were barely getting by. Abi was sure at least a few were abandoned and boarded up. Dog could hole up there for a few days, scoping out opportunities, while Abi rejoined Midsummer and Renie and the rest.

Then when she knew what was proposed for the protests, she and Dog could lay their own plans.

It turned out the direct route from the gate to the car took less than ten minutes. Abi didn't know whether to be impressed or freaked out by the scope of Silyen Jardine's brain-bending Skill, and settled for both.

"I'll drive," she told Dog. "Get in."

"Nice not to be—in the back," Dog said, and cackled as he pulled on his seatbelt.

Apart from the carrion stink, he proved to be an excellent traveling companion. On the outskirts of a riverside town, they pulled into a twenty-four-hour supermarket so Abi could buy a few basics for them both—sandwiches and water, toothbrushes, clean underwear and T-shirts, and a couple of cheap mobile phones. Wet wipes to get the blood off Dog. She came out to find that Dog had tugged the license plates off another vehicle in the parking lot and fitted them to Layla's car. He tossed their plates in the trunk.

He also had the radio working in time for the midnight news bulletin. Abi's hands shook on the wheel as she heard Jenner's voice pledging a full inquiry into the "unlawful" events at Fullthorpe secure unit. She wanted desperately to switch it off before anyone mentioned Dad's name. She thought she might throw up if there were any more lies about his violence, and how Security guards had supposedly risked their lives to end his.

Instead, Abi turned up the volume. Like her fear, her courage was a wild animal. She could feed it with fury or starve it with grief.

Right now, she needed it fed.

Dad's name wasn't the only horror the bulletin contained. It named four prison officers and Security staff also killed during the breakout.

"Impossible," she said, fingers clammy on the radio dial. "None of us were armed. Well, apart from a giant with two huge hammers. But Midsummer was controlling him."

"The death toll may rise further," the reporter's voice crackled out from the dash. *"And the public is asked to refrain from speculation while a full investigation is ongoing. However, should this prove to be the work of the same cells that have acted with such callous disregard for life in Millmoor, Riverhead, and the Bore, Chancellor Jardine has vowed that they will be pursued with full force, in order to keep Britain safe."*

"Maybe deaths from friendly fire." Dog shrugged. "When they were—firing at you. It happens. Or false flag."

"What?"

"False flag. You do something bad. Then blame it on—your enemies."

Was that even possible? To ramp up outrage over the Full-thorpe breakout, could Whittam Jardine's regime not only have murdered Dad, Oz, and those others, but also have stage-managed deaths among its own officers? Who could do that and ever sleep again?

Listening to the radio bulletin had been the right choice. Abi had once boned up on the ethics problems you had to study at med school—seemingly daft questions, like whether you'd push one person onto a railway track to block a runaway train that would otherwise crash and kill five passengers. If you just considered the numbers, it should be an easy choice. But some-how, the fact that *you* had to push the unfortunate made almost everyone hesitate—Abi included.

Not anymore. If the person you were pushing was Whittam Jardine, Abi would shove him with every ounce of strength she had.

As they drove through the sodium-lit night, Abi sketched for Dog the barest outline of Midsummer's plan. This included the day of protest and the possible addition of large-scale arson, just to show that the Equals could be hit where it hurt—their assets and centers of privilege. She sensed he wasn't especially interested. Perhaps because his motives were purely personal, or maybe because no killing was involved.

"This list of yours," she asked, although she didn't really want to know. "Who else is on it?"

"All of them."

Dog patted the bulging front pocket of his overalls, where he'd stashed his monstrous glove. But his reply disturbed her. Could he really mean Lady Thalia, who might be cold and in-different, but was nothing like her husband? Or Gavar and Jen-ner? Even Silyen, although Dog had been living under his roof and had managed not to kill him just yet?

"All the Jardines?"

"All the Equals."

Abi's skin crawled as she shifted lanes to take the route into London's heart. Her ally's moral compass was as busted as that of her enemies. Well, you could still do a good job with bad tools.

It was nearing two in the morning, and traffic was sparse when a Security officer waved them down just outside Romford. Should she speed away? But the officer's patrol car was parked on the shoulder, so it would only invite a chase. She pulled over and wound down the window.

"I need to see your license, please, miss." The Security officer was a young man, and though his Essex accent was cheeky, his expression was serious. "The Chancellor's raised the alert level across the capital and we're doing spot checks. No cause for worry."

"I don't have a license," Abi said, sounding as contrite as she could. "I'm really sorry. I mean, I've got a provisional one, but not on me. My test is next week, so I just begged Dad to take me out for a quick practice."

How had that word come out of her mouth so easily? Abi could have wept.

Frowning, the officer ducked down to peer at Dog.

"Funny time for a driving lesson, sir. Your daughter should be getting her sleep."

"Sorry, Officer," rasped Dog, rubbing a hand wearily across his face. "I'm a shift worker. Only chance I get. Anyway—she's a night owl."

The Security guy's face softened at Dog's profession of paternal duty.

"You should be displaying learner plates, sir. I'm afraid I may need to take a few details."

"It's my fault," Dog rasped. "So tired I forgot 'em. Don't want my girl—getting penalties—before she's got a license. They're in the trunk."

Filled with trepidation, Abi watched Dog get out of the car and wave for the officer to follow him. *Please let Dog not lose it.* He'd probably think nothing of making her drive through the capital with a dead body stuffed in the back.

But he simply lifted out one of the discarded number plates and whacked the officer round the head. Then he carried the unconscious man behind his patrol car and laid him down out of sight from the road. When he returned, it was with another gun, two extra magazine cartridges, and a triumphant expression.

"Wait," Abi said. "We can do even better." And, blushing all over—trying hard to imagine he was just a patient—she went and stripped the officer down to his underwear.

"It should fit you," she said, dumping the uniform in Dog's lap. "And now we've got to do something about the fact that when he comes round, he'll have everyone on the lookout for a kinky father-daughter duo in a beat-up blue Ranger."

An idea came to her and she took the next exit off the highway, half a mile farther on. She urged Dog to change into the uniform in the front seat while she cruised the local streets, looking for the right sort of place.

The right sort of place revealed itself as a run-down pub with blacked-out windows, a crooked sign proclaiming it to be "Open all nite," and three cars parked outside. They sized up the best vehicle, and Officer Dog went in to summon its owner on a plausible pretext. Once the man had shuffled outside— from the state of him, he shouldn't be anywhere near a steering wheel for at least forty-eight hours anyway—Dog performed a simple choke hold that sent him down into unconsciousness.

Dog took the wheel of the new car and followed Abi as she ditched the old one several streets away, hiding it in an endless row of residential parking. Leaving it at the pub would have established an easy connection between their old car and previous crime, and this new vehicle. Then Abi took the wheel again and they were off into central London.

"You've taken to—a life of crime."

"Just as well," she said ruefully, "because I'm not going to have a whole load of career options once this is over."

The closer they came to the center of the city, the more armed Security officers were visible on the streets, even at this early hour. That was definitely a new development. It didn't bode well for Midsummer's plan to get huge numbers of people assembled peacefully. Because of course, if the Jardines had known in advance about Fullthorpe—and that had to have been Gavar, however much Abi wanted to believe otherwise—then they probably knew about the planned protests, too.

Here in East London was where the common folk lived. Abi wondered if there were as many Security patrols over in posh West London, or the public spaces of the center, around Westminster, Aston House, and, of course, Gorregan Square.

Just thinking about the square made Abi shake, and her palms grew slippery on the steering wheel. She could have been over the water in Dublinn with Daisy. What was she doing here?

How could she contribute anything when she was this afraid? And she should stop thinking like this, but she couldn't. The gun she'd given Dog would surely be damaged from where she'd mishandled it. It would misfire and shoot someone innocent, probably a child, and they would find her and take her away to Astrid Halfdan and then there would just be pain and more pain until . . .

A hand wrapped round her wrist on the wheel and she yelped. The nails weren't clawlike anymore, but they applied pressure.

"It keeps you alive," Dog said brusquely. "You can always tell the ones—that don't feel fear. 'Cause they're the ones—that don't come back. But you can't let it—master you neither."

Abi focused. Blinked. The hand on her wrist was an anchoring pressure.

"Thank you," she said. "I needed that. I used to take pills if my anxiety and panic attacks got really bad, like around exam time. I reckon I'm due an upping of my dose."

Dog laughed—and the sound of it made her miss her father even more. Dad had always been her quiet cheerleader, but also the one who pushed her out of her comfort zone. He'd taken the training wheels off her bike, and had let go of her in the swimming pool before she'd felt ready. In both cases, though, Dad had been right and she'd managed just fine.

She was going to have to go through the rest of her life without him.

The tears that she'd held back the whole day suddenly came uncontrollably.

She pulled the car over to the side of the road and killed the engine, then laid her face against the steering wheel and cried and cried.

Sometime later, she felt a bony hand on her back. Heard a ruined voice rasping.

"Easy now. Good girl. Breathe."

Abi breathed. And wiped her face.

"You and your brother," Dog growled. "Stronger than you think."

"I could have gone through life quite happily never finding

out," Abi said, and hiccupped. She wiped her streaming nose. "Luke, too, I bet."

"He's safe. With Silyen now."

Abi's head snapped round so fast it pinched a nerve, pain slicing up the side of her skull to stab the back of her eye.

"Luke is with Silyen? What do you mean—at Far Carr? Why didn't you say anything?"

"Wasn't important."

Abi could have strangled him. Instead, she asked a million and one questions, which Dog mostly answered with shrugs. But the little she gleaned was that Luke had made a friend at Eilean Dòchais who had helped him escape. (And wasn't that just her little bro all over?) He had come to London to try to rescue Abi from the Blood Fair, but lost her in the chaos, whereupon Silyen had taken both Luke and Dog to Far Carr and woven them into the estate boundary.

"And he's safe?" Abi asked, over and over again. "You said he's safe?"

"I said he's with—Silyen Jardine. They seem to be—getting on fine."

Dog wheezed a laugh. Who knew why. Presumably because the idea of being safe in the vicinity of a Jardine was risible. And yet . . . that estate wall. Luke was somewhere neither Crovan nor Whittam Jardine would be able to find him, just like Daisy.

Abi leaned back in her seat, limp with relief and disbelief. She was full of regret that Dog hadn't told her earlier, so she could have insisted on seeing her brother and hugging Luke till her arms hurt.

But it would have changed everything.

She couldn't have *not* told Luke about Dad. But going through that again, so soon after telling Mum, would have been unbearable. And how would Luke have reacted? Knowing him, he would have decided to shoot Whittam Jardine himself, which could only have ended in absolute disaster.

It was better this way.

She wiped her face. "Thank you for not telling me back there," she told Dog. "That was the right call. Now let's get on with this."

She pulled the car away from the curb, and drove them deep into the dense, run-down streets of East London.

Dog craning at the window caught her attention, so she ducked and looked, too.

A body was hanging from a railway overpass. It was swollen from exposure, the face so tight with black bloat that it was impossible to guess at age, ethnicity, or gender. The one thing you could tell was its crime, because a sign pinned to the body bore the word "SABOTEUR." Near its dangling feet, a Security officer patrolled, presumably to deter any attempt to cut it down.

Abi's mouth went dry. The words "KEEPING BRITAIN SAFE" had been stenciled along the inside of the underpass. The body spun as a train went overhead.

Once past the swinging corpse, it was just a few more turns to the railway arches. They encountered no more Security, and Abi let out a sigh of relief. It was a little after three in the morning and the grimy cul-de-sac was deserted. As she had remembered, an auto-parts yard with a roll-down metal shutter was the only business unit that appeared still to be trading.

Abi led Dog to the unit that looked the best combination of deserted yet habitable, and pushed open the door. There was a scuffling within, and she froze. Rats? But there was no further movement, so she gingerly stepped inside.

Only to be slammed against a wall as something slashed toward her arm.

At her cry, Dog sprang snarling through the doorway. Whoever had assaulted her was now attacked in turn, and screamed. Abi's heart raced.

"Stop! Please!" came a cry from the dim recess of the cavernous space.

It was a child's voice.

The person Dog now had in his grasp called out something in a language Abi didn't understand. And though the voice was male, it had that wobble Luke's had when his voice was breaking between child and adult.

They'd been attacked by children?

A light sputtered into existence—a small battery-powered lamp. Its pool of weak light revealed a pair of unkempt children, one maybe eight, the other younger, and held in Dog's grasp was a struggling boy of perhaps twelve.

"I speak best," said the middle one, in heavily accented English. "Please don't hurt us."

They looked to be from the Mesopotamian region? It was hard to tell. A few blankets on the filthy concrete floor showed where they had been sleeping, and empty sandwich cartons lay scattered around.

"We won't hurt you," Abi said, motioning at Dog to release the boy. He did so, though not before shaking the kid's wrist until a penknife fell to the floor.

"Are you Security?" asked the child. Its small sibling began to cry.

Dog was still wearing the uniform.

"No. Who are you? Why are you here?"

In halting but clear English, the child poured out a story that

Abi had already half guessed. The family had fled conflict in their homeland and been smuggled to Britain. They'd been here for six months. Their parents were both teachers, but had worked as a laborer and a cleaner to pay the rent on the single room they all occupied. Then a week ago, Security's immigration team had come knocking.

"She said we were thieves," the child said. "Because we use schools, have jobs, walk in the street, but do not do slavedays. My parents cried. They said: 'We will do days, we just want that our children are safe.' But they were taken. We were told to stay, a child dee-poor, dee . . ."

"Deportation," Abi supplied. Her eyes were watering with the dust in this place.

"Child deportation officer would come in the afternoon. But we ran. We hide here."

The smallest one sniveled against its sibling's side. Their brother looked on, fingers clenching, having lost his only means of defending the remainder of his family.

"'Keeping Britain Safe,'" Dog rasped. "I fought in their country, against—their persecutor. Now we need to keep this country—safe from them?" He spat on the floor.

But Abi knew many would approve of such expulsions. This narrative fitted into the bigger lie Whittam Jardine was telling the British people. If folk felt poor, it was because of these sponging refugees, not the greed of the Equals. In the same way, those who protested against the slavedays were being cast as the lawbreakers, when it was the days themselves that were unjust.

Whittam was terrorizing the people of Britain under the guise of being their protector. The man was a monster. And a genius.

She and Dog would be the end of him.

Abi drew Dog back outside, away from the children.

"This can't go on. Something needs to happen—and soon. I need to get back to Lindum and find out what Midsummer's plans are. When we do this, it has to be in a way that doesn't implicate her, but I'm betting on the fact that what she's planning will draw him out. He won't be able to resist grandstanding: addresses to the public, some kind of counter-demonstration, flags, that sort of thing."

"I'll watch Aston House," Dog said. "And Westminster. People on the offensive—often forget the defense. If there are weak spots—I'll find them."

"Good. But remember, we have to see if this can end peacefully first."

Abi could tell from the look in Dog's eye that he didn't believe it could.

And neither did she.

TWENTY-ONE

BOUDA

"It starts the night after tomorrow," Jon said.

"So soon?" Bouda couldn't hide her skepticism.

"They're drawing on networks that have been in place for years, remember. There are people here from Exton, Portisbury, Auld Reekie, you name it. All my mother's shadier contacts, too. They want to keep up momentum after Fullthorpe. There are three stages planned. First, targeting property—there'll be takeovers of empty mansions. They're going to call those 'house parties' and invite people to turn up. It's a way of getting people turned out, ready for the march the next day.

"Then second, while Security's distracted with all that smallscale disruption, I've got her sold on the large-scale targets we discussed. There'll be major arson strikes through the night. Then when London wakes in chaos, to pictures of Equal buildings burning, there'll be a massive march through the city that will end up in Parliament Square. It'll finish with a rally."

Bouda pressed her lips together. Thank goodness Midsummer had taken the bait on the arson, because otherwise it would be a tame sort of protest. Nothing at all that would justify reprisals. And nothing that would give Bouda the opportunity to show the people of London what *she* had to offer.

"That's a pretty innocuous finale," she said. "A rally? Let me guess: speeches and a megaphone. She seriously thinks she'll change things like that?"

"That's the point." The line crackled and Bouda could hear the distant hooting of an owl, and wondered where Jon was. No doubt somewhere in Lindum's grounds, while inside, behind those dirty old brick walls, Midsummer and her band of traitors were scheming. "If Security or the military start shooting at the crowd, then you've instantly lost moral credibility on the claim to be 'Keeping Britain Safe.' They figure you're a hostage of your own slogans."

Bouda drummed her fingers on the bedside table. They sported a bright turquoise manicure. Gavar's inexplicable and uncouth visit had left her thinking about DiDi, and on a whim she'd dug out the little bottle of polish her sister had once done her nails with. On that morning, Bouda had thought her sister was just back from a shopping trip to Paris. In reality, Dina had been breaking a prisoner out of Millmoor—Oswald Walcott. He had foolishly come back to Britain later, so was picked to die at Fullthorpe. You didn't thumb your nose at authority without consequences.

Her darling sister had worked against everything Bouda believed in. She had collaborated with Midsummer and others who wished to destroy the Equal way of life and overturn their country's history.

Bouda had utterly mistaken the person closest to her. What else might she be getting wrong?

"Bouda? Are you still there?"

"Sorry, Jon, I was thinking. It's late. Update me tomorrow when timings and locations become clearer."

She cut off the call.

It was time for sleep, but sleep eluded her. She drew the coverlet off her bed and curled up with it in her armchair instead. And in the shadows of her unlit room, one by one, she seemed to see them: Mama, killed in Portisbury slavetown by a commoner's act of sabotage, when Bouda and DiDi were girls. Bodina, whose final words were that everything her sister believed in was wrong. Daddy, who showed his love by just giving her whatever she desired. Gavar, her longed-for and hated husband, turning away with pity in his eyes. Whittam, who used her as an ally and coveted her as an ornament. Jon, who desired and respected her Skill and her body.

Who was she, without this Skill and the skin she stood up in? She was nobody's sister now. Felt like nobody's wife. Might soon be nobody's daughter.

But she wasn't nobody.

She shouldn't get so caught up in Midsummer's plans that she forgot the other person she needed to take care of: Whittam.

Because there were two ways to rise—you could climb, or your enemies could fall.

Manage both, and you'd rise so high no one could touch you.

She threw the coverlet aside, pulled on some warm clothes, and padded through the corridors. Security at the front door touched their helmets in salute as she exited.

The fountains caught her eye first. Even though it was a mild night, they had somehow frozen. Bouda touched one, and it melted back to bubbling liquid. Then the second and third.

When the fourth was flowing freely once more, she sent them jetting high into the sky, even though there was no one there to see them except her and the sentries. She laughed as the water rained down, wetting her face and hair.

Poor Midsummer, plotting to overthrow Whittam through the so-called power of the people. Did she not realize that the people had no power, and never would have, in a world in which Skill existed?

Bouda inhaled, and the night air held the river's briny tang. She let her Skillful awareness reach toward the Thames. The tide was turning, and she could feel the great river flex like an animal shifting in its sleep as she petted it.

Her sense of mastery felt greater than before. Was the mere exercise of her Skill increasing its strength?

A chill went down Bouda's spine. She remembered when she'd first encountered a notion like that. It was a year ago, in the House of Light, when Whittam had told her of Silyen's scheming for an abolition proposal. The only explanation they'd come up with to explain the boy's motives was that, as a devotee of Skill, he wanted the Equals to use their neglected powers.

Well, he'd got his wish.

He might be only eighteen, but her precocious brother-in-law knew more about Skill than anyone alive, Bouda was certain. Had he anticipated events building to a confrontation like this? Engineered it, even? Because that proposal had sparked the Millmoor riot, which had snowballed into the Bore burning, and then Riverhead—and everything since. Where was Silyen, anyway? And what was he up to?

He'd never appeared interested in politics. And yet he'd levered himself neatly into the House of Light. If the rest of them were discovering that the more you exercised your Skill,

the more you wanted to, might Silyen find that the more political power he had, the more he wanted?

Bouda curled her fingers. Everywhere you looked were people with their own slippery agendas. Why did this have to be so
hard? There was no question of this country not being ruled by
the Skilled. Anyone with an iota of common sense could see
there was no alternative.

Yes, the slavedays and the country's economic footing required adjustment, to ensure that people's qualifications and
experience were being put to best use. That, coupled with improvements in living conditions in the towns, should satisfy the
vast majority.

That was what was needed. Not Midsummer's abolition.
Not Whittam Jardine's tyranny.

And if she could just hold her nerve through these next
forty-eight hours, Britain's future would rest in Bouda's hands.

Working through these problems had helped settle her
thoughts, and when she returned to her apartments, Bouda
slept.

The next day, she was at her desk first thing. The office felt
strangely empty without Jon, but soon warmed up with a hum
of activity. Across the country Bouda's monitoring stations
were reporting gatherings and departures—busloads of people
slipping out of the great cities of Britain and heading to the
capital. Tomorrow night, these people would kick off the
"house parties" across Mayfair, Chelsea, and Kensington. The
day after, they—and everyone they'd drawn onto the streets
with their fun—would march.

It was a tough call, deciding when and how to intervene. If
Security's response betrayed too much foreknowledge, it could
alert Midsummer that her plans had been compromised beyond
the little that Gavar had gleaned. But for Security not to react

at all would be even more suspicious. Bouda didn't want Midsummer sensing that she was being led into a trap, and spooking. This showdown needed to happen.

She picked up the phone and called Speaker Dawson. She knew from Jon that his mother still used the number listed in the parliamentary directory. When the woman answered, Bouda demanded to speak to Midsummer.

The muffled and confused exchange down the phone was almost entertaining. Bouda could just picture the panic among the plotters. But Midsummer's voice was strong and confident when she came on the line.

"Bouda. I take it you're not ringing for a chat. What can I do for you?"

"I appreciate you're busy, so I'll keep it short. I hear you have some fun planned for us, and the traffic and people-movement data I'm seeing suggests it might be happening soon."

"Your husband reported back like a good boy, did he? I wish I could say I'm surprised. Are you calling to tell me how you'll put a ring of steel around London? The people won't be denied, Bouda."

"I'm sure they won't, Midsummer. But they might have a difficult time making their voice heard if I shut down London's main thoroughfares. Block off any place that might be used for gatherings."

"You can't close down everywhere. We'll find a way."

"What if—" Bouda jumped in quickly, because it sounded as though Midsummer might be about to hang up. "What if I *didn't*? What if I gave you and your rabble a free pass to the very heart of London? Gorregan Square, maybe. Or even parliament."

"We don't need your permission, Bouda. We'll be marching peacefully. I've invited members of the international press.

Global observers. Citizen journalists. The minute one of your goons lifts a baton against us, it'll go around the world. You'll be even more of a pariah regime than you already are."

"Midsummer, I know you took an advanced degree in Thinking the Worst of People, but you may have misheard me. I said I would let you through. You can come down the Mall. Do your thing in front of the House of Light itself, if you want."

"Because it makes us easier to round up and arrest in Parliament Square? You must think I'm stupid."

"No. Because it seems to me that the current leadership—which is to say, the emergency leadership of Whittam Jardine—may be failing in several respects regarding the welfare of this country. Speaking as a committed parliamentarian, I would have no objection to hearing valid criticisms of that leadership voiced."

Midsummer went quiet. Bouda knew she'd be processing that. Good.

Then she heard the woman's throaty laugh.

"You're good, Bouda. Or bad. Or whatever. For the record, I regard you as part of that leadership, and I'm not making deals of any kind with you."

"I'm not proposing any deals. All I'm saying is that should, at some point, the people of London—"

"Britain."

Bouda could almost hear Midsummer smile. She smiled, too. ". . . the people of *Britain* spontaneously decide to voice their dissatisfaction with the current leadership, then I would require our Security forces to be respectful of their right to free and open protest."

That laugh again.

"I'd volunteer to dog-sit your sister's flatulent pooch in a broom cupboard before I trusted you, Bouda. But this has been an interesting conversation. Thank you for calling."

The line went dead. Bouda let it whir in her ear a moment before ending her call. She replaced the handset and contemplated it.

Tomorrow was going to be interesting.

She received a text from Jon at lunchtime the next day. All it contained was a time and a list of place names.

All of them were locations on the list of possible arson targets that she and Jon had drawn up.

Well, Midsummer might have "citizen journalists"—kids with cameras—but Bouda had the professional media at her disposal. She put in a call to a correspondent whose reporting she'd always found irreproachable, and suggested that he and his crew be at the parliament gates at eight o'clock that evening.

The word came through from Security a few minutes after eight, at which time Bouda and Astrid were already in her ministerial car, parked in front of the Westminster complex alongside the crew's satellite truck.

Even burning, the first target looked beautiful. It was one of London's most iconic department stores, its pillared facade dominating the main shopping street. The store was Equal-owned and, like the luxury shops on Mountford Street, sourced much of its stock from slave labor, where there was no constraint on how many hours might be spent crafting a single, exquisite item. The fire department was on the scene, their hoses playing across the building. Astrid ran to instruct them to redirect their attention to the corporate headquarters behind the store. Preserving the company's office space was the priority, they were told.

Which left the facade clear for Bouda. Flame was licking through the windows. Over the main entrance was a vast art deco frontage, a delicate lattice of glass. The TV crew got in position just in time to see it blow.

Perfect.

Bouda filtered her Skillful awareness down through the tarmac into the subsoil of the city. She felt for the city's wet arteries—those buried and forgotten tributaries of the Thames. There were two close by: the Tyburn and the Westbourne.

And she called them.

Her heart was racing, her Skill was thrumming, and this was it now. These next twenty-four hours were all or nothing. Bouda wouldn't sleep again until Britain was transformed.

The result was even more spectacular than she'd hoped. She could feel the two sunken rivers strain upward, and was almost thrown off her feet as they erupted at the surface. They geysered high into the air, and Bouda heard the TV crew's astonishment.

"Are you getting this?" the producer asked the cameraman, who made a scathing response.

Then she had no more attention for them, because she was directing the jets across the store's elegant exterior, where the flames were fiercest. She didn't need to gesture to do this. She knew by now that the water simply bent to her will. But for the sake of the cameras she played it up—crisp, precise movements, like a musical conductor.

This wasn't just about what she could do. It was about what she was *seen* to be able to do.

Jon had first hit on the idea—something that would fit in with Midsummer's rebellious plans, while actually showcasing Bouda's Skill. And his instincts had been spot on. He'd even suggested the red suit she was wearing. "To make you more visible. Pale clothes will get filthy; in dark colors you won't stand out. It has to be red."

The heat from the flames was ferocious, but nothing that Bouda's superior Equal physiology couldn't cope with. Again, the cameras wouldn't miss that she stood closer to the flames than anyone else—another subtle signal of both her bravery and her superiority.

The arson strikes were expected through the night. Jon's text had told her the second target, but the location was an anonymous set of offices in an unphotogenic section of Vauxhall—something that wouldn't look good on camera. And as in their conversation earlier, Bouda didn't want Midsummer knowing exactly how much detail she had. If the woman sensed that Bouda was going to steal the thunder for each act of arson, she might call off the attacks. And Bouda didn't want *that* happening before target number three.

The third target was one side of Canary Wharf's main plaza, behind which loomed the gleaming corporate skyscrapers of international banks and investment firms. It was the HQ of an Equal-owned commodity trading firm, whose origins lay in partnerships opened up by the voyages of Bouda's ancestor Harding. That was a nice detail for the reporter to pick up—a reminder that Bouda wasn't just an Equal, but from a family that had helped build Britain's economy. She hoped he also remembered what she'd said about using her maiden name of Matravers, instead of the double-barreled version she'd adopted since marrying Gavar.

Once word came from the fire department—Bouda didn't want to arrive too early, to give the blaze time to catch hold—their car sped through the streets, flanked by motorbike outriders. The TV crew's outside-broadcast truck raced after them, capturing every moment. As they drove, Bouda drafted a short statement to deliver on arrival, condemning the arson attacks. Overhead, the whir of helicopter blades told her that an airborne filming crew was also tracking them. Perfect.

Canary Wharf at night was a diamond grid against the sky. Each lit window in its towering office blocks was a pixel in a billboard thirty stories high that advertised London's prosperity to the world. The blaze had already taken hold, though, and even though only one building was on fire, the mirrored glass on several of the office blocks gave the impression of a vast, raging inferno.

Both the skyscraper lights and the flames reflected off the black water that surrounded the central plaza on all sides. To the west was the Thames, Blackwall Basin was to the east, while north and south of the plaza were the former docks, now yacht-filled marinas. When Jon had suggested a Canary Wharf target, Bouda had initially dismissed it. Too challenging. Too much. But then she'd come and walked around here, and realized it could be her finest moment. The water in the docks and basin was shallow and would be much easier to manipulate than the open channel of the river.

"And we're hearing about homes—mansions, I should say—across central and West London being occupied by groups of protesters," said the reporter, once Bouda had delivered her statement against the blazing backdrop. "Can we expect tough action on those, too?"

"I'm monitoring the situation," said Bouda. "Property ownership is the well-deserved reward of hard work, and its destruction will not be tolerated. But let me say this: I will never authorize the use of undue force against those peacefully protesting. The events of this evening are a message from the people of Britain—one that I, Bouda Matravers, will be listening to carefully. Now, please excuse me."

"A busy night for Bouda Matravers-Ja—" she heard the reporter telling the camera as she jogged toward the burning building. "Miss Matravers heads the Office of Public Safety, and as you can see, she's taking that responsibility very personally indeed this evening. I'm seeing feats of Skill here with my own eyes like I never imagined. And just look at this. . . ."

Bouda stood in the center of the plaza and turned slowly on the spot, arms outstretched. Skill vibrated through every cell of her and the sensation was ecstatic. The river, her power, and the fifty percent of her body that was composed of water felt like one indistinguishable whole.

The water spiraled up from all four sides of the plaza, rising like an inverted tornado above the long, low blocks of offices. Bouda, her entourage, and the film crew stood beneath its dripping, foaming pinnacle.

As she held her breath a moment, the Skill quivering through her, Bouda gave devout thanks to Midsummer Zelston and her ragtag revolutionaries. They couldn't have provided a better opportunity for Bouda to show what she was capable of. Then she inverted the point of the churning cone of water, and with a balletic dip of her knees and a powerful downward swing of both arms, pulled it down to douse the fire in one surging instant.

Water sluiced across the plaza, carrying burning debris with it. The office was gutted (if the fire hadn't been allowed to take hold, the pictures would have looked pathetic), but with one drenching, the blaze was now entirely extinguished.

"That would have looked even more amazing from the air," Astrid said, hurrying to her side once the cameras had moved off Bouda to pan up Canary Wharf's glass towers, saved by her actions. "How are you? Is it exhausting?"

It wasn't. Bouda had never felt more alive. This was what she was born for—to work Skill, and be a strong leader for her people.

They caught up on reports of further explosions—another two, bringing the total to five. According to Jon's text, only two targets remained.

One would be the historic buildings in the heart of Mayfair that housed the neighboring embassies of Japan and the Confederate States of America, Britain's partners in the Skilled Bloc of Three. The other was the London headquarters of BB Enterprises—the Matravers business empire that Daddy had named for his two girls, Bouda and Bodina. It was Britain's biggest employer of those doing days, and Daddy kicked back generous payments to parliament each year for the right to use their labor.

As Bouda had anticipated, these final attacks broke simultaneously. These were the two most high-profile targets, and the saboteurs would want to ensure that London's firefighters were fully engaged elsewhere before they took them out.

"We have reports of fire at the headquarters of your family's business, Heir Bouda," one of the TV reporters said, pushing a microphone into her face. "I imagine you'll be heading straight there."

"The goal of these devastating attacks is quite clear," said Bouda. "To damage British-owned businesses, and jeopardize the livelihoods of tens of thousands of ordinary men and women. Now, I'm very confident that BB has every firefighting procedure in place. My concern is for Britain's crucial economic and diplomatic relationships with our great allies, Japan and the Confederate States. I'll be putting national interest above my own family interests tonight—as anyone would."

"Smooth," Astrid murmured as their car sped across London.

The embassies would be her pièce de résistance. The nearest water source was the Serpentine lake in Hyde Park. Like the Gorregan fountain, it was fed by a deep borehole.

Well, Serpentine by name, serpentine by nature. The entire lake lifted from its bed as a vast, coiling wyvern, like that which had done battle with Midsummer's animated dragon. Unlike her first creation, raised from the Thames, this serpent had to move without contact with its now-drained source. It was phenomenally unstable as it flew across Hyde Park, its every molecule held together by nothing but Bouda's Skill and her will. Sweat was running down her face and spine, and her hands shook.

But it was a short flight and a glorious ending.

The wyvern set a collision course for the embassy buildings, annihilating itself against the pillared porticoes and elegant frontages, and extinguishing the flames in an instant. Astrid had instructed Security to allow onlookers to remain at a safe distance, rather than evacuating the whole square. And as the fires died in a gout of smoke of which a real dragon would have been proud, noisy cheering and applause went up from those gathered to spectate.

Bouda didn't turn to acknowledge them—that would have been unseemly grandstanding. But the cameras missed nothing. And inside, she was exultant.

Dawn was breaking.

Round one to Bouda Matravers.

TWENTY-TWO

ABI

Whoever coined the phrase "on the run" was right.

Abi felt like she'd barely paused for breath since the day she ran from Kyneston, after Luke's trial. But one way or another, this was where the running stopped.

This gamble was too big. If they won, everything changed. If they lost, they lost it all: the country, their freedom, possibly even their lives. Crovan would destroy Midsummer's Skill, just as he had Jackson's. And then there'd be another Blood Fair, at which no lions would come roaring to the rescue.

After leaving Dog lying low in Dalston, she'd returned to Lindum. On the drive back, she'd wondered if they would let her in. After all, she'd vocally supported Gavar, who turned out to have betrayed them, and had just disappeared herself without warning. Perhaps Midsummer would suspect her, too.

She had an explanation ready, though, when she pulled the car up to Lindum's front gates and waited for the Equal to come out.

"I needed to be alone," she told Midsummer. "I went back to Manchester, to look at our old house. I wanted to think about my dad, about how we were before all this happened. And I couldn't face having to say goodbye to my mum. Has she gone—you've got her away to Ulaidh?"

And when Midsummer said "Yes," Abi genuinely broke down in the noisiest, snottiest, most helpless crying jag imaginable, and the Equal had yanked open the gate and pulled her into a hug.

There hadn't been any questions about her absence after that.

Lindum had been frenzied. Jon was there, and Abi was glad to see him.

"I hear your info is being put to good use," she said.

"I hope so. Major targets with minimum risk to life. We'll deliver tip-offs to any night watchmen or cleaning staff so they can get out, and then . . . burn, baby, burn. It'll send the message loud and clear that the Equals *can* be hit." He flashed that disarming smile, then turned more serious. "I think Midsummer has something else up her sleeve, though. Some surprise planned. You've no idea what that is?"

It was news to Abi. And given that Midsummer was now so busy that she seemed almost to have used her Skill to clone herself, there wouldn't be any opportunity to ask. Besides, after the whole Gavar thing, Abi wouldn't blame her if she kept back parts of her plan from absolutely everyone except those they concerned.

She wondered what it was, though.

And she was still wondering now, even as everything was unfolding around her in the heart of London. Midsummer had delegated responsibility across three teams: Mac from Auld Reekie had joined with Emily from Exton to mastermind the riotous house parties. Speaker Dawson was using her networks to bus in protesters from around the country for the march, with Jon at her side coordinating the logistics. And Renie's uncle Wes was working with unflappable Bhadveer from Portisbury on the arson strikes. Portisbury's factories specialized in chemical engineering, and several men of the Bore, responsible for the original arson across the slavezone, had chosen to stay and help after their release from Fullthorpe. This team of guys knew what it was doing.

Layla had been clear from the start that she wasn't leaving her girlfriend's side. She was running the base they'd temporarily taken over—an office building that had been mothballed pending redevelopment, where everything from the phones to the loos was still working.

The whole place smelled of industrial cleaning products that tickled Abi's nose and throat. She couldn't sneeze, though, because Renie's head was in her lap and the girl was dozing. The pair of them had been out on one of the arson hits. They'd acted as lookouts for a team of the same guys from the Bore who'd leveled the Queen's Chapel.

Abi had heard about Bouda Matravers's response to the fires. They'd gathered round the office's TV screens to watch the rolling news reports, Layla rubbing her bump and mouthing swear words of which no mother would approve whenever Bouda delivered some trite condemnation of what was going down in the city. But they'd all stood openmouthed when she'd flown the water dragon smack into the burning embassy. Jon had stepped away from the telephones to watch, and Abi had heard his awed intake of breath. Had he known what his erstwhile boss was capable of?

Midsummer just stood there grimly, watching. And Abi remembered what she'd heard about Renie's capture at the House of Light. How Midsummer had raised a dragon from its roof to buy Renie time to escape, or pluck the girl to safety—and how it had almost succeded, until Bouda conjured a creature from the Thames to do battle with it.

There was a rumor going round that the Equal had actually telephoned Midsummer to taunt her. Who knew if it was true? But it was clear that Bouda Matravers was good at more than just feats of Skill. Abi felt a flicker of apprehension. If her plan to take out Whittam Jardine succeeded, would Bouda merely be waiting in the wings to continue his brutal policies?

But the people were rising. Across the city, the parties were drawing more and more Londoners onto the streets. Updates were coming in—someone was tallying the numbers on a massive whiteboard—of busloads of people arriving in the capital. And many more were disembarking from trains. Even though social media was regulated and closely monitored, two hashtags were trending: #unEqual and #takeback. Hilda had been on standby to knock out any attempts to block them, but it looked like nobody in Bouda's Office of Public Safety was particularly concerned about hashtags.

"They're technophobes," Jon explained. "Computers, social media. They don't see the point. I think it's something to do with their Skill as well. Silyen Jardine won't even get in a car unless he has to."

Abi didn't much care why. The important thing was that it left one more tool at their disposal.

They could do this. They could. Despite Bouda's spectacular interventions, and the fawning coverage of the broadcaster she'd taken along with her for the ride, the journalists and observers Midsummer had embedded in their night of protest were sending out the true story. It was headline news across the international media and on pirate channels, like Radio Free for All. Jessica was managing them, providing quotes from Midsummer and Speaker Dawson and suggesting other people for them to interview or house parties to check out.

"Oz did a few stints on Free for All," she told Abi, with a sad little smile. "I always told him he had a face for radio."

There was so much pain and loss gathered in this place, Abi thought, looking around. But so much hope and passion, too.

On the floor above Midsummer's ops room, groups of students were working on signs and placards, and Abi wrinkled her nose at the spray paint in the air. She remembered Luke's tales about Meilyr's love of signs and slogans when she spotted several "UN-EQUAL" placards. And she felt a stab of regret when she read one wide banner spread out on the carpet tiles to dry: "WHEN I GROW UP, I WANT TO BE A ~~SLAVE~~, DOCTOR, TEACHER, ENGINEER." Surely for these students, that was still possible.

As the sky lightened through the windows, a palpable sense of calm descended. Midsummer called together the whole HQ, apart from the core crew who never stepped away from the phones.

"It's nearly time," she said. "The march will begin at ten, reaching the House of Light by twelve. Bouda Matravers herself assured me she won't let Security block off the route to Parliament Square. If you didn't hear her on TV last night, she was talking about 'listening to the message from the people of Britain.' I reckon she might be looking to squeeze out her dear daddy-in-law, Chancellor Jardine, by acting good cop to his bad cop in all this."

"More like bad cop, worse cop," someone jeered.

"Quite. But assuming that intel is correct, the goal is to have Parliament Square and the surrounding streets filled by midday. Then we'll hear short testimonies from around the country about how the slavedays devastate lives. Just before half past, I'll take the mic and do my thing.

"We must be prepared for a hostile response. But remember, the cameras will be our witnesses and our safeguard. We have our own among us. Foreign observers will be livestreaming the whole thing, too. Bouda may well have her pet news crew in tow, though, and as we know from Fullthorpe, some cameras really do lie.

"Today won't be the end of Equal abuses in this country, but let's make it the beginning of the end. If I want to send one message today, it's that the Equals can no longer use their power to tyrannize and beat down the people. Someone I once knew liked to say that *there's no magic more powerful than the human spirit*. Let's prove him right today."

Listening to Midsummer, Abi wanted to believe it, too. Wanted to believe that this brave, passionate woman and those who worked with her—from veterans of the resistance, to students Abi's age fired with idealism—would be enough to overturn centuries of wrong.

She hoped it could be done.

Dog's finger wasn't yet on the trigger that would take Whittam Jardine's life. It wasn't too late for a miracle. For Bouda Matravers to really mean it when she talked about listening to the people. For Lord Jardine to see the streets filled with people demanding reasonably and peacefully not to be treated like dirt, and to grant their wish.

The thing was, Abi didn't believe in miracles.

"I need some air and a bit of downtime," she told Renie. "I'll find you later. I'll be there in the square."

Then Abi slipped out into the morning. The sky across London was a haze of smoke, and the rising sun turned it gold. It lay over London like a fog of Skill, radiant yet smothering, and Abi shivered at the sight of it.

She had a lot of London to cross, and took a few wrong turns as she jogged through the streets, but was there by half past eight. She knocked on the door and stepped back, should Dog come barreling out, knives first.

The door opened a crack, and she saw only his lean face. That broke into a grin, and as he pulled the door open she saw a gun ready in his hand. He probably slept holding it.

Sounds of sleepy complaint came from within, and to her amazement Abi saw that the three children now had makeshift beds and bedding, and that a few books were piled beside them. Plainly Dog hadn't been prowling the streets only to observe Security patrols. She felt remorseful about taking him away from them. When everything at Westminster was over and done, Dog would be able to come back for these kids. Maybe.

"It's time," she told him. "The Security uniform would be a good idea."

Abi placed Dog's knives and overalls and the gun she'd picked up in Fullthorpe into her backpack. He slipped the second gun into the holster of the officer they'd taken it from, and they set off.

The march was beginning at Hyde Park. It would follow Oxford Street and Holborn, go down the Kingsway to Embankment, then flow along the river before bending back up to Gorregan Square. From there it would funnel down Whitehall to parliament. Assuming that Bouda kept her word and there were no obstructions, Midsummer and the speakers would be saying their piece in Parliament Square, directly outside the Westminster complex.

"D'you really think—Whittam—will show up?" Dog asked.

That was the question, wasn't it?

"I think she's going to challenge him personally to come out and answer to the people. Let's see how that goes. I don't *want* us to have to do this. . . ."

But it was probably already too late for that. She had brought Dog into this, and now he had the scent of Whittam Jardine's blood, she didn't think he would just walk away, the job not done.

Midsummer's determination to keep the protest peaceful filled Abi's mind with misgivings. It wasn't that she presumed to think she knew better than a woman who had worked for commoners' rights for so long. It wasn't even—as she had once thought, when with Meilyr and Dina—that there was something inherently wrong with Equals giving commoners their freedom, instead of the people taking it. At the end of the day, that freedom was the thing.

It was that the Equals, none of them, even the most empathetic, really understood what it was like to be powerless.

And because of that, none of them, not even Midsummer, really understood just how difficult—how inherently violent— the process of seizing power would have to be. Abi knew her history. Not as well as Silyen Jardine, perhaps, but she couldn't think of a single bloodless revolution. Just look at the Equals' own. Lycus Parva had executed the Last King in the bloodiest way imaginable: publicly, over several days.

That hadn't been necessary. But there was something in the act itself that was cathartic. Conclusive. That marked a point of no going back. Abi knew that she stood on the brink of another such moment now, and the thought was dizzying.

Don't look down, she told herself. *It's a long way to fall.*

TWENTY-THREE

ABI

As they neared Lambeth, they heard the demo before they saw it. Even at a distance, the noise was phenomenal: shouts and chants, whistles and drums, vuvuzelas and football rattles.

It resembled a human river flowing along the Thames Embankment, and Abi's heart swelled to see it. There were so many of them, so united. Bouda Matravers might be able to bend the river to her will, but this stream of people was all Midsummer's.

As Bouda had promised, the roads weren't barricaded off. What was the woman playing at? Was she truly intending—as her words last night had suggested—to listen to the complaints of the people? She was young and intelligent. Was it conceivable she was inclining toward reform? Jon had been in her office as a plant, but perhaps his influence really had rubbed off.

Abi couldn't smile at the notion. She remembered Bouda unflinching beside Gavar at the Blood Fair—telling him to sit down because this was "the justice they deserved." She remembered the pain and the blankness that had followed what Silyen Jardine said was a brutally administered Silence at Kyneston. One inflicted merely to cover up a trivial row with her husband-to-be.

No, Bouda Matravers would do nothing that wasn't in her interests. Given that, Abi could see two possibilities as to why this protest hadn't been closed down already. One was that it was entrapment. How might the trap spring shut? Not with free-fire on the protesters at least, given the large media presence. The other alternative was that this was Bouda the pragmatist, putting on a show of listening in the hope of defusing the unrest. Perhaps she also wanted to burnish her image on the world stage as a strong but fair-minded politician.

And would Lord Whittam appear? Everything depended on it.

They crossed the river at Lambeth—it was the same route Abi had taken to meet Jenner at Aston House, and she dug her hands into her pockets to stop them trembling at the memory.

On the far side, they were stopped by two Security men, their uniforms the same as Dog's.

"Awright," one of them said. "Who you with?"

"London Met. I'm her escort," Dog growled. The two officers looked Abi up and down.

"You're looking like you've never seen a plainclothes officer before," she said witheringly. "But I guess you wouldn't, sitting at your desks all day filling out paperwork for bicycle thefts."

That put them on the back foot. But not entirely.

"ID?"

Dog held up the badge of the officer she'd undressed. The photos weren't a great match, but they were both dark-haired white males and Dog angled it so the tamper-proof hologram flashed in the sun.

"You really don't know CID if you think we carry badges," Abi said. "The kind of places I work up north, you might as well have a sign round your neck saying 'Cop—shoot me.'"

"Up north? Didn't think you sounded like you were from round here."

"CID in the best city on earth: Manchester," Abi said. "I'm the lucky baby-faced bastard that gets the call whenever they need someone who looks like a teenage girl. Pimps, traffickers, molesters, you name it. It's a nice change being an angry student for the day. This is the only badge I need."

She lifted the bottom of her shirt to display the gun in its Security-issue holster. When they'd spotted the patrolling officers from the far side of the river, she and Dog had paused in Lambeth Gardens to work out their shtick.

"We expecting trouble then?" one of the officers asked.

"Best to expect anything, when our lords and masters are involved," she said. "Now, let us crack on, eh?"

She walked past them with a confidence she didn't feel. Ahead lay the Jewel Tower—which had once been the royal treasury, and had survived the Revolution. The sight line it offered was too narrow for Security snipers, needing to scan the entirety of the square. But it had a clear line onto both the gates of the parliamentary complex and the small raised stage that had been set up for Midsummer and the speakers. The tower was usually open to tourists, but surely couldn't see more than a handful a day given that directly over the road was the dazzling House of Light, free for anyone to gawp at.

The custodian had, luckily, already been given warning to secure the place and leave. Dog battered the lock, and the pair of them crept in and up the stairs to the roof. Perfect. Or so Abi thought.

"Too far for the—effective range," Dog sniffed, tossing down both of the Security pistols. "Toy guns. Wait here."

Abi waited, her heart in her throat. And waited. The noise of the demo was getting louder and the front row of marchers was coming into view. There was Midsummer, and Renie alongside her uncle Wes. Other faces she recognized, shining with optimism and confidence. Were they wondering why she wasn't with them? The scale of it looked incredible. She'd have to make sure that Dog held fire until they were absolutely certain it was the right thing to do.

What if Whittam came out onto that stage and started making the same placatory noises as Bouda? To kill him then, in the middle of a reasonable response, would appear inexcusable.

But in her heart, Abi knew he never would. Whittam's way was dominance, not compromise.

Then the door of the tower banged and Abi heard something heavy being pulled across the floor of the tower gift shop. Expecting the worst, she leapt down the stairs. Over Dog's shoulder was slung what even Abi recognized as a powerful sniper rifle, and he was dragging a limp man in a bulletproof vest. He rummaged beneath the till counter, and emerged triumphant with two rolls of packing tape.

"Help me—wrap him up."

Abi was reassured by the man's firm pulse and lack of visible injury. Dog must have used a choke hold. She laid out their victim as considerately as she could, making sure his airways were open, before they mummified him with tape. She balked at Dog's proposal to tape up the man's mouth, and they compromised on using a souvenir tea towel as a gag.

Then Abi heard the first testimony begin, and it was time they were back on the roof.

The stories were everything she could have imagined, but it still broke her heart to hear them. A woman whose two sons had drowned when a poorly maintained fishing boat from the Ipswich fleet had capsized. A man left quadriplegic in an industrial accident. A woman for whom the contraceptive implants mandatory for females doing days had failed, who lost her baby and was left infertile after complications the slavetown clinic wasn't equipped to treat. A young man whose father was sentenced to slavelife after complaining about victimization by his shiftmaster.

Midsummer gently took the microphone off the last speaker as he broke down in noisy sobs that echoed round the square.

"We could keep listening to these stories all day," she said. "All of you standing here will have a story of what has happened to you, or your friends or loved ones. But we've not gathered here to make the case that the slavedays are dangerous. We all know they are. Nor are we here to argue that the slavedays no longer make economic sense, forcing talented people into a decade of rote labor, and keeping our country stuck in the past as the factory of the world, churning out junk. This is obvious, too.

"We're here to say that *even if* conditions in slavetowns were improved, and *even if* they were modernized and reformed, so that we use people's talents and broaden Britain's economic base . . . even then, the slavedays would be wrong. Because they're based on a fundamental untruth—that not all are Equal.

"I tell you—and I say this as one of them—the people that rule over you, that imagine they mock you by calling themselves 'Equals,' truly *are* your equals, and not your superiors. They are not cleverer than you. Not kinder than you. Not wiser or more responsible. There are only two things that set them apart: their Skillful gifts, and their wealth. One they are born with, the other they have hoarded. Both they have used to strip each one of you of freedom and dignity."

Midsummer wasn't holding back, Abi thought, admiration coursing through her. This was stirring stuff, simple and true.

And yet unease prickled her palms. Why had Bouda and Lord Whittam allowed Midsummer to continue unchecked? Were they really going to make some show of conciliation— even if they subsequently tried to ignore it and carry on as usual? Surely they must know that today's protest wouldn't be the last of it?

"Here they come," said Dog gruffly, sighting through the scope on the top of the rifle. He moved to let Abi see. Bouda and the Chancellor were exiting the door at the base of New Westminster Tower. They'd be at the front gates of the complex in two minutes. Perhaps another two to reach the stage where Midsummer stood.

"Not yet," Abi urged Dog. She laid a hand on the rifle barrel.

"This building behind us is beautiful," Midsummer said. "But its beauty is a lie. It is called the House of Light. But it is where dark hearts gather, and use their dark gifts to keep this country in thrall. It's time to tear down this system, and build a better, fairer one."

Midsummer handed the microphone to the person at her side—Layla—and threw her hands in the air.

What was she doing? Abi's heart sped up. The crowd had fallen deathly silent.

Then as one, it gasped.

The two bronze dragons that curled around each pinnacle of the House uncoiled as fast and as forcefully as the chain of a dropped anchor. They sped into the sky, bright shining streaks. Their scales glowed with Skill and sunlight.

Circling lazily, the creatures twined till you could hardly tell where one sinuous shape ended and the other began. Beneath them, the soaring windows of the House of Light pulsed. The sheets of glass seemed hammered from molten gold.

Abi had forgotten how to breathe. Even Dog was looking up, distracted from his weapon and his revenge. Had Midsummer planned this all along? Or had Bouda's water serpent yesterday reminded her of their earlier aerial duel?

Either way, the dragons' target was clear: the radiant House itself. The gleaming symbol of all that the Equals represented.

This was spectacular. It was perfect. It was violence without harm, and it was even more beautiful and terrible than Bouda's showy displays across the city last night.

The dragons writhed and separated, climbing higher with great languid wingbeats.

Then as one, they pivoted, angled—and dived.

People in the crowd were screaming in terror and wonder and awe as the dragons fell. One toward the great East Window, the other the west end. Like god-thrown spears of burning gold, they lanced into the building, crossed inside, and burst up through the roof, wings spread wide.

The windows caved in, the roof sprayed up in a shower of wood, stone, and lead, and golden Skill-fire burned into the sky like a detonating incendiary bomb. The roar and crackle of it was deafening, and it was too bright to look at. As Abi shielded her eyes she heard Dog mumbling and cursing—he'd be too dazzled to sight accurately for a minute or two.

The roof and upper parts of the House had been entirely destroyed. The walls still stood, at half their previous height.

Their broken remnants were wreathed in a miasma of golden mist.

"You see," said Midsummer's voice. "It can be done. Four hundred years of cruelty and oppression can end, here and now. Because all are Equal! *All. Are. Equal!*"

Those assembled took up her cry. It began as a low rumble as the crowd found its rhythm, then swelled as it spread up Whitehall. The crowd continued as far as Abi could see—all the way back to Gorregan Square. And it chanted in one voice. *All. Are. E-qual.* The rhythm of it drummed in Abi's brain, and she found herself silently mouthing along.

The dragons writhed, crossed, swooped again—and the walls of the House were leveled beneath the rake of their wings.

Half the crowd cheered. The other half kept up the chant.

How on earth were Lord Whittam and Bouda going to respond to this?

Abi strained her eyes to look at Midsummer. She'd done it. She had achieved what Abi had thought was almost impossible: a peaceful act of destruction, an unignorable protest. And she hadn't compromised her ideals in the process. She should be exulting right now.

She probably was, inside. But on the outside, she appeared to be struggling. Her arms were jerking, no doubt under the strain of controlling her creatures. This was more, even, than she'd attempted at Fullthorpe.

"Here they come," said Dog, bent low over his rifle. His eye was trained on the two Jardines, not on what was happening on the stage.

The dragons turned, coiled, and climbed again. Midsummer's gestures had become frantic. Abi's heartbeat went off the scale. Something wasn't right.

The creatures plummeted a third time: side by side, emitting a horrible screech of triumph. And they didn't fall upon the ruins of the House, but toward the stage. The protesters gathered nearest to it began to stampede, but there wasn't time for them to get away.

They weren't the target, though.

As the paired dragons lifted upward again, a single struggling body could be glimpsed clamped between two sets of needle-sharp metal jaws. And as their sinuous bodies arced away from each other, the pitiful figure tore in two, spraying blood and gore over the onlookers.

Through the microphone, inhumanly loud and inhumanly awful, Layla's scream went on. And on. And on.

What had happened? What had just happened?

That tiny, torn figure had been Midsummer.

Abi felt as though the dragons had fastened their claws in her heart and ripped that apart, too.

The double gates of Westminster swung open. The crowd on the pavement immediately in front somehow found room to scramble back. In the space revealed stood Whittam Jardine. A short way behind him was Bouda Matravers.

There was no doubt about it, thought Abi. Whittam had somehow caused Midsummer's dragons to turn on her. How, she had no idea. But she was as certain of it as she'd been of anything in her life.

He deserved this. It was right.

"Now," she told Dog. "Jardine. Do it now."

Dog's finger tightened on the trigger.

But maybe the gun was damaged, or perhaps Dog had failed to release some catch, because it made a dull, thwarted sound and no shot came.

TWENTY-FOUR

GAVAR

From where he stood at the edge of Parliament Square, Gavar saw it all.

He listened to the testimony of those who had suffered in slavetowns, and found himself wiping his eyes. He hadn't cared for all the commoner girls who had warmed his bed over the years. There were plenty whose names he hadn't even known. But he'd cared enough for some of them that to imagine them enduring shattered bodies, lost babies, and wrecked lives filled him with anger.

He'd seen Millmoor, of course. Twice. He'd convinced himself that it was particularly nasty because it was the oldest slavetown, and because Mancunians were a bunch of troublemakers who brought it on themselves. But the tales he'd heard when among the men of the Bore, and from those rescued at Fullthorpe, made it plain that Millmoor's atrocious conditions were the norm, not the exception.

He listened to Midsummer's passionate denunciations of the Equals, and found himself unable to deny a single thing that she'd said.

He watched, as stunned and awed as the rest of them, as she ruined the House of Light. The gout of Skill-light made him shudder. No less so the golden mist that settled over the wrecked remains. He thought of Meilyr Tresco, broken and howling on the floor of the House. His Skill ripped from him by Crovan and flung upward, to evanesce through the roof into that pulsing world of light.

He held his breath for a moment, wondering if something more might happen. Something like Aunt Euterpe's destruction of the Kyneston ballroom, which had warped the air itself. But no disaster came. The world wasn't sucked through a wormhole into some glittering and cruel alternate dimension.

But this one was cruel enough. He saw Midsummer's alarm, then her panic and fear. Her arms were moving awkwardly. Unnaturally.

As the dragons turned on her, Gavar watched, horror-struck. The creatures fell in perfect unity, as if harnessed to a chariot. Angling their jaws sideways as they neared the ground, they snatched at her legs and shoulders. This was no attack that Skill could repel, because it was her own malfunctioning Skill controlling them.

He heard Midsummer scream as she was taken up, and looked away from what he knew would come next.

Then the Westminster gates swung open, and Father was there. He had that look of easy authority that left his face only when he was drunk or furious. The man tugged at his shirt cuffs, as if he'd just performed a trifling task and acquitted himself well. As he made his way to the stage, Bouda clipped after him in heels. She'd spent the night Skillfully saving some of London's most priceless assets from arson. But she hadn't been able to—or wanted to—save Midsummer.

That tweaking of the cuffs nagged at Gavar. It was one of Father's little mannerisms, indicating self-satisfaction. Why was he so pleased with himself?

The answer to that was immediately and gut-churningly obvious.

Father stepped up to the stage. His face was grave but calm. As the terrified protesters looked up at him, they quieted under his gaze. He radiated reassurance.

And something more, too. Skill.

No one had ever considered Father especially Skilled—which was, of course, curious in a man of such eminent lineage. Gavar supposed that until the country had started going to hell, none of them had really had much cause to display what their Skill could do. Gavar broke windows when infuriated. Mother tended to her garden and grew flowers that took the cup every year at the Kyneston village fête. Silyen could be found lying floppy and blank-eyed as he "visited" Aunt Euterpe. Father had done none of those things.

So what *had* he done, over the years? He had won political power, despite being a cruel and unpleasant man. He had bedded women without restraint, despite being both a drunk and nothing like as good-looking as his son and heir. Both of those things could be attributed to awe of the Jardine name, of course.

But they could equally be attributed to Skill. Specifically, that quality the scholars had labeled "persuasion."

Father was up there on the stage, speaking quietly. The crowd hung on his every word. He appeared to be eulogizing

Midsummer much as he had done Dina Matravers. She was a brave, bighearted young woman, wickedly led astray. (Father was surely running out of culprits to do the misleading.) She was impressively Skilled—but had overreached herself. Had lost control of her monsters and suffered a tragic accident trying to bring them back under her mastery.

If Father was gifted at persuasion, a lot of things suddenly made sense. Such as why Mother, who had been famously spirited in her youth, was so perpetually compliant. Why Zelston's abolition proposal had been so decisively defeated, when Gavar knew—as Meilyr Tresco must have known, when he campaigned for it—that there were other commoner-sympathizers in the chamber. Why no one had yet pushed to end Father's emergency Chancellorship and elect a new incumbent. Or had raised a voice in opposition to the elevation of the Jardines to the position of First Family.

Why Gavar had never renounced his inheritance and run away with Leah.

Although that could simply have been because Gavar was a coward.

Well, he was through with blaming his own mistakes on his father, but he was damned if he wasn't ready to lay everything else at the bastard's door. That was why Midsummer had looked terrified. Father must have been *persuading* her to call her dragons down upon herself. He'd been close enough for it to work—just behind the Westminster gate.

And now look at this. A crowd that only minutes earlier had been shouting angrily about Equal abuses, that had cheered as the dragons ruined the House of Light, that had chanted "All are Equal" with one voice. Now listening raptly as Father offered false sympathy and empty promises.

He even had his arm around Midsummer's girlfriend, Layla. Her head rested on his shoulder, as if his strength was the only thing keeping her up. Gavar saw the swell of her stomach. Another baby that, like Libby, would grow up missing a mother.

And that thought decided it.

Gavar Jardine, the marksman—that was how he'd been taunted, when Leah's death had been passed off as a hunting accident. (And how had so many people swallowed that absurd story? Gavar suddenly wondered. Had that been Father's persuasive Skill, too?)

The taunt had been considered amusing because Gavar really was a marksman. The best shot in Hampshire, able to take down songbirds in flight.

He reached beneath his leather coat for the gun he always carried. It had taken Leah's life. This wouldn't bring her back, but it was long, long overdue. He kissed the cool metal and whispered her name.

Gavar offered up a silent apology to Midsummer Zelston— that he was doing this too late to save her, and promising to do everything in his power to protect her unborn child. Then he named Dina and Meilyr, too, and the men dead at Fullthorpe, for all of them had died at his father's behest. So very many of them.

He lifted the gun. Sighted along its barrel.

You bastard, he thought. *I'm through.*

And he pulled the trigger and saw his father drop.

It was chaos, of course. With his father's hold over them broken, and a second death right before their eyes, the crowd started screaming again. Midsummer's girlfriend collapsed to the ground, spattered with bloody pulp. Bouda stood on the stage, her head turning this way and that.

This would be the moment for Gavar to hide. To draw his Skill about him like some cloak of invisibility. To whisper in people's ears as he passed them: *I am not here. Look away.*

Instead he stuffed his gun back into place, fastened his coat, and moved toward the stage. People parted in front of him and he ascended the steps. Bouda was there, watching him. It was like their wedding day in reverse—except Gavar felt calmer walking to his doom today.

He paused to crouch down at the girlfriend's side. She was being supported by the scrappy kid, who managed to look both fierce and absolutely broken.

"I'll watch over you," he whispered to the sobbing woman. "You and your baby, I promise."

What about his own baby? Whatever happened to Gavar, Libby needed to be safe. He would have to be on his guard.

He picked up the microphone from where it had rolled on the stage, and stood up, glancing at Bouda. She appeared as outwardly composed as ever, but he could detect her confusion and uncertainty.

She was a cold bitch, but was she a monster? He'd sensed her vulnerability the night he'd paid her that impromptu visit. Perhaps together they could do what they'd never yet managed, and wrest something good out of this utter fucking mess.

And then at last, because he could ignore it no longer, he looked at his father's dead body. The force of the bullet had taken off the top of his father's skull, and with it, his lion's mane of red-gold hair. His face looked somehow naked without it, as if he were the old man he'd never lived to be. Death had relaxed his features, smoothing the scowl lines that Gavar had seen—and no doubt caused—all his life. He bent and closed his father's eyes.

Gavar supposed he should feel sorry. And he did. Sorry that

his father hadn't been a better father, and that he, Gavar, hadn't been a better son. But the only regret he felt was that he hadn't done it sooner.

Drawing in a breath, he turned toward the crowd. He was about to own up to murder in front of the world's cameras.

"It's over," he said. "You're all safe—please stay calm." He drew in a deep breath, because his chest felt as if his lungs had turned to lead. How did politicans do this every day: addressing crowds, explaining, persuading, justifying? Who in their right mind would want to?

"I'm so sorry any of you had to witness what you just did. Those who have children here with you, I can't apologize enough. *I* shot my father."

The crowd heaved with something that could have been revulsion or relief, Gavar could hardly tell which.

"I did it, because he was responsible for what we just saw—the appalling death of an amazing woman who was brave enough to defy her own class and fight for what she believed in. I did it because my father has killed many others. He reinstated the Blood Fair—abolished more than a century ago for being too inhumane even then. That 'violent uprising' at Fullthorpe prison you all heard about? There was no such thing. It was a breakout of the innocent and falsely accused, in which the only people harmed were those my father murdered to tar his enemies.

"Who led that breakout? The young woman who just lost her life—Midsummer Zelston. I know. I was there. I went to her at my father's request, to spy on her plans. What I found was a woman of principle and courage, and I will always regret deceiving her."

Gavar paused to collect himself. He wiped the sweat from his brow. At his side, he could almost feel Bouda quivering. She had been complicit in some—perhaps all—of what he had just mentioned. Should he try to bring her down, too? Or could she be trusted to act in the country's best interests?

What even were those? Gavar didn't know anymore. The end of Equal rule? Some kind of power sharing with elected commoners and Equal advisers? Speaker Dawson was up on the stage with Midsummer's crew—she'd doubtless have some opinions. Alongside was her son, Jon Faiers. Gavar had thought that Weasel Boy was part of Bouda's clique. Whose side was he really on?

Gavar gave up. He'd just shot and killed his father. The man he had spent his whole life simultaneously hating and yearning to be loved by. He couldn't figure out his country's future on the spot. In fact, he had zero right to do so.

He could only speak from his heart.

"As my father's eldest child, heir of the Founding Family, I was told from the moment I was born that I would rule this country one day. My daughter, though, is common-born. No one in my family ever said the same to her. I don't want Britain to be a country where one child's opportunities are greater than another's simply because of their birth. I take no pride in being the son of a man who thought that's how it should be.

"I'm not a good person. And what I just did certainly wasn't a good thing. But it was necessary."

He turned to Bouda and handed her the microphone.

"Please get it right," he said. "Because I don't know how."

Then he bent down to the girlfriend and the kid—Layla and Renie—and helped them up. Others of the Fullthorpe breakout team were there, too. Meilyr's Millmoor friends.

"You can come with me," he said. "If you want. You need somewhere to recover from all of this. I'll keep you safe."

"Where?" Renie asked skeptically. The kid had plainly never trusted anywhere to be safe in her entire life. It wasn't as though experience had proved her wrong.

"My house," said Gavar. "It's not far. About a ten-minute walk, in fact."

He nodded away across Parliament Square toward St. James's Park. At the far end of it—the flags just visible above the trees—was Aston House.

"Doesn't *she* live there?" Renie jerked a thumb at Bouda.

"I've a feeling she'll be playing down her connections with my family, after what I just did. Her family has its own place in Mayfair. Or, knowing Bouda, she'll take over the Chancellor's suite. Layla, may I?"

When the poor woman simply nodded, Gavar picked her up with infinite care and made his way down the steps. The crowd parted to let them through.

"I can promise a full investigation," Bouda was saying behind him. "All those found to have a case to answer from what has happened in recent weeks will be held to account. I will consult with key members of the Justice Council and other advisers, including the Speaker of the Commons, whose son is a member of my own personal team. Together we will find a way forward for Britain after these shocking events."

Held to account, Gavar thought grimly. There wasn't a single one of them, in any of this, who didn't have something to answer for.

"Wait! Gavar, wait."

Someone was pushing slantwise through the crowd. Abigail Hadley. He hadn't noticed her absence from the group around the stage. She had a Security escort. Had she been arrested, and wanted him to assert her innocence?

Then Gavar noticed the identity of the uniformed officer, and nearly dropped Layla.

"You."

His late great-aunt's dog bared his teeth in what could have been either a threat or a smile—and was probably both. Gavar noticed that he had somehow acquired a sniper-class gun, slung over his shoulder.

"Nice shot," the man rasped. "You beat us to it. Here, let me—clear the way."

"To Aston House," said Gavar.

"Wait."

Abi hesitated, and it took a moment for Gavar to realize why. Jenner.

"I'm pretty sure he's at Westminster. He's been rather thick with Bouda lately. If he *is* there, I'll keep him away from you."

She nodded, and their strange procession made its way through the crowd. Bouda had finished speaking and people were dispersing, streaming away from the square, doubtless fearful of being implicated in two terrible deeds: the destruction of the House of Light and the death of a Chancellor.

This should have been a morning that changed everything.

It still was, but not how anyone had anticipated.

The gates of Aston opened for him, clearly not objecting to his patricide, and Gavar kicked open the heavy front door and led his fugitives in. (When had they become *his*? The moment Midsummer had died, perhaps.) He yelled for the servants, who came hurrying—and Mother with them.

"Will you check she's okay?" he murmured to Abigail, setting Layla down. "One of the staff can call our family doctor, if you think she's needed."

"What has happened?"

Mother's pale complexion went even paler at the sight of the blood that covered them all. One of her dark curls had come loose as she ran, and Gavar smoothed it back behind her ear. She was so tiny and birdlike. Father had kept her caged for all these years.

He led her to one of Aston's many salons. Telling her was almost harder than the deed itself.

"Father's dead."

Her hand came up to her mouth and she gripped a chairback for support. But she didn't cry. She'd never say it, but she was glad he was dead, Gavar knew.

"How?"

"I shot him."

But Mother flew at him then, with a scream and flailing fists. He had to grab both her hands in one of his and hold them till she quieted. When she'd fought herself to a standstill, she looked up at him. The wet streaks of mascara made it look as though her black eyes were leaking.

"You're *sorry* to see him gone?" he asked. "I thought—"

"Not him. Not *him,* Gavar." And she collapsed against his chest, her narrow shoulders rising and falling. "This ruins everything. For you."

When she'd calmed, she eased away from him.

"Take me to his body. I need to see it. And people need to see me with you—to know that you have my full support."

"You think it will get that bad? Everyone in parliament knows me—knows what sort of a man Father was. My wife will effectively be running parliament."

"That's what I'm afraid of. Go and change. We need to show your remorse and your duty."

And so, a short while later, Gavar and his mother went back

down Birdcage Walk. Gavar wore a black suit, had shaved, washed, and neatly parted his hair. He looked every inch the grieving son.

Mother gasped when they reached Parliament Square and saw the yawning space where the House of Light had been, now filled with nothing but a pulsing golden miasma. The bronze dragons lay broken across the high railing around the Westminster precinct. They must have fallen when the Skill animating them died.

When Midsummer died.

Parliament Square was empty, although its perimeter was now ringed with Security guards. Father's body had been removed. The abandoned stage, churned mud, and detritus of trampled placards and banners were the only evidence of the presence of tens of thousands of people. Gavar took his mother through the events of the morning, showing her where he had stood, where Father had fallen. He hadn't seen where the remains of Midsummer's body had dropped—they were gone, too—but he steered Mother away from a patch of grass that was darkly slicked with blood.

Equal bodies were never released to hospitals, so they must have taken Father's inside the parliamentary grounds. Gavar may have killed a Chancellor—something he now had in common with the Hadley boy—but Westminster's gates recognized him and swung open. Patricide or no, he was still Heir Gavar Jardine. Was, in fact, now Lord Gavar Jardine.

Perhaps he could really do what he'd threatened to all these years, and make Libby his heir.

Once behind the railings, they could see more clearly the extent of the destruction. The House of Light had fallen in such a way that the surrounding buildings were unscathed, so not a single life would have been in danger. Gavar knew intuitively that Midsummer would have planned it that way. Even as she destroyed, she spared.

What a leader the country had lost in her. Who would run things now?

The ruined House filled the courtyard: a mass of blocky rubble, shattered beams, grit, and glass. Dust still hung in the air, and the Skill-light that pulsed there rendered it almost opaque, like bright cloud.

Laid over one section of broken wall was a black cloth. Dust clung to it and glittered. And on top was Father's body. Former Chancellors were always laid in state in the House before their funeral. That hadn't been possible with Zelston, of course, but plainly someone was observing the niceties with Father, and that touch of ritual and routine was reassuring.

Gavar took his mother's hand and led her over. Father's skin had gone waxy; the cheeks were beginning to sink in. The flesh was cold to touch. His salamander-print neckerchief had been folded decorously over the missing top of his head.

The Chancellor's star of office had already been unpinned from his chest.

Mother circled the body. She didn't bend to kiss it, but paused every now and then to touch it with light fingertips. The lines on Father's knuckles, the graying gold hair that peeped at the neck of his shirt, no longer concealed by the neck scarf. Gavar looked at the body and wondered how it was that even though death had not wiped out his fear and anger toward this man, he still felt a profound sadness at having never won his love.

It was overwhelming, and Gavar stepped away, nearly turning his ankle on some masonry. He looked down, only to find an expression very like Silyen's staring blankly back: the head of the statue of Cadmus Parva-Jardine that had once stood in the chamber. It was where Father had liked to converse discreetly with his allies, and Gavar had been forced to listen, as part of his political apprenticeship.

"The fall of the House of Jardine," said a voice. "How very appropriate."

Gavar looked up. "Bouda."

His wife stood there with her two cronies at her side: Astrid Halfdan and Jon Faiers. Well, that cleared up whose side he'd been on. Someone else Midsummer had mistakenly trusted.

"It's your house, too," he said, "so I wouldn't speak too quickly."

"Oh, I don't think so." She stepped a little closer. "I gave you the chance to be a proper husband to me two nights ago, and you refused. And now I can hardly stand by a man who murdered his father and his Chancellor. No, I'm afraid I'll need a separation, Gavar."

He shrugged. "I suppose. But I thought your priority was 'finding a way forward for Britain'?"

"You're quite right. That—and other things. Such as, first, your confirmation as the next Lord Jardine. Seeing as you have no legitimate offspring, that makes me, as your wife, your next of kin and heir. Second, your trial for your father's murder. Third, once you're found guilty, the stripping of your title. That title and the accompanying assets then pass to—well, your next of kin and heir. Me. So I guess the House of Jardine gets reborn after all."

"You jumped-up little bitch." Mother appeared at Gavar's side. He could feel the fury quivering through her, and wondered why he'd always assumed he'd inherited his temper solely from his father. "You're a tradesman's daughter. Every inch of standing you have you owe to us—to my husband's family and to mine."

"But don't you see, Thalia? It's a new world. Oh, you Parvas and Jardines played your part in your day. You established the rightful rule of our kind. But you've not kept up. The slavedays have become inefficient and the Equals irrelevant. That's going to change.

"I intend to modernize the slavedays. We'll extract maximum use from every man and woman in this country. And they'll love us anyway, because your little freak Silyen is right— we've forgotten what we're capable of. I won't give them spectacles of terror, like your husband's vulgar Blood Fair. I'll give them feats of wonder. People will be better fed, better educated, better employed. They'll have rulers to marvel at. They'll neither notice nor care that they're still not free."

Father had known what he was doing when he'd picked this woman for Gavar. She had enough ambition for the two of them, and no heart at all.

Bouda came closer. Gavar tensed, but she passed him and went to where Father lay. Bouda bent to inspect the corpse. She lifted the folded neckerchief, wrinkled her nose, then dropped it carelessly back again.

She was practically purring, like she'd had it all worked out, yet the only thing that had given her this opportunity was Gavar's own rash stupidity.

"What would you have done, if I hadn't killed Father earlier and handed you all this on a plate?"

"Your father would have got a bullet one way or the other. Your talk about snipers rather inspired me. I got his permission to have a few marksmen planted in that crowd, to take down Midsummer in case there was no opportunity for him to do it Skillfully. But unlike Riverhead, these shooters were *mine*.

"They answered only to me, and they all knew there were *two* possible targets: her or him. You throwing yourself into the middle of it was an unanticipated bonus. But it just shows what a hothead you are, Gavar. People like you will make it hard to build a stable new administration. So, come along quietly and your mother won't get hurt."

"*Come along quietly?* You think you've got a prison cell that can hold me?"

"Who said anything about a prison?"

Bouda's smile was as lovely as it had been on their wedding day as something stung the back of Gavar's neck.

"You gave us the idea for this, too, when you faked the rescue with the Hadley girl," Astrid murmured in Gavar's ear, as her clever fingers depressed the needle's plunger. "Who knew you had *so many* good ideas. . . ."

Ice spread through Gavar's veins.

And his scorching Skill froze over.

TWENTY-FIVE

LUKE

Meeting the Wonder King, Rædwald, had blown Luke's mind.

Properly blown it, like a lightbulb, into little pieces that couldn't be put back together in any way that would work.

In the year since Kessler had pulled up in front of the house in the slavetown van, and Luke had experienced the first queasy feeling that something was horribly wrong, he had been thrust from one incomprehensible situation to another. Millmoor. Kyneston. Eilean Dòchais. Gorregan Square and Far Carr. He'd learned to adapt fast.

But this? A world in which people could just step into thin air and disappear?

A world that was just one of *many* worlds.

He still couldn't quite believe it, despite having seen it happen. First with Coira, then again with a king who should have died one and a half thousand years ago, and who had been only

a legend until he walked into Luke's mind and then onto Silyen's beach and showed them both marvels.

They'd stayed on the beach after Rædwald had departed, attempting to follow him. Trying and failing to open a door in
the sky. A door that might lead them to Coira.

The Equal was pacing up and down talking to himself, while
Luke attempted to offer constructive input, or just occasionally
snorted as Sil swore effusively after another fruitless attempt to
reach into thin air and pull another dimension out of it. They'd
been at it for hours now, and their patience was growing as
frayed and tattered as Rædwald's cloak.

Luke could still find no way of rationalizing what had happened—or, no way that would make sense.

"The 'door' we went through to his memories was like the
'doors'"—Luke drew air quotes around the word—"in those
mind-places of ours. Our bodies stayed here, just like they did
when we met him at Eilean Dòchais. But then he and Coira
physically went through actual doors to actual other worlds.
And that doesn't make any more sense now than it did the first
time I said it. If Mum could hear me, she'd have me down the
clinic for a drug test."

"Your family sounds terribly narrow-minded." Silyen made
a show of examining his fingernails.

"And yours is better, is it? Maniacs and narcissists and murderers."

"Harsh. Only a few of them are murderers."

"That's not funny, Silyen."

Luke turned his back and bent over the fire, poking it with a
charred stick. It was nearly down to embers, although they
soon wouldn't need its light, because far out over the sea the
sun was rising. As he watched the fiery sparks float and eddy,

Luke thought about how Silyen had looked when Rædwald had shown them the Skill that shimmered everywhere.

He had dazzled with it.

The dance of the embers was hypnotic and Luke evidently nodded off, because when he opened his eyes next it was bright day and the sun stood high overhead. Was it past noon? He sat up, and felt something slip off him. It was Silyen's riding jacket. The Equal must have put it over him while he slept.

He looked for the boy himself, wondering if Silyen had figured things out while Luke dozed, and had walked off into some strange new world without him. The thought provoked an inexplicable ache. But no, there Sil was, facedown on the stones on the other side of the fire.

Luke scrambled over. The Equal's constitution would protect him from any chill—hence the loan of the jacket—but had he overtaxed his strength? Then Luke's alarm escalated to panic as it occurred to him that maybe the boy had remembered Rædwald's gruesome murder and tried to off himself in the hope that his Skill would both save him—and super-power him.

But no, Sil was breathing deeply and evenly. His skin was warm, if still disconcertingly pale. Luke rolled him over to double-check, gently shaking his shoulders.

Silyen groaned and cracked an eye, then opened both on seeing Luke.

"There's a nice sight to wake up to."

Luke glared. "Just checking you weren't, you know, *dead*."

"Good as"—Silyen yawned—"until I've got some coffee in me. Come on. Let's head back."

And he jumped to his feet, hooked his jacket with a finger, and strode off along the beach.

The remainder of the day passed in more thwarted discussion about what exactly Rædwald had done on the beach. Silyen stood glaring at the canvas in the great hall as if the tiny painted figure of the Wonder King might come to life and squeak out all his secrets.

It was that evening they first noticed Dog's absence. One of Far Carr's freezers had contained an abundance of sausages, and they'd got used to Dog filling a sizzling pan with them and poking with his finger-knives to check if they were cooked through. But he wasn't around, so they shared a sorry-looking ready meal instead.

Luke didn't sleep well that night. Partly because his sleep pattern was out of whack, but mostly because he lay awake pondering his next move. With the failure of their best efforts to follow Rædwald, he had to accept that there was nothing more he could do for Coira. She was hopefully safe, but was *definitely* somewhere he couldn't find her. Mind-blowing though this whole doors-to-other-worlds thing was, it wasn't a challenge that was playing to Luke's strengths.

He needed to start thinking about finding Abi. About making sure that his parents were doing okay in Millmoor, and that Gavar Jardine was still treating Daisy right. Where was Renie? Silyen had said that the woman who rescued her was Midsummer Zelston, the late Chancellor's niece. Dared Luke hope that she might see past his role in her uncle's death, and let him see Renie?

He didn't launch straight in with it the next morning, but after another couple of hours that were no more productive than the previous afternoon, Luke spoke up. Silyen looked at him incredulously.

"You've just witnessed the most astonishing feat of Skill this country has ever seen—something that makes the acts of my ancestors Lycus and Cadmus look like a game of hopscotch— and you want to *walk away*?"

"Be honest, it's not like I'm much use. What do you want me to do? Stand around looking pretty while you think? No, *don't* answer that. I'm serious, Silyen."

An awkward silence fell, then stretched on and on.

"Excuse me," the Equal said tightly. "I find that music aids my thought process and I haven't practiced since we came here."

And he brushed past to a piano in the adjoining room, that even Luke could tell was out of tune, where he proceeded to violently play a piece that sounded like it required at least six hands.

Fine.

Luke knew what would help his own thought processes. Getting the heck away from Far Carr and its lord. Silyen had said he was free to leave this place, and that he would be able to see the wall and find his way back to it if he did. Time to put that to the test.

He hiked across the estate to the gate, and put his hand to the latch. The gate swung open. Luke drew in a breath, and stepped through. Nothing.

He felt for the car key that he never took out of his pocket. He wasn't planning on leaving right this moment. But it would be good to check that the vehicle was still in working order. Back home, rowdy kids sometimes let the air out of people's tires for a laugh. It didn't seem likely that vehicles parked at a magically protected Equal estate would have the same problem, but you never knew.

Which was when he saw the tire marks in the woodchip of the path. At first Luke thought they were the ones he'd made when they arrived. Then he realized they belonged to a second vehicle.

Someone had come here and gone again.

The thought was unnerving. Who had it been? Had Lord Jardine sent someone to investigate the freeing of the estate slaves? Had Security been prowling around Far Carr's hidden wall?

It looked as though the vehicle had at one point pulled up behind what Luke was now calling "his" car. Why would it do that? He clicked the door lock—all in working order—then inspected his vehicle thoroughly. No one had tampered with the tires or brakes. The fuel gauge still showed half a tank.

He could see scuffing along the dirt trail that led off the track and into the woods. He followed, noting that the track had been trodden either by several feet or by one person several times. Inside the tree cover, the picture was more confusing. What had been a clear trail turned instead into a churn of movement among the trees, across a wide area. Whoever had come here must have walked back and forth for ages—maybe even hours.

Luke's skin prickled to think of Silyen's Skill causing this, with Silyen himself nowhere near. His resolution yesterday had been correct. Far Carr was no place for him, even if he and Sil had reached a strange understanding. And his conscience wouldn't allow him to sit safe behind the estate walls while everyone he loved was still somewhere out there and in danger.

He turned to give the car a final check, then to head back and tell Silyen what he intended, when something smacked him in the face. A branch, hanging down at an odd angle. As he tugged it out of his way, he realized it was broken already. It had been fastened in place.

By a hair tie.

Luke wasn't sure if he was imagining things, because frankly any teenage boy paid as little attention to a sister's grooming routines as he possibly could, but it looked a lot like one of

Abi's. You'd find them all over the house. They were good for pinging at annoying younger sisters.

He must be imagining it, though, because why would Abi have come here to Far Carr?

Unless she had been looking for him. And looking harder than he had been looking for her.

That settled it. He was going, as soon as he'd packed a few things. He'd tell Silyen—he owed the Equal that much—and hoped he wouldn't object. Sil would have much more time to research the mystery of what Rædwald had shown them without Luke under his feet.

He was relieved to still see the gate, and let himself back in before hurrying to the main house.

Silyen wasn't there, of course. He was always inappropriately close when you least expected, but vanished without trace when you needed him. Luke went and packed a bag of all the things he might need, and slung it over his shoulder. Once he'd alerted Silyen to their visitor, and explained his own departure, he'd be off.

When there was still no trace of the Equal in the house, Luke went down to the beach, frustrated to see that the light was already beginning to fade. He staggered up and down the stones, calling for Silyen, then nearly jumped out of his skin when a voice spoke into his ear.

"Going somewhere?"

When Luke was done with his half a heart attack—how was it possible to walk soundlessly on shingle?—he whipped round.

"What?"

"You went out the gate earlier."

"How do you know?"

"Skill, mostly, but the travel bag is a bit of a giveaway." The Equal tweaked the strap. His face wore an uncharacteristically neutral expression. "Listen, have you seen Dog? I haven't seen him since before the king came. That was two days ago now."

"I haven't. He must be off somewhere hunting. Silyen, someone's been here. I went outside the gate. There's been another vehicle. Someone in the woods . . ."

Silyen's eyebrows lifted. "Why didn't you say so earlier?"

And Luke rolled his eyes and followed him. Evening was drawing in as they circled back to the gate. Sil laid a hand on it and closed his eyes.

"Dog," he said. "You, recently, but Dog before you. I must not have sensed it because we were . . . *elsewhere* with the king."

"Look." Luke led Silyen to the vehicle tracks. "Someone came for him."

They stood side by side, staring in silence at the marks in the dirt, Luke debating whether to tell Silyen his theory about Abi.

"You can leave if you want to," the Equal said quietly. "There's nothing keeping you here. I can try and unpick that thread of ours, too. I improvised it in a hurry, so it's a bit messy, but if you want, I'll have a go."

Oh.

Oh. Luke touched his stomach, where there was, of course, no outward sign of his connection to Silyen. It flared sometimes, when they were in one of their mindscapes, trying to see if they could open a door to somewhere that wasn't either the mind of the other, or the conscious world where their bodies slumbered. It had disturbed Luke at first. But not now. Now it felt almost a part of him.

He remembered Crovan's golden collar at Eilean Dòchais. The sickening moment when he had touched it and found it was barely distinguishable from his flesh. That had made his skin crawl. This connection with Silyen was the opposite. The less obtrusive it became, the more comfortable he was with it.

Or maybe he was just, finally, comfortable around Silyen. Because amoral and frankly alarming though the Equal was, he was also just another teenage boy, with a ferocious sense of humor and a willingness to eat whatever unidentifiable thing they fished out of the freezer each night.

There was still the not-so-small matter of him having allowed Luke to be taken by Crovan. But even with what the Equal had discovered about Rix's role in the murder, could he have prevented Luke from being Condemned? Luke doubted it. Someone had to pay the price for Zelston's murder, and that person was Luke. When a Chancellor died, there had to be consequences.

"You've gone very quiet," Silyen said. He put a hand on Luke's shoulder. "I'm almost concerned."

And Luke wasn't quite sure what he intended to do next when, rather than step away, he turned to Silyen and—

"Ahh!"

The Equal's face twisted, and now it was Luke's turn to reach out.

"Are you okay—does something hurt?"

"Not *hurt*, exactly, but . . ."

Silyen took a deep breath and exhaled, rubbing at his temple.

"What it is?" Luke said. "Something to do with the king?"

"I have no idea. I don't think so. It's someone using Skill. One of my family. It's very strong."

"Your family is hundreds of miles away, in London. You're telling me you can feel every time they use Skill?"

"No. Only rarely. I felt Aunt Euterpe, the night you shot the Chancellor. It was what brought me back to the house. And again, when Gavar did that thing in Millmoor. You remember."

Luke did remember. *That thing* where Gavar had taken down

an entire square full of people with one horrifying blast of pain.

"Just the big stuff, then," he said, and Silyen nodded.

"When Gavar caught that bomb on the balcony at Aston House, too. I visited him after, when he was recovering. Sat by his bed and told him how remarkable he'd been. I've always been aware of my family's Skill. I don't know if that's because of . . . the way I am."

"You mean, what the king said—that you have his ability to take more? That's why Jenner's the way he is, isn't it?"

"I believe so, yes."

"You *believe* so?"

Silyen sighed. "I have no memory of it. None at all, though I would have been a baby, so that's maybe not surprising. He's asked me so many times. But I can't remember, and neither can he. Which only makes it worse. The defining moment of his life—the moment that wrecked it forever—and it happened without either of us knowing.

"I have theories. Maybe I was seriously ill, or injured, and somehow needed more Skill than I had to heal myself. Maybe I simply took it because I wanted it. Because that's what babies do, and Mama hadn't yet trained me that nice children don't just take—and certainly not things that you can't give back. And I *have* tried to give it back, or to provoke some sort of Skillful response from him, but nothing works. Each failure only makes it worse."

Luke thought about that for a moment. Then thought about it some more.

"I wouldn't want it," he said. "If you offered me Skill right now, I wouldn't want it. I know it's only a tool, and not good or bad in its own right. But it's power, and power always seems to get abused."

"Someone's always got to have power, Luke. If it wasn't Skill, it would be money. Or intelligence. But you know what they say: the only ones who should be trusted with power are those that don't want it. *Ahh!*"

"Again?"

Luke peered at Silyen's face. And dammit, he was packed and ready to go, *so* ready to leave this boy and this place.

But he couldn't. Not with Silyen like this. With Dog gone, too, he'd be entirely alone. The Equal could barely operate a microwave and didn't know how to drive. He'd starve or something.

No. Luke's departure could wait one more day. He might even persuade Silyen to forget about the king's mysteries for a while and come with him. If Dog really was with Abi, Sil might have a way of finding them.

"This calls for a cup of tea," he said. "Let's get you back."

In the great hall, he steered Silyen toward the sofa and covered him in a blanket, despite the Equal's protests—"I'm *sensitive,* Hadley, not sick." Then Luke made a pot of tea and settled in the armchair opposite. It was just how they had been after Silyen exhausted himself renewing the Far Carr boundary.

The strange spasms came through the night, and on the fourth one, Silyen gasped, "Bouda." Then, "I always knew she had it in her. Ever since Gorregan."

"But she's not your family," Luke objected.

"She is. That's part of the marriage ceremony. Your Skills touch and entwine. She's a Jardine, now—*for better or for worse,* as they say, though I think Bouda mostly signed up for the *better.*"

"What on earth is she doing, using so much Skill in the middle of the night?"

"Who knows." Silyen pressed those deft pianist hands to his

forehead. "Maybe the mother of all rows with Gavar. I'll call him in the morning."

But just like two days ago, the morning was half gone by the time they woke, Luke uncurling awkwardly from the armchair. While he made coffee, Silyen tried telephoning Gavar, but there was no response. Then he tried Jenner, who also didn't pick up.

"Your mother?" Luke suggested, after further calls to Gavar didn't connect.

"I guess. But she worries so much about them already. I don't want to alarm her." The Equal peered into his coffee cup as if the answers might be swirling blackly in there.

Luke was checking the dismaying transmutation of frozen bread to charred cinders in the toaster when something smashed behind him and he almost jumped out of his skin. He turned to see Silyen's coffee cup in bits on the floor, and the boy himself doubled over.

The Equal's dark eyes were wide and large in his sharp, pale face. When he moved his mouth, for a moment words didn't come out. Was he having a stroke?

"Something just . . . broke."

"Broke? Our boundary?" Could whoever had been at the Far Carr gate have come back? "The Kyneston wall?"

Sil shook his head. "Bigger."

But what was bigger and more brimful of Skill than Kyneston? Nothing, apart from the House of Light, and Luke couldn't imagine anyone attempting—let alone managing—to break that. What was going down in the world outside Far Carr's walls?

"Tell you what, never mind the phone calls. Let's just get you to London. I'll drive. I presume you'll handle the explanations if anyone stops us for driving a stolen vehicle. Or me for being an escaped murderer."

Sil nodded. Luke found his bag, grabbed the boy's jacket, and steered him toward the door.

They'd barely made it over the threshold when Sil screamed and collapsed to his knees.

"Bloody hell!" Luke fought down panic. That wouldn't help either of them. He crouched at the Equal's side.

"What is it now? The same thing?"

"Not some*thing*. I think . . . some*one*. One of my family."

Shit. Silyen's family was about the worst pack of people Luke could possibly imagine, and the Equal himself wasn't keen on most of them, apart from his mum. But this sounded serious. Luke hauled the boy up and wound one of his arms around his shoulder. The three miles from the hall to the estate gate had never felt so long.

Luke bundled Silyen into the car, where he rested his head against the window, either lost in thought, recovering from the pain, motion sick, or all three at once. Luke didn't want to disturb him, but if this was something big, it might be on the news. So as they left the cover of Rindlesham Forest, he stabbed on the radio and tuned it to one of the talk channels, keeping the volume low.

At the announcer's words they both reached to turn it up.

"And if you're just joining us," the announcer was saying, *"here's what we know about the shocking events of the past hour. That is, the destruction of the seat of parliament—the House of Light—by Heir Midsummer Zelston during a large-scale protest. And the fatal shooting, at that protest, of Chancellor Whittam Jardine."*

TWENTY-SIX

LUKE

Luke nearly ran them off the road he recoiled so hard. Horrified, he looked over at Silyen, who was hunched forward in his seat.

"I'm so sorry," he croaked, but Silyen held up a hand for silence.

"After the shooting, Lord Jardine's son and heir, Gavar, addressed the assembled protesters, claiming responsibility for the act. No move was made to arrest him at the scene. However, he and his mother, Lady Thalia, the late Chancellor's wife, have just been seen apparently voluntarily entering the parliamentary compound, without any escort. Security has now established an exclusion zone around the parliament buildings, so joining us live from the other side of that in Gorregan Square is . . ."

Luke's heart was pounding. Lord Whittam dead. Gavar Jardine responsible. The House of Light destroyed. That answered the question of what Silyen had felt earlier. Luke held the steering wheel in a death grip as the on-location reporter took up the story.

"Yes, that's right. It is not known at this time whether Gavar Jardine is being detained, or is merely providing information of his own free will. Here's what we do know. The individual who has moved to take charge of the situation is Bouda Matravers. Matravers is known to be a member of the late Chancellor's inner circle, and only earlier this year she married his heir—and now self-proclaimed killer—Gavar Jardine. Given this potential conflict of interests, we understand that Matravers has already summoned to Westminster other key figures, including Lord Arailt Crovan, who is expected to arrive in a few hours' time.

"Lord Crovan, a senior member of the Justice Council, is the man responsible for the incarceration of Britain's most dangerous political prisoners. For example, in his custody is the Millmoor terrorist responsible for the slaying of Chancellor Zelston."

Shit. Luke knew who that was. Though Crovan had evidently kept quiet about Luke's disappearing act.

"Will Lord Crovan soon be taking into custody another—wholly unexpected—murderer of a Chancellor? Or has he been summoned to begin talks about the future direction of this country's government? We'll be keeping you updated as the picture here develops."

"The House," said Silyen, snapping off the radio and throwing himself back in his seat. "That's what I felt. We're lucky that London even still exists. I don't know what Midsummer was thinking."

He sounded almost angry. No—definitely angry.

"And your father?"

"Had it coming. I'm only amazed Gavar didn't do it earlier. That *anyone* didn't do it earlier."

"That's it? That's your response?"

"Oh, I'm sure in five years' time I'll have some sort of de-layed breakdown, and hit the bottle and cry about my lost father. But you know, he really was a complete bastard. And besides, I've always been more of a mummy's boy."

He attempted a halfhearted smirk, then huddled against the window and didn't say another word. What was going on inside that head of his? Luke didn't want to imagine. For all that Silyen had said, he must be feeling his father's loss. Luke would be in bits if anything happened to his parents or his sisters, though admittedly his kind and somewhat dorky dad wasn't a psychopathic dictator.

A three-hour drive had never felt so long. Crovan would have flown from Scotland in less time than that. And when they finally approached the outskirts of London, it was to the unwelcome sight of a flashing sign warning of Security vehicle spot checks ahead. Luke didn't exhale until they were through, not having been pulled over.

"Where are we heading?" Luke asked. "Aston House? That place of yours? Westminster?"

"Westminster. Bouda will have everywhere sealed off, but let's park and we'll go through on foot."

"On foot? Did you hear that special mention earlier for 'the Millmoor terrorist who shot Chancellor Zelston' et cetera? I won't be able to cross a Security cordon."

"Yes, you will. And it probably won't even take Skill. People rely on what they're told, rather than their own common sense. That way it's always someone else's fault if things go wrong. They've been *told* that the naughty young man is under lock and key. Therefore, he *can't* be walking into Westminster. You'll see."

Luke did. The Security line was at the top of Whitehall. Silyen went straight up and pushed the crash barrier aside.

"I'm pretty sure you know who I am," he said haughtily,

when three officers hurried over. He spread his palms in a show of having no weapons, but actually to let Skill writhe and crackle intimidatingly around his hands and wrists. "Though I'm happy to demonstrate, if you need."

"No need, my lord. But . . . who's this?"

One of the Security men tapped Luke's chest with his rifle butt, and Luke was thrown suddenly, hideously, back to Millmoor and Kessler and the baton smashing his ribs. He could feel his pulse race at the memory. There had been no Skilled people in Millmoor, but there had been people who abused their power all the same.

"He's with me."

The camera crews had caught on to the arrival on the scene of another Jardine, and Luke could hear reporters shouting questions as they hurried over from their fixed positions by Nelson's Column—right where the Blood Fair had taken place. He swayed on the spot, momentarily paralyzed by awful memories.

Then Silyen grabbed Luke's wrist and yanked him through. Behind them, Security bunched together to prevent any further incursion.

"You okay?" the Equal asked, once they were out of earshot.

Luke tried to shake himself out of it. "Remind me to take you along next time I try to get into a nightclub."

Silyen smiled, but it was wan. "Gavar uses that 'Do you know who I am?' line all the time, even though every doorman in London knows who he is and is desperate to let him in." The Equal looked down at the crumpled placards scattering the street, and kicked one viciously. "I've no idea how he's going to talk his way out of this, though."

The wide thoroughfare was eerily empty. On both sides of

the road stood the great departments of state—Treasury, Foreign Office, Home Office—that did the bidding of parliament. Luke imagined they were usually a hive of activity, but no one was going in or out today. The surface of the road was sticky with spilled drinks, dropped food, wrappers, and rubbish. The news had said that hundreds of thousands had marched here, peacefully.

How had it all gone so wrong?

At Luke's side, Silyen had stopped. His gaze was riveted on the House of Light.

No. On where the House had stood. But not anymore.

In its place was a pulsing golden cloud—an incandescent fog. Silyen picked up his pace. When they reached Parliament Square, he didn't look at the spot where his father would have died, nor at where his brother could have stood to shoot him. He had eyes only for the dazzling ruins of the House.

Luke marveled at the bronze dragons that lay speared and broken atop the railings. The reporter had described how the creatures had swooped through the House, tearing it to pieces—then turned on Midsummer and did the same to her. He shivered.

"Oh, is that . . . ?"

It was. Whittam Jardine had been laid out in state, as all Chancellors were, before being given an elaborate funeral. All except Zelston, because the body had been too much of a mess by the time Luke's gun was through with it. And now that there was no House of Light any longer, the corpse had been laid on a low stretch of unbroken wall.

But Silyen wasn't looking at his father's body. He was gripping the railings and staring intently through into the brightness.

Here was the shining, golden power of the Equals. Luke's skin would never not prickle at the sight of it. Bleeding from Jackson. Swirling around Silyen and King Rædwald. Had it spilled like blood in the death throes of the House of Light?

Sil was gripping the railings so tightly his fingers were bone white, and when he turned, Luke recoiled. His eyes shone pure gold, like the owl eyes of Rædwald.

"Just what do you think you're—oh!"

A hand grabbed Luke and spun him around. A Security man stood there, a gun strapped across his chest. But he let go of Luke pretty damn fast when he caught sight of Silyen's face.

"I am Lord Silyen Jardine of Far Carr, and I have come to pay my last respects to my father." Sil's voice could have frozen the Thames.

You could see the Security man practically shrink before him. "Ah, come with me. Yes. Your brother's child came in only ten minutes ago. Very well-behaved little girl, a credit to her nanny, though she's on the young side herself. Family summit, yes? My condolences."

Libby Jardine? Libby's young nanny?

Fear squeezed Luke's heart with its cold fingers. Daisy was here. And suddenly the stakes rose again.

They'd come to London simply to find the cause of Silyen's Skillful pain. Now they'd found it—and had been thrust into the middle of a national crisis. The situation had escalated almost unimaginably. What had Sil been planning, those hours he'd spent brooding in the car? Luke had assumed that he was here to be some kind of voice of reason. To help secure his eldest brother's release and to look after his mother.

He'd always made a show of disinterest in politics—of laughing at Gavar's paranoia that he'd maneuvered himself into the House of Light to leapfrog him in their father's favor. But this was turning deadly serious. Crovan was here. Libby Jardine was here. What was being planned?

And did Silyen intend to bring peace—or seize power?

Well, Luke had his sister to worry about now. And if he could do the right thing by Gavar—who had rescued Abi and kept Daisy safe while Britain melted down around them—he would, whatever Sil was up to.

The Security man led the pair of them to the main gate.

"It's your sister-in-law's office you'll be heading for, right?"

"Where they took my niece, yes."

"We'll need to alert Heir Bouda's staff," the Security man told his colleague, running a scanning wand over the pair of them to make sure they weren't concealing any weapons. The other officer nodded and pressed her radio.

"Calling for Chief Kessler, repeat, Kessler. We have Silyen Jardine plus one incoming for Heir Matravers's office."

The radio rasped and crackled.

Kessler.

Well, bloody hell. It was going to be a complete reunion, wasn't it?

Luke looked at Silyen. Could he really trust him? Things had . . . changed between them in the past weeks. Changed in ways Luke couldn't put his finger on. Silyen was the same brittle, brilliant, and astoundingly selfish person he'd always been. But Luke thought he'd found some humanity beneath it all as well.

He'd better hope so, because he might need this boy more than he'd ever needed Jackson or Renie or his friends in Millmoor.

"Out of range? Okay. Well, someone from Public Safety,

then," the Security woman said. There was more buzzing from the radio. "Right. We're sending them in now."

"You know the way?" the first officer said. "Staircase Four on the Great Quad. They're all in there. Someone from Heir Bouda's staff will let you in, then Chief Kessler will take you through to where your family are."

Silyen nodded and strode ahead. Luke hurried after him.

"My sister Daisy," he said.

"I realized. And Kessler? He's that bastard from Millmoor who . . . ?"

Luke nodded.

"And my brother," Silyen said. "What a mess." He ran his hands through his hair.

"And Gavar's little girl," Luke said. "I want them all safe. That's what we're going to do, right?"

Silyen's mouth twitched. His eerie golden eyes had thankfully faded to black, but they gleamed all the same with something nameless and terrifying.

"Have you forgotten so quickly, Luke? You don't get to save everybody."

A staffer met them at the staircase entrance and took them into the corridor. On the right, slightly ajar, was an elegant oak door that a shiny brass plaque proclaimed as the entrance to the Office of Public Safety. But the woman led them past it to a door at the far end.

"They're in Astrid Halfdan's suite downstairs," she said, using a fob to buzz them into a small, sparsely furnished waiting area. The only other exit was a metal door on the far side, with a touch keypad beside it. "Heir Bouda's head of Personal Security, Chief Kessler, escorts everyone through personally. Wait here and he'll collect you. He'll know you're here."

She pointed up to a pair of CCTV cameras on either side of the room, then turned on her heel and left. It was only once the door shut behind her that Luke saw there was no means of opening it from the inside, no handle or lock, except the smooth square where the fob touched.

"I don't know about you," Silyen said, "but I get terribly bored just waiting around."

He went over to the keypad. Luke remembered how he had reached for the padlock on Dog's cage in the Kyneston kennels and simply plucked it off, so he wasn't remotely surprised when, just a few moments later, the door popped open with a series of clicks as the bolts drew back.

Somewhere in there was his little sister and Gavar's tiny daughter. What a nightmare. Luke pushed the door open and recoiled as the stench of hot, fresh blood washed over him. The corridor was dimly illuminated by strips of emergency lighting. There was enough light, though, to make out the body on the floor.

Luke squatted and rolled it over.

TWENTY-SEVEN

ABI

What Abi had realized, the moment Gavar brought them over the threshold of Aston House, was that Daisy was here with Libby.

She was overjoyed at the thought of being reunited with her little sis—but hard on its heels came a sick sorrow that she might have to break it to her that Dad was dead. Could Daisy cope with that, on top of everything else? Could Abi? It might be better simply to say nothing for a while.

But once Gavar and his mother had left to go back to parliament, Abi went to find the nursery, and the look on Daisy's face as she pushed open the door told her everything she needed to know. Her sister had heard about Fullthorpe. And as they cried and clung to each other, Abi could at least give assurances that yes, Mum was safe.

And Luke? Neither of them had any news there.

Abi took her sister and little Libby through to the salon,

where those whom Gavar had led from Parliament Square were
gathered. Perhaps Layla could play with Libby, and that might
distract the poor woman for a little while. Speaker Dawson was
pacing up and down, a phone clutched tight in her hand. She'd
been trying to call Jon.

He hadn't come with them, but had remained on the platform with Bouda as she said her piece. It was a terrible risk, but
Abi saw the logic. Bouda was talking about listening to the
common people. Perhaps Jon imagined that she would finally
heed his words.

And yet, even more than she worried for Jon, Abi feared for
Gavar. She shouldn't care what happened to him now. In fact,
she should hate him. He'd helped compromise the Fullthorpe
raid. Yet she didn't believe he'd known her father would be a
casualty—didn't believe he'd known there would be casualties
at all, until that conversation she'd overheard at Lindum. And
she believed that his shooting of his father was at least partly an
atonement for his own mistakes, and in revulsion at the man's
evil.

Maybe Abi was foolish for wanting to think the best of him,
after so much cruelty and compromise. But the day you lost
the ability to hope that people were better than they seemed
was the day your heart hardened to nothing more than a me-
chanical pump.

It had been two hours since Gavar and his mother had left
Aston House to go back to Westminster, and Abi was getting
uneasy. The two Equals had believed that such a public display
of propriety would be the best way to proceed, and they knew
the ways of their world best. But Abi feared they were underestimating Bouda's ruthlessness.

When Renie sidled up and said that she'd just heard on the
TV that Crovan was on his way, Abi knew she had to act.

"I want to go and check on Gavar and Lady Thalia," she told the room. "I know we've all had reason to wonder about his loyalties, but what he did and said this morning was powerful. He's not a good person, but he did the right thing. I'm worried about what Bouda intends. Who'll help me?"

Layla sat motionless, her eyes burning. But Dog came to Abi's side, as did Renie and several others. They went up to the Aston House balcony, from where you could see the emptiness of Whitehall and Parliament Square, the blocked-off road entrances and vans of Security officers.

"We'll have to go in—as them," Dog said. "Security. We managed it this morning."

It would have to be something like that, Abi thought. With Security now crawling all over the place, there'd be no climbing over walls. Straight through the main gate, legitimately, was the only thing that would work.

But how? Even if they had convincing ID and uniforms, the compound would be on maximum alert. They wouldn't let in a random pair of officers for no reason.

What would get them in—without question and without hesitation?

When the answer came to her, Abi felt sick. But it would work.

Libby Jardine.

They would say they'd been instructed to bring her in, then take the little girl to find Gavar and Lady Thalia.

If everything was fine, and Abi was just overreacting, they could safely leave Libby with her grandmother, and hopefully her father. This might even be a wonderful turning point in the little girl's life. Gavar would no longer have to worry about Lord Whittam's rages and threats toward his daughter.

But if Abi's worst fears were correct, and Gavar was being

questioned or even detained, then she and Dog would be in the right place and able to work out a plan of action. If it was something that required Skill, then Lady Thalia could help.

Renie mutinously accepted that she wasn't old enough to pass for Security. But her larcenous skills were definitely required.

"I'm going to need a uniform," Abi said. "The 'plainclothes' excuse won't work for this job, and we won't be able to fast-talk our way in. So, I need you and Dog to get the necessaries—that includes fresh ID for him, too. We won't be able to use the one he has now, because if it's electronically scanned, it'll flag as stolen several days ago. Be as quick as you can—and for goodness' sake make sure he doesn't actually kill anyone. A bit of strategic rendering-unconscious-and-gagging is what we're talking about here."

Renie saluted. Then frowned.

"You really think you gotta do this, don't you? That Gavar's in that much trouble?" the kid asked. "I remember the first time I saw him, great big bastard in his leather coat, makin' us all fall down screaming, his Skill hurt so bad. I can't imagine anyone getting the better of him."

"Fingers crossed we'll find him taking tea and cucumber sandwiches on the terrace with his mother. But if not, yeah, maybe he is in that much trouble. Crovan is never a good sign, you know that."

The kid's face darkened. She knew it.

"You can't use the front gate," Abi told the pair of them. "That's controlled by Skill. But there are other entrances along the boundary: doors in the wall, and a garage door for delivery vehicles. Use those and be as quick as you can."

And they were quick. Abi had barely had time to hunch with Asif over the screen of an illegally networked laptop, to glance

at maps of the parliamentary complex, before the pair were
back—short of breath and triumphant. They burst into the
salon and high-fived each other noisily. Abi thought, wonderingly, of the refugee kids hiding out in the railway arches, and
wondered if Dog was weirdly good with children.

Then she remembered his original crime—the murder of an
entire Equal family, innocent children included—and winced.
He was good, she decided, with people like himself. Those
whom the system should have broken, but hadn't.

"We pulled out all the stops with this one," said Renie,
dumping a woman's Security uniform into her lap. "And no
one's even hurt. Well, not badly."

The kid showed her two sets of ID. In both cases the photographs on the cards were only a loose match: one fair-haired,
youngish woman; one brown-haired, thin-faced man. But Asif
pulled out his laptop. Give him fifteen minutes, he promised,
and he'd be able to alter the photos on the Security database to
a morph of the original plus Abi or Dog. When the gate check-
point scanned the IDs, the images that flashed up on-screen
would look a lot more like them.

"And that's what they'll look at," Renie said. "Jackson always told us that. People trust the tech more than they trust
their own eyes, so you just gotta worry about foolin' the tech."

Dog cocked his head, and Abi listened, too. Chopper blades.
Dog bounded up to the balcony, while Abi changed into the
uniform in a swanky bathroom. The trousers were too short
and too wide, but she belted the jacket tight and hoped the
boots concealed the leg length.

"Crovan," Dog confirmed grimly when she got back.

"Time to go, then. Libby, we're going to see your daddy."

"Me, too," Daisy insisted, standing between her sister and
her small charge. "She'll be scared otherwise."

"I'm not taking you," Abi said. "For goodness' sake. It's too—"

"Too dangerous?" Daisy said, and kept on talking when Abi protested that no, that wasn't what she'd meant. "'Cause if it's too dangerous for me, then I'm surely not letting you take a two-year-old. No way."

"I was going to say 'too complicated,'" Abi said. "I can take Libby in and leave her in there if I have to, with her family. How can I leave you?"

"If Gavar's not in trouble, there's no problem," said Daisy stubbornly. "If he is, someone's gonna need to get her out of there while you do the rescuing. I'll bring her straight back here."

There was no arguing with that, Abi supposed, her heart heavy. One more reason to hope she wasn't making a terrible mistake. She watched as Daisy put a coat on Libby and hooked a toddler-size backpack containing a teddy and some books over her little arms.

"We're ready," Daisy said brightly, as if they were off on a picnic.

Libby Jardine reached trustingly for Daisy's hand and beamed.

It all went flawlessly, though Abi's heart was in her mouth the whole time.

She and Dog escorted Libby and Daisy across from Aston House to the main entrance of Westminster. An officer came and greeted them, asked what they were there for, and was satisfied by Abi's reply. He took their ID to his colleague in a booth, and the woman scanned them, looking up from the screen to check the identity of each of them. Satisfied, she motioned them forward and her colleague ran a scanning wand over Daisy and Libby.

"I've got a magic wand like your daddy, eh?" he said to Libby, making her giggle.

And this, Abi thought, was why Midsummer had been so insistent on doing things peacefully. It wasn't just her protesters she was looking out for. It was the men and women of Security, of the armed forces, who had signed up to protect their country and who never deserved to be collateral. Well, she'd do her utmost to honor that. First, do no harm.

Except when she'd explained the concept to Dog, he'd bared his teeth and laughed. "Then second—if you have to—ignore the first rule."

The female officer was on her radio, which crackled.

"Go to the Great Quad, Staircase Four," she said. "A staffer will take you to Chief Kessler."

"But we're here for Lady Thalia," said Abi. "Surely she's in the Chancellor's suite in the tower?"

"Couldn't say," said the woman. "But Kessler needs to see you first. My colleague will walk you over."

Kessler.

Abi exchanged a quick glance with Dog, hoping to convey her alarm at hearing the name. The four of them followed the officer across the front precinct of parliament toward the Great Quad. Another woman, dressed in office clothes, waited on the steps to one of the staircase doors.

Abi knew where this was. The wing of Bouda's Office of Public Safety. It was where Renie had been held, when she and Gavar had broken the kid out.

They must have Gavar down in Astrid Halfdan's suite.

Her heart rate surged and raced. The one good thing was that she knew the layout of what lay ahead. But that was outnumbered by a legion of bad things. The space was confined, with nowhere to hide. Controlled by doors to which she did not, this time, have a fob. And if it contained Gavar, there was a good chance it also contained Bouda, or Astrid, or possibly Crovan.

Or even all three.

The officer turned back and the woman took them in. They passed Bouda's headquarters on the right. "That's where Daddy's wife works," Daisy whispered to Libby.

With her fob, the woman buzzed them through a door at the end. Abi recognized the sparse waiting room with its molded metal furniture.

"The next door has restricted access. Heir Bouda's head of Personal Security, Chief Kessler, will be with you shortly to take the child through. He can see that you're here."

She pointed out two CCTV cameras in opposite corners of the ceiling, then left. The door clicked and beeped shut behind her.

"Why don't you read to Libby while we wait?" Abi told Daisy. As the pair settled themselves onto chairs, she and Dog looked around them.

"Not good," she said softly. "Beyond that door are the cells and Astrid Halfdan's suite. She's Bouda's in-house torturer."

"This Kessler—Bouda's head of security—he'll have—all the keys we need. And he's a bastard—the kid said."

"Yes, but—" Abi said.

But then the inner door beeped open and Dog was already upon him.

His momentum took the two men back through the door, and Abi grabbed Libby's backpack and ran to wedge it open before it shut. In the dim corridor she heard a wheeze and gurgle.

Dog wouldn't be fooling anyone anymore that he was a normal Security officer, because his face was drenched in gore. In one hand he held a knife—he must have had that stashed some-where. The other hand clamped shut the mouth and nostrils on a broad, meaty face that Abi had last seen puce with fury as Kessler clawed at Renie around a door. The wheezing sound was air passing through Kessler's opened trachea, but it wouldn't save him, because his lungs were drowning in his own blood.

It was horrifying. Every bit as unbearable as seeing Meilyr Tresco die. Except it was Abi's decisions that had led to this death.

Please let it be the last one.

Abi kept Libby and Daisy behind her, shielded from the awful sight, until Kessler's final, sodden breaths had subsided. What should she do with the two girls? Nothing good could be happening to Gavar and his mother if they were being held in here.

Somewhere on Kessler's person would be the fob to open the outer door they'd just come through. Should she tell Daisy to take Libby and flee back to Aston House? But that would alert Security to the fact that their mission had gone rogue. More officers would come and investigate. And the girls might not even make it out. Perhaps they'd be kept at the gate until the officers received further instructions—and who knew what those might be? Could Abi find a place for them to hide in this wing of the quad? Maybe a storage cupboard. She'd tell Libby they were playing hide-and-seek, and lock them safely in.

And yet . . . Abi touched the gun at her hip. Looked at Dog, now stripping Kessler's body of anything useful—a key chain with a fob, a taser.

"You two stay here and keep quiet," she told Daisy, then went to Dog's side.

She took the taser and keys from him, and watched as he helped himself to another gun and snapped off Kessler's radio transmitter. Together they rolled the body over, to conceal the worst of Dog's butchery and the dead man's staring eyes.

Abi returned to where Daisy and Libby waited, and picked up Libby's backpack, letting the door close softly behind them. Leaving it propped open would alert anyone on the outside.

She'd keep the girls with them a little longer, until they knew how things lay on the other side of that door. If Gavar and his mother were simply captives in a cell, they might yet be able to pull this off.

"Don't look," she warned her sister. Then she scooped up Libby, and pressed the little girl's head to her chest as she stepped over Kessler's body.

The corridor was short, and ended in another door. This one wasn't locked, but was heavy and soundproofed. She and Dog looked at each other.

"Stairs down, and then the cells and the interrogation room," she told him, and he nodded.

Abi remembered the horror of that white-tiled room, so like a hospital, but devoted to pain, not healing. She swallowed down her nausea.

"Wait here," she told her sister, then readied and lifted the taser.

She pushed the door open, and Dog went ahead of her down the stairs. The door of Astrid's torture chamber was ajar. The cell doors were all closed. Abi crept around them, and saw in one the unconscious form of Lady Thalia. No Gavar. Which meant there was only one place he would be.

The pair of them flattened themselves against the wall by the partially open door.

"I would like you to try," Bouda was saying. "I'm aware that it's not been successfully attempted, but wouldn't it be good to know it can be done?"

"It would be dangerous," replied a voice. Scottish. Crovan. "Besides, his brother has already tried."

"To transfuse dregs of his own Skill." And Abi knew that voice. Jenner. Still seeking the reward for which he had betrayed her. From the corner of her eye, she saw Dog finger his gun. "This wouldn't be the same. Here, you would be *removing* it from Gavar—we know you can do this—and placing it entirely into me."

"Foolish boy," Crovan sneered. "Do you imagine Skill is like water and can be poured from vessel to vessel? In any event, you are a broken vessel. What Silyen has told me makes that perfectly clear."

Abi shifted to try to see farther into the room.

And saw Gavar, restrained in a chair. He was injured, though not grievously—a split lip, bruising and cuts to his bared chest—but he was limp and unaware. You might almost think him dead, were it not for the shallow rise and fall of his diaphragm. By his side stood a watchful Astrid Halfdan, a hypodermic in her hand.

"I have another suggestion, Arailt," Bouda said. "How about we make a trial of this procedure using someone unSkilled?"

"A commoner?" Abi could hear Crovan's lip curl.

"Not exactly. My friend Mr. Faiers here is the baseborn son of the late Lord Rix. He is the same age and sex as Gavar. Why not attempt it?"

Abi froze.

Jon.

Jon at Bouda's side—and being offered Gavar's Skill? So he had fooled them all along. That was how Bouda had known about the locations of the arson attacks. She must have planned in advance those spectacular demonstrations that had stunned the whole of Britain and were surely already making her a global celebrity. How much had he known and passed along?

Another betrayal. And was this one, like Jenner's, done for the sake of Skill? It certainly sounded like it.

Abi trembled with fury. This awful ability the Equals had. It twisted both those who possessed it and those who did not.

But Jenner was shouting, and Bouda replied scornfully, and when Jenner walked out of the interrogation room and saw Abi, his eyes went wide—

—and Dog's arm was around his neck, twisting, and Abi heard the crunch as it broke.

Dog eased Jenner's lifeless body to the floor and laid it in the shadow along the wall.

That swiftly, it was over.

There would be no last words between them. No recriminations for this boy who had betrayed both Abigail and his own better nature. No chance to offer a final forgiveness that Abi hadn't known, till this instant in which it became impossible, that she wished to give.

Spasms shook her body, and she fought to steady herself. This was no time for shock or grief. They needed a plan and they needed one now. Dog couldn't just lurk outside the door and murder them one by one as they came out.

Or could he?

At any rate, one of the others might come out any second to chase after Jenner. They couldn't risk being caught here like this. Abi laid a finger to her lips and motioned toward the stairs. Dog moved up them soundlessly. Abi didn't disguise the tread of her feet, opened the soundproofed door, and once Dog was through, slammed it shut behind her. Hopefully, they would think that was Jenner, making his exit, so no one would investigate when he didn't return.

Daisy and Libby looked up. Abi had no idea what she could

say to them. She leaned against the wall, her chest heaving, trying to get her thoughts under control.

Crovan. Bouda. Jon. Astrid Halfdan. And Gavar their prisoner and unconscious.

Tasers didn't work on Equals. Dog would be able to shoot one of them, but it would have to be fatal, as he'd only get one shot, and then the others would be alerted. Their protective reflcxes would go up, and they'd be on him in a trice.

Wouldn't the best thing be simply to gather up Libby and Daisy and quietly creep away before they were all discovered and a terrible situation became a tragic one?

She and Dog looked at each other. He would kill and kill and kill, she knew. But there was surely enough of the soldier in him to resist the needless throwing away of life. Wasn't the harder, better thing to do to leave a man behind for the sake of the rest?

And maybe they would merely take Gavar's Skill and let him go—the same punishment given to Meilyr Tresco. It would be shattering, but Meilyr had survived and found purpose in life. Gavar had his little daughter—and she was also Skilless. He'd come through it.

But in her heart of hearts, Abi didn't think Gavar was getting out of that room. He was only alive at this moment so that Crovan could harvest his Skill.

Abi silently offered him an apology. She had tried. The best thing she could do for him now was keep his daughter safe.

She motioned for Daisy and Libby to get to their feet.

Which was when she heard a hiss and crackle from the far end of the passageway. The bolts popped back, and the door opened.

TWENTY-EIGHT

LUKE

The body was Kessler. That brutal bull neck had been slashed so ferociously you could see right into his gaping windpipe.

Whoever had killed him knew what they were about. They'd also stripped him of weapons—apart from a baton, which he presumably still carried for old times' sake. No matter how grand you got, the fancy might take you now and then for a bit of old-fashioned rib-breaking.

Luke could make use of it. Silyen might be *the most Skilled for centuries,* blah blah, but not even he could stop a bullet he couldn't see coming. Someone still needed to watch his back, particularly if there was a killer this effective on the loose.

He was tugging the baton from Kessler's belt when Silyen's boot gave an urgent *tap-tap-tap* against his ribs. Looking up, Luke saw movement at the far end of the corridor. It was too dim to make out who was there, or how many they were—it was definitely two people, maybe more.

He stood up slowly, shielding the Equal.

"Can you see?" he whispered.

"I think . . ." said Silyen. "You won't believe it." And was that honestly a curl of amusement in his voice?

The Equal spun a ball of golden Skill-light in his fingers and released it down the passageway. Luke froze in horror as he heard a small child's laughter, and saw a tiny figure toddle down the corridor toward it.

"My brother does it to amuse her," said Silyen into his ear. "Excuse me while Uncle Silly goes and says hello. And before you freak out, the door down there is soundproofed, and not even two-year-olds scream as loudly as torture victims, so I'd say we're okay."

Luke barely paused to push shut the door they'd come through, because he'd realized that if Libby Jardine was here, then . . .

But where he'd hoped he might find one sister, he found two. Unbelievably, along with Daisy, was Abigail. Luke felt as though his heart would burst. He picked up his little sis and crushed her against Abi as all three of them were reunited for the first time since the fatal Kyneston ball. He decided to test his strength and leaned back to lift Abi off her feet, too. Daisy was having silent hysterics. Luke could feel her little body huffing against his.

Then he heard a noise from Abi, and put her down. She was crying—very, very quietly.

"Your brother," she said to Silyen. "He just . . . came at us. I'm so sorry. Both your brothers."

"What?"

Silyen looked up, shock so plain on his face that Luke wondered how he had ever thought this boy didn't have feelings.

"Jenner's dead," Abi said. "He was with them. They've got

Gavar shackled down there, under some kind of sedation. Bouda told Crovan to take Gavar's Skill, and Jenner asked for it, but Bouda wanted it for someone else instead. The Speaker's son, Jon Faiers. So Jenner stormed out—and surprised us, and . . ."

Abi lost it, and Luke held her as tight as he could while she shook.

"It was quick," rasped a voice. "Reflex."

The only person not currently being reunited with family stepped away from the door where he was leaning. Dog. So Luke had been correct—Dog and Abi had somehow teamed up. Well, that would be a story for another day.

"But you know," the man continued, "I might have done it anyway."

"You animal," said Silyen coldly. "The only one of us that can't fight back."

"None of *us* can fight back—against any of *you*. And if I'm an animal—your family made me one."

There would never be a good time for a conversation like this, but right now definitely wasn't it.

"You say Gavar is in danger," Luke said. "And we've got these two to think about."

He put his hand on his little sister's head. Her hair was soft and tangled as ever, and his need to protect her and Gavar Jardine's kid was overwhelming. To hear that Dog had killed Jenner was unreal and would presumably hit him later. Abi must be in bits—or would be soon. She needed to be out of here, too.

"Tell us quickly what we're facing down there, Abi. And then you need to get this pair away from here."

So she did. And it was bad. Crovan, Bouda, Astrid bloody Halfdan, whom he'd seen pin a man to a table with her dinner knife. Plus some commoner called Jon Faiers, about whom Abi was particularly bitter. And Gavar Jardine, restrained with Astrid standing guard. She'd surely kill him if they gave her a moment's opportunity. Luke's brain raced, trying to find a way through it.

Dog would be able to get in a shot and take one of them down. Probably Astrid, from what Abi had said about the layout of the room. The protective reflexes of the other two would kick in, making normal weapons or attack useless, so it'd be Silyen against the pair of them: the cruelest and the most ruthless Equals in Great Britain. And there'd be nothing Luke could do to help him other than make sure the Faiers bloke wasn't a problem.

But Silyen had been doing some thinking of his own.

"Luke needs a weapon. Give him your knife," he told Dog, jerking a thumb at Luke. "The one you used on that chap back there. It's obviously nice and sharp."

So at least Sil didn't think he'd be useless.

"Didn't you wipe it?" the Equal said as Dog produced the sticky blade from down the side of his boot. "Nasty. Hanky, please, Libby."

Little Libby beamed as she pulled a crumpled white square from her cardigan sleeve and handed it over. Silyen cleaned the blade fastidiously, then passed it to Luke, handle first. The blade was short and thick, yet plainly razor sharp on both sides. It didn't have a proper handle, but notches at intervals down the haft, where it had been sewn into a leather glove. One of the knives from Black Billy's deadly gauntlet.

"Keep it to hand. You'll know when to use it. Now, how about something in exchange?"

Luke narrowed his eyes. You never just agreed to Silyen's bargains.

"A kiss for the hero who's going to save everyone," the Equal said.

And Luke was halfway through laughing at him when Silyen's hand went round the back of his skull and Luke found that he was kissing him instead. It was . . . startling. It was absolutely mortifying.

It was quite possibly the best thing ever.

He felt dizzy, and reached out to steady himself, one hand on Silyen's shoulder, the other on the Equal's hip, pulling him closer. Something coiled and fizzed inside his chest that had nothing to do with Skill. He heard himself groan and felt Silyen smile against his mouth.

Luke was having none of it. The boy should be busy kissing, not smirking. He angled forward hungrily, and heard a squeak that could have been either one of his sisters. Luke felt himself flush bright red, but couldn't care less.

Silyen's hand was at his neck, gripping possessively. Through his giddiness, Luke realized that the boy was pressing his thumb insistently in one spot, just below and behind his ear. Luke's pulse was hammering, and its beat was almost painful beneath Silyen's fingers.

Then Silyen whispered something. Just a few words. That wicked tongue gave a parting lick around the curl of his ear, and the Equal leaned back. Luke stood there, dazed and reeling.

"That's a good look," Silyen said with satisfaction, "if I say so myself."

Abi looked almost as stunned as Luke felt. He wiped his mouth with the back of his hand, not quite sure what had just happened. He glanced at Daisy to make sure she wasn't too traumatized. She gave him two thumbs up.

Yeah. He'd kissed Silyen Jardine and it was brilliant. That was what had happened.

Then Silyen's whispered words came back to him. They had been instructions. The Equal's kiss had left him trembling, but those words made Luke sag against the wall for support.

Had Sil been serious? He shot him a look, but the boy was as inscrutable as ever.

"Now I know," Dog said, "what you two were doing—on all those 'walks.' "

He gave his horrible wheeze.

That was quite enough. Luke straightened up. Anything could be happening to Gavar down there. Silyen didn't think Crovan knew how to take or transfer Skill, only how to destroy it, but why even give him the opportunity to try?

"Let's get on with it," he said.

Abi nodded. "I'll get these two out safely. That's our most important task, and it's my job, because I brought them here. We'll be back at Aston House. Join us there afterward—that's an order. Lady Thalia is in one of the cells downstairs. She looks okay, but she's out cold, too."

Abi picked up Libby's bag and marshaled the two girls.

"Stay safe, big bro." Daisy snaked her arms round Luke's neck and planted a wet smacker on his cheek, then whispered, "Sorry I don't kiss as well as him."

Luke reddened to his scalp and gave his sis a not-so-gentle shove along the corridor. Libby Jardine waved a small hand. Luke hoped to goodness she wasn't scarred by any of this. She seemed to be taking it in her stride. He wondered what she'd seen in her few years to be this unfazed.

"Don't look at the sleeping man, or it might wake him up," he heard Daisy instruct Libby, as she steered the little girl around Kessler's body.

"What's the plan?" rasped Dog.

Luke knew what the plan was. His palms sweated.

"The plan is that we go down there," said Silyen, "I'll unlock my mother's cell, then Luke and I will enter the room where they have my brother and cause a distraction. During it, I will incapacitate the Equals. You remain outside until it's clear I've been successful. Then you'll need to strip them of any weapons or other means of doing harm—search Astrid very carefully—and take care of the commoner."

" 'Take care of'?"

"Try not to kill him, but apart from that . . ." Silyen shrugged. "Now, you still owe me two debts: a life, and an escape. The life: I give you *one* of the Equals—not my mother or Gavar, obviously. You can't have them all, because people are going to need someone to blame when all this is done, and the living make better targets than the dead."

Dog nodded, his expression exultant and ferocious. "Crovan, of course. The escape?"

Silyen leaned forward and whispered in the man's ear. And if that wasn't him all over, Luke didn't know what was. Sil was the only one who knew exactly what their plans were. Luke and Dog each had only half the picture.

Luke knew what he'd been tasked with. And it felt more impossible than pulling a door to another dimension out of thin air.

What would happen if he did it?

What would happen if he didn't?

"Shall we?" said the Equal.

Silyen threw open the soundproof door and gave a small bow as Dog went through. As Luke passed, Sil reached out and brushed his fingers lightly across his jaw. Luke had seen Abi touch, in the same way, things in shops that she coveted but was unable to afford. It made him feel like he was worth more than every precious thing in Kyneston.

He started trembling again. Those too-clever fingers of Silyen Jardine's. Who the hell knew that one human being could do this to another just with a touch?

He hurried down the stairs, as far away from the boy as he could manage. This was going to be hard enough as it was. In fact, Luke was terrified that he would find it impossible.

He stopped short at the bottom. Lying against the wall, head lolling at an ungainly angle as if drunk and sleeping it off, was Jenner Jardine. Luke moved to let Silyen pass. The boy crouched next to his middle brother, brushing the floppy bronze hair back from his freckled face. He closed his brother's eyes, then ran a finger down the line of his strong nose. He stooped to kiss his brother's forehead.

Luke ached just watching him. If it had been Abi or Daisy lying there, Luke didn't know what he would have done.

Abi had told them which cell Lady Thalia was in—thankfully one away from the sight line of the main door. No sound emerged from the interrogation suite, though the air was heavy with static that Luke knew meant the working of Skill. So he was relieved when the door to Lady Thalia's cell popped open noiselessly. Silyen went in, and Luke saw him bend over his mother's motionless form.

His father dead, his brother dead. His mother and older brother captive and drugged. Silyen was the last Jardine standing.

For how much longer?

After a few moments, Silyen emerged again. He nodded at Dog, as if to remind him of his promises, then squared back his narrow shoulders and took a breath.

"I'm telling you, Crovan hasn't the faintest idea what he's doing," he said loudly, walking into the interrogation chamber.

Luke's heart lurched like he'd just taken Kessler's taser direct to his sternum. He wiped his hands down his trousers, touched the knife in his pocket, and followed Silyen in.

It was even worse than he'd imagined—like they'd interrupted some creepy sacrificial rite. Gavar was bound to a chair that looked like something you'd find in a dentist's or hospital. Clinical. Designed to give someone else access to your body. The heir's hands were cuffed behind his back, his legs were bound at each ankle to the chair legs, and around his neck a restraint kept his head partially upright against a headrest, though his chin lolled. His eyes were open but unseeing, and the corner of his mouth gleamed with spittle.

It gleamed gold, because a pale, glittering miasma hung about him. There were cuts and grazes to his face, and visible on his chest where his shirt had been ripped open. Those, too, bled gold. His unseeing eyes were limned in gold, like a pharaoh's, where Skill was pooling, ready to spill out.

If Silyen was as sickened by the sight as Luke was—how could he not be, this was his brother?—he concealed it well. He walked over to the chair and inspected Gavar, wiping the drool from his mouth with a finger and cleaning it off on the ripped shirt. Gavar swung his head and gave a low, distressed moan.

The Equal tutted.

"Silyen," Bouda said, keeping her voice level. "Your company is unexpected."

"You know me, Bouda. Always interested in promising research. I wasn't there for Meilyr Tresco, of course, so I'm fascinated to see the process. Astrid. Arailt." He nodded genially, as if bumping into the pair of them at a cocktail party, then frowned at the fifth person in the room. "I don't think we've met? I'm Silyen Jardine."

"Jon Faiers," said the man. He was smooth and silky-looking, this guy Abi was so furious about. As Gavar groaned behind them, the pair shook hands.

"Your . . . friend?" Bouda said, those blue eyes so like her sister's turning on Luke. And that feeling was back, of being a mouse beneath the claws of these people. Luke fought it down.

"I'm sure you all remember me," he said with bravado, smiling round the room.

"Zelston's killer. I thought you were at Eilean Dòchais," said Astrid.

"Oh, I have him on a kind of extended loan from Arailt here. He's a rewarding experimental subject. Aren't you, Luke? Very rewarding."

He reached out and pinched Luke's cheek, a mocking, proprietorial gesture. Luke stared at the floor, his face burning. His hand went to his pocket. Yep, the blade was still there.

"So, Jenner was telling me—I just met him on his way out and he seemed awfully upset about something—he was saying that you're going to try and transfer my brother's Skill to Mr. Faiers here. Of course, as the heir of his late father, Lord Rix, I'm not entirely sure how I feel about that. Might it give you a claim on the estate, Jonathan? Though I have to tell you, Far Carr is a damp old place and pretty dull. I'm sure we could work something out like gentlemen."

They were all still looking at Silyen like he was speaking another language. It took a brittle laugh from Astrid Halfdan to break the tension.

"Strangest of a strange family, you are. Funny, how your father always preached about the Jardines, the bloodline, the Founding Family. And yet you've all turned on each other, one by one."

"Family," said Silyen. "Such a quaint notion. Well, shall we?

It's not every day you get to see history being made. And if I can contribute anything to the proceedings, I will."

Luke knew exactly what Silyen planned to contribute to this little gathering. As the boy gestured toward Crovan, Luke's hand found the knife and gripped it. *You'll know when,* had been three of the words Silyen had whispered in his ear.

When was looking a lot like *now*.

Crovan frowned and made a taut gesture in the air. Gavar howled. The assembled Equals in the room watched as the golden miasma around Gavar Jardine pulsed. A single molten tear spilled from the man's eye and ran down his cheek. That broad, muscled chest heaved with exertion, as if in a tug-of-war with an opponent too strong to defeat.

Luke whipped out the knife and jammed it up into Silyen's skull, right behind the ear.

There, Silyen had breathed, as his thumb rubbed Luke's throbbing pulse. *Up and deep. You'll know when.*

Silyen dropped to the floor, already dead. Luke had sunk the knife to the hilt, and not only had it severed the boy's carotid artery, several inches had driven into his brain.

Blood fountained everywhere. More blood than you'd think someone as pale as Silyen could contain. It sprayed all over Luke, startlingly hot.

Luke began to shake. He loosed his fingers from around the knife and tossed it to the floor. He felt dizzy.

Someone was screaming. Bouda Matravers?

Luke dropped to his knees. Crovan had turned his head to regard him quizzically. The round lenses of his glasses were once again golden discs, as they had been when the chopper first angled over Eilean Dòchais at dawn. Death offerings for a journey to the next world, Luke had thought then.

Wouldn't that be nice. Was there a next world? Was there really any other world than this?

Luke's brain felt fuzzy and a pain had begun to gnaw at his gut. He looked down, expecting to see a bright golden thread leading from him to Silyen Jardine, but of course there was nothing. Maybe its absence was the pain? Silyen Jardine was dead and the wide pool of his blood was already soaking through Luke's trousers. Luke plucked feebly at his T-shirt, to lift it and check, but the task was too complicated for his clumsy fingers.

Someone stood over him. Black trousers. Black hair. Astrid Halfdan.

She backhanded Luke across the face, sending him sprawling to the floor.

Then howled and dropped to a crouch, both hands clutching her head.

Luke twisted his neck. His eyes were clouding over—or was the golden mist in here thickening?

"Bouda," someone was saying urgently. A man. Luke couldn't remember his name. "Bouda!"

A gunshot rang out. The man screamed and crumpled to the floor, clutching his knee. He sobbed and wailed and whimpered. Luke had never heard someone make so much noise.

Then Dog was there, standing over the man, with the gun in his hand. He angled the gun down at his other knee, and fired again. The man cried out, then fell silent.

Dog crouched next to Luke, laying the gun down.

"You okay?" he rasped. "Hang on in there. You two—did great. Watch. You'll like this."

Dog lifted Luke's head gently and turned it, so that it lay facing the other way. Luke felt Silyen's blood trickle down from the already soaked side of his face. It tickled his nostrils, and ran in rivulets into his eyes and along the seam of his mouth. He parted his lips and licked them. He was glad that he had kissed Silyen Jardine before he had killed him, though in the fog that was clouding his brain he was no longer sure why he'd done either.

It wasn't like Rix and Zelston, though. No one had made him drive a knife into Silyen's skull.

He'd chosen to do it. There had been a reason. A good one. But the pain in his abdomen was growing worse and it was all too hard to think about.

Dog was sitting on the chest of the man on Luke's right—a man who wore glasses. Crovan? He was struggling weakly, but Dog's legs pinned his arms to his side. Dog raised a knee and released one of them. It fluttered in the air and Dog caught the hand like a bird. With surprising delicacy, he snapped the little finger. Then the next. Then the next. It shouldn't have been possible. The man's Skillful reflexes ought to have protected him. But Silyen had done something, or Luke had—or maybe both of them—and now it was possible.

When Dog was finished, he let the broken-winged hand drop to the ground, released the man's other arm, and repeated his actions.

You'll like this, Dog had promised. But Luke didn't. He didn't like any of this. Why was power always about inflicting pain? Couldn't it be different?

Something was coiling up from Crovan's chest. A thick, bright vortex of golden light. It spiraled upward, then arched back down again, falling somewhere close by that Luke couldn't see. It didn't seem to bother Dog, who plucked the man's glasses off and pressed downward with both his thumbs. Crovan screeched and his heels drummed the floor.

Luke closed his eyes. He didn't need to see this.

Silyen's blood was cooling, and the pain in Luke's gut was almost unbearable, as if something inside it was being stretched to its utmost limit. Would it snap?

He held a hand to his stomach and moaned.

The golden haze was thickening up. It was as bright as if the room was burning. There'd been a fire on the beach at Far Carr. Luke could almost smell the woodsmoke and the sea. He and Sil had sat, knees touching, and on the other side of the fire had been a king.

And inside the flames was a door.

Luke opened both eyes and stared into coruscating brilliance all around him. If he looked long enough, he might see a door opening.

He stared.

And stared.

But there was no door.

The light was too bright to bear now, so he closed his eyes again and lay there. He wasn't sure for how long. Then arms were under his shoulders and beneath his knees and someone was lifting him. The last thing Luke heard before he blacked out was Dog's rasping voice.

"Come on. Time for that escape—I promised."

TWENTY-NINE

BOUDA

It had been a week, and still they had said nothing about it. Not publicly. Not formally. It wasn't as though the common people had been used to seeing Equals using Skill anyway.

And there were many forms of power. Wealth. Capital. Land. Inherited advantage, from the schools open only to Equals, to their superior beauty and intelligence, cultivated through generations of dynastic marriage.

All that power still belonged to the Equals.

And it was all trash compared with what they had lost.

Bouda drew her sister's cashmere robe around her—she'd had a servant dig out the garment, because it really was cold up here—and looked down from the tower window of the Chancellor's suite.

Where the House of Light had once stood was now just rubble and ruin. She'd watched it fall, after Midsummer woke her dragons, and hadn't believed the woman's audacity. *I gave you your targets,* she'd wanted to scream at her. *Office skyscrapers. Embassies. Weren't those enough?*

They hadn't been enough. More than a building, Midsummer had wanted to destroy a symbol.

But had she destroyed Skill?

Was the fall of the House of Light what had ripped the Skill out of Bouda, and every Equal in the realm? If so, why hadn't it happened in that instant? Instead, a golden cloud had settled over the ruins. The House had gone, but not—at that moment— the Skill.

Perhaps it had been Crovan's attempt to strip Skill from Gavar? Maybe that act had been somehow fatally amplified by the Skillful residue of the ruined House.

Or could it, somehow, have been the work of Silyen Jardine? But that made no sense. Silyen had lived for Skill. Its destruction would have been the last thing he wanted. Just as well that he was dead now.

The commoner boy, then? The terrorist. He'd knifed Silyen just as pitilessly as he had gunned down Zelston—and that had been the moment when Bouda had felt it. Had felt something tug inside her. What had followed was so horrifying she could hardly bear to examine it.

It was as if a thread had been pulled out of her, and everything that she was had unraveled inside as the bright thread unspooled. And when it was all gone, she was simply a Bouda-shaped bag, shaken out and emptied. That bag was what she walked about in now, secretly astonished that it didn't just crumple around its own unbearable hollowness.

Had the commoner boy known that such a deed would bring such a result? If so, *how* had he known?

And where was he? He had disappeared, along with the man whose Security uniform had initially prevented her from rec-

ognizing him as Hypatia's dog. The way the animal had muti-
lated Crovan was unspeakable.

Bouda would have begged a Quiet from Astrid to hide the
memory. But neither Astrid nor anyone else in Britain would
be able to perform a Quiet now, or ever again.

The current official line was that the shocking destruction of
the House of Light had rendered Skillful abilities "temporarily
erratic." It wasn't just British Equals that were panicking.
Skilled foreigners in the country when it happened had been
similarly affected: envoys from Japan and the Confederate
States. International students at Britain's celebrated Equal-only
boarding schools, and the two Oxbridge colleges. All were
being told to remain calm while the disturbance was "resolved."

It would never be resolved. Bouda felt as if every last trace of
Skill had been painstakingly scraped out of her, like flesh off
the back of an animal hide. The others surely felt the same. It
was never coming back.

She understood now why Meilyr Tresco had fought Crovan
so desperately. How Jenner Jardine must have felt all those
years. His body had been found outside the interrogation room,
his neck broken. The only mystery was how he had managed to
resist killing himself years before.

Bouda didn't want to die. But she wondered what she had to
live for. She had pursued political power her whole life, until
she had finally discovered something even more astonishing—
the surging brilliance of her Skill. And no sooner had she found
it than she had lost it.

She went to the wall of portraits—that unbroken line of
Chancellors. So many Jardines. The occasional Rix or Esterby
or Occold. She touched the gilded frame around beautiful
Aristide Jardine, the Harrower of Princes.

Had he thought that this was all there was? The climb, and

the Chancellor's Chair, and your face on a wall? Slowly and deliberately she pushed a sharp fingernail through one corner of the canvas and watched it tear. That was what political power was. A magnificent facade, stretched thin over nothing at all.

She walked along the line to the very end. Two more would need to be added: Zelston and Whittam.

Perhaps a third. A Last Chancellor, just as there had been a Last King.

At the knock on the door, she turned.

"Come in," she called, though there was no force to her words beyond mere permission. There would be no more conversations behind Skillfully sealed doors.

It was Rebecca Dawson, the Speaker. The pair of them stood awkwardly, facing each other. When Dawson extended her hand, Bouda shook it.

"The others are on their way," Dawson said.

"My people, too." She poured the woman a glass of water from the carafe that stood where Whittam's whisky decanter had once been. "Shall we?"

There were eight chairs around the oval dining table in the suite. Bouda considered sitting at one end, with Dawson at the other, but changed her mind and took a seat in the center. Dawson sat opposite.

"Your son?" Bouda asked. She had visited Faiers in hospital, but only briefly, and on both occasions he had been unconscious. Medicated to the eyeballs to deal with the pain. Once, a simple touch from Bouda could have eased that—and even if healing shattered kneecaps wasn't something she could be confident of performing, she would have had a go. As it was, he'd need weeks in hospital, and months of physiotherapy if he was to walk again. The same few minutes that had stolen Bouda's

Skill had robbed Faiers, too. He'd also lost an ability that had once been as natural as breathing.

Dawson gave her an update.

"You genuinely care for him?" the woman said, when she was finished. "I always knew he admired you—far too much for me to approve of, but . . ."

Bouda didn't think she could care about anyone or anything ever again, but she nodded.

"He believed in me."

More knocks at the door, and one by one they arrived. Bouda's team: Daddy; the Elder of the House, Hengist Occold; and Lord Esterby.

Not Astrid. Bouda had sent her to Eilean Dòchais to establish if the castle's wards were still operational (they weren't), and to impose order before the Condemned realized they could now just walk out of their prison.

Dawson's team: a woman named Emily, who had been an activist at Exton slavetown; a pleasant-faced man named Bhadveer, from Portisbury—and Armeria Tresco. No surprise there. Bouda and Dawson directed them to sit in alternate seats around the table, so there was no sense of one side facing another.

"Our Skill has gone," Armeria said, in her usual forthright way. "What you did to my son, to punish him, has somehow fallen on all of us. And don't give me that nonsense about it being erratic, or a disturbance. Meilyr said it was like a hole inside him that the wind blew through. That's how we all feel, yes?"

Bouda nodded. There was no point denying it.

"We'll have to be straight about it sooner or later," she said. "But we need to acknowledge the risks of such an announcement. . . ."

"Risks to you Equals," said Emily. "Not to the rest of us."

"*Yes,* to the rest of you," Bouda said. "For centuries, our country's governance—our whole way of life—has been based on the slavedays. And the foundation of the Slavedays Compact is quite clear: labor given in exchange for Skillful protection. Now there is no Skill, there is no longer any basis for the slavedays."

At her side, she heard Daddy exhale.

"Words I never imagined hearing from *you,*" said Armeria.

"Simple fact," Bouda said. "While our class possessed Skill, we were superior, and the slavedays was a rational and effective expression of that superiority. We still are superior, of course, but not in the same way or to the same degree, and so the nation needs to be reordered to reflect that."

"Still not admitting that you were wrong? That the slavedays are cruel and inhumane?"

Such useless words. What was right or wrong? Only thinking made it so.

"If my sister were still alive, Armeria, she'd be sitting here saying the same as you. Your son, too. That was what they believed. I believe differently: my assessments are based on logic, not sentiment. Speaker Dawson's son, Mr. Faiers, works for me. And for some time we have been discussing ways in which the system might be improved. Now I see that those improvements need to go further. That wholesale reform is needed."

"Reform?" Bhadveer sat forward. "When something is as broken as the government of your people, it cannot be reformed. It can only be scrapped and remade."

"Let me be clear," Bouda said, pressing her fingertips against the polished wood of the tabletop. "This *is* a remaking. I am proposing democracy: direct elections. I am proposing the abolition of the slavedays. But transition is needed if we are to keep our country strong and maintain our place in the world.

Some changes can begin right away. We will act upon slave-town conditions immediately, for example."

"How kind," said Emily, unappeased. "Vague promises of elections, improvements. We could put your entire class on trial for crimes against humanity—do you realize that? Many countries in the international community would support such a move."

"And many would not," snapped Esterby. "Japan and our Confederate cousins, for a start."

"You think they'll care about you now?" scoffed Bhadveer. "You are their worst nightmare. A country where—poof!—Skill just disappeared in an instant."

"Enough." It was Dawson. "Miss Matravers is correct. She's made us a big offer here. The two things we want most: abolition and the vote. The rest will take time, if the country is not to collapse into anarchy and economic ruin."

"Time for them to find a cure for this loss of Skill," said Emily.

Armeria Tresco reached over and laid a hand on the woman's arm.

"I saw it with my son," she said softly. "There is no cure."

"Let's hear what you're proposing, Bouda."

Dawson sat back in her seat, and Bouda saw in her qualities that she recognized in herself: a love of country, a fierce defense of her own class—and a yearning for power that circumstances had long denied her.

Perhaps she and this woman could talk.

Perhaps things need not change so very much.

Bouda pulled her folder toward her and opened it.

"This is my proposal," she said.

★ ★ ★

It was late afternoon by the time Bouda made her way to the small, subterranean chamber where Whittam's body was being kept after his lying-in-state. Equal bodies now decayed as fast as normal ones, so he had been removed here, to what had been a former cold-storage room for the parliamentary complex, before electricity.

The corpse was being prepared for dispatch to Kyneston. The funeral was tomorrow. But Bouda wouldn't be going.

She circled the body where it lay, all those old feelings swirling through her: admiration, resentment, fear, and a longing not for who he was, but for what he represented.

"It's just as well you never lived to see it," she told him. "It would have finished you off. Gavar took you just a few hours early, nothing more."

A wig had been placed over Whittam's blasted scalp. The handkerchief that had covered it had been cleaned, and was tucked into his top breast pocket. Bouda tugged it out and crumpled it in her fist, suddenly overcome with emotions to which she couldn't put a name. Tears were hot on her face.

"I'm the Last Chancellor," she said. "They're giving me five years, and I'll work alongside an elected cabinet to transition the country. My picture will hang next to yours on that wall. A woman among you all, at last.

"After that, everything changes. There'll be a Prime Minister, or a President, or something. It might even be one of us. Who knows. Old habits die hard, and while they'll take Daddy's factories, I won't let them take our estates. We'll still be the elite, we'll just have to adapt. You always said a confident politician never compromises. Well, I guess that's one more thing you were wrong about."

"Heir Bouda?"

She turned. It was a minor functionary in the Office of Ceremony, the third son of an obscure lord. She imagined he spent most of the time polishing the trumpets that heralded the Chancellor's approach. They would sound one final time, for her installation.

"What should we do with this?" The man tipped up a section of wooden board from where it had been leaning against the wall. "It's the only bit that survived the destruction of the House. We laid Chancellor Jardine out on it, but should we send it to Kyneston?"

As he angled the wood, Bouda saw what it was. The carved back of the Chancellor's Chair. The old throne of kings and queens. It had outlasted the monarchy, and now it had outlasted the Equals.

Her fingers traced the carvings upon it. Age had rendered them dark and smooth, and the wood was freshly pockmarked, where flying masonry and debris had struck the chair as the House fell. But she could make out fanciful images. A dragon. A crowned man. A winged woman holding a sword. A sun surrounded by stars. Wavy lines that could have been water, or could have been something else entirely. Nonsensical pictures from a more primitive time.

Was that how history would remember the rule of the Equals?

"It's of no use," she said. "Burn it."

EPILOGUE

ABI

Abi held Daisy's hand, and Daisy held Libby's as they watched the three bodies being carried out of the great house, each draped in scarlet-and-gold cloth. On Libby's other side was Gavar, his mother on his arm. A black net veil was pulled down over her face, this woman who had lost her sister Euterpe, and now her husband and two sons.

As they stood on the high curve of the hill, Gavar bent low to answer his daughter's curious chatter.

Abi had never imagined she'd be back at Kyneston. She'd worried about coming at first—fearful it would drag up bad memories and trigger an anxiety attack. But she was glad Daisy and Griff had persuaded her. The old woman had stayed at home. She didn't want to see young men she'd known as babies put into the ground, she'd said. And besides, someone needed to keep watch over Luke. Although unharmed, Abi's brother hadn't regained consciousness since Dog had carried him out of

Astrid's basement, and he now lay sleeping in a room at Griff's cottage.

Abi breathed in the warm summer air. It was good to be out of the house, and she drank in the sight of open parkland, the lake sparkling in the sunshine, and the loud cooing of wood pigeons from the trees. The water was the only thing about Kyneston that glittered now. The coruscations of Skill were gone from the house's great glass wings. Its boundary wall possessed merely the warm, dull patina of aged brick. The gate was now just a perpetually visible arch of intricate ironwork.

Skill had died in Britain when the House of Light fell.

That had been a week ago. Midsummer Zelston hadn't lived to know it, but the change she had fought for was coming.

It had to.

The Equals still weren't admitting it—though reports promised a "joint statement" from Bouda and Speaker Dawson on Monday—but the disappearance of Skill was unignorable. One of the first clues had been when a helicopter of holidaymakers bound for the Scillies had seen an entire island shimmer into existence beneath them, topped with an extravagantly spired and turreted castle. Their blurrily snapped pictures of Highwithel had gone worldwide.

Abi liked to imagine Renie on the castle's summit, flipping the bird at the tourists as they flew by. She and the club had taken refuge there with the Trescos. Layla and the men of the Bore had gone to Lindum.

No one knew where Dog was.

Abi had seen the moment it all changed. She had led Daisy and Libby out of the main gates of parliament without challenge from the Security officers, and they were almost across Parliament Square when it happened: a soundless, near-blinding explosion of light.

They'd turned back to look, Abi shielding Libby's eyes. In place of the pulsing golden cloud above the House of Light swirled an incandescent vortex. Then in an instant, soundlessly, the light funneled down into the ground and disappeared.

Not knowing what it had meant, still desperately anxious about the safety of Luke, Gavar, Dog—and, yes, Silyen—Abi had hastily scooped up Libby. She'd urged Daisy to follow, and run to Aston House. She'd headed for one of the back gates but had noticed, as they passed, that the flames and fiery salamanders that had adorned the front gate had been extinguished.

They never burned again.

From where she stood now, on Kyneston's hill, Abi could make out the marble salamander curled on top of the Jardine family mausoleum, granite flames licking about it. Beneath, along the lintel of the Roman-style structure, was the Parva motto: *Uro, non luceo.* "I burn, not shine." The front of the mausoleum was a pillared portico, and the Jardine motto was carved within, above the heavy bronze door: *Sapere aude.* "Dare to know."

But what was there to know after you'd been carried inside? Abi thought. There was nothing to learn in there. Death held no last, great secret.

The three biers were closer now, the bearers trudging slowly toward them. Gavar led his mother away from the group of mourners, up to the mausoleum gates.

Abi watched the small procession. The first body was a man she had been prepared to kill, if she had to. She had realized something important in that moment: that sometimes the best thing isn't always the good thing. In the end, Gavar's bullet had felled his father. But Abi had given Dog the order, and felt as changed by that as if she had shot Whittam Jardine herself.

She wasn't sorry.

About the second body, she was more sorry than she could ever say.

What she'd felt for Jenner hadn't been love—she knew that now. But it had been something that had felt bewilderingly, beautifully, deceptively like it. And though it had ended in horror and betrayal, she had learned something from Jenner, too. That loving someone didn't mean you could save them. And that you didn't save yourself simply by the act of loving.

It was a cruel irony that he had not lived to see a world in which he would, finally, have been the equal of his now-Skilless peers. Abi made no attempt to stop the tears that welled in her eyes as his body passed. Their sting was somehow cleansing. Abi forgave him, and forgave herself.

The third body, she almost didn't believe. But she'd seen Silyen's pale, cold face when the three Jardines had been laid out in Kyneston's great hall for mourners to pay their respects.

No one knew exactly what had happened in that basement room of Astrid's. In the chaotic hour that followed that explosion of light, Security had ventured into the interrogation suite—and found a scene of carnage. None of those who survived had spoken of what happened. Maybe Luke would tell her, one day.

Much though she longed for her brother to wake up, Abi dreaded what she would have to tell him. He still didn't know about Dad. Abi had asked for her father's body to be cremated, and when Luke woke up and Mum was back from over the water, they'd all go and scatter his ashes somewhere special.

And depending on what had happened in the basement, it was possible he didn't know about Silyen's death, either. Their moment in the corridor had taken her completely by surprise— though now she'd thought about it, there had been clues. Like the time she'd spotted Silyen watching a shirtless Luke chop down trees in these very woods.

Luke's enthusiastic response had been rather more startling. But then, Abi and her brother had been apart for most of the past year, and they'd each changed in ways both obvious and invisible.

Not Daisy, though. Abi squeezed her little sister's hand. Stoical, steadfast Daisy. She'd seen the good in Gavar long before the rest of them, and had stuck loyally to him and his little daughter.

It remained to be seen whether anyone else would see the good in Gavar. The bad was rather more conspicuous. And of course, he had confessed before thousands—not to mention the assembled news cameras—that he had killed his father.

And yet the country's mood had shifted, just as Midsummer had dreamed it would. Already, that father was no longer seen as a great statesman to be wept over, but as a tyrant. His death might not go unpunished, but would definitely go unmourned. Gavar's words were played over and over by the media: *"I don't want Britain to be a country where one child's opportunities are greater than another's simply because of their birth. I take no pride in being the son of a man who thought that's how it should be."* Pundits freely debated whether he would end up in prison or running the country. Both were equally possible.

Here he was now, unlocking the door of the family mausoleum as the biers of his father and brothers drew near. A sweet, tarry odor wafted out—the phenols of late-stage decay, before the last flesh had rotted off the bones. That would be the remains of Euterpe Parva. Abi thought of Jenner lying in there in the darkness, his freckled face hollowing out, skin shrinking tight to bone, then falling away, and found herself sobbing again for a world that hadn't been kind enough to any of them.

She couldn't face the reception that followed, and after letting Libby and Daisy gorge on sandwiches, she drove the pair of them back to Griff's house. They'd all moved in, while Gavar divided his time between there and Kyneston. In the absence of their Skillful protections, he had private security patrolling the boundaries of both places—already a few Equal great houses had been ransacked, and at least one had fallen victim to arson.

Abi knew he was considering shutting up Kyneston altogether. His mother was moving back to her childhood home of Orpen Mote. Gavar was still waiting to see if he would end up in a prison cell.

She called a greeting up the stairs to Griff, and settled the two girls at the kitchen table. Daisy reached for a stack of art paper and some pencils, to get Libby drawing pictures of their afternoon, and opened up a book for herself. Abi intended to have her sister back at school in September. Mum would rejoin them in a couple of days. What Abi would do with herself, though, wasn't yet clear. It depended on whether Luke's condition improved.

She made two mugs of tea, left one on the counter for Griff, and, carrying the other, went upstairs to relieve the old nanny's watch over Luke. After filling Griffith in on the funeral, Abi settled into the armchair she'd vacated, put her feet up on the end of the bed, and looked at her little brother. *Not so little,* she corrected herself.

Abi rose to check his vitals again. Her brother's heart rate was steady and his breathing strong. Sitting on the edge of the bed, she told him about the funeral. Silyen had looked very handsome, she said, and they'd interred him in his beloved riding boots and jacket.

"They'd had as much success as ever getting a comb through that hair, though."

She wondered if Luke had enjoyed winding his fingers in that messy tangle, and found herself crying again.

Wiping her nose, she turned up the radio they left burbling for Luke, and retreated back to the armchair. The program was discussing Midsummer Zelston, and the unconfirmed rumors of the disappearance of Skill.

"Never mind Cadmus Jardine, the Pure-in-Heart," said one panelist. "Or Bouda Matravers, holding these talks with Speaker Dawson and commoner representatives. The one who'll go down in history is Midsummer Zelston, the Pure-in-Deed. This is the end of the slavedays. The woman needs a statue in every town."

Statues were all very well, but Midsummer would have preferred to be with her Layla, getting ready for the birth of their child. Abi tugged the armchair blanket around her shoulders, and tuned out the radio.

They all lived in a new world now. And things might get worse before they got better. If it truly was the end of the slavedays, how would that work? Those millions of people who at any given time were in the process of spending a decade shut away would all need jobs and houses. And Britain's economy was based on the junk the slavetowns churned out for export. Its people were fed on slave-processed meat and slave-grown crops. Everything could crash down in an instant.

A year ago, as they'd boxed up the house ready to begin their days, Abi had been a girl who followed the rules. A girl who loved her mum and dad and her adorable, though annoying, little brother and sister.

This past year had broken her, her family, and the rules. It might still break the country.

But she had to believe it was the beginning of something better.

Could Abi be a part of creating that? She'd never be a doctor now. She had violated the physician's vow to do no harm before she'd ever taken it. But perhaps she could help heal the country.

In this fragile aftermath, people were still cautiously disbelieving of the new state of affairs. But in the weeks and months to come, when it became clear to all that the Equals' Skill had gone for good, joy at the people's newfound freedom might yet turn to fury and further bloodshed. After centuries of oppression, wouldn't Britain's commoners seek revenge for it upon the remnants of their ruling class?

Perhaps, having struggled to overthrow the Equals, Abi might find herself defending them. Having to remind people that Midsummer's final speech cut both ways. That the Equals were no wiser, no kinder, no more intelligent or more responsible than the rest of them.

But also no less human.

And that better futures should never begin in blood.

If that was what it took to bind up this broken country, Abi would do it.

Lost in her thoughts, she wasn't sure how much time had passed when she heard the phone ring downstairs and Griff answer. It wasn't a long conversation and Abi's leg had cramped from so much sitting, so she went down to investigate.

"Master Gavar," Griff told her, out of earshot of the two now playing in the living room. "He won't be back tonight. Seems there's been some trouble—someone's already vandalized the mausoleum. They found the door half broken off. He sounded horribly upset."

Abi felt sick. What a disgusting thing to do. Whittam had been a monster, Jenner unkind, and Silyen unnerving. But to desecrate the tomb in which they lay? Surely there was no satisfaction in vengeance against the dead.

She gave Griff a hug—then a noise from upstairs turned her dismay to joy. Had that been Luke's voice?

She looked at Griff. The old woman had heard it, too. There was faint laughter. Then the sound of a door closing.

Calling her brother's name, Abi raced up the stairs. She pictured Luke on the landing, wobbly-legged and triumphantly clutching the banister. But he wasn't there.

She burst into his room. The bedclothes were thrown back, but he wasn't there, either. Frantic, she went along the landing, checking the bathroom, the other bedrooms, even barging into Griff's room and peering into her en-suite.

Luke was nowhere.

They would have seen him come down the stairs. Perhaps he'd fallen. He must have tried to get out of bed. He'd be lying there on the floor, unconscious again.

But when she hurried back into Luke's bedroom, he still wasn't there. Not on the floor, not under the bed. She even checked the window, in case he'd been delusional and had opened it and thrown himself out. You never knew what brain-injury patients might do.

Nothing. Abi stood in the center of the room, chest heaving.

Which was when she noticed an inexplicable scent.

Woodsmoke and the sea.

ACKNOWLEDGMENTS

A trilogy is a huge undertaking—it's just as well the summit is hidden above the clouds when you first contemplate the ascent. The air gets thin up there! That I've finally planted a flag atop the Dark Gifts trilogy is down to many tireless and brilliant people.

My inspiring editors, Bella Pagan and Tricia Narwani—the truly Skilled.

My phenomenal agents, Robert Kirby, Ginger Clark, Jane Walsh, and Yasmin McDonald, who started me off on this journey and have been alongside the whole way. The United Agents assistants who keep the wheels turning—I see you.

The wonderful folk at base camp (aka Del Rey and Pan Mac): Alice, Abbie, Phoebe, Jo, Don, Kate, Lorraine, Emily, Julie, Keith, Scott, Ryan. My foreign editors, translators, cover artists, and publishers. It's been a joy working with you all.

Bloggers, booksellers, librarians, those who've come to events or conventions, and quiet readers, your love for these books warms me more than a down onesie. Seeing *Gilded Cage* picked as a 2018 World Book Night title was an honor and a true #lifegoal.

My TV colleagues, you make program-making such fun I can't bear to give it up, even though I should be writing: Greg, Cam, Rita, Jay, Grant, Suzy, Al, Sam, Paddy, Mike, Fiona, and Jacques.

My friends, you make the world go round. Thank you, Hils, Giles, Tanya, John, Taran, Joe, Rowan, Kristina, Debbie, Rachel, Mark, Mira, Nick, and so many more. I got lucky when I met each one of you.

And my family: Jonathan and Justine, Isabella and Rufus. Dad (if you're out there somewhere). And my unstoppable, remarkable mum. Heartfelt thanks.

ABOUT THE AUTHOR

Vɪᴄ Jᴀᴍᴇꜱ is a current-affairs TV director who loves stories in all their forms. Her programs for BBC1 have covered the 2016 U.S. presidential election and Britain's EU referendum. She has also twice judged *The Guardian*'s Not the Booker Prize. *Gilded Cage* was her first novel, and an early draft of it won a major online award from Wattpad for most-talked-about fantasy. She has lived in Rome and Tokyo, and currently lives in London.

vicjames.co.uk
Facebook.com/VicJamesAuthor
Twitter: @DrVictoriaJames
Instagram: @DrVictoriaJames

ABOUT THE TYPE

This book was set in Bembo, a typeface based on an old-style Roman face that was used for Cardinal Pietro Bembo's tract *De Aetna* in 1495. Bembo was cut by Francesco Griffo (1450–1518) in the early sixteenth century for Italian Renaissance printer and publisher Aldus Manutius (1449–1515). The Lanston Monotype Company of Philadelphia brought the well-proportioned letterforms of Bembo to the United States in the 1930s.